B...
LAND&SEA
SPLASHDOWN

BLAINE LEE
PARDOE

BOOK
01

You have no idea how lucky I am to work with such an incredible team at Creative Juggernaut. It is to these comrades in arms I dedicate this first book on our long journey together.

Brent Evans
Eric Crew
Joan Melgaard
Melissa Wrenchey
Ryan Zimbelman
Kevin Hughes

CYCLE I

Charter fishing boat *The Badge,*
twenty miles off the New Jersey coast

No matter what, it's better to be paid to transport drunken idiots than arrest them. Despite his mantra, Captain Mike Cole, former police officer now charter boat owner, had to admit that this had not been one of his best days. The small party of men that had chartered *The Badge* were more drinkers than fishermen. Two had been heaving the moment the seas pitched a little. They had been goofing around on deck as well. His customers were just-out-of-college-age men with far more money than brains or balls. At least their credit cards were good. On days like this, Mike could at least be happy for that.

Two of the men had gotten into a shoving match over some bullshit thing. Mike's police training had been more than enough to quell the argument. That cop voice, that cop stance and bearing, had silenced the issue quickly. Snot-nosed spoiled-ass rich kids . . . they were all the same. He had seen it for fifteen years on the force up in Jersey City. These kids wouldn't have lasted twenty minutes in some of the neighborhoods on his beat.

Now it was dark and only two of the men had caught any striped bass worth note. They had insisted on staying out a few more hours, which Mike didn't want to do, so he told them he'd do it for an extra 300 dollars. They paid, so he let them get a little more shitfaced.

The waters had picked up a little chop when the sun went down. He had switched on the running lights and was using his navigation system as much as his own eyes and ears. In the dark during the spring on the shoreline, you had to keep sharp.

It was around 9:45 p.m. when he saw the light. It appeared almost directly above his ship. A massive ball of light, like a shooting star or a meteor. This was different; most shooting stars moved fast across the skies. This one looked like it was coming down right on top of him. The sky lit up like twilight. Even the drunks he was hauling leaned out and stared upward.

Then came the roar. It was not like a jet—more like a freight train. It hit the water off to port, well over a mile away. There was a boom, supersonic air pressure from the impact. The sound hit *The Badge*, followed a moment later by a huge wave. It slapped into the hull so hard, he was sure one of his passengers was going to tumble off, but apparently God favors idiots because they managed to stay on board. It was followed by a searing hot wind, a pressure wave in the air that made his skin feel like he had been sunburned.

Out in the ocean where the ball of fire had hit, he saw a massive orange glow, sinking deep into the green and darkness of the sea. He watched it for what seemed like the longest minute of his life. Whatever had hit was big, and he was wondering if it really had been a meteor. *My God, I hope it's not an airplane . . .*

Mike grabbed his microphone and dialed to the emergency station. "Coast Guard Atlantic City, this is *The Badge*, skipper Mike Cole." He rattled off his coordinates quickly and got a confirmation back.

"This is Coast Guard AC. Go ahead, Badge."

"Something just went down in the water less than a mile from my position. Big ball of fire. Hit us with a six-foot wave."

There was a long pause. "Give us your coordinates again, Badge." He complied.

"Roger that, Badge. We have logged it."

"Was it an airplane? Do I need to move in looking for survivors, Coast Guard?"

Again a long pause. "Negative. We have no commercial or military flights in your vicinity all night. We didn't pick up anything on radar, either."

"What am I supposed to do?" Frustration tinged his voice.

"We've had a few of these reports up and down the coast, Badge. It must have been space debris or a meteor shower."

Mike looked out in the distance where the object had hit. It didn't make sense to him, not in the least. Even a meteor of that size should have showed up on radar. "Okay, Coast Guard. It's your call. I'm heading into port. I'm making for South Amboy."

"Roger that, Badge. Have a good evening and thanks for the call."

Mike frowned. *This is bullshit on a stick* . . . He checked his navigation system and angled *The Badge* back to the New Jersey shore.

Port Orford, Oregon

Greg Brimsford and his wife, Mandy, stood at the end of the Pacific Ocean and drank in the last bit of warmth from the sun's rays. The afternoons were getting shorter, and usually the beach at Port Orford was nearly abandoned at this time of year. But Indian summer had made a surprise visit, and it was warm enough for Greg and Mandy to take Angela along the beach. Soon the winter storms with their bitter winds would come and such trips to their favorite beach would be nothing more than a distant memory.

Angela was five years old, a strawberry blonde like her mother, and her eyes—they were just like Mandy's. Even though she couldn't get into the cold waters of the surf, she got as close as any kid could to the waves. She had raced ahead of them nearly fifty yards, as always, scouring the sands for shells or anything else that washed up for her collection. The late afternoon sun seemed to make her pink Hello Kitty wristwatch light up like a beacon for Greg as he walked.

It was the perfect day.

Angela called for Greg. "Daddy, Daddy, come look at what I've found!" Greg had heard it dozens of times. He didn't want to go just then. It seemed as if it had been weeks since he and Mandy had enjoyed such a period of quiet.

"You'd better go and see what she's found," his wife prodded.

"You know it's just driftwood, or a bottle," Greg replied, half a plea in his voice for her to change her mind.

Mandy didn't respond other than to slightly cock her head, as if to say, "Really?" He stared into her eyes for a moment. There was no rebuttal to something not spoken. He let his hand slip from Mandy's and started down the beach toward his daughter.

He saw the objects in the sand near her feet but couldn't make them out clearly until he got closer. "What is it, honey?" he asked, squinting as he walked.

3

"Crabs, Daddy!" Angela said. Her face was red with excitement as she pointed to them.

Greg got close to her and saw what indeed looked like crabs. Oregon was home to red rock crabs, but you never saw them on the shore. What washed up was molts, essentially abandoned shell husks. That usually happened a month or so earlier than this, at the end of summer. As Greg looked down at the crabs near his daughter, he was struck by their size and pale gray, almost white color. Their bodies were thicker than the crabs he had seen before, and somewhat larger. And these crabs were alive: they were moving at the edge of the water, all seeming to face his daughter.

"They are crabs," he said slowly, still looking at them in the wet cold sand. There were things that didn't look right about these crabs. They had too many legs. He counted the appendages on one and came up with ten . . . *that doesn't make any sense.* Their front claws were oddly shaped too, much more curved, and they seemed more . . . menacing. Their bodies were not just thicker and more pale than red rock crabs, these looked more tough, almost as if they were armor plated. Their eyes were like black balls on little stalks. *These are not crabs like I've seen before.* Greg took a step toward them, but they did not scurry away as he imagined they would.

"They look funny," Angela said.

"They sure do, honey," he said, looking at the three crabs in front of them.

"We should catch one and take it home," Angela said with a hint of hopefulness in her voice.

Greg took a step back to where his daughter stood. His eyes swept the surf and he was surprised to see at least five other crabs just at the edge the water, almost obscured by the foam hitting the beach. It felt as if they were watching him and Angela.

"We can't, honey," he said, keeping his eyes on the water. "Besides, I'm not too sure about these crabs." He glanced farther up the beach and saw four more that had climbed out of the water and onto the sand, only ten feet away. They turned to face him and Angela, almost in unison.

Greg's iPhone 24 pulsed in the pocket of his shorts. It was a Saturday, no one from work would be calling him. "Hang on, Angela," he said, reaching down to his pocket to pull out the device. As he extracted the phone, he thought it might be worth getting a photo of the crabs and looking them up on the net.

"Daddy!" Angela's voice squealed, this time with a hint of fear. He glanced down and was shocked to see that one of the crabs had moved right up to her feet. Others were starting to come out of the water now. *How had they moved so fast?*

Greg reached down and grabbed her arm to pull her away. Suddenly he saw one of the crabs move toward his own Docksides. He stepped back, pulling Angela with him. He forgot the phone in his hand. Something was happening . . . something he couldn't define.

Angela reached down to grab at one of the crabs that was moving at her feet. He saw a needle-like stream of something shooting out of the claws of the crab. It hit her left wrist, just above her Hello Kitty watch. Greg watched in horror as a mist of crimson blood sprayed the air and Angela's hand fell off—watch and all, as she screamed in a piercing high pitch of pain. He felt a searing pain in his leg. He dropped the phone and tried to run, pulling his daughter. His footing disappeared under him. His last memory was of her scream echoing in his ears. Ripples of agony burned at the edge of his consciousness. His vision tunneled, becoming a dark abyss that seemed to consume him. He tried to scream but could only feel the crush of wet sand on his face.

Container vessel Hanjin Harmony, 128 nautical miles from the western coast of Japan, Pacific Ocean

Randy Banks made his starboard pass for the third time that day and carefully checked the guylines to make sure the cargo was still intact. The massive container vessel *Hanjin Harmony* was on a return run from the United States via Japan. His job, like it or not, was boring, simple, and paid good money. Cargo handler. On a trip like this, he was to make sure the deck cargo stayed secure. In easy weather like they had been experiencing, it was simple work.

The trip had been anything but boring this time out. There had been an incident where one of the crew, Jack Harmon, suffered from some sort of seizure. The Japanese coast guard had airlifted him off the ship two days ago after it had taken four men to secure him. Jack had claimed to hear voices in his head at night. The crew had ignored it. Randy had assumed he had been drinking. Others said some men went a little stir-crazy at sea. When he didn't report to the engine room for duty, a check was made of his bunk and he was found in a puddle of his own vomit, urine, and drool, shaking like a mad man. No word had come down identifying his condition.

As Randy logged the condition of the starboard cargo, he tucked the clipboard into his armpit and made his way to the bow railing. He looked out over the ocean and drew a long, deep breath. Two more years of this work and he would have enough banked to go to college. Randy had been smart and didn't blow his earnings when the ship made port, like so many of the crew. He didn't have a family he was fleeing from or a life he was attempting to dodge. This was a job; nothing more, nothing less. It paid good money and he saved it up like a miser.

The air was clear and the sun deceptively warm, though the wind managed to find every tiny gap in his coat and sting at him whenever it penetrated anything larger than a pinhole. He watched the shallow waves and ran his fingers through his brown hair in a valiant but wasted effort to keep it straight. He was going to need a trim soon and was counting on Juarez in the galley to do it. Every penny he saved counted.

As he held the rail, he felt a momentary wave of dizziness. It came and went. His stomach lurched slightly. Randy gripped the railing a little harder. *That was odd . . . I've never felt that on the ship before.* He looked down the railing and felt it again, a wash of unbalance that seemed to make him lose his footing, if only for an inch or two. *What the hell?*

Dusty , another cargo handler, came from around the forward cargo containers and made his way to the rail. Dusty was a bit of a stoner; he used his job to travel the world, spending his pay on a variety of drugs. He was hardly ever high on duty—at least, that was what everyone liked to believe. How he passed his urine drug screenings was worthy of a book. "Did you feel that, man?" Dusty asked as the wind whipped his long stringy hair, reminding Randy of Shaggy on the old *Scooby Doo* cartoons.

"Yeah. I think we're losing speed," Randy said, and again, the feeling of disorientation swept him. This time it was stronger, more substantial. Something was happening to the massive *Hanjin Harmony*, something wrong. His grip on the rail was all that kept him from losing his balance completely.

A klaxon sounded from the bridge. Three long blasts. He had never heard them before other than drills. It meant, "All hands to emergency stations." Something was definitely wrong. He looked over at Dusty. "We've got to get to the forecastle."

The moment he finished his sentence, there was a sickening lurch, as if a giant hand had grabbed the container vessel from the rear and stopped it. He and Dusty tumbled to the deck, rolling forward nearly fifteen feet before Randy managed to grab the railing to stop his slide. If not for grabbing Randy's free hand, Dusty might have continued to roll forward on the deck. "Thanks, man," the stoner managed as he fumbled for the railing.

There was a metallic snap and pinging noise, almost musical in tone. One of the guylines had broken. Randy glanced up. The cargo containers had shifted; more than one of the lines had given way and the others looked strained to their maximum. "What the hell is happening?" Randy asked as he made his way to his feet.

The massive ship was no longer moving. The gusting wind had dramatically diminished. "Did we hit something?" He looked forward but saw nothing.

He was about to make a run for the forecastle and his emergency station when suddenly he lost his footing again. This time, it was as if the ship was dropping, sinking down into the water. He watched as the waterline of the ocean seemed to rise all around him. *This can't be happening!*

Pulling himself up, he looked over the railing. The ocean was frothing around the massive cargo ship, the churning water sucking the ship straight downward. He heard and felt a groan of metal, as if the ship itself was straining against the unseen force. The black water only seemed to be moving right below the ship . . . ten feet out, nothing seemed to be moving at all.

"Dude, what's happening?" Dusty said from beside him, seeing the same thing.

7

Randy didn't know. Things like this simply didn't happen. The emergency klaxon continued blasting. His mind raced. Container ships didn't go down in calm seas. There was no explosion, no sign of attack or massive failure. It was as if the ocean was opening up directly under the ship and swallowing it.

The klaxon changed to a long, continuous blaring noise. "Abandon ship!"

"What do we do, man?" Dusty asked.

Randy grabbed a life vest for himself and tossed one to Dusty. "We're going to have to jump for it."

"Are you crazy?"

"The ship is going down." As if to accentuate his point, another guyline snapped mid-ship. One of the cargo containers, a brilliant green in color, rolled from the top of the stack, landed on the deck and rolled into the water. Its contents, apparently clothing, spilled out everywhere as the mangled container hit the side of the vessel and seemed to disappear into the blackness under it.

"We've got to jump out as far as we can. Get clear of whatever is taking the ship down," Randy barked. He made his way down the rail as the ship continued to sink deeper and deeper into the sea. In a matter of moments, it would be beneath the waterline. He didn't know what would happen then, but he was sure death was soon to follow.

He opened an auxiliary gang gate on the rail. "Come on!" He took a running jump and leapt out into the ocean beyond where the ship was going down . . .

CHAPTER 1

Defense Intelligence Center,
the Pentagon, Arlington, Virginia

Captain Ashton Slade slid in behind his JT-13 workstation deep under the Pentagon and removed his black-framed eyeglasses for the retina scan. He was in the bowels of the Pentagon, in the second sublevel of ring three. Some people complained about the lack of sunlight, but Slade wasn't the outdoors type . . . he'd had enough of that during the war. His workstation was cramped and the lighting was kept low in the work pod area of the Defense Intelligence Center, or DIC as it was called by the Defense Intelligence Agency (DIA). Everyone who worked there hated that name. Intelligence had a bad enough reputation in the annals of military history without having one of its hubs labeled with an acronym that was pronounced "Dick." It had been the brunt of plenty of jokes over the last few years. Glancing around quickly, he saw there were only five other analysts in his section at their stations. With all of the defense cutbacks since the war, the staff seemed smaller every month. There were days you came in, found more tasks in your inbox, and realized a face was missing.

Slade sighed while he waited for security confirmation. The cool air in the subbasement was sterile in his nostrils, filtered and devoid of aroma or a hint of humidity. The DIC was almost hospital-like, adding to the cheeriness of the self-inflicted darkness. *All part of the fun of working under a bunker.* While some officers had issues working underground for prolonged periods of time, Slade enjoyed his work and where he worked. Having been in the field and been shot at during the war, he enjoyed the more secure aspects of his work environment.

The flat-screen terminal beeped twice, indicating that the retina scan had been accepted. It looked antiquated compared to the commercial holodisplays used in homes and in the corporate world, but according to the FedGov contractor who supplied the hardware, it was more secure than a holographic display. The only holographic displays were in secured conference rooms—bunkers within bunkers. *Bottom line: we never seem to get the fun toys.* Captain Slade unrolled his auxiliary keyboard on the desk and put on the wristcomp bands used to manipulate his data. Each was fitted with a neurofeed sensor that translated his movements and basic commands into processing or display tasks. He felt that he had a more sophisticated e-system at home, certainly a better processor—but this was the price for higher security. Another effect of White Monday.

Damned Russkies . . . White Monday was an open wound for anyone in the military when it happened. On 2 April 2029, almost every website in the United States came under cyber-attack, going white. In a matter of a few hours, attacks shifted to personal devices. Everything went down and stayed down for weeks. Some companies simply evaporated as a result of the attack. Intel said it was the Russian mob, the Bratva, which had been responsible, striking from over two dozen countries. In the end, most Americans had settled on who was really behind it: the Russian government. It was one of a long list of things for which he could never forgive the Russians. Slade had been a raw lieutenant then and had fought the Russian shock troops in Prudhoe Bay, some of the most brutal fighting of the war. His role had been battalion intel, but the Russian's third counterattack had suddenly put him on the front lines. Ashton heard some armchair generals and new recruits, men who hadn't seen combat, say they respected the Russians as warriors. Slade didn't subscribe to that bullshit at all. They were brutal, vicious, highly trained murderers—plain and simple.

He glanced down at his wrist and saw the jagged scar from his wound. He wore the scar more proudly than any of his medals. When he had enlisted, it was to prove to the world that he was more than just brilliant. Before White Monday, geeks were popular. After the crash, the world soured on people with tech jobs, blaming them for the crash by association. That was why he liked the Army; it had toughened him up. Combat . . . that toughened him even more. Ashton had watched men and women die around him in battle. He had killed men too: those memories were hard to shake, especially in winter when the snows of Virginia tugged at his memories of Alaska. He had taken shrapnel from a grenade in three places. When he recovered, he didn't have anything else to prove to the world. So he slid back into a role where he used his mind more than his trigger finger—military intelligence.

The wristcomp relayed his commands to the workstation, accessing the daily report and initiating the first three data-filtering algorithms. Data came in from around the globe to the DIA from a mind-blowing number of sources and feeds. He began to use his hands to whip through the information almost without thinking. To anyone passing his pod, he would look like a musical conductor leading an imaginary orchestra.

Slade had planned on leaving the military after his tour of duty in Alaska. When the opportunity came to take a job at the DIA, he did it purely so that he would be outside of Washington, DC. He reasoned that if he retired from the DIA, he'd be well poised for being picked up by one of the defense contractors that sucked the government's bounteous teat. When the war ended, though, the inevitable cutbacks to defense spending came. Contractors weren't hiring as Congress and the nation turned away from the memories of the war and wanted to spend money on domestic programs.

Rumors ran rampant that the DIA would be merged with the Department of Homeland Security and/or the CIA. That rumor had been around for decades, since the War on Terror. His colleagues gossiped and speculated about what it would mean for their jobs. Slade didn't take part in that speculation. Attempting to predict the Russians was hard, but possible. Attempting to wrestle with the mind of Washington politicians, that was impossible.

The result was that Slade had been trapped at the DIA, though he had come to love the job. He surveyed Russian army movements in the Eastsec (Eastern sector) of their country, logging anything out of the ordinary. He even got to present to the Joint Chiefs twice on troop movements that were deemed significant, resulting in a commendation in his file. If the economy ever bounced back, he was sure that commendation would help him get a different job. After all, it was all about making yourself stand out, and there were a lot of veterans from the war in the job market out there.

During the off-shift, he had three lieutenants who processed the raw datafeeds. After they did the heavy lifting of the data, his processing filters crunched the mix of data dumps from satellites, observation stations, and other intel sources. Slade then could extract the material that came up as anomalous. That was when the *real* work began. Computers could massage and compact the data, but in the end, the work of the DIA still relied on human beings, smart people, to wade through the material and see if there were patterns or trends that were worthy of note. Slade followed the DoD (Department of Defense) approach diligently for this process, with his own nuances. Those nuances had paid off. Some of his data-handling techniques were up for review to be standard processes, testimony to the skill he brought to his role.

Using his hands in the air in front of his screen, he moved the information blocks around, arranging and rearranging them. Data he deemed insignificant, he set aside in special virtual containers on the screen, where they would be filtered with routines he had written. Other information he read, digested, and filed for later analysis. Many people considered it tedious work; traditionally, there was a high turnover in analysts. Slade had a knack for it though, and found it almost therapeutic.

He didn't pay attention to the time: he simply buried himself in his work. With no social life, time was practically irrelevant for him. This day, 13 January 2039, the Russian Army seemed to be relatively quiet. Oh, they were redeploying several air defense batteries, but nothing that seemed to be a sign of a larger play on their part. Some of the reports he had read from the CIA pointed to their economy suffering after they had settled in with the Armistice. *Good. They deserve it.*

He felt a shadow fall over him and he dimmed the screen with a flick of his wrist. He turned and saw his commanding officer, Colonel Harper, standing behind him. "Morning, Ashe. Anything going on in Eastsec today?"

He shook his head slightly. "Mostly quiet, sir. I did pick up some convoy traffic last week, but today's dump seems to indicate it was nothing more than routine maneuvers. Other than that, they are still moving those air defense batteries around."

"You run that by the Air Force boys yet?"

"I was going to shoot it over this afternoon in time for the 1500 sitrep."

Harper was a stern, by-the-numbers officer. He didn't press much into Slade's personal life like some of the younger officers did, which Slade appreciated. It wasn't like he had much of a life outside of his job anyway. He read history books and had been doing some research to write his own on the WWII battle of Eben-Emael. He had written a book on the history of medieval siege weapons a few years before, not exactly a bestseller. It was the closest thing he had to a hobby, and he didn't have to interact with other people while doing it. Some commanders were too nosy for his taste. It was part of the "humanizing the Army" trend that had started before the war. Slade didn't have a life outside of work, and the last thing he wanted to do was talk about that gap with his CO out of some feigned sense of obligation. He didn't even know his neighbors' names and didn't feel any lesser for that. Thankfully, Harper wasn't one of the new generation of officers; he was old-school, right down to his Army underwear.

"Look, Slade, I have an assignment for you."

"Yes, sir," he replied. Additional assignments were rarities. Some of the analysts grumbled when they came up; they saw them as additional work. Slade saw them as a chance to do something new and was enthusiastic about the opportunities.

"You know Commander Franks, your counterpart in the Navy?"

"Yes, sir. We've presented together several times. He handles the Pacific, so we've done some coastal Russian defense analysis together."

"Good. His wife is pregnant with their first kid. Any day now he's going on leave. We're going to need someone to take over his tasks for the next few months while he's out. Your name was at the top of the list."

For a moment, Slade said nothing. "Doesn't the Navy want to have one of their own take the job, sir?"

"They don't have someone cleared and up to date on the latest protocols. You'll have access to the Navy desk during this, but I thought it would be a good opportunity for you."

Should I tell him I get seasick just thinking about the ocean . . . no. "Yes, sir. I'd be glad to. Do you have any thoughts as to who I should hand off my workload here to?"

"For a while you'll get double duty, though I would send any excess over to Lieutenant Waterson. She's got some free pipeline, despite what she'll tell you." Slade understood the comment. Waterson was always complaining about her workload, but had the lightest assignment out of the Army Intel Desk.

"Understood, sir," he said, keeping his opinions of the lieutenant to himself. *It would be better for me to simply do both jobs than have her screw up the last six months of work.* Slade was pretty sure that the colonel had been thinking the same thing, but had offered up Waterson out of a sense of obligation. The Old Man knew his stuff when it came to his staff.

"Good. Slot some time this afternoon with the commander and get up to speed on his assignment load."

"Yes, sir." It was a good thing he didn't have anything going in his private life . . . his work life was about to double.

***

"I'm glad the colonel chose you, Ashe," the lanky Alistair Franks said. "I recommended you, but sometimes the upper echelon has their heads up their collective brass."

"I appreciate the opportunity. Congratulations to you and your wife," he said.

"Thanks. It's our first. I served aboard a carrier during the war and I wasn't as nervous then as I am with her being pregnant."

"I have to tell you, Alistair, I don't know much about the Navy. You might have been better served with one of your own branch."

"Bull," he said with a wry grin as he pulled up his own daily data dump on the screen. "Intel is intel. Nautical data is the same, just some nuances are different. You're the smartest guy in the analyst pool, everyone knows that. And you have been in battle, which is more than the other officers. I'd prefer to have a guy who knows what he's doing handle my desk, even if you are just Army." He winked at the snide reference to the competing branch. "Let me show you a typical feed and filter routine." His narrow fingers danced in the air in front of the screen, and blocks of data danced on the screen in response.

Captain Slade looked at the datafeeds that Commander Franks was analyzing and some of the filters he was using. "Hey," he said, pointing at one chunk of data. "That routine is one I wrote."

Franks smiled. "No shit. Like I said, you are one of the smartest guys here. Navy desk is using a few of your algorithms."

Slade allowed himself a flat grin of satisfaction. The Old Man had not said anything to him about sharing the routines. *Secrets within secrets*: that was the Old Man's favorite saying . . . now he understood it better. He felt a lot of satisfaction with the results.

The two of them spent the better part of three hours going over Pacific data that Franks, now Slade, was responsible for. As the day came to an end, Slade noticed one block of data off to the side. "What's that?" he said, pointing to it.

"Oh, that's stuff I set aside that doesn't fit into any of the known categories for how we slice and dice the data. The Pacific is a big pond. You always get things, sightings—events and such, that just don't fit into any known patterns. They are disconnected bits and bytes, really. I set them aside and in my downtime I wade through them every few days or so, looking for anything that stands out that might be part of a bigger pattern. So far, we haven't been able to make heads or tails out of it. Maybe you'll have better luck."

Slade perused the list in the data container. Ship disappearances. Radar anomalies from naval ships—they were odds and ends of disassociated reports. For an Army analyst, the data was something new, something oddly enticing. He ran his fingers through his short-cropped black hair as he studied the information scrolling by. "What about these unidentified radar readings?"

"I usually run those by the Air Force desk. They corroborate or dispel them. You know Colonel Hasting and his team's reputation." Slade understood completely. The Air Force DIA desk was a bit arrogant for his tastes. Colonel Harper never put up with their attitude, but when he wasn't around, they could be pains in the ass.

"Yeah," he replied. "And those missing ships?"

"You have to bear in mind, at any point in time we have about 130 ships in the Pacific that are unaccounted for. Most pop up within a day or two. I have a subroutine that filters those out. The others show up in this container. Some will drop off as they are located over the next few weeks."

"And the others?"

"Pirates, storms, incompetence on the part of their captains and crews . . . they are gone. The Pacific holds her secrets dear—that's what they told us at the Academy. Unlike the Army, you're going to learn on this desk that Mother Nature is a nasty bitch with an attitude when it comes to ships and planes at sea."

Captain Slade studied the material with his eyes, mentally processing it. The anomalies file enticed him. Like a woman flirting with him, it had a draw that he could not resist. "Yo Ashe, you okay?" Only when Franks had spoken did he realize that he had been staring into the data for several moments.

"Sure. It's just there's a lot there."

"You're going to find that most of it is nothing. But who knows, maybe you can uncover something out there that we've missed? I'm willing to bet that's why the colonel is putting you on this assignment. It seems to fit his management style."

Ashton Slade stared at the megabytes of information for a longing moment. He couldn't wait to wade deeper into the material. *This assignment just might prove to be fun . . .*

CHAPTER 2

Andersen Air Force Base,
Guam, Pacific Ocean

Lance Corporal Natalia Padilla Falto stepped off the transport aircraft and was greeted by a wave of heat that made her skin tingle. The bright sunlight made her lower her shades off her crew-cut black hair and on to her eyes, just so she could focus. The digital display in the sunglasses told her the temperature, 96°F, 88 percent humidity, and a newsfeed scrolled at the bottom edge of the lens covering her left eye. She ignored all of the data. She didn't need displays to tell her it was sticky weather.

As she trudged down the ramp onto the scorching tarmac of Andersen AFB, she drank it in. Guam. There were palm trees in the distance, green plant life, but it was not a tropical tourist trap. She knew all the stats. There were just over 170,000 civilians on the island. It was only 212 square miles, a dot in the Pacific. She had read the summary of the fighting there during World War II, but it was hard for her to imagine the jungles from the tarmac of the air force base. Guam was one of the forward bases of the 7th Fleet and a major Forward Force Projection Base for the US military. She hadn't come for the views, the history, or to soak in the tropical rays. This was a chance to get away from her past.

Her journey had begun with her enlistment in the Marine Corps. Falto's father had abandoned the family when her brother was born. It had torn her mother apart, working full time–plus and taking care of two children . . . it had aged her prematurely. Her brother, Francis, "Franco" as he liked to be called, had contributed to her mother's aging. His solution to money problems was to sell drugs, mostly "Duke," out on the streets of South Los Angeles. With a cop drone on almost every corner, selling drugs required more brainpower than Francis possessed. He spent his teen years in one juvenile facility after another.

The United States Marine Corps had been her solution. Her mother fretted over Natalia's decision to enlist. "What if you are sent to war?"

Natalia had assured her mother that there was no war going on. "What are the odds, Mom?" The Russians had learned their lesson. NATO had all but dissolved during the last war, so they wouldn't be dragging the US into a future conflict either. This was a peacetime Marine Corps, she'd assured her mother. She'd get good education and training. Latino mothers were masters of worrying though, and no matter what she told her, Natalia knew her mother would worry until the moment she mustered out of the Corps. *She's going to have to wait a long time.*

What she didn't say to her mother at the time but felt in her soul, was that she did not want to end up like her brother. She loved him, but he always tried for the fast, easy path in life. Natalia wasn't that way at all. For her, the harder the path, the better it made her. She refused to be another gang member or criminal. One was enough for the family.

She spotted the staff sergeant standing rigid at the end of the tarmac, pad in hand, so she adjusted her duffle and marched smartly toward him—followed by the other five replacement Marines. She stood at attention in front of him. "Lance Corporal Falto, reporting as ordered."

The tall black man seemed to be carved of pure muscle and discipline. Every line on his face was etched with strength or marked from battle. His campaign ribbons told a story too. He had been in Korea and Alaska during the Russo-Bratva War. Korea had been a mess. Once the US and Russia had gone at each other and the Russians had swarmed over Alaska, the North Koreans had struck at the UN garrison there. The North Koreans had proved to be brutal opportunists, where the Russians were downright diabolical. For him to have fought in both places, Falto knew, he had to be one serious badass.

"Orders," he said in a flat tone.

She held out her right arm. The chip implanted in her forearm digitally held everything the Marine Corps had ever said or thought about her. An identical one was in her lower back. They mostly were used for tracking or identification of your body if you managed to get yourself killed. They were scrambled and coded so the enemy couldn't tap into them, at least that's what the Corps medics who implanted them said. Falto always wondered what else the chips did that they didn't bother to tell her.

Tapping his pad, the staff sergeant dumped down her transfer order. "Very well, Falto, welcome to the 4th Infantry Division, 1st Battalion, 2nd Regiment, Bravo Company, 1st Platoon. I'm Staff Sergeant Andrew Rickenburg." He rattled off the chain of command as if it were tattooed on his arm. "It looks like your sorry ass has landed you under my direct command." The staff sergeant paused in thought. "Falto . . . Falto—oh, I remember *you*. Your SRB was impressive as hell except for that one little blemish."

She knew what he was referring to. It had happened three months after basic. She didn't talk about the incident, the memories and the investigation afterward had embarrassed her. *I keep hoping it will go away, but it keeps coming up.* It had been two years ago, but it was like a scar everyone seemed to see.

"Yes, Staff Sergeant," she replied.

"Board the transport." He hooked his thumb over his shoulder toward the vehicle. "We'll be heading over to Big Navy in a few minutes, once I process the rest of these snot-nosed kids." She grabbed her gear and headed to the transport, then climbed aboard. She remembered the recruitment officer when she had enlisted. "If you join the Marine Corps, you'll get to see the world." Falto allowed herself a chuckle. *It isn't much, but it sure beats the hell out of LA.*

***

Staff Sergeant Rickenburg dropped off Falto as his last stop of distributing the reinforcements to their new quarters. He stopped the transport and turned his head toward her slowly, deliberately. "Welcome to one of the most isolated backwater assignments the Corps has. Nothin' happening here since WWII. Guam exists for tourists and in support of our bases here, plain and simple. We call the main base here in Apra Harbor, Big Navy—and don't ask me why, I have no idea.

"If you were looking for a place to relax, though, this isn't it. I run a tight ship. I don't care what race you are, or that you're a woman. I intend to push you and push you hard. I will make you do things that you can't imagine yourself doing. I also don't give a damn about what happened in your past. What matters is how you perform *for me.* Some of my men break under the pressure. Those who don't, are something a cut above the rest. Do we understand each other?"

"Yes, Staff Sergeant," she replied. *I don't expect any less.* More importantly, he was telling her that the "incident" in her past was going to stay there.

Rickenburg leaned in so that he was close to her face, close enough for her to feel his warm breath even in the heat of the Guam sun. He spoke low, so his words wouldn't travel—and did so through gritted teeth. "And before you wonder if you'll be treated different because you're a woman: I know the regs require me to say you'll be treated like any other female Marine, that your standards are lower than the men's because of your sex. For the record, I follow orders like that. In reality, I've had women fight alongside me in the war. I've saved some of their lives and more than one has bailed my ass out of a tight spot. I don't disrespect females in the Corps; in fact, quite the opposite. I've found it best to treat you just like every other Marine in my command. Now, you may disagree with my methods and the standards I'm going to hold you to. You may be compelled to go to the lieutenant and tell him that I'm treating you against the regs. He'll haul my black ass in and chew it, but come the next morning, I will be here and so will you. You want to transfer to some other platoon, where their NCOs are a little more fluffy and soft on you female Marines—I'll help you with the paperwork."

He paused, as if to take in her reaction. "But if you do want to transfer because of my high standards, then know this. I have fought in every major battle in the last war. I have been pinned with three Purple Hearts, two Bronze Stars, and the Marine Corps Commendation Medal. I was at the siege of Anchorage from the start. I *earned* those honors because I am one of the best. No bragging—just the facts. I qualified for the first and second generation ASHUR suits, and I piloted several rigs with honor when we broke the Russies in the Kobuk Valley." His pronunciation of "Russies" made it sound like "pussies," and she was sure it was deliberate. Everything about the man seemed deliberate. "I personally chose you out of the transfers because I saw your combat ratings and evaluations. You're good. Stick with me and I'll make you one of the best." She stared at the stylized Assyrian winged god Ashur on his shoulder, one of the many marks of an ASHUR pilot.

She was paralyzed for a moment. Two things stood out in her mind. Being ASHUR qualified—Augmented Soft/Hard Unconventional Combat Rigs—said a great deal. Dubbed "Ironman" suits, they were the early generations of augmented battle armor. Only the best of the best were even given the honor of trying to qualify to wear a rig in battle, and then you had to test for each model of suit. His having piloted a rig in combat told her quite a bit about the man beside her. She found herself trying to see if he sported the traditional tattoo on his hand that marked ASHUR pilots.

The second bit of information was the mention of the siege of Anchorage. The Marines and Army troops there had taken the city back from the invading Russians, only to be surrounded in a vicious counterattack. Anchorage had been under siege for twenty-two days. It was now mentioned in the same breath as Tripoli and Iwo Jima. The veterans of that siege were nearly gods among men in the Corps. Falto drank in that knowledge carefully, slowly, like a scalding hot triple-caff coffee.

"Staff Sergeant. Permission to speak freely," she replied slowly, and in a low tone of voice almost a match to his own.

He nodded once, slowly.

She gritted her teeth, just as he had done. The look was impressive, and she was going to use it from now on. "I have no problem whatsoever if you want to hold me to a higher standard. My whole life has been a struggle, so I'm not afraid of the challenge. I was born of two parents whose parents crawled across the Arizona border. My father deserted my brother and me. My mother raised us both. I had to fend for myself in one of the worst schools in LA. At seven I was in my first fistfight and sent that kid to the hospital. At seventeen, I was nearly raped at knife point by a boy whose hand I crushed in a car door. When he and his brother showed up the next night to pay me back, I broke the arm on one and the jaw on the other. I was smart enough to avoid getting sucked into gangs or drugs, and managed to avoid getting pregnant.

Fighting is a part of my character. The Corps has made me better at it, taught me technique and control. It has put an edge on my blade."

She continued on with a firmness in her voice born of experience. "You're tough and smart: I recognize that and respect it. I'm tough and smart too. I'm not as good as you . . . yet. But one day, I will be. I'm not going to go ask for no *damn* transfer. I'm going to prove to you and everyone else in the Corps that I'm as good as I think I am."

He seemed to take in her words. The staff sergeant didn't smile—but he didn't frown, either.

"I'll be the judge of that, Falto. Stow your gear. We have a night march at twenty hundred—light jungle gear. We'll see if you're half as good as you think you are."

She grabbed her duffle and entered the barracks. It was a typical Marine bunking, women with their own room on the right, men on the left, both at the rear of the commons area. The air had a tinge of sweat mixed with a whiff of military-grade disinfectants. She entered and felt the cool breeze of the air conditioner hitting the tiny beads of sweat on her skin. The personnel of 1st Platoon were in the commons area. Four were playing pool, the others were either relaxing in front of the e-unit or cleaning their gear. Falto stepped in and closed the door behind her. For a moment, all eyes fell on her.

"Who are you, fresh meat?" asked a massively muscular Marine. She'd seen the type before, a pumper, or so they were called. Pumpers were not to be screwed with, that much she had learned, at least not deliberately. *I hope this isn't going to be some sort of macho-ass attempt to intimidate me or put me in my place as the noob.* She wasn't about to put up with that kind of shit. *I earned my stripes and I don't need to prove that to anyone.*

"I'm Lance Corporal Natalia Falto," she said coolly.

The pumper stared at her for a moment. "Lance corporal, eh? Who would have thought it?" He laughed and was lightly goaded on by two other Marines.

Falto stepped in, closing the distance between them. "Is there a problem?"

"Not yet," he replied with a sense of confidence. "Where you from?"

"Los Angeles. Does it matter?"

He shook his head. "Probably not. I'm Foster, fire team Baker, grenadier." He extended his beefy hand. Natalia worked out quite a bit herself, but her hand seemed almost lost in his. "The hombre you are replacing was my buddy—Cox."

"What happened to him?" she asked.

"Wounded . . . free fire exercise. He popped up at the wrong time. Even with his body armor, it dislocated his shoulder. Nasty stuff."

She nodded in response. Others in the unit got out of their chairs and started to move around her. She caught a flurry of names. One of the women, a tall redhead with spiky hair, was named Hernandez. There was a stocky lance corporal at least ten years older than her whose face reminded her of worn and cracked leather. His name was Appleton. There was a runt of a kid too, almost too skinny to look like a Marine. His name was Reid Porter. When she shook his hand, she worried she might hurt him.

"You met the staff sergeant already?" Foster asked.

"We had a discussion," was all she replied.

"Let me guess," Hernandez said. "You got the 'I treat men and women the same,' lecture, right?"

She nodded.

Hernandez gave her a flash of a knowing smile. "Well, for what it's worth, he's telling you the truth. We take care of each other in this platoon. The staff sergeant, he's as tough as petrified dinosaur shit. His standards are a hell of a lot tougher than the Corps's. That incident with Cox? That was training way above and beyond the norm. He caught a lot of flak for it, but in the end, they only reprimanded him. Anybody else might have been drummed out. The staff sergeant will bust your balls and crack your cervix. He doesn't do it for fun, he just wants us to be ready."

"Ready for what?" she asked naively.

"Fucking war," Hernandez replied. "What else? He'll tell you that peacetime is the best time to prepare to fight the next war. And you know what? He's right. One more thing you need to know. In this platoon, we stick together for one reason, right, Marines?"

In unison they all spoke the response. "It's us against the staff sergeant!"

She found herself chuckling, just one little laugh. Until she had joined the Corps, she had almost never laughed. Life had been too rough. Now, here, these were people she could understand. "Where can I stow my gear? The staff sergeant said we have a night march at twenty hundred. I need to break out my gear and get hydrated."

The platoon members seemed to freeze. Foster broke the moment of silence. "You saying we have a night march tonight?"

She nodded.

"Fuck a duck," he replied. "Well, at least we got notice this time. Thanks, Falto. Usually he springs these things on us. You're already proving useful," he added in a sarcastic tone. There was a collective moan and groan that rose from the platoon members at the realization that they would be running. The runt, Porter, looked like he was on the verge of crying upon hearing the news.

Appleton tossed her a palm-sized gear pack. "Pop two of the tabs for electrolytes about an hour beforehand. The heat on this island is your second worst enemy after the staff sergeant," Appleton said in a hoarse voice that sounded like he had been hollering at a concert for a few hours.

The tabs, short for tablets, were common in the Corps. There were tabs for night patrol which juiced you up. Foster was clearly a Ster-tab junkie—soaking up military-grade steroids. Some were pain deadeners. Others were designed to heighten hearing or give you better night vision. The Army used them too. Side effects were known, and Appleton's raspy voice was a clue that he had wired himself up with Night-tabs quite a bit. Natalia had always shied away from the ones that band-jacked your body and brain. Elect-tabs released boosts of electrolytes; that was about all she had been willing to take.

Falto was led to her bunk by Hernandez. As she opened her bag and started to stow her gear, she realized that she was home . . . the best home she ever had. Nothing could take that feeling away from her.

CHAPTER 3

USS *Virginia*, just outside of Kitsap Naval Base, Pacific Ocean

Commander Titus J. Hill stood on the bridge of the USS *Virginia* as she left port at Kitsap Naval Base. The nuclear attack submarine SSN-774 was the tenth US Navy ship to bear that proud name. Getting slotted for the executive officer of a boat was a distinct honor. The ship had been stationed in the Atlantic until the war with Russia. Since then she had remained as part of the Seventh Fleet —a deterrent against further Russian aggression.

Or so the propaganda said.

During the Cold War, there had been a deadly game of cat and mouse between the superpowers. With the collapse of the Soviet empire came a pause in those tensions. When the Russians had backed the events on White Monday and had responded to US surgical strikes by an all-out invasion of Alaska, the era of tension had returned. The naval battles had been vicious dogfights under the waves. Even years after the war, the Russians were aggressive in their patrols, forcing others to respond in kind.

The *Virginia* was a potent weapon of war. Weighing in at 7,800 tons, she was capable of moving at over twenty-five knots on paper, but Titus knew that what was public and what was reality were different. Depending on conditions, the *Virginia* could top thirty-five knots for short periods of time. Her armaments included a dozen Vertical Launch System tubes which could unleash the new War Hatchet missiles, capable of hitting a variety of programmable targets. Her four torpedo tubes could deliver her Mk-50 Enhanced Torpedoes against any man-made target in the sea or below it. Hill had a deep respect for the boat and what she represented. The *Virginia* was not just a vessel of war, she was a projection of US might in the Pacific.

Captain Jacob Stewart of the *Virginia* was shorter than Titus, but his presence was not based on height but on his commanding authority on the boat. Titus towered over most of the crewmen he had met since joining the ship two days earlier, but that was not unusual. Since he had enrolled in the Naval Academy, he had always been a few inches taller than his colleagues and fellow officers. Stewart's mere presence seemed to tense up the crew . . . he had that kind of air about him.

Captain Stewart was almost the opposite of him in every way, not just height. Stewart had a slight paunch at his waist, where Titus was, as his mother had called him, "skinny as a rail." Stewart's voice was crisp, concise. Titus's had a bit of a nasal twang to it. The biggest thing that he could see that they had in common was the Naval Academy graduation rings that both of them wore. It was a pass card of sorts in the US Navy, membership in an elite club.

"Mister Hill," Stewart said with no hint of emotion. "Set a course for the Brown Bear—two thirds."

He nodded. "Aye, sir. Navigator—plot course for the Brown Bear Seamount from our current bearing."

The navigator replied and began his work, huddled over the digital plot map. Twenty-five years ago, plotting was more manual, even with the computers. The *Virginia* had undergone two major overhauls since then. She was an aged grand dame, with enough firepower to devastate cities or naval task forces.

"Course plotted, sir," he replied.

The chief of the boat, a master chief named Tyrone Simmons, leaned over the display, touching it several times. Simmons didn't look like other chiefs Hill had met. Most were "grizzled," tough-looking. Simmons didn't have that kind of rock-hard facial expression. *I wonder how that appearance reflects in his style?* As the senior chief, his role was as important as Titus's role as executive officer. "Course verified, XO."

"Very well, Chief. Get us underway."

Simmons barked out the commands as if he had rehearsed them for weeks. "Helm, lay in the new course. Set speed for two-thirds."

Titus watched as the helmsman adjusted the course, then he turned back to Captain Stewart. "Course laid in, Captain."

Stewart nodded once. The older man's eyes seemed to drift around the command center smoothly, from station to station. "Mister Hill. Would you join me topside?"

The request caught him off guard. They had set sail only two hours ago at 2200, twisting and turning through the complicated Strait of Juan de Fuca and past Port Townsend. Going outside was pointless, but Hill didn't question it. In the vast ocean at night, there was nothing to see. Still, when the captain asks you to go topside, you go topside.

"Yes, sir," he said, following Stewart. Both men donned their cold weather gear and wet-gear coats.

When the hatches were opened, there was a blast of wetness and stiff, cool ocean air. Stewart scampered up the ladder as if it were a race, Titus right behind him matching his pace. *The captain is a fast mover . . . that much is for sure.* There was an energy in the older officer that seemed younger than his years.

Standing room atop the mast was only large enough for the two of them. In every direction there was blackness. The moon was obscured by clouds which had a bit of a silvery shimmer to them. In the places where the stars poked through the clouds, they seemed brighter, starkly brilliant in the vast openness.

"We didn't get much of a chance to get to know each other before we set sail, Mister Hill," Stewart said, staring out in the darkness.

"No, sir. I guess we didn't."

"I picked you personally for this command. I'm sure you're aware that you weren't exactly at the top of your class on your PXO exams. Some captains pick their XOs based on tests. I don't."

Titus understood the comment regarding his grades all too well. The three-month Prospective Executive Officers course was designed to weed out men. He had passed, but had not excelled. His mind raced for something to say but Stewart started speaking again, probably sensing his XO's hesitancy.

"What won me over was your tour aboard the *Mississippi*. Mike Crofton and I went through the Academy together. That fire aboard ship was nearly a disaster. He credits you as one of the reasons the ship didn't go down. Tests tell you one thing, action under pressure tells you another. Your actions were outstanding—you may have saved the Old Miss."

Fire aboard a submarine was one of the worst fears of any seaman. Aboard the USS *Mississippi*, a frayed electrical wire sparked, the worn element overlooked during the construction and inspection of the boat. When flames engulfed the torpedo room, the sub was at risk. Titus had organized the firefighting team himself. They lost two men in the blaze, but managed to save three others and put out the flames. The mention of the fire made Titus reach up unconsciously and touch the scar on his right brow. He had hit his head on a bulkhead in the frenzy of leading the firefighting detail, leaving him with a concussion and a permanent reminder of the incident. "All I did was what I was trained to do."

Stewart drew a long breath. "Son, that's what we all do. The fact that you stuck to your duty and got the job done despite personal risks, that says a lot to me."

"Thank you for the opportunity, sir." It was tempting to kiss the old man's butt. Titus had done his digging on Captain Stewart, too. He had commanded the USS *Missouri* during the war and had taken out two Russian attack subs in the Bering Strait, which tied him with another captain for a record in the war. He wanted to ask the captain about those battles—he wanted to congratulate him—but now was not the time to look like he was cuddling up to the new boss.

When the war had broken out, Hill was fresh out of the Academy. He earned his dolphins, slang for certification as a submariner, aboard the Ohio-class USS *Tennessee*. She was a missile boat and spent most of her time hovering in the far North Atlantic, awaiting orders that never came to disgorge her missiles. It had been a good career move for him—it was duty in a time of war—but there was a part of Titus Hill that wanted that taste of battle. That was why he had transferred to the *Mississippi*. *Attack subs are always on the forward patrols*: at least that was his thinking. He wanted to be able to prove himself just once, but that opportunity had slipped away when the war ended. Other men, brave men like Captain Stewart, would earn their reputations and much deserved honor in another sea.

The naval war with the Russians had been brutal. The United States technology was better—the Russians were using antiquated submarines with cobbled-together refits and gear. What the US possessed in terms of grace, the Russians countered with brute force and their Air Force dropping torpedoes. Several billion dollars' worth of submarines had been lost before the momentum of the naval fighting had turned in favor of the Americans. The ghosts of those lost men haunt the Bering Straits, or so submariners say. The men that came out of that conflict were icons in the US Navy, used as proof-positive that the United States had been training its men right and building the best boats.

"I'll go over our orders with you in detail. Suffice it to say, we are heading to the western Pacific along a new patrol route. This glimpse of the sky and breath of fresh air is the last you are going to have for a while. Soak it in."

"There's not much to see," Titus said as he looked around.

"There's the stars." Stewart gestured toward the horizon. There was a moment of quiet as Hill looked up.

Stewart continued, "On this cruise, I want to you to pay close attention to our sonar gear. Watch it carefully."

"Why is that, sir?"

"Our last cruise out, we started to pick up anomalies. Big readings like subs in some cases, but larger than any submarine ever conceived. I'm talking things the size of aircraft carriers. I ordered the ship to pursue them, but they seemed to move twice as fast as we could and we lost the signals. A few days later, we started to pick up readings that sonar read as whales, but their profiles were off the charts in terms of size and speed."

"What did Kitsap say about our gear?"

"I had them go over it three times, top to bottom. They purged and reloaded the software too, but no one could find anything wrong with it," Stewart said, his eyes never leaving the stars on the horizon.

The information made Titus a bit cautious. "Is there any chance that this is a new form of Russian or Chinese jamming or some sort of countermeasure?"

Stewart turned toward him slowly, looking into his eyes. "I had the same thought. The yard assured me that we are good to go, but you and I both know that this ship lives and dies by our sonar. But we didn't pick up any other submarine activity in the area. In fact, the contacts came up outside of normal Russian patrol lanes. I raised the point with the Naval Intelligence officer with COMSUBPAC, gave them a full dump of our readings too."

"What did they say, sir?" Titus agreed with the captain about how crucial sonar was to an attack sub. If it wasn't working one hundred percent accurately, their lives could be over in a matter of seconds.

It was the first time he had seen any emotion on the face of his new captain, and this was little more than a very faint grin—and then only for a moment. "Intelligence officers—well, they are spooks. They take in info, but don't share much. They thanked me for the information and said they would look it over and forward it up to the DIA for analysis. They also told me that we should consider ourselves good to sail."

"Meaning?"

"This isn't my first rodeo, Mister Hill. I've done the dance with the spooks before. When they say something like that, it's usually an indication that someone else has had the same readings. Otherwise they would have told me nothing or told me to keep my boat in port until the defect was found. The fact they told me I was good to go was a clue . . . a clue that someone else has encountered the same problem."

It makes sense. The Navy would never put us in harm's way if it was a bug or glitch. More importantly, Titus learned a useful bit of information from his new captain about intelligence issues that wasn't in the manual or book. "I'm not sure that's good news, if it *is* some sort of countermeasure or jamming technique for fooling us."

"I will offer you a bit of advice, Mister Hill, just in case you didn't know it. The Navy isn't about procedures and regulations. Procedures and regulations are what we do, so we do things consistently and don't screw up. If you want to survive in this man's Navy, the real key is your network of peers. Now that you're my XO, you need to start developing relationships with other XOs. Trust me, you'll learn a lot and it'll be good for your career in the long haul. If you're going to be with me for more than a few months, you need to get comfortable with my style."

The problem is, I don't know how long I'll be here. Hill had been appointed Executive Officer on the *Virginia* just a week before she put to sea. Her normal XO, Paul Sanders, had come down with kidney stones. His treatment had some complications and he wasn't going to be ready. His illness had been a boon for Hill, landing him a seat that he might have had to wait on for months or longer. During wartime, such positions opened up fast as new boats were launched. In an age of defense cutbacks, new command positions were a rarity. *For all I know*

I might just be here for one patrol, until Sanders feels better . . . He suppressed those thoughts. *Best to focus on the here and now, not speculate about the future.*

"I take it you spoke to some of the people in *your* network Captain?"

Stewart nodded. "Unofficially, of course. We didn't break regs, but I found out from the yard crew and another captain that they'd had similar strange readings. We didn't plot on a map where these took place, but I have a pretty good idea of patrol stations after the war. Here's the kicker—I think we were nowhere near each other at the time. They said they picked up one large reading the size of *Nimitz* under water—and fast too."

"Sounds like your Sierra."

Captain Stewart nodded.

Titus crunched his own intelligence. The only other boat in dock when the *Virginia* was there was the USS *North Dakota*, also a Virginia-class vessel. Knowing that told him something of Captain Stewart's network of colleagues.

"Did they pass on their data too?"

"Yes, they did. They got the same thing. My 'friend' told me that a similar set of readings had occurred eight months ago in the Indian Ocean, picked up by a cruiser on anti-pirating patrol."

"That doesn't mean that it isn't the Russians or some other country that has developed a new technology," Titus responded as he felt a misting of salt air hit his face. In the breeze, it was cold—but it was clean air, unfiltered, not sanitized, not manufactured.

"Correct, Mister Hill. That's not for us to figure out. The boys in the DIA need to see if there's a trend and try to determine what it means. In the meantime, we patrol as planned, but keep our eyes and ears sharp."

For a moment Titus stood mute, deep in thought. Stewart cocked his head just a few millimeters to the left. "What's on your mind, son?"

The question shattered his concentration. "Well, sir, it's just that . . . if it is not the Russians or some other country . . ."

"Yes?"

"Then who or what is it?"

CHAPTER 4

Blown Sun Media Headquarters, Los Angeles, California

Dana Blaze was less a person and more a creation of the mind of Donna Horton. Donna had graduated from the University of Central Florida seven years before as a communications student. She knew then that creating Dana Blaze would take meticulous planning—and taking full advantage of others. Both of which were things Donna was willing to do. There were no lines she was unwilling to cross in order to get ahead. Hesitation . . . that was something with which others burdened with petty morals had to cope.

She knew she wanted to be a media figure at the age of four. Sure, her mother pushed her into those beauty pageants, but Donna did not fault her for that. In fact, she was glad her mother had gotten her used to the limelight early. Donna had sidelined her mother by the time she got into college and landed that role on the reality program. The two of them had not spoken in years. Donna didn't mind. Just part of the price you had to pay to get ahead.

As she entered the office building in downtown Los Angeles, "La" as many of the hipsies, or hip people, had called the city for the last decade, she stopped in the restroom she spied off the lobby and went to check herself before going up. Dana looked in the mirror and adjusted her blouse to show more of her ample cleavage. She tapped her wrist-feed and pulled up the inflation controls for her breasts, increasing them a notch—straining her blouse a tad more. Adjustable breasts were just part of what she had paid for with her reality show money. The name change to Dana Blaze was another. She flicked her fingers through her genetic-weave blonde extensions. Her hair had been treated with a custom mix. It would retain its shape in winds and even without washing for several days. The color was a special creation designed for highlights that the camera would pick up. Again, it was all part of the image, and in her case, the image was the reality she had crafted.

She took the elevator up and entered the Blown Sun Media office with a sweep of the glass door that demanded that anyone in their reception area take notice. She stepped up to the desk and the bland nameless receptionist tried to flash her a smile. "Good morning. May I help you?"

"Dana Blaze for Ryan Jackson," she said, looking down at the receptionist. *Poor girl. It would take 50K in surgery to make her even remotely a contender.*

The receptionist spoke into the deskcom and Jackson appeared. He was twenty-eight years old. She'd done her research . . . otherwise she wouldn't have wasted her time. He was skinny, with an Oxford button-down shirt and a loosely fitted tie which looked like it was wired. No surprise there—he was, after all, a digital entrepreneur. "Miss Blaze." He stuck out his hand and she gave it a firm shake, as firm as any male. "Shall we step into my office?"

"Certainly," she replied. As she sauntered out of the reception area, the closed-stream feed from her ring picked up the receptionist leaning out, admiring her. The image was transmitted to her contacts and Dana smugly grinned to herself. *That's right, honey . . . soak it in. This is what it takes to get ahead.*

Jackson's office was impressive. He had one of those new stand-up office chairs, where you half-stood, half-reclined. Thin holographic displays drifted in a slow orbit around the office. That technology had been one of Jackson's first innovations and had earned him billions. She took her chair, a more traditional deep leather monster . . . real leather, not the synth that the hemp-huggers insisted on. Dana could smell the leather—the power. *Why not? He is worth almost a quarter of a billion dollars. If he wants the trappings of power, he's earned that right.*

"You have a nice office—may I call you Ryan?"

"Thank you, Dana, and yes, Ryan will do. I take it you were intrigued enough by the offer I sent you to agree to this interview."

She leaned forward, deliberately letting her breasts strain against the fabric of her blouse. "Let's just say you got my attention."

"I have big plans for Blown Sun Media, Dana," he said, rubbing his hands together as if they were cold. "We're going to reinvent news media, more thoroughly blur the lines between information and enter-tainment. It's the final nail in the coffin for the traditional news agen-cies. You and I both know it's more about entertainment than news. I'm going to make it grittier, grinding in reality elements. We are going to change how people get their news."

He was excited, she could feel his energy. Dana was smart enough to not let her reaction show. "I read the offer you sent. It sounds excit-ing. But how many anchors are we talking about?"

"Four was the original plan."

This was it. Time to play her cards—she could feel it. "I'm going to be the star of your new network, Ryan. That's the price for getting me on board. I need to be the center of the lineup, first chair. I choose the assignments, and I get the best ones. I'll pick my own producer and camera tech—I have someone in mind already. I don't like being part of a team. Teams always play to the weakest member. Put me in the spotlight, and you'll get the kind of ratings you need to build this new network." She had rehearsed her lines the night before and her delivery was crisp and clear.

There was a pause as Ryan reached out and grabbed one of the ho-lographic displays. "You're making some interesting demands, Dana. But you're asking me to purchase something that seems to be a bit of an unknown quantity."

"Meaning?"

"Dana Blaze—your persona. I'm pretty good at data manip—but five years ago, there was no Dana Blaze. I can't seem to find out who you were before then."

"Does it matter?"

"You're asking me to put down a lot of money on someone who didn't exist before 2034," he said.

"Who I was before is of no consequence. All that really matters is what I am *now*, your star. That is really all that you need to know."

After looking over the holographic data file once more, he tossed it out, returning it to the other newsfeeds and data chunks that were in a slow virtual orbit of his office. "I own the majority of this compa-ny—but I have shareholders, Dana. I have a degree of accountability. It's not just my money, but theirs too. They will have questions about you, and right now, I can't answer anything about you before five years ago. How do you suggest I explain spending millions you are likely to demand from me?"

She licked her lips. It was not just a seductive measure. The pheromones in her lipstick were activated by her saliva. Her breath would float them into the room and into the nostrils of the supergenius sitting across from her. It was a fabulously expensive tool in her arsenal. While he would not spring an erection in front of her, it would lower some of his defenses . . . at least it was supposed to.

Reaching down to the tiny concealed compartment in her belt, she pulled out a disk that was the size of an old-timey quarter. She slid it across the glossy surface of his desk. The surface of the disk shimmered and her own holographic image flickered to life. Most corporate presentations were boring, dull. Dana had had a movie producer friend make this for her. The image was her in a stunning red outfit, covering the United Airlines crash a year ago that won her her first Emmy. The data bullets popped up around her image as she covered the disaster.

"You should tell your shareholders that my ratings are through the roof. I get into places that other reporters don't even try. My demographics with men 17–24 are fired missiles. I'm solid with women as well, and that isn't easy to pull off. You can assure your shareholders that if you bring me aboard as the foundation of your new network, I will deliver you scoop after scoop and ratings that anyone in this town would drool to have. You can see by my demos, I can and will deliver the kind of impact your new venture needs."

Ryan studied the data points as she spoke. She had chosen to use the sophisticated portable holo-emitter because he was a techno-geek himself. Dana always did her homework on her prey. If she wanted this job, she was going to have to demonstrate to him that she was as savvy as he was with technology. It was a matter of respect, and might level the playing field during their negotiations.

"Your ratings are what got my attention in the first place, Dana. I am curious, though. You seem to have a knack for being in the right place at the right time. There was that train wreck in Mexico where you happened to be on vacation at the time. When that gunman went psycho at CalTech and took out fourteen people . . . you were one of the first on the scene. It's happened over and over again. There are rumors out there about you—out there in the darker corners of the net—

that you might actually have orchestrated some of those incidents." He stared into her face. She could tell that he was looking for a response, an indication that might lend weight to what he was saying.

Dana had heard the rumors before, of course. In fact, she had paid to have some of those rumors started and spread. She had turned them into a media event of their own, all aimed at boosting her own ratings as she demanded that her faceless accusers produce their alleged evidence. Her passionate counterattacks on the air had gotten her record ratings. In the end, no evidence ever was produced. *They can't produce the evidence . . . and never will be able to.*

The network had been supportive. After all, she was being painted as some sort of sinister villain who was killing innocent people to get a story. There was the *People* interview: the news special where she talked about how the accusations had devastated her—but she was somehow prevailing despite the pressure. Some well-placed death threats had kept the story alive when it should have petered out.

It had all been choreographed, a carefully planned and staged media event. Even better, it had been a media event inside a media event. *If they knew the full truth, it would have been an even bigger story.* She let the moment spin out. *Chances are he's got poly-devices in the room. Well, I'm prepared for them as well.*

"Those allegations have been out there for a long time—and I have refuted them online and in print. You of all people should know that you can't believe what the pundits on the net say about you. When you are as good as me, there are a lot of people who will do and say anything to try to drag you down. You'll find that I'm a competitor, Ryan. I know this game and I play it well." As she spoke, she gently let her hand drift to her belt. The small stud there would disrupt any devices aimed at trying to determine if she was telling the truth. She wasn't worried, though. Her response was calculated and careful. She hadn't lied.

Ryan Jackson nodded. "I meant no offense, but I'd be a fool if I didn't bring it up. To be blunt, we've hired our own investigators. None of them have come up with anything untoward in your involvement."

What he didn't say was . . . *so far.* Dana heard the words in her mind, though.

Ryan shifted in his seat. "You have a reputation for being a bit heavy-handed with your colleagues. There was that incident with Bob Rollins last year, for example."

She flashed her award-winning smile at the mention of her former colleague. Bob had made a flip comment about her off-camera. Her crewman managed to capture it and leak it to social media without having it linked to her. It put Bob in a bad position. To try to save face, he apologized live on the air for the faux pas. Everyone expected her to be gracious and forgiving. She wasn't. Dana had recoiled like a cobra and punched him hard, breaking his nose—live—in front of millions of watchers. *One thing I know is how to punch people's buttons.* She had granted interviews to say that Bob had been disrespecting her as a woman and journalist since she had joined the network. His denials had fallen on deaf ears. The network, facing pressure from several women's groups, had given Bob his walking papers. He had been at the top of his game and in a matter of a few weeks, she had taken him out, hanging him on his own snide comments. It was one of her proudest moments. "What I did was wrong," she said with only a hint of pensiveness in her voice. "But what Bob did was a thousand times worse. You have no idea how big of a bigoted jerk he was when the cameras were off. I was just lucky that the clip surfaced so the world could learn the truth."

"It had to have been leaked by your crewman, though," Ryan said.

"What can I say? My people are loyal to me. I can't fault them for that. You should know, if you hire me, I plan on bringing my crew. They know how I operate. We're a well-oiled machine . . . and in a cutthroat business, we look out for each other."

Ryan flashed a wry smile. "If we get to the contract stage, I think that's something we can work out. But we're not there just yet, Ms. Blaze. What about your current employer? Da-News is highly respected and they have deep pockets. For all I know, this is a ploy to press them for more money."

Ryan was not stupid, that much she was sure of. He understood how many in her industry operated. "I've gone as far as I can with Da-News. I need a challenge. Your start-up offers that kind of incentive for me. Challenges are what drive me." She let her voice hint at a giddy young-girl tone. It was a measured response. She had researched

Jackson carefully. He had answered a similar question with an almost identical response. She had studied and rehearsed her response to subtly manipulate him. *Use every bullet in your gun, girl.*

His eyes drifted to one of the slowly orbiting holographic displays, but only for a heartbeat. "I understand that feeling," he replied, and she knew she had struck a chord with him. He seemed to be lost in thought; she wasn't sure if it was her or something he had seen on the displays behind her. "Do you have any questions for me, Ms. Blaze?" he finally said.

"When do I start?" she replied with a bat of her eyelashes.

He grinned ever so slightly. "I'm impressed, I'll give you that much. You cut quite a swath. You *are* the kind of person I want on our news team. I envisioned more of a team, though, an ensemble—"

"We both know what you want: ratings. I can deliver that."

Ryan nodded. "I bet you can. Let me ask you this. I need a killer interview, something we can hype up. I'll talk to my lawyers to work out a deal, but you have to promise me something for our first few weeks—something that no one else has ever gotten. I need something sensational. You do that, and guarantee it in writing, and I'll work with you on terms."

He was good . . . very good. "Give me a name. You obviously have someone in mind."

There was that wry smile. "Jay Drake," he said flatly.

It was a challenge, that much was for sure. "JayTech's Jay Drake?" Ryan nodded. Jay Drake never gave interviews to anyone in the press. His company had been a rising star since the dark days of White Monday. JayTech had saved the United States, at least that was the story they liked to spread. The public sure bought it. But their founder was elusive, or reclusive. No one had been able to secure his time . . . ever.

Dana stood and leaned forward across the desk, her hand extended. "Deal!" Now all she had to do was figure out how to pull it off.

CHAPTER 5

The Torn District of Montebello, Los Angeles, California

Antonio Colton sat tilted back in the battered old chair outside the abandoned church that served as his home. The sun was warm, almost too hot for his liking. While the scant few people he saw walking around wore shorts and skids, cheap flip-flop sandals, he wore full-length denims. It wasn't for the comfort. He hated the looks he got from people when he wore shorts . . . so he rarely did anymore, at least not in public.

His right leg throbbed and he unconsciously rubbed it. *When it heats up, it gives me ghost pains.* The sophisticated metal prosthetic under his pants seemed to reassure him that his leg was gone, compliments of a Russian Volk RPG. The round had hit his antiquated Bradley during the fighting for Seward. He had been at the back door of the armored personnel carrier when the round had exploded. There had been a *whoosh*, then a sound like thunder that engulfed his entire body with a strange vibration. He remembered gasping for breath, his eardrums popping, and the muffled haze of smoke and dirt.

The concussive force had tossed him from the vehicle. The memories of his leg feeling like it was on fire still stung him. There was a smell he caught, just a whiff, the smell of bacon cooking. He didn't need therapists to tell him it was someone burning to death. When he looked down, he saw crimson-soaked muscle strands and exposed, stark white bones poking up at him like daggers. He had crawled away, getting some distance from the blast as the Russians fired into the wreck. Just before he blacked out, he used his belt to fashion a tourniquet around his thigh.

It wasn't until a week later that he learned he had been the sole survivor of the attack. Rodriquez, Jakes, Sally-Jo, Franklin, Stalker—all gone. They had been on the front lines for two months, fighting in several battles. The men and women in that beat-up old Bradley were closer to him than any family he had ever known. Now, years later, he still remembered what they had gone through, but their faces were blurry in his mind. Even when he tried to concentrate on them, he found his memories fading. *Once I'm gone, no one will remember them as they were.*

The Army had repaired the damage of his wounds. His lost leg had been replaced with a bionic prosthetic. Wired right into his nerves in the stump of his thigh, it moved just like his real leg. To him, it just looked like he was half-machine. His new leg had synth-skin which was supposed to be blended with his own dark skin color, but it was obvious it was a biomechanical replacement, even at a distance.

The VA repaired his body and gave him drugs for the sleepless nights. The counselors told him all about his survivor guilt. The sleeplessness was diagnosed as part of his Post Traumatic Stress Disorder. He hated that diagnosis. Sleeplessness wasn't a disorder, like a weakness. In a society where labels were abhorred, the VA had no problems labeling him. *I don't have a disorder, I just have issues.* They taught him meditation techniques. He had hypnosis sessions—deep-brain suppression therapy, the works. Even with drugs, he only managed to get four hours a night of sleep at best, so he eventually just tossed them into the toilet. All of the therapy and support groups didn't seem to be able to shatter his restlessness.

"Hey, AC," Gio said as he rounded the corner. Gio was a veteran too, the 101st Airborne. He met Gio in a bar during his drinking period. Antonio had turned to drinking for six months as a way to cope. It didn't help; in fact, it made matters worse. So, like his medication, he discarded booze as a solution to his issues.

"Hey, Gio," he replied as his friend sidled up next to him.

"You scannin'?" Gio asked as he surveyed the nearly abandoned street. This section of Los Angeles had been the Montebello neighborhood before the war. The Russians had launched some missiles at the city from subs during the war. Some neighborhoods had caught it bad. Montebello had caught fire in the attack and almost a third of the homes and businesses had been lost. Then came the looting, the heavy-handed police response, the riots and street fights. Now Montebello was one of a half-dozen Torn Districts, abandoned and still unrepaired/un-refurbished parts of the city; left to rot until it became profitable to buy them up and tear them down. The people who lived there were like Gio and Antonio—people who couldn't afford to live somewhere else.

Colton nodded. In his lap was an old-model pocket pad. Even the homeless had a right to be connected—or so the lawmakers said. The VA had given him his. He had loaded a semilegal app to run scans on police drones in the area. "They buzzed us about ten minutes ago, a class three." Keeping track of the police patrols was a part of his business. "That means we have about a half-hour before they swing through again."

Gio grinned. "Class three? It's like they don't trust us or somethin'."

"All part of the mayor's 'Clean up the Torn Zones' campaign."

"Yeah. I don't want any more trouble with the cops than I've already had."

Antonio nodded. He himself had suffered at the hands of the La PD a few times. *I deserved it . . . but that doesn't mean I'll invite it.* "You're carrying?"

Gio nodded, still scanning the street with his bloodshot eyes. "Of course I am. I'm a businessman, same as you."

Not quite the same. Finding work after the war and in the tight economy had been hard. There were a lot of veterans flooding the workforce, all looking for a good living. Gio had helped him, though. He was living in an abandoned apartment when Gio told him how to make some fast money selling designer drugs. Before the war, he would have been appalled at the thought of being a drug dealer. He had plans then—going to college, being an engineer. He had even tried picking up on that after the war, but he couldn't seem to fit in with the other college students. Still trying to cope with the war and taking classes was too much to do at the same time.

Antonio sold both Wire and Duke. Wire was a slick chemical mix you wore as a tiny sticky tab that you pressed on your skin, where it slowly seeped into your body. It was a complex amphetamine-like substance that was complicated to manufacture. Rich people bought it to help them work long hours. It did some strange things to your metabolism, burning fat and energy. Wire users looked like they were starving. As a result, people started taking it to lose weight, which drove up demand. It worked—but it consumed you as a person too. Most people were willing to take the risk.

Duke was a pill that induced a near-coma state for hours. Your dreams become so incredible, so intense, it was like you lived in them. People got hooked on it after one hit, making it a great street drug. It was expensive—God only knew where Gio got his supplies given it took a sophisticated lab to make it—and people paid for it.

"You know," Gio said slowly. "You might just enjoy trying some Duke yourself, AC. If anyone deserves some happy times, it's you."

Colton shook his head. "You know I don't use that shit."

"You don't know what you're missing, my man. You used to drink. Using this stuff is no different."

It's very different to me. Drinking until you passed out was one thing. Colton didn't want to become one of those dealers hooked on the stuff they sold. That, from his perspective, was a spiral into doom and death. He only sold a little stuff, just enough to pay the bills. He had started to stash some of his profits. He sold the stuff as a means of getting out of the Torn Districts and back into the real world. Drugs were a means to an end—nothing more.

A car rounding the corner three blocks up caught their attention. Cars were not a rarity in the Torn Districts, but they were usually cobbled-together rust buckets called "rat rides." When people had moved out of the war-battered neighborhoods, it was free rein on what they left behind. This car was nice, a Benz, and it was obviously trolling.

"First customer of the morning," Gio said. "Can you see if they're transmitting?"

Colton stabbed at his digipad. Police vehicles out to sting sellers usually were tied to headquarters sending live-feed data of their patrol. This car was dead according to the apps he was running. "She's black on my scopes. That doesn't mean the cops aren't playing us. They do that sometimes—run silent, run deep."

The car cruised toward them at less than ten miles per hour. Gio seemed to get excited. "Those aren't cops," he said, squinting down the street. "Looks like kids to me."

Antonio winced at those words but said nothing as the vehicle approached. It pulled up in front of his church/home and came to a halt. The car had one of those new fiber-panel bodies where you could download your own colors and images to display on the vehicle. It was a silvery gray color now—but in a few minutes it could be something else entirely. *The Germans seemed to produce the best cars since the war.*

The driver's window came down and Colton could see the two occupants. Gio wasn't wrong—they were kids, probably sixteen. They wore expensive clothes, adaptive gear, fully wired. It was in stark contrast to the stained olive-drab T-shirt that barely covered Antonio's slight paunch. "Hi," the driver said with a false sense of bravado that only made him look more afraid.

"Yo," Gio said, taking one step toward the car, looking up and down the street. "You lost or trolling?"

"We're looking for some royalty," the kid replied, attempting to seem cool with his response. "Royalty" was how people asked for Duke in the movies. Nobody on the street actually said that. The boy driving the car was nervous, Antonio could see it in his face. These kids were on the wrong side of town doing something illegal and potentially dangerous.

"I know some royalty," Gio replied. He turned his head back to Antonio and winked. "It's gonna cost you, though."

The kid held up a coin-like object—a money transfer chip. "How much?"

Antonio pulled himself from the old chair and stood. Where he had been sweaty, the air cooled him for a moment. He took one step and put his hand on Gio's shoulder. "No, Gio."

Gio looked back at him with a mix of anger and confusion. "Why—is it the cops?" He flashed his eyes up and down the street but saw nothing.

"No," Colton replied flatly. "You don't sell to kids."

The boy in the Benz jumped in. "I'll pay the going rate!"

Antonio glared at him. "Get your sorry white asses out of here."

"What are you doing, man?" Gio snapped.

Antonio ignored his friend and took another step toward the car. "Kid, you need to get out of here. You're going to get your ass robbed or killed." His words were not spoken like a parent, but more like a threat.

Gio twisted and got Antonio's hand off his shoulder. "What are you doing, man?" he repeated.

The driver's face went red. He hesitated for a moment then stabbed the accelerator and the gray car took off down the street, leaving Gio and Antonio standing next to each other. "You mind explaining to me what the fuck just happened here?" Gio demanded.

"I don't sell to kids, that's all."

"Well I *do*!"

"Not when you're with me, Gio," Antonio said in a flat tone of voice. "You want to get some rich starch-shirt juiced up, I don't care. Hell, I'm in favor of it. But I won't be a part of getting some kid hooked on this stuff."

"You *do* realize that he's just going to drive somewhere else and get it, from my competition, don't you?" Gio's anger was slowly ebbing.

"Maybe," he replied. "Maybe not. Either way, I'm not going to be a part of some kid getting hooked." *I still have a soul. I still believe I have a purpose beyond this.*

"AC—we are drug dealers. We sell drugs. Why are you getting so holier-than-thou on who your customers are?"

He paused. Gio had never asked him that before. "I don't know for sure. I'm selling this stuff because I have to, to get by. My mom would not approve of that, but she would kill me if she knew I was selling to kids."

Gio tilted his head, puzzled. "Your momma is dead . . . you told me that!"

Antonio allowed himself a thin smile. "Does it matter?"

"It does when you are interfering with *my* business. You want to get all preachy and high and mighty on who you sell to, that's up to you. Don't fuck with my business, man."

Antonio stopped slouching and pulled himself up to his full six-foot-four height, towering over his friend. He felt that surge of excitement, just like before going into battle. His heart thumped loudly in his chest. It felt . . . good. "If you are going to peddle this shit to kids, you're going to have to do it somewhere else. I won't have a part in it—that's all."

"You're going to trash our friendship over something like this?"

"No. We are still friends. You want to sell to kids, I think it's wrong and I don't want you doing it in my presence or in front of my home.

This isn't about us being friends, it's about doing what's right—that's all."

Gio shook his head. "Whatever happened to you in the Great North, it messed with your head, man." Gio tapped his own temple. He started walking away but after a few steps, turned back with a softer expression. "I'll swing by tomorrow, man." He walked away around the corner.

Antonio walked over to the chair and picked up his digipad, then climbed the steps up to the old church. The bionics in his leg made him "feel" the steps as he went up. The big oak door creaked and groaned as he entered.

The air inside the old church was stale. There was a thin veil of dust in the air, lit up by the beams of sunlight. The pews were all still as they had been left when it had been abandoned. Two windows were broken, and he had nailed up plywood to cover them. The light in the church was tinted from the stained glass that was still in place.

As the door closed behind him and snapped shut, Colton leaned against it. He wiped the sweat from his brow with his hand and took a ragged breath. Anxiety attack, that was what the therapist had said about it. Every time he had a tense moment, he felt this wave of uncontrolled nervousness wash over him. All part of his PTSD, that's what they told him at the VA. He took several deep breaths.

He gained control over his racing heart and closed his eyes to regain his composure. "I don't have a disorder," he said out loud, the words seeming lost in the vastness of the church. "I just have issues." He walked down the aisle toward the church rectory, two small offices in the back, where he had a cot set up.

Maybe tomorrow will be better.

CHAPTER 6

JayTech headquarters,
Los Angeles, California

Jay Drake didn't do interviews. He didn't do them because he didn't have to. His corporation employed a large public relations department whose whole purpose was to make sure anytime he spoke, it was carefully scripted and controlled. A lot of CEOs had lost their jobs through poorly executed media interviews—having been caught off guard or saying the wrong thing. The stock market could be influenced by a facial twitch. Drake never gave interviews because of that. His Communications Director Frank Cole had always told him that he would never recommend Jake doing an interview. Cole had always told him that it was part of his image. Being elusive to the press was part of the mystique they crafted around him. *Besides, the whole world knows who I am . . . or they* think *they do.*

Now, suddenly, Cole had reached out to him and told him he had to do an interview with Dana Blaze. When Drake had balked at the request, Cole had hammered him with a long list of reasons for doing the interview. There was the congressional investigation into his contracting practices; the recent Commerce and State Department's inquiry into the data block allegedly stolen from the Chinese Navy which had caused a minor diplomatic incident; a slight slump in stock prices—a seemingly endless list of excuses. The more he argued in favor of the interview, the more Jay doubted Frank Cole's sincerity and motivation. Jay's business practices had always been the subject of scrutiny by his competitors and those jealous of his success. *Somebody's gotten to Frank to make him change his position so radically and so out-of-the-blue.* That thought caught his attention. Cole had been hired because he was rock solid. *Anyone who can shake him like that—I need to get to know.*

The press had called him "The Boy Wonder" when he was seventeen years old and had created the first commercially viable neural interface. It had changed computer interfaces, bionic limb control, dozens of other industries and fields. He disliked the nickname because he read comic books and Batman's sidekick was Robin the Boy Wonder. They were on the seventh Robin in the series, but he was still hopelessly un-cool. While the nickname had been meant as a compliment, to him it was a curse. *Nobody likes Robin—even Robin doesn't like Robin.*

His invention of an inexpensive and workable neural interface would have been enough accomplishment for any man for a lifetime, but Jay liked to think that he was more than just a normal man. When the war had started with White Monday, his company was well poised to take advantage of it. Almost every tech device in America had been corrupted, as had months' worth of backups. Everyone panicked, but not Jay. He had been working for three years on a new operating system: the key was to make it *loadable* around the embedded programming hooks that had taken everything down. While everyone tried to fight the viruses and the widespread corruption of data, Jay and his company rushed out a new operating system that was, at least for four years, immune to the attacks that had so injured the US. The harsher members of the press had labeled him a crass opportunist, but it was a name he took to the bank.

He used a prototype chip-implanted neural interface to signal his admin to send in Dana Blaze. He had chuckled when he had first heard of her two years earlier. A carefully crafted persona, replete with a corny name that reminded him of a stripper more than a reporter. But he knew her reputation as well—she was ruthless in an industry that hid behind that word. When he realized that she had somehow corrupted or blackmailed his communications director, he'd decided that she was worth getting to know. Jay had done his homework on her. His resources had discovered who she had been before the name change, which had taken some time. Dana had covered her tracks very well, his people admitted that. His own intelligence team had learned that she had cultivated a strong network of "research associates," a civilized phrase for spies. The meteoric rise in her career had been at the expense of those she'd destroyed on her way up. Jay couldn't find fault with that;

it was something that he appreciated himself. *You can't take time for the regrets . . . they only slow you down.*

She entered his office followed by her cameraman and Jay immediately sent a brain impulse to shut off his holographic display. He rose from his rather plain chair and managed to fake a smile. "Miss Blaze," he said, gesturing to a chair opposite his old wooden desk. As she entered the office, his eyes were drawn to her breasts. She wore a dress with a circular opening over her ample cleavage. His office sensors had flagged her breasts as implants, but they were high-end, he could see that. The sensors were designed to scan people and feed data to his right contact lens, a fringe benefit of JayTech having developed the tech for the military. The scan also told him they were probably adjustable. *She's using everything she's got to get ahead.* This was no ordinary reporter and cameraman.

"Mr. Drake." She flashed a smile and licked her lips. "This is my vidtech, Theodore Hart." Drake gave him a nod acknowledging his presence. His camera was miniscule. Jay recognized it as one of the top-of-the-line Japanese systems. "It is a pleasure to meet you."

He tipped his head once. "I've heard of you, as well."

"Good things, I hope." She was faking her sincerity quite well.

"You have a reputation for being hard-hitting."

"It's a difficult business." She adjusted her top slightly. "If you don't mind, maybe we can begin?"

Jay waved his hand. "Whenever you're ready."

"Fizz," she said to her camera tech, "if you could just roll—we can edit this down to the key points," she said, turning her attention to Jay. "This is Dana Blaze and I'm here for a worldwide exclusive—the first media interview with Jay Drake, the renowned CEO and President of JayTech," she said, looking at her cameraman. Slowly, she turned to face Jay. "Thank you for allowing me this exclusive, Mr. Drake."

"As you know, I usually don't grant interviews, Ms. Blaze," he replied. "You must have been very persuasive with my communications director."

"I have been told I am just that—persuasive." He wasn't sure how she made her eyes twinkle, but he was confident that it was through artificial means. "I understand from sources in the FedGov that a congressional investigation is going to be calling you to Washington to testify on the recent data theft from the Chinese military on their stealth submarine technology. Was your company responsible for that theft, Mr. Drake?"

This is the reason that I don't give interviews . . . the ambush question. Still, he appreciated the tactic. No preamble, no false build-up of feigned friendship. Dana Blaze tried to topple him in a knockout punch. "Ms. Blaze, the technology market is intensely competitive and the government contracting market even more so. JayTech gets accused of many things by our competitors or lobbyists who are working against us. Such allegations rarely have merit. And when they do, there is often more going on than the public knows."

"So what does the public know or need to know?"

"That JayTech has done nothing illegal. We did not steal the data block from our customers in the Chinese Navy. In fact, my people have recently informed me that a Japanese firm largely financed by the South Korean government was actually involved with the alleged theft. We secured these assets via intermediaries." That much was true. Anyone scanning him would have found his physical reactions to be perfect. Not because they were rehearsed, but because he was telling the truth—just not all of it. His operatives in the Far East had engineered the entire theft and the passing of the data. More to the point, there were others who were involved and potentially implicated. Data blocks were massive slabs of Big Data. Truly tech-savvy people would have questioned how that much data could be so casually moved around in the first place.

"Did the FedGov have knowledge of this?"

Jay flashed a smile. *Good, she is playing into my trap.* "I cannot say without potentially putting myself in the unenviable position of compromising my security clearance and the position of my company as a contractor. I'm sure you understand." A rogue CIA agent had full knowledge of the operation and had endorsed it, in writing. Dropping this hint ensured that he would never testify before Congress, because the Agency would block such testimony to protect itself. Even if they tried to unravel the web of hands that had touched the data, they would be misled to a radical element of the Chinese government, the Russians, and even the Vietnamese. It would take years to unwind the maze of digital blind alleys and false leads, as it had been designed. Rogue intelligence operatives were a rare commodity, and he was pleased to have several in his employ.

"So, an agency of the FedGov did have knowledge of the transfer of this security data?"

"Again, it would be inappropriate and legally risky for me to say. I will say this, however—if Congress does want me to come to Washington and share what I know, I'm more than willing to do so, as long as *all* agencies of the government concur." *There, let the people make what they want out of my answer.*

"This isn't the first time that JayTech has come under scrutiny. Do you chalk all of that up to your competition?"

"My company was responsible for this country's recovery after White Monday if you'd care to remember. What we did was patriotic. When every device in this country was reduced to worthless metal and plastic, we breathed new life into them. When we did this, I was hailed as a hero—hell, the president gave me the Medal of Freedom. Then the pundits came after me. They claimed I was a war profiteer . . . that I was exploiting the conflict for personal gain. Americans like to try to topple people at the top—I guess it's our love of the underdog. I appeared before a half-dozen congressional subcommittees and all that ever came out of those investigations was the conclusion that I was a gifted businessman, in the greatest sense of our nation and our tradition of free enterprise."

"You had the country over a barrel," she replied coyly.

He waited a beat. "If that were really the case, don't you think I would have done more with the opportunity? If I had that kind of leverage, I could have made myself a dictator or run for political office. Did I? No. Why? Because that is not who I am. People who know me know I am a good person. Look at JayTech's charitable donations list. Look at the schools we have built, the communities that we have helped." *The truth is no one knows who I really am.*

"Who are you, then?" Suddenly, he felt as if the trap had turned on him.

He paused. "I am a young man who built a major corporation on nothing but my intellectual capital and effort. I was the kid in school who got bullied . . . beat up by the soccer team just because they thought it was fun and I wasn't able to defend myself. I didn't go to prom because girls thought I was odd. I went off to college and didn't fit in well there either—and I subsequently dropped out. I had an idea for a new neural interface—a medical tool that would change how we could use computers and other devices. I changed people's lives for the better," he said, hearing his own words with a sense of pride he rarely felt. "And I changed the world after the crash of White Monday. You want to know who I am—I am *that* man," he replied, locking his eyes onto hers.

She paused for a moment herself. "I see. Yet I've done some digging, Mr. Drake. That high school you claimed you got beat up at? You purchased that school for an outrageous sum of money five years ago through one of your shell companies. You had it plowed into the ground. The college you dropped out of: your charitable arm, the Drake Foundation, made an anonymous donation of $55 million with the stipulation that your former dormitory be razed. Were these the acts of a man changing lives for the better, or retribution?"

He said nothing. This woman was good—almost exceptional. No one else had even noticed those acts. *I wonder what else she may have stumbled across?* Jay knew that these examples were only the tip of the iceberg. Yes, he had done those things, for revenge. His past had been unpleasant, and he responded with vengeance. "Did one of my subsidiaries purchase my old high school? I was unaware of that. JayTech has grown so large and complex, it is hard for a single man to know every transaction of every division. It's too bad it was torn down; I would have liked to have seen it one more time."

"Yes, your real estate management company did it. I have spoken to several representatives there who said you verbally gave the orders."

"I'm sure those people are mistaken—I would have remembered something like that, I assure you." *Not only are they mistaken, they are fired—or worse once I find out what they told her.*

"So my sources are lying?"

"I would be happy to look over any documentation you may have related to this transaction, rather than respond to some potentially disgruntled employee's false accusations."

Her eyes darted down only for a millisecond. "I'm afraid I don't have anything digitally or otherwise—short of their recorded discussions with me."

"I would think that such a conspiracy would leave some sort of audit trail, wouldn't you?" Jay replied.

"Unless the person who performed the actions had incredible power and influence," she replied.

"I'm willing to play along, Ms. Blaze, but only so far. This is, of course, a hypothetical discussion. If I had that kind of power, why would I waste it on something so incredibly petty? I have been called many things over the years, but never petty."

"Perhaps it wasn't a waste. You were wronged and you simply were administering a form of justice."

"Such actions would be a waste of power." He shrugged.

"Interesting," Dana replied. "What is power to you?"

"Some people think power is influence or control."

"But what do you think?"

"Plain and simple," he said, leaning back in his seat and feeling it creak slightly. "I measure my power with money."

"Your company is privately held and with some of the new laws in place, it is difficult to get a good idea of your net worth. Forbes had listed you as number three on the Forbes 400. They estimate your wealth at twenty-one billion dollars."

Jay chuckled at the amount. Forbes had gotten it wrong for years, the result of masterful deception on his part. But Dana Blaze was proving herself quite resourceful. Was this another verbal snare on her part? "Ms. Blaze, what do *you* think my wealth is?"

"My sources say that it is nearly twice that."

"You're still short, I'm afraid," he finally replied.

"Really? What is the amount then?"

Jay smiled and glanced down at his watch. "I'm not willing to reveal that for personal security reasons. Let me just say, I'm comfortable."

"You do know the exact amount, don't you?"

"Of course I do," he said, suppressing his grin. "In the game I find myself in, you always need to know the score." The timer on his desktop that he had set prior to the meeting beeped audibly. "Unfortunately, I have another pressing appointment." He rose abruptly and extended his hand. "Thank you so much for taking the time to come in."

Dana nodded to her cameraman to stop recording and rose to shake his hand. "Thank you for this opportunity. It was a pleasure to meet you." Her eyes darted over to a place on his desktop and the feeds scrolling by, if only for a second.

He smelled her perfume and felt his face flush. She must have a custom mix—pheromone-embedded. "I have to admit," Jay said as he gestured toward the door, "your research was impressive. I have not found many people that have done as much digging into my past as you have done."

She offered a flirtatious smile. "This is one of the most important interviews I've ever done. I don't come in unprepared."

"Your intelligence sources were less than accurate. But I'm impressed with what you did learn about me. Perhaps we should continue our discussion in a more private setting?"

She looked at him, tilting her head slightly. "Mr. Drake, are you attempting to influence my report by asking me out on a date?"

"Call me Jay," he replied. "And I just want to get to know you better. Anyone who does that much research is worth getting to know."

She flashed a perfect smile. "I will give my contact information to your admin."

Jay flashed a grin. "Dana, I assure you, that isn't necessary."

CHAPTER 7

Applebee's, Riverside, California

When he entered the restaurant, Sergeant Adam Cain removed his mirrored wraparound sunglasses and slid one temple into his duty-shirt chest pocket. Even wearing his sunglasses, coming in from the outside, his eyes took a moment to adjust to the darkness. Squinting, he finally spotted his wife and daughter sitting in a booth at the back of the Applebee's.

Seeing his daughter generated a smile. With long, confident strides, he moved through the restaurant and arrived at the table. His wife, Julie, looked up at him, her jaw already set. *She's ready for a fight. I wonder what I did this time?*

Before she could say anything, he extended his hand that held the small bouquet of flowers. He had purchased them on the way, which was why he was so late for lunch. It was getting harder to get real flowers. There had been a blight a few years back, and tulips became tricky to find. Once they were declared rare, the green groups had moved to prevent their sales. Still, Adam knew a guy that knew a guy who had hooked him up with a half-dozen of the brilliant yellow flowers. "I brought these for you, Julie," he said.

With a sneer, she took them from his hand, almost tossing them on the table. "You're late, Adam."

He didn't let his grin fade. Moving to his daughter's side of the booth, he stood there, waiting for a moment before she moved over for him to sit. "I'm sorry. I wanted to pick up the flowers for you. It took longer than I expected."

"You're an hour late."

He remembered that tone of voice and why he hated it so much. "I said I'm sorry. My phone got trashed on exercise last week and the Army hasn't gotten me the replacement yet." Sliding in next to his daughter, he noticed she seemed to look forward toward her mother rather than at him. Her expression was, *Here we go again.*

Adam agreed.

"Have you ordered?" he asked.

Julie's temper seemed to ebb. "Yes, and we've eaten too. The reason we pick a time for us to meet was for you to actually show up at that time." She sniffed the air between them. "Have you been smoking a cigar? You know that's against the law."

"Guilty as charged," he replied. "And, for the record, that law is stupid. California is full of tree and weed huggers. We can finally get cigars from Cuba and they go and ban them. Don't get your undies in a wad, I didn't do it outside—just in the privacy of my car."

"So it's okay to break the law?" his daughter Amy said in a snide tone.

Oh great, now it's two against one.

"No. I honored the spirit of law. Nobody had to get my second-hand smoke."

Amy rolled her eyes and leaned away from him, just a little more.

"Look, I didn't come to fight with you."

"So why did you want to meet?" Julie asked flatly, in a tired tone.

And in that breath, a dozen memories flooded his mind. Their marriage had lasted eight years, eight hard years. Looking into Julie's face, he saw the crow's-feet around her eyes. Gone was that girl he'd met at the bar and who rode with him with the top down in his convertible. The memories of their time living on bases all over the world showed in her wrinkles and sags. Adam understood that. When he looked in the mirror, his own face looked like worn leather.

But things are going to get better now. "I've just gotten word that I'm being reassigned. They are sending me to Washington, DC. Third Infantry Regiment. It's a plum assignment." He wanted to tell them it was the capstone for a great military career, but he knew his occupation had always been a point of division with his wife and daughter.

"Okay," Julie said slowly, apprehension creeping into her voice.

"Well, I'm going to be across the country for the next two years, then I muster out." He couldn't help sounding excited.

"So what about visitations?" Julie said, glancing at Amy, who turned her face farther from him.

"They'll be a little different, that's all. I was going to ask you what you . . . and Amy, of course, think about her coming to the East Coast once I get settled in? We can adjust the terms of our agreement. I can't do it every month, not on a sergeant's pay, but a couple times a year, yes. You can come too, Julie, if you want." He had made more money in his career when he'd been at a higher rank, but circumstances seemed to work against him . . . that, and a nasty right hook.

His excitement was met with an awkward pause. For a full second, his ex-wife's mouth hung open and no sound came out. "I'm not sure what to say to that," she finally managed to respond.

"Look, I know it's a bit of an inconvenience and all, but this is an honor guard assignment. No combat. With the medals and commendations I've earned, I was a good fit. The Third Regiment does all of the formal ceremonies—White House detail, the whole nine yards."

Julie shook her head once. "Um, Amy—honey, how do you feel about visiting your father?"

"Do I have to?"

Adam Cain had been at war since he was seventeen years old, in the last of the Gulf conflicts. He had slogged his way through heavy fighting in Korea and Alaska. He had been wounded four times. He had won two Silver Stars and a Bronze Star. Her words hit him harder than any piece of shrapnel ever could. He felt his excitement wash away.

"What is that supposed to mean?" he snapped back. The sergeant emerged in his voice.

"You're never around anyway," his daughter replied, facing him with an angry glare in her green eyes. "Most of our visits consist of me sitting with you watching a movie and ordering in Domino's pizza or sushi."

"I took you to Disneyland," he retorted.

"That was four years ago. I'm seventeen years old. In a year, I'll be an adult and we can end all of this lame shuffling around, me pretending you're my dad and you pretending you know me. Most of the time you cancel our visits anyway. There's not a lot for either of us to do on post."

This time the pause was his. *She has a mouth like a machine gun when she starts.* "My job often requires me to be on-call."

"Other dads somehow make the time."

"Other dads are not responsible for the lives of twenty-two snot-nosed junior-college pukes who couldn't find their asses without a flashlight and both hands. My 'job' means I have to take care of those kids and protect our country." This was not the first time they had gone over this ground. *How many more times am I going to have to take this hill?*

"I get it," Amy replied. "I've heard this routine my entire life. Look, it's not a big deal, okay? You and Mom are divorced and you can't be around. I'm not complaining. You don't have to keep trying to force yourself into my life. I'm almost an adult."

Her pushing back was an insurmountable force, he could feel it. The sergeant in him wanted to yell. It took a lot for him to suppress that. "Honey—I'm sorry I wasn't there more, I really am. But things can be different. Just a few years in DC and I'll be out. We can spend more time together."

"You always say that. Every base, every new assignment, it's always going to be better. You don't understand. It's too late for that. I'm not a little girl anymore. I'm certainly not *your* little girl anymore." Hurt rang in her voice, years of it.

"I—we can fix it, Amy."

"What makes you think I want to fix it?"

"I'm your father," was all he could respond.

She stared at him. Gone was the girl with ponytails who wore braces. Gone were the cute dresses and the hugs. What was left was a teenager—no—an adult. She was another woman in his life who wanted nothing to do with him. He wanted to say something like, "What has your mother told you about me to make you hate me so much?" It wasn't necessary. Julie wasn't that way. Oh sure, Julie had been bitter in the divorce. She was as much as a fighter as he was. The only difference was that he liked it more than her. No, this wasn't about Julie poisoning her mind; this was about him.

He could lead a platoon into battle, seize the objective, fight the good fight. As a father though, he had made a lot of mistakes. His broken promises, most not deliberate, hadn't helped matters. There was the time he caught her making out and threatened to break the young man's skull . . . that had not gone over as planned. The arguments had been in their relationship for some time, but he had always chalked them up to her being rebellious and him not being around. Now he realized that there was no resetting the clock. She was grown up and didn't want a relationship with him.

It hurt. Adam didn't show it. Years of having a rigid jaw and wearing a permanent tough expression made his emotions seem distant. It was the Army way. For the first time in a long while, he felt old.

"Can I go? Mom, I'll meet you outside." She scooted over next to him, her hip touching his.

For a moment he didn't move. Then he slid out of the booth and watched her as she left. She was on her wristcomp even before she hit the restaurant door. Adam slid back into the booth and put his elbows on the table, wringing his hands.

"Adam," Julie said with actual compassion. "She feels grown up. What did you think she was going to say?"

He looked at her and let the years melt away, so he saw the twenty-four-year-old girl of his youth. "I don't know," he confessed. "I just assumed she'd want to come out and see me. I thought that she'd look forward to the trip out east."

Julie shook her head slightly at his words. "You never change. That's part of the problem. You're looking at her and hoping to still find your little girl. She's outgrown everything you remember."

"The last few visits we had were great."

Julie rolled her eyes. "Seriously, Adam? She told me about them. You took her out for pizza and you streamed a war movie."

"Jules—she said she didn't want to go out at all, I had to drag her out for pizza. And for the record, she's the one always ordering Domino's sushi. I asked her what she wanted to watch and she said she didn't care. She enjoyed the movie—she told me so."

"She told me something different, Adam. Jesus, you never could understand women."

"I understand women—"

She waved her finger in the air to cut him off. "Let's not go there. Look, she told me she was bored. She didn't want to be there in the first place, that's why she didn't want to go out. And a war film? Really?"

"It was that latest John Wayne flick." A decade before, Hollywood had come up with the means to cast dead actors in films, digitally duplicating every aspect of them. John Wayne was a star again, decades after his death. "It's going to be a classic. She said she didn't care what we watched."

Julie shook her head. "You treated her like one of your Army buddies."

Her words struck home. He hated when his wife was right.

"Julie—I just want to set things right. I know I was rarely around. I know that was mostly my fault. I get it. But I'm going to be out of the Army in two years. I want to try to connect with her. She's just about all I have that doesn't fit in a duffle bag—her and you."

She looked into his eyes and said nothing for three seconds. "Adam . . ."

"Maybe you can come out with her. I can arrange for quarters, nothing trashy like that dump at Fort Hood. DC is a blast. There's museums, monuments, tours of all the FedGov sites. It will be great; just like old times."

Her eyes became suspiciously bright for a moment. "Adam, I'm not coming to Washington. We're divorced. I have a life here now. Our life together is over, gone. In fact, once Amy turns eighteen and moves out on her own, you and I will have no real reason to meet."

Adam stared at her. The divorce had been her idea, not his. Oh, he had gone to court, signed the paperwork, everything his lawyer said he had to do. He didn't mind cutting the checks for alimony and child support every month. He was never late, never bitter. She had divorced him—but he had never left her. He realized it all over again as she spoke. It was a tug at his emotions, feelings he had buried a long time ago. Inside him was a young man who idealistically thought that time might reverse and his girlfriend might return.

The soldier in him overtook the youth. The mission was over . . . he could see that now. He had learned a long time ago about the risks of pushing a bad position. There were times you had to retreat, fall back, live to fight another day. "I know," he growled, as if his voice didn't want to form the words.

She reached up and put her hand on his shoulder. "Do you, Adam? We're just about at the end of this."

He hated what she was saying. Anger swelled in him. Fifteen years ago, he would have exploded. He pushed those feelings down, hard. His hand swept up across his brow and back across his tightly cropped hair, and he rubbed the top of his hair where he was going white. He struggled for composure. "I *do* understand. I know you've moved on with your life. There was always a part of me that thought you might come back. You moved on. I didn't. Now I have an ex that doesn't have any reason to talk to me and a daughter that has no inclination to." His daughter was almost his only evidence that he existed outside of the Army, and now she didn't want to spend any time with him.

Her hand moved from his shoulder to the leathery side of his face. "This has been coming for some time, Adam. You were always away, carrying the damn flag all over the globe. Every time you got a promotion to get ahead, you did something to lose it. During the war there was at least twice I thought you were dead. While you went off to fight, I had to battle it out at home raising a daughter alone. Now you are ready to spend time with us and that moment has passed. I'm sorry." She was, and that made it hurt even more.

Julie tugged his head down and kissed him on the cheek. Before he could say something stupid, she spoke again. "I'll talk to Amy. Let me see if I can sway her into coming to visit you."

"I appreciate it."

She turned and walked out of the restaurant. Adam stood there, watching her leave. Out of the corner of his eye, he spotted the tulips he had bought her, still sitting on the table. *What was I thinking?* A part of his life had just walked out the door, leaving him in the darkness of the restaurant.

Well, he still had one lady who never left him—the Army. He reached down to his breast pocket and pulled out the cigar next to his sunglasses. He bit off the end, spit it on the floor, and shoved the brown Cuban cigar into his mouth. The Army asked a lot, but in the end, it was the only family he knew he could count on. Julie would be true to her word, but it was time to move on. He reached into his pocket and pulled out a lighter. *Screw this . . . screw the flowers . . . screw this sentimentality.*

He brought up the lighter and a waiter appeared in front of him as if out of nowhere. "Sir—that's against the law." The whiny tone of his voice didn't help his position in the least.

Adam flicked open the lighter and took a long drag on the Cuban. "I don't give a flying fuck at a rolling doughnut," he replied. He headed out of the restaurant before the police could be called.

Hooah . . .

CHAPTER 8

Cassidy Chen sat down in front of her breakfast packet and tore it open. The smell of eggs and simbacon rose on a blast of steam. Her mother had three kinds of nukeable breakfast packets in the house. Cassidy preferred the maple bacon oatmeal, but her mother had warmed up the scrambled eggs fiesta. With the right amount of hot sauce splattered on it, it was acceptable.

"Cassidy, honey," her mother called from the family room, where the holodisplay showed the morning news and entertainment, "make sure you say goodbye to your father, you know he leaves this morning."

Nobody called her Cassidy outside of the house. She was CC to the rest of the world. Her mother knew that, but refused to concede. She had been named after a grandfather on her mother's side, a man she had never met. While he was originally from the old world in China, he had taken an American name and wife. Her mother said she had his eyes, that was why she had gotten the name. Everyone she knew had a handle—a nickname. Being raised with a predominantly boy's name was a good enough reason for her to hate being called by her given name.

She had inherited more than his name. Her father was second-generation American from Japan. The mixing of genes made CC look more Asian than either of her parents. It came with benefits and curses. On the plus side, she wore a lot of the more trendy clothing imported from the Far East and it made her stand out. On the minus side, other students presumed that she was above average intelligence academically and they asked for help on H-work and assignments. She didn't mind. In this case, the stereotype was close to reality. She was in the top percentile in the freshman class at Barbara Walters Academy, something her parents were more proud of than she was.

The mention of her father's trip made her roll her eyes. *Another one of his boring trips.* He was gone often, the nature of his work. He worked for a civil engineering firm downtown and was assigned to major construction projects around the world. When he left, he was gone for months at a time. Sure, he connected with her every night, but it wasn't the same as him being there. Her friend JZee said she felt sorry for her that her dad missed so many school events and field trips. CC didn't feel slighted, though . . . *not too much.* When her dad was home, he devoted himself to her and every aspect of her life. Even after the arrival of her brother Donald two years ago, her father's time seemed focused on her and she loved that. He never missed soccer practice when he was in town, nor a single parent-teacher conference. Her mother, on the other hand, spliced her time between her work at a prestigious law firm in downtown LA and her family. David Chen was the rock in the family. While his trips took him abroad, his priority always seemed to be her and CC loved it.

She shared a special bond with her father; there were things she could tell him that she wouldn't share with her mother. He had been an only child, just like she had been until Donny was born. *He understands me, whereas Mom just gets frustrated.* Her mom was judgmental, always telling her how to act or what to do when she opened up with her. Not her dad. He just listened and tried to relate how he had dealt with a similar issue when he was a boy. Mom wanted to solve everyone's problems: then again, she was a lawyer. Her father looked to build connections to her—even at the age of fourteen she could see that. She gulped down the processed eggs and simulated bacon and as soon as she swallowed it, headed for the stairs.

Donny was adorable, even she had to admit that, with his blond hair (*where did that come from?*) and dimples. CC tolerated him and the way he drew their mother's attention. Ivanna, the au pair, spent more time with Donny than her mom did. *I swear she's teaching him Romanian.* Donny was a fast learner. She loved him too, but she made sure she didn't show it often in front of her parents. CC never forgot that for the first part of her life, she didn't have to share her parents' time.

At the top of the stairs she turned right and went into her parents' bedroom. Her father was adjusting his tie. He was tall for his family. CC always felt she had to look up to him. Now, it hit her that she was nearly as tall as he was. She sauntered in and plopped down on the bed next to his suitcase.

"Hey, kiddo," he said, his eyes fixed on the mirror for a moment, then turning to her. "What is up with you today?"

"We're doing a VFT to the city grid control," she said with a hint of boredom in her voice.

"VFT?"

"Virtual Field Trip," she replied. "I might as well watch a Red-ray of the tour."

He flashed her a smile. "Look, the grid is pretty important. I mean, it provides us access to the net and supports pretty much everything we do. I know a guy who helped architect their facility downtown. It's a pretty impressive piece of work. Try to enjoy it."

She faked a quick frown. "I will pay attention, but they can't make me like it." She bounced once on the bed, for no reason at all. "So, Dad, how long are you going to be gone this time?"

"Three months. I'll be working on the new Marine facility on Guam. It's not anything that'll win me an award or anything like that—typical FedGov project. Still, the base is getting its first real facility upgrade in the last forty years. I'll be back once a month for a few days, promise."

"So you're off to a tropical island and I have to go to school."

He smiled and shook his head. "It sounds a lot more glamorous than it is, kiddo. Sure, we've got grid there, but I won't have lot of time to lay on a beach or anything. The sooner we get this project done, the sooner I'm back with you and Mom."

"You're still gonna be able to help me with my math—right?"

"We're a few time zones off—but I will make the time on my calendar. With the international dateline and all . . ." he looked up, running the calculations in his head, ". . . when you are usually doing your homework, I'll be just starting work the next day."

This wasn't CC's first experience dealing with time zone changes. Her father worked on projects all over the globe, though this was the first one on a tropical island. She really didn't need his help often on homework, but he liked math and it was an opportunity for them to connect. Neither of them said that out loud, but both understood it.

"Are you going to have Mom and me come out and visit you?"

David Chen shook his head. "I don't think so, not for the first month or so. Your mom is working that big class-action lawsuit and is going to be tied up. Besides, there are very few commercial flights to Guam; it's not exactly a big tourist draw. By the time you guys got there, you'd have to turn around and head back."

CC had hoped to go to the island. She had studied up on it secretly when her father had begun talking about traveling there. It looked very much how you'd picture a tropical island. There was a lot on the net about the island during World War II, but that was ancient history. While she liked to study history, in this case, it didn't get her any closer to spending time with her father. In fact, Guam was keeping the family apart, so she automatically didn't like the place.

"You know there's a dance at school in two weeks," she said coyly.

Her father was at his dresser picking up cuff links. He turned to face her. "There is, huh?"

"Not a big thing, really—only until ten o'clock. It's the first dance of the year."

"I see," he said, taking a few steps toward her. "I went to my first high school dance when I was about your age."

She knew the quickest path to approval required her to engage her father and his memories. "Did you have fun?"

He cocked his eyebrow and winced. "Not really. Loud music, bad punch, girls lined up on one wall, boys on the other. A few kids dancing—really badly. Most of us didn't know what to do or were too nervous to ask."

"Oh," she replied, hoping that there would have been a better story to go with her father's memory.

"You want to go, right?" he asked.

"Well, I guess—yes. My friends are all going."

For a moment or two he said nothing, just studied her face. "I'm not entirely comfortable with you going, CC. You're just a freshman, and younger than a lot of the kids." That was always the case. CC's birthday was late in the year, and testing had allowed her to skip first grade. She was one of the youngest students that would graduate in the class of 3043, four years from now. She hated that—and the fact that everyone else would have their driver's license before her. "I just want to go so that I fit in with the other kids. I want to see what it's like."

"Have you asked your mom?"

CC winced, which told her father the answer before she opened her mouth. "I did. She said I was too young. She's all worried about boys and drugs. But there'll be teachers there—chaperones. None of my friends who are going are troublemakers. You know JZee and Storm."

"If your mother said no—"

"She said I could check with you," CC blurted.

Her father said nothing. Then, "A dance. This is a big deal for you, isn't it?"

"Yes."

"Is there some boy involved in this?"

Was there? If it had been her mom asking she would have just replied quickly with a "no." But this was her father. There wasn't a boy, not specifically. There *was* a cute boy, Arnold Fletchman, whom she liked. His handle was Spiked, compliments of his spiked hair. She liked him, but didn't understand why. There was just something about him, maybe his sense of humor or his looks—she couldn't really say. She didn't know if Spiked was going to be at the dance or not; they barely talked in class. Still, if he was, it would be an opportunity for them to talk. There were few chances for social conversation at school other than at lunch and the bustle between classes. "Not really. I just didn't want to miss out. Everyone else is going." Her voice wasn't quite pleading, but was close.

He smiled. "Alright. I'll talk to Mom. No promises. She's in charge of the house when I go, and if she says 'no' then that is that—understood?"

"Thank you, Daddy," she said, standing up and hugging him. She felt his arms wrap around her body and hold her close. Again, she noticed that she was almost as tall as her dad.

As they pulled apart, he leaned forward and kissed her on the forehead. "I need you to behave while I'm gone. It's hard on your mother when I'm out of town. Listen to Ivanna and your mom. Help out with Donny—especially when it's time for him to go to bed. Do your chores around the house and no back talk. Got it?"

"Got it," she replied, giving him another quick hug.

"Cassidy!" her mother called up from the kitchen. "The shuttle is about three minutes away. Say goodbye to your father then get down here and get ready."

"I love you, kiddo," he said softly, in a way that only her father could.

She moved away from him and toward the staircase. She turned and looked again at David Chen. He was standing there in his black suit pants and white starched shirt, putting on his cuff links. He flashed her a smile and a quick wave.

CC turned toward the stairs and felt an unfamiliar tug at her emotions. She gave her father another quick glance. He was no longer looking at her but working on a stubborn cuff link. Somehow, something about this trip felt different from his other business trips, but she didn't know why she felt that way.

As she started down the stairs, the feeling seemed to fade, but still lingered. CC walked into the kitchen and saw her mother standing there with her pack. Her mother kissed her, but CC was numb, still attempting to process the strange sensation she had felt. As she left the front stoop and moved toward the school shuttle, she pushed away the last bit of the weird emotion. *It's just another business trip . . . nothing special. Why worry now?*

CYCLE II

Dunbar V oil drilling platform,
Buzzard Oil Field, the North Sea off Scotland

Albert Ferguson was a man with a problem. The Dunbar platform was one of British Petroleum's most advanced rigs operating in the North Sea, and he was her chief engineer. For the four years since the rig had begun drilling and pumping, it had been a complex, challenging, and strangely fun job. But in the last two weeks, things had changed.

It started when the rig began to tilt. It wasn't a massive tilt. In fact, none of the ninety-two people on the platform even noticed it. Only the sensitive control room instruments detected the list. He had tried at first to prove it was an instrumentation error, but it wasn't. Now it kept him up at night, because even with the correction systems, the tilt was there and increasing.

The legs of the platform were constantly being checked by monitors and everything seemed correct. So he adjusted the sensors and moved the cameras as far as possible. It was then he spotted it: Leg 3 was buckling. The bend was minor, but enough to give the platform a slight tilt. But the buckling, that was what ate at him. It shouldn't be happening. The platform had weathered North Sea storms like a Titan, but this stress had come out of nowhere. There hadn't been a major storm in over a year. So why was the leg bending? There had to be a hell of a force working on it, or something wrong structurally. Could the warping be stopped?

Today, he was going to get up close and personal with the problem. He was going to pilot down Dog One—the remote-controlled robot used for close-up work under the water. With her cameras, he knew he could get close to the damage and hopefully see what was causing the issue.

In the control room, he inserted his hands into Dog One's control arms. His implanted neural interface gave him command of her movements. Even with her brilliant lights, it was hard to see through the debris swirling in the water. The North Sea was an unforgiving bitch. Twice on the way down, Dog One bumped into the leg, victim of the currents that dominated the drilling site.

When he got within twenty-five feet of the bend, he slowed Dog One's descent and activated the recorder. *It can't be a design flaw . . . we built this thing to last fifty years.* He snaked the remote control deep-sea probe down along the leg until he saw something, a bump on the metallic surface.

It was a sea creature of some sort, but not like anything he had ever seen before. It was attached to the leg by its mouth, as if it was sucking on it. Its body, however, did not look at all like a normal fish. The light struck a luminescent glow from the creature, in broad-painted brush-strokes of different colors—yellows, greens, oranges. Without light, the stripes were all but invisible. The creature's eyes seemed to glow brilliant green. Its jawbone was hyperextended, and appeared to have nasty bone-like protrusions jutting out like barbs or extra teeth. The creature was almost a yard long and seemed oblivious to the probe's presence beyond the strange glow from its stripes.

"What the bloody hell are you?" he muttered, while looking at the display. He angled Dog One past the fish and saw something in the next three feet that stunned him. A hole in the leg. It was relatively small, the size of a cricket ball, but a hole nevertheless. He spun Dog One to be perpendicular to the hole and moved in closer. The edges of the hole were relatively smooth. This was not a hole cut by an acetylene torch. The hole was not a perfect circle but close to it. *How can that be?*

He dipped Dog One downward along the leg and saw another pair of the strange creatures. *There's more of them.* Between the two of them was another hole. *No . . . it's not possible . . .* One of the creatures dropped as his camera focused in on it. It left behind a hole in the leg, and the creature's bizarrely striped markings seemed to pulse a dull crimson as it fell away. He watched the pulsating maroon light on the creature's body fade into the depths. *It's like some sort of beacon . . . but for what?*

He swung Dog One around and backed it away from the leg of the oil platform. Then Albert activated another light on the remote unit. With some distance between him and the leg, he was able to see more of it.

His jaw fell open. There were more than a dozen of the strange creatures hanging vertically on the massive leg of the platform, at least that many in the beams of the light. Each pulsed a dull green or yellow as the light hit their otherwise invisible markings. There had to be more than that outside his field of vision. *Hundreds of them?* He also saw the holes. *Over twenty of them . . . my bloody God!* The farther down he angled the light, the more holes he saw. The creatures weren't fish, not in the traditional sense—there was something very different about them. They reminded him of a prehistoric creature, like a mutated form of Coelacanth. *Maybe that's what they are—something hiding in the deep all of these centuries.* Now they had come up to devour his rig.

"These damned-dickhead fish are eating the platform leg!"

That isn't possible. The leg was high grade structural steel coated with three layers of special sealants and anti-corrosive agents that made it some of the strongest material used underwater. Cutting it required special torches and other gear. Yet here these creatures were, and wherever they left, a hole.

The engineer in him kicked in. Two issues popped into his brain. One: how could these fish be eating the alloy? Two: why are they doing it?

As he took Dog One lower and saw the number of holes near the bend in the leg, he came to a realization. No matter how they were doing it, the damage to Dunbar V was so extensive, he'd have to seal the wells and evacuate. *They are eating my rig right from under me.*

Albert Ferguson didn't know what those creatures were on his rig, but he knew he hated them.

***

The ferry *Hansa*, twenty minutes out from Thoothukudi, India, the Palk Strait

Anish Deo had been a deckhand on the *Hansa* for the past five years. The ferry made the run twice a day between Thoothukudi and the island, loaded with cars, passengers, and light cargo. It was not a glamorous job, but it paid good money for a good day's work.

The *Hansa* herself was one of the newer ships in the fleet of ferries owned by Kanesta Corporation. Newer meaning it had been built in the current century. There were older ferries in the fleet that were cobbled-together pieces of junk. Getting assigned to those ships was a form of punishment, from what Anish knew. Many of them leaked, had bumped the docks so often that their hull plates were mauled or split, and others had barely functional engines. More than a few times, the *Hansa* had been called to tow one of the older ships whose engines had failed. While no one said it out loud, it was common knowledge that working on this ship was a privilege compared to others, so even when there were problems on the *Hansa*, her crew rarely complained.

This was the last run of the evening. The sun had set and twilight had wrapped the warm waters of the Palk Strait. The air stank of seawater and a hint of garbage, probably overflow from some barge that had passed earlier. As Anish stood at the railing for his first true break of the evening, he watched the last seconds of sunset in the distance. This was his favorite run with the ship. The passengers were generally quiet, the heat subsided enough to be tolerable—it was a great time to be aboard the ship.

He had no illusions about being a ferryman as a career. Anish had been saving his pay diligently, as his parents had insisted. When he had enough money, he was planning to emigrate to another country and get a job there until he could afford to go to college. Anish, at the age of eighteen, had a plan and was sticking to it. For now, the *Hansa* was his source of income and his stepping stone to his future. As he watched the sun wink out of sight and full darkness descended, he wondered if he would look back on these days fondly in his old age? Would he ever want to ride the ferry again when he was a successful graduate and wealthy in another country? *No. My memories here are just of work and the smells of people and the water.*

As these thoughts cooled him, he looked out in the distance and noticed a shimmering green light. The light was moving fast at the edge of the horizon. Anish had made the trek across the Palk Strait many times and did not remember seeing such a light before. It was low, almost as if it were on the water itself. From the speed it was moving, it had to be a private vessel of some sort, perhaps a yacht or speedboat. His eyes fixed on the light.

The light seemed to turn, as if it had suddenly noticed the ferry, like a shark stalking its prey. Then it began to move toward the ferry. It was fast, very fast, quicker than a jet ski. There was a massive wake in the distance behind it.

And the light—the green light got brighter. Then he realized that the light was not on the surface—it was a brilliant light *under* the water. *Is that some sort of submarine? How could it move like that?*

Whatever it was, he realized, it was heading straight for the starboard side of the *Hansa.*

Anish didn't have time to think, only time to act. He sprinted down the rail to the emergency warning alarm. He broke the glass and pulled the lever. A warning siren whooped loudly. The light was rapidly closing with the ship. Other people were gathering on the railing, pointing at it too. *It's going to hit us!*

He grabbed a life preserver ring hanging on the railing and yelled to the passengers. "Get your life preservers! It's going to hit us!" There were shrieks and cries of panic. He could see some of the people following his commands over the whooping sound of the siren. Others were mesmerized by the approaching light.

It was upon the *Hansa* in a matter of seconds. He saw it under the water, barely—it was like a long fish of some sort, but was clearly a vessel. There was a metallic grinding sound as it hit the ferry. The ship rocked hard to starboard. Anish slammed into the railing and went over the side. His mouth opened to scream but he didn't hear it. There was a rush of water, and bubbles everywhere. The sounds of metal on metal and of thuds and bangs under the sea seemed to fill his mind. He clung to the life ring with his left arm, struggling to kick his feet—to put some distance between him and the ferry.

He burst into the air, gasping and panting—spitting up water that he didn't even realize he had swallowed. As Anish turned his head he saw the *Hansa*, half rolled over on her starboard side. Cars and scooters on her deck toppled into the water only twenty feet from where he bobbed. People bobbed through the surface of the water too, flailing and screaming. His ears were filled with water but through the muffled noise he could hear crying and the sounds of human panic.

Whatever that ship was, it had torn through the hull of the ferry and now people were dying all around him. He wrapped his right arm through the life ring and watched in horror as the lights on the ferry flickered twice and went dark.

What hit us . . . and why?

CHAPTER 9

Conference Room Bravo, Defense Intelligence Center, the Pentagon, Arlington, Virginia

Captain Ashton Slade took the first two weeks in his new temporary position at the Defense Intelligence Agency to acclimate himself to the role. It wasn't too different from his Army position, but the data was new and interesting. Commander Franks's team had been very supportive and helpful. He'd anticipated some interservice rivalry issues, but they seemed to evaporate as soon as he began to lead them. Once he'd settled in and started looking at the data using some of the tools and techniques he had developed for use by the Army team, he saw them . . . the anomalies and odd patterns that Franks had mentioned.

Analysts mined big data looking for trends and patterns that are not normally observable. It was a science, and at the same time it was an art. What Ashe had seen first were strange occurrences that didn't fit into the statistical norms. These then formed patterns of their own, which opened them to additional analysis. Slade had become obsessed with the new data and the strange trending he saw. His nights had been spent writing new algorithms attempting to make sense of the patterns and connections.

The anomalies that kept him up at night were not major or massive in nature. Many were small, barely warranting reporting. They did stand out, however, at least to him—and to his team, once he started sharing his findings.

A few members of the Navy intel team initially balked. He was, after all, filling in for Commander Franks. What could an Army analyst know about the high seas? Slade encouraged them to challenge him, to wade into the stats themselves and prove him wrong. The doubters were silenced after only a few days of crunching the numbers.

He classified the anomalies as disturbances tracked by military- and civilian-reported events. Slade tended to favor those submitted by military sources. The disturbances were broken into additional categories, all tied to the Pacific Ocean. There were airborne instances, nautical instances, and those along the coasts. The supporting evidence was remarkably abundant. The patterns were there—he saw them, as did his staff. The data *consumed* him. Working in a semi darkened secure conference room, he projected the trends on the holographic displays and plotted them against the maps. The bits of light, the scrolling data, the maps, they held him in their grip, compelling him to stare into them as if they could speak. They could, only if you knew what you were looking for—and at this point he didn't. A knock at the door brought him back to reality. He condensed the images into the tabletop and called, "Secured—enter."

The door opened and Colonel Hastings and Captain Diaz entered. He shook hands with the colonel, then the captain. Both were US Air Force, and Colonel Maxwell Hastings was a presence in the room. Looking as if he had stepped out of a 1960s Cold War movie, he was rigid, tough, and his reputation as a combat aviator was well known from the days when pilots actually climbed into the cockpits and faced down their enemies.

Captain Diaz was his colleague in the analyst pool. They had worked together before. She was cold, emotionless, and from what he could tell, brilliant. Oftentimes when he was working late, he would see her doing the same in her pod of workstations. She was conservative with her words, thoughtful, clear and articulate.

Slade gestured to the chairs and the officers took their seats. "Thank you for coming down, sir. I appreciate your time."

"You asked that we bring our radar tracking data for the Pacific for the last five years," the colonel replied. Captain Diaz put her thumb on the small black case she carried and, once it read her biosig, it popped open. She pulled out the coin-size access disk and slid it toward him on the desktop. "We don't get this kind of request every day. So what have you come across?" Curiosity and skepticism rang in her voice, the marks of a good intelligence officer.

Slade put the disk on the datafeed portion of the table and accessed the radar data. With his left hand he pulled up one set of data that he had extracted. "I'm filling in for Commander Franks at the Navy Pacific desk. I started crunching his data and discovered a strange set of sightings—many military, some civilian. I wanted to see if your tracking data detected anything out of the norm that matched."

A map of the Pacific came up. Tiny red dots appeared in several locations—one grouping south of the Hawaiian Islands, some out in the middle of the ocean. Some were random, but there were clear patterns, clusters of red on the vast blue of the sea. "Where you see these red dots, there have been sightings of ships, usually at a distance, vessels of abnormally large size."

"Captain," the colonel began. "You do know that we are Air Force. We're not going to get radar readings on the surface unless they are close to our monitoring stations."

Slade suppressed the urge to smile at his comment. "I know that, sir. These vessels were not just seen in the ocean. They were seen flying in some cases. Their physical descriptions are similar, but the vessels involved were seen both in the skies and at sea."

Colonel Hastings narrowed his eyes. "You have my attention."

"Here're the dates and locations," he pointed to a holographic list. "Can you compare that against your radar histories—see if there is anything that can match up?"

The weathered colonel nodded to Captain Diaz. Silently she pulled up her own list and began to filter it. As she worked, Hastings leaned back in his chair for a moment. "You said these are of abnormally large size—are we talking bombers?" His tone meant one thing: he was thinking of the Chinese or the Russians.

I have to be careful about what I say here . . . so he doesn't shut me down. "Sir, they were larger than bombers."

"Larger? Just how big are we talking?" Hastings pressed.

Slade felt his face redden slightly. "Two different sizes, sir. One roughly the size of an aircraft carrier. Another larger than that."

Hastings looked like he was about to explode in anger or laughter—Ashton wasn't sure which. "That's pretty damn big, son."

He was prepared to share his data and weather the potential ridicule, but Captain Diaz cut him off. "Data's up, gentlemen."

The red dots were matched up with a series of green and yellow dots. It became clear that there were few green dots and many yellow.

The dots were scattered over the Pacific, but again, there were detectable patterns. Many were near the red dots of Slade's observations. For a moment no one in the conference room said anything, their eyes transfixed by the dots.

"The green dots indicate confirmed readings unaccounted for by our radar operators," Captain Diaz said.

"That's a lot of instances," Ashton said, staring at the massive holographic map.

"It's not uncommon to pick up momentary blips—they can be anything from dropping space debris to atmospheric disturbances. I'm more concerned about the yellow dots."

"What are they?" Slade asked.

"Abnormally large or apparently errant readings that trigger equipment diagnostics. Sometimes we pick up readings that indicate that the equipment is out of calibration. When we get those kinds of readings, the officer in command usually orders diagnostics. I included them in my query because they may have misinterpreted a reading and assumed it was an equipment error." *She's good.* There were many yellow dots, all clustered around the areas where he had recorded sightings.

"Are those numbers correct?" Colonel Hastings asked.

"Yes, sir."

"Pull up some of the reports. Are any of them linked to large readings, the size that Captain Slade here mentioned?"

Her hands flew in the space over the desk, data lists dancing in the air in front of the map. "Sir, I'm pulling out those not related to abnormally large readings." The number of yellow dots diminished, but not by much.

"What in the hell?" Hastings said in a low tone. "Can you pull up some of the readings they received before they ran their diags?"

She did, in only a few seconds. The images that appeared in the holographic space over the conference table showed as black blobs, some larger than others. "What are they?" Slade asked.

"Damned if I know. These readings have to be wrong. Those there," Hastings pointed to two off to his right, "those are nearly 360 yards across. They're beyond massive. The others," he pointed to several of the reports as Diaz brought them up, "they're smaller—but still they are close to the size you are reporting. Why the hell didn't they report these things?"

Captain Diaz replied, never once slowing her manipulation of the data in front of them. "Simple, sir. Readings of that magnitude would have been deemed as equipment malfunctions. The sizes of those readings are larger than anything we've tracked before. Our men were following procedures."

"Procedures," Hastings spat out with contempt.

"You can't blame them," Slade commented. "The larger class of these vessels is as a big as five or more aircraft carriers. One report from a fishing vessel reported a wave of four feet in height, and they were at least eight miles out from the sighting. That's another thing too, sir. Rogue waves. The Navy analysts have been trending them. Usually they are linked to some meteorological occurrence or seismic activity. In the last five years, our instances of rogue waves in the Pacific are up."

"How much are they up?"

"From seventeen sightings to one hundred and thirteen. NOAA's buoy network is fairly good at tracking them," Slade replied. Hastings's jaw extended slightly and locked, but he didn't respond.

Diaz, unfazed by the information, stared at the reports she had pulled up, sifting through them with her fingers in the virtual space above the table. "Sir, these radar reports all indicate a downward trajectory. They were coming from suborbital space downward."

Into the ocean. "Do you have reports like this from before October of '35?"

A moment or two passed as she parsed the information. "Only two. Why?"

"We have nothing in our records of these sightings prior to that. When you look at the numbers after that, and the correlation of locations, this can't be coincidence," Slade said.

Diaz went into motion again, moving information around quickly. "I wonder . . ." she muttered to herself.

"Wonder what, Captain?" Hastings prodded.

"I've been crunching some data of my own, sir. Over the last five years, we've had an increase in the loss of satellites over the Pacific. It's a little side project of mine. The numbers show as an anomaly, but we've never been able to compare it against anything else. I'm lining up the

lost satellites' last positions, dates, times, and these clustered patterns."
A series of triangles which Slade assumed to be the satellites in question
appeared on the map. All but two were lined up with the clusters of
dots.

"Oh," Diaz said in surprise. "Most match right up with these radar
incidents."

"Why hasn't Space Force command been raising a stink over
downed satellites?"

Diaz shook her head once. "You would have to talk to them. My
guess . . . Space Force looks for deliberate acts by aggressor nations.
Satellites go down, gravity does that. If they didn't pick up anything
hostile, like one satellite targeting another, they wouldn't have known
to raise a red flag."

Hastings squinted at the data, rubbing his jaw as he thought. Slade
said nothing else for a few moments then shattered the silence. "These
are not coincidences. There is a distinct pattern here."

"Could the radar readings be the satellites coming down?" Hastings
asked.

"They certainly wouldn't have come up as readings that large, even
if they did break up. Even the biggest one, Centaur 17, was relatively
small."

Hastings continued to massage his massive jaw. "What could those
readings be? A craft of some sort. They would have to be Russian or
Chinese."

*The next few words could determine if I'm sent for a psych evaluation
or not, so I need to choose them carefully.* "Maybe not, sir. None of our
intel sources show the launch of any vessel of this size from either nation. Just to build something this big would draw resources that would
have caught our attention, sir."

"What are you saying, Captain?"

*He knows exactly what I'm implying, he wants me to say the words out
loud.* "Sir, the fact that we've lost satellites, picked up these radar readings on descent into the sea, and have multiple sources reporting seeing
vessels of massive size in the air and sea in those same areas—well, sir,
they had to have come from somewhere other than Earth.

"And Colonel, there's more, sir."

"Okay . . ."

"The Japanese reported that their listening post on Futamata Island in the Sea of Japan was taken out four months ago."

"I saw the report on that. The CIA said they believed that it was the Russians."

"With no evidence to back that up, sir. I read the Agency's reports. Pure speculation on their part. No trace of the eighty men on the base was found, nor anyone in the fishing village on the south end of the island.

"We've also had strange reports of missing ships, more than usual, near these same general locales. Same thing with aircraft. Most have been civilian cargo transports, but they've gone missing, some pretty close to these zones. And our ships in the 7th fleet have picked up an abnormal range of sonar signals. Some biological, some not, all within five hundred miles of where these sightings took place."

Hastings shook his head. "I wonder if this is some sort of Russian ECM—something that tricks our radar and sonar."

"I can't attest for radar, because I wasn't sure if your team had data that corroborated my own. As for sonar, Naval Intelligence has not come across anything like this before. Adding to that, there is no Russian submarine activity in these areas. They are way off the known Russian sub patrol corridors. Our active sonar buoys would have picked them up if they wandered too far off known patrol paths."

"If it was anything other than extraterrestrial . . ." Hastings said, half to himself, half for the junior officers in the room.

Ashton drew in a long breath. "There is more, sir."

"You're kidding."

"We've had strange reports from a number of Pacific coasts. Crabs that have attacked and even killed people. Other reports describe sea creatures we have never seen before—some outright hostile." He waved his hand over the table and extracted the additional reports, allowing their summaries to scroll where the colonel and his aide could see them.

"And you think these are tied with the sightings of these large—things—out over the ocean?"

"I had one of the Navy analysts check the reports. Until four years ago we had two instances of such sightings a year, usually attributed to erroneous reports. These were the statistical norm for the previous two decades when this reporting was tracked."

BLAINE LEE PARDOE

"And now?"

"We are now trending at over thirty-two instances a year. All *after* these ships, or whatever they are, dropped into the ocean. We've also had spikes in shipping losses. So far, the media and everyone else has chalked them up as nothing out of the ordinary, but I've started plotting them as well. There's a 67 percent increase in commercial and private shipping losses in the Pacific Ocean in the last five years, increasing every year."

"Why the oceans?" Hastings said. "Why not land in Nevada or anywhere else for that matter?"

Slade shook his head. "Unknown, sir. As with all of this data—we find ourselves with more questions than answers."

"Have you reported this to anyone else, Captain?"

"No, sir," he said. "I wasn't sure if my data was correct. Not until now," he gave Captain Diaz a slight nod and she offered him a solemn nod in return.

"Have you validated with analysts in other sectors, Atlantic Command, the Indian Ocean?"

"Only the Coast Guard, sir. The Air Force was my next logical stopping point." *And it turns out, a good call on my part.*

"Okay. We proceed carefully here. We're in uncharted territory. We need to get our shit in order before we take it to the top brass. We need to try to rule out everything we can. Boil this thing down to the facts and support our conclusions with data, not wild-ass guesses. We need to figure out what this means and if the problem exists with other commands. I'm appointing Diaz here to work with you. Both of you need to make discreet inquiries with other commands. Compile your findings. I need to know what this means."

What does it mean? Invasion? Perhaps some sort of contact? "The bottom line, sir, is we don't know what we don't know."

"Correct—we're in the dark here. Keep digging. In the meantime, I'm going to lay the groundwork so I can do my job with this when you're ready."

"Sir?"

"My job is to inform the people in charge of this five-sided clusterfuck of a building what we are able to verify and ascertain. In other words, I'm going to bump this one upstairs. Somebody in a higher

81

pay grade may be able to offer insights. If not, they can't say we didn't inform them."

Hastings rose to his feet and Diaz did the same, retrieving her access disk and securing it in the transport container. The images of data disappeared from the holographic display. "I'd tell you good work, Captain, but I'm not sure what in the hell kind of Pandora's box you might have just cracked open. I can't tell you what you're raising is going to help your career at all."

"I understand, sir. This isn't about my career. This is about doing my job," Slade replied.

"Good answer," Hastings replied.

As he watched the two Air Force officers leave, he had to agree with them: he wasn't sure what he had started, either.

CHAPTER 10

US Marine Corps training grounds,
US Naval Magazine Complex, Guam,
Pacific Ocean

Lance Corporal Natalia Falto flattened her body as thin as humanly possible as she snaked her way through the low brush. Her movements were slow, deliberate, careful to not disturb the jungle brush. She wore BA/2 J (Body Armor Class 2, Jungle), older-model stuff, not nearly as flexible as the more standard STG—but Staff Sergeant Rickenburg set the terms of the engagement, and she had learned to play by his rules. Making them wear older model armor was deliberate, to force them to work harder and think more. It was a mix of ceramic plates and bullet-proof weave, with some parts equipped with STF (Shear Thickening Fluid) packs, flexible fluid packs that hardened to the strength of ceramic blast plates when hit with kinetic energy. In BA/2, this was augmented over vital areas with actual ballistic plates. It was hot, wet work. Her body was soaked with sweat and stinging with determination. Her target, a sentry, was from her platoon but assigned to be the "enemy" in this mission.

In the United States Marine Corps, there were two kinds of aviators, flyboys and joyboys—and neither of them were joining in the mission today. Flyboys actually climbed into the cockpit and flew missions—close-in combat support ops and troop transports. Joyboys piloted aerial drones, and there were a lot of them: the last Natalia could remember, there were fourteen different types of drones. Most were innocuous; they were outfitted as sensor platforms that digitally mapped out the battlespace, pegged enemy forces, and relayed that information to a special visor in a Marine's Mark III Enhanced Combat Helmet, which would give them a full tactical layout of the terrain. In battle, it even painted the opposing forces. Other drones had specific combat missions and appropriate armaments. In a perfect battlefield situation, the joyboys would map out the battlespace and use their drones for fire support, giving the Marines on the ground the upper hand.

The staff sergeant felt differently. "Perfect battlefields don't ever happen in the real world, boys and girls." So he often stripped out the drones and air support in their training. Then he had them go out in BA/2 armor. Sometimes he even took away their Hounds, the gear-toting and sensor-sweeping ground robot drones, as he had done for this exercise. Everyone bitched and moaned about it, but in the end, she understood. The staff sergeant was preparing them for the real world. If war came, it would never play out the way they hoped.

The company had tried this scenario two days earlier, and she had gotten overconfident and had been "killed." She had kicked herself in the ass enough about it, and Hernandez piling on didn't help. Their soft-fitted Remington ACR-25 (Adaptive Combat Rifle) were fitted to fire blanks and used tiny pulse lasers to simulate hits on the targets. Her weapon was slung over her back. Falto was not going to make the same mistake she had the day before. Rather than squeezing off a round and taking out the sentry, alerting everyone to her presence and position, she was going to fight her favored way—hand to hand. *I learned my lesson the hard way . . . not again.* Sure, she had taken out the sentry, but thanks to the dense growth, she had done it at relatively close range. Falto had been converged upon from three axes and had been taken out before she could respond.

As she moved through the wet dark soil, creeping closer, she could make out the back of the sentry. *Porter—I'm doing that kid a favor taking him out.* She would have shaken her head if she wasn't suppressing even the tiniest of movements. Reid Porter was a good guy and all, friendly as anything. But the short, skinny farm boy was a walking clusterfuck as a Marine—at least that was what Staff Sergeant Rickenburg called him. Taking him out, even in a simulated fight, might actually prove beneficial to the opposing team. At that thought, she allowed herself a smile.

Private Porter leaned back against a tree, his adaptive camouflage combat gear flickering as he brushed the tree. The adaptive gear was good and in the shadows of the jungle, it would've made him almost invisible if he hadn't moved. Porter's leaning up against the tree forced the uniform to overcompensate and flicker as it tried to adjust the colors and shading—making him easy to spot. She had shut hers off and was relying on its printed camouflage to cover her. Otherwise her movement crawling on the ground might have exposed her the same way.

Using a rapid eye movement right to left, she commanded her Mark III ECH helmet to drop a heat signature filter in the form of a visor over her left eye, one of three visors Natalia had access to. She swept the area slowly, smoothly. Porter was running cool; at least he had enough sense to do that. His thermals were at a minimum. If she wasn't as close as she was, he would have been hard to detect. From her position on the ground she surveyed the area, looking for even a hint of someone else from the opposing team. She flicked her eyes again and her helmet retracted the filter.

Falto maneuvered to put the tree between Porter. As she moved, she could feel something, a centipede or something like it, slither into her uniform. She focused her attention and ignored it. When she reached the tree she rose slightly, out of the low foliage, and reactivated her adaptive combat suit to blend in. Reaching down, she pulled out her combat utility knife. The blades had been removed at base and replaced with plastic for the exercise, making it feel light in her hand. She tossed and twisted it slightly, catching it with the edge down, ready to strike. She could still feel the insect on her torso, but pressed ahead.

She moved like a jaguar, not jumpy or violent, but smooth in her motion. From behind the tree, she brought the dull plastic blade up against Porter's throat. With her other hand, she covered his mouth. "Press your stud, Porter, or I will. Either way you are dead," she whispered into his ear. "You're dead." The shorter Marine nodded and reached down to his belt and hit the manual "dead" button, signaling that he was officially terminated.

"Slide down the tree and sit like a good boy," she said, taking her hand off his mouth and resheathing her knife. She crouched down low, hugging the tree, instinctively checking her six o'clock and flanks. Once she was convinced she hadn't been seen, she tapped her CCS (Combat Communication System) wristcomp which tied to her helmet. "This is A5. Target terminated." In the tiny bud in her ear, she heard the faint voice of Lance Corporal Appleton. "All sentries eliminated. A5, move to the left flank, 20 yards, four x-ray." She knew the code 4X—prepare for a general assault, overwatch position. Her fire team would move in first, get the attention of the target, while the other two moved to flank it. "Four x-ray confirmed," she whispered. With a fluid movement, she swung her ACR-25 around from her back and readied it. It was hot in her hands from having been in the sun, but it felt good—natural.

She felt the bug in her uniform begin to move and she reached to her side and pressed hard and fast. Whatever it was, she had crushed it, or so she hoped.

Keeping crouched low so as to present a smaller target, she slid left. Staff Sergeant Rickenburg was out there with the other team, and that added to her caution. This was a training exercise, but the staff sergeant always treated it like the real thing. There was a part of her that wondered if he was reliving the battles he had fought in his youth. The Marines under his command had several nicknames for the staff sergeant, but the one they used on training missions was always the same—Hannibal, his formal call sign.

She moved behind a massive tree, careful to not touch it to make the same mistake that Porter had. As she rounded the tree, she once more lowered her heat filter visor and made a sweep. She spotted a thermal near a tree off to her right. With her right eye she couldn't see it, but from the size, she was guessing it was Fitzsimmons. Like her, he was running hot. She was tempted to kick in her personal coolant mesh but she found that when it was on, it was stiff enough to hinder movement. Fitz was like her, he preferred mobility over comfort. Besides, thermal sweeps by the enemy in the middle of the hot steamy jungle were not too good—especially since they lacked joyboy support. From the way Fitz was standing, he was looking off to where she had been five minutes earlier, toward where his teammate, Porter, had been taken out. *Probably wondering what happened to the farm boy . . . wondering if he is running silent or dead.*

She raised her ACR-25 and looked at his heat outline through her scope. "Target acquired," she said softly into her ECH's chin-mike.

"Go on one," came back Corporal Appleton. "Three, two, one . . . Go!"

She slowly squeezed her trigger as the sounds of rounds being fired off to her right and rear began. Her own ACR-25 bucked only slightly as the dummy training round fired. She fired another, just in case, but she could tell that the laser in her barrel had painted Fitz downrange. It was the Marine way. *Anything worth shooting is worth shooting twice.* He was angry, she could see it in the thermals. He deactivated his adaptive camouflage suit, and she could see that he was furious at having been picked off before he could fight.

"Move in on the flanks. Seven marked down. Hannibal is unaccounted for. Keep crispy out there," he warned.

Falto pulled her ACR low and dropped to a crouch again, moving faster than before, but closing in on where she had taken out Fitzsimmons, who was now sitting against the tree as a dead body.

"What the fuck!" came Hernandez's voice in her earpiece. Another voice bellowed, "Holy shit! Where did *that* come from?"

"Fall back, lay down suppression fire. A7, dispense smoke! We need to fall back. Bring up the Gustaf!" Something was going on, and it was going bad.

Natalia tried not to react, but it was hard. Something was happening, something was going down, and she needed to see what it was. There couldn't be too many of the enemy team left. They had been on this exercise for three hours and by her mental tally she could account for most of the opposing team. That only left the staff sergeant. How much havoc could one man cause? She winced. She had seen the staff sergeant in action several times and had been taken out by him in hand-to-hand training more times than she could keep track of.

The smoke from someone's grenade filled an area of the foliage and she headed toward it. The ragged pop of gunfire was intermittently filled with someone firing full auto bursts. Contrary to what the movie-going public believed, full auto was generally inaccurate and usually was used as a last-ditch effort. In two heartbeats, she could tell that there were at least two, if not more, members of her unit, firing full auto. *That can't be good.*

She waded low into the smoke, weapon at the ready. Suddenly she came clear and saw it. Towering almost three yards tall, it was a battle armored suit. Not just any suit. She identified it quickly. A Russian Grizzly-class armored combat suit. The wearer's feet stood at the knee joints on the thick pile-driver-like legs. The suit was boxy, with sharp edges defining the armored torso. Its arms had actuators just behind, allowing the operator to move them easily. Falto had come up on its side. She saw that it was just opening up with a chain gun slung under its left arm. For a moment, the firing didn't sound simulated as the weapon tore through the dummy ammo. The two men from her team she could see through the smoke were diving for cover—attempting to outrace a stream of ammunition. They were goners. *If I run now, I will only die tired.*

Small arms fire could take down a Grizzly, she remembered that from her training. It took a *lot* of it and quite a bit of luck to hit the combat suit in the weaker actuator joints. Two grenades, training-only FBs (Flash Bangs), went off near the feet of the Russian monstrosity as it moved forward. Those simulated explosions stirred her memory. Falto's mind rapidly flipped through what she knew about the power armor and how to take it out. She hit the quick release on the strap of her weapon and tossed it down. Grabbing a grenade from her belt, she gripped the handle and pulled the pin. Sprinted the ten yards toward the Grizzly and jumped. She wanted to land high enough to slide the grenade into the shoulder joint. A blast there and she might injure the operator and at least take out the arm.

Midway through her jump though, the Grizzly pivoted at the waist, swinging its left arm and attached flamethrower assembly right into her. It moved fast, much faster than she had thought it could. The mechanized, heavily armored arm nearly caught her, forcing her to dive to avoid being hit. The grenade slipped from her grasp. Falto fumbled in the foliage, hitting the soft, wet soil and grasping around for the grenade. The flash went off before she could find it, simulating a blast. The burst of light seemed to shake her out of her daze a little. Her right side ached from the dive onto the ground in full gear.

Slowly, painfully, she sat up. Her belt monitor flashed red. She didn't even have to press the stud, she was dead. Looking through the smoke, she saw the Grizzly advance, firing into the jungle after what was left of her team. She didn't need to see who was piloting the suit: she knew. It was the staff sergeant. Hannibal had entered the fight in a markedly unfair way. *I was stupid to even try that—I broke doctrine. I should have fallen back.* She braced herself for the lecture that was going to come.

Ten minutes later, she made her way to the clearing for the debriefing along with the other walking dead. The last to arrive at the rally point was the hulking armored Grizzly suit. The entire front of the suit popped and hissed open as Staff Sergeant Rickenburg hit his releases and pulled the neural feeds off his head. He was drenched in sweat, just like she was, but he was victorious—she could see it in his eyes. He seemed to explode with energy and power, even out of the suit. *That is what victory looks like.*

"Well . . . that was entertaining," he said, surveying the hot, sweaty members of the 1st Platoon. Falto winced as her STF armor returned to its soft state. The fluid in the plates had reacted instantly to the impact, hardening like the old ceramic plates, but that had served only to spread the impact out to her entire side.

"Can anyone here tell me what went wrong?"

Hernandez spoke up. "You came in piloting that thing, Staff Sergeant. How could we have expected that?"

"You're Marines. Combat isn't a chess game, but it also isn't a vidgame—it is a blend of the two. Unexpected things happen every second of a battle. You're expected to Improvise, Adapt, and Overcome." He turned back and patted the war machine. "This is the Russian GR-17 Grizzly Bear. Their very rough equivalent of our ASHUR second-generation Rhino rig. She's a monster in a firefight, as you have all just learned. She ain't the biggest bitch in their arsenal, but she's the one you are most likely to fight. This beastie is equipped with a Glagolev-Shipunov-Gryazev Model 20 gas-powered minigun capable of firing 6250 rounds per minute. Of course, five of you already know that, since I mowed you down with that purring monstrosity. She has a flamethrower, two AK-27s, and can mount up to six RPGs in shoulder racks when fully configured." Falto looked up and saw that the staff sergeant hadn't even bothered to fire the RPGs; they were in their launch boxes, still ready to go. "This is one of the weapons your enemy will send to kill you. We captured a lot of these in the fighting in Alaska; this one is set up for training." His hand flattened and he appeared to caress the raised armored plates as he looked at the beast almost longingly. "I took out three of these in the fighting." For a moment, he was far away, in a blinding snowstorm—Falto could see that in his face. He turned back to the platoon. "She can move quick when she has to. The Russians don't go much for style, they favor hitting power." She could hear respect for the war machine in his voice.

The US Army had embraced the concept of powered/armored tactical suits in the early 21st century. The earliest models were cumbersome and limited by their power needs. Innovations in fuel cells and battery storage finally made a powered rig feasible. The program, dubbed ASHUR (Augmented Soft/Hard Unconventional Combat Rigs) was named after the Assyrian god of war.

There were the Mongoose light recon suits, and the heavier models of assault suits dubbed Badger and Rattlesnake. Each was modular to a certain extent and could be outfitted quickly with a number of different weapons systems, offering flexibility. Each consisted of a reinforced spine that supported the armor and weapons, as well as a sophisticated set of hydraulics and neuro-interfaced miniaturized servos and actuators that gave the pilot incredible control and precision in terms of movement. Wearing a fully outfitted rig gave the pilot the ability to not only move faster with no loss of control, but they could lift an incredible amount of weight and the rigs could be outfitted with a staggering amount of firepower. At the start of the war with Russia, this was what the Army and Marines fielded.

The second generation of tactical suits emerged as the war dragged on: the Recon rigs, Mongoose II and Hyena; the Medium rigs, Mamba, Gator, Cougar, and Badger II (aka the Honey Badger); and the Assault rigs, Rhino, Wolverine, Armadillo, and Lion. Every Marine could identify their distinctive shapes by sight.

To even qualify for ASHUR, you had to be in the top 10 percent of your MOS (Military Occupational Specialty) and have been certified as a marksman with at least two heavy weapons. The soldiers who wore them were the best of the best, men and women who underwent a rigorous evaluation and training program that washed out 75 percent of those who enrolled. Graduating the program wasn't the end. Pilots were trained in every suit, but were tested and matched to the suit that best fit their skills, psychological profile, and capabilities. Soldiers had to certify for the program and qualify individually for each suit. Pilots often wore patches on their sleeves for each rig they were rated to pilot. It was a badge of honor to be selected to wear an ASHUR in battle.

The ASHUR program proved to be one of the turning-point weapons systems deployed in the war. In the summer months, tanks could become bogged down in thawing tundra, where the ASHURs were able to move virtually unimpaired. Carrying enough firepower to take out armored vehicles, the ASHURs and their drivers were seen in the same light as fighter pilots generations before.

The augmented hydraulic systems made the ASHUR pilots more like walking tanks than armored infantry. They called themselves "pilots" rather than "drivers" because they were more like ground-based fighter pilots. It also added an air of glamour to their role on the battlefield. The ASHUR program was credited with helping win the war against the Russians. There were rumors of a third generation of ASHUR rigs, but Natalia chalked that up to the usual bullshit grapevine gossip. Until it showed up in the field, it was just a rumor.

"If you're going to fight and survive, you'll need to know how to fight one of these. I know you got the orientation in boot on these. Answer me this: Why didn't you take me out?"

"You were on us so fast and our fire apparently was not damaging you. You moved in on us and made us susceptible to catching our own people in the crossfire," Lance Corporal Appleton said.

"Don't feed me excuses, Appleton. Only one of you had the balls or the brains to do the right thing." He turned and looked at Falto. "Falto here had the right idea. Tell your dead comrades what you did."

She stiffened slightly. "I pulled a grenade and made a jump for the shoulder. There's plenty of unarmored space there. Drop in a grenade and you will likely kill the operator or disable most of the systems. If nothing else, it might cut a few hydraulic lines or mangle the actuator joint." Her tone was flat, almost dejected. She had tried to take it out and had failed.

The staff sergeant actually smiled at her response. "Exactly. You are Marines. You did some minor simulated damage firing all of those bullets at me, but she went for the known weakness and the kill shot. I took out your team members with the Carl Gustafs early on.

"When you deal with an ASHUR, you want to keep it at a distance, but in this growth, you stumbled on it at almost point-blank range. If it can happen here, it can happen in the real world. These things can shrug off small arms fire. What Falto did was dangerous, probably foolhardy, but it had a chance of crippling this rig. You shouldn't break with our doctrine, but if you do, do it for a damn good reason.

"Falto here remembered what she knew about the enemy and went for the kill. Her only mistake was coming at me from the side. This thing has relatively good peripheral vision, which was how I saw her coming. If she had cut to the rear and come at me there, Alpha Team would have won the exercise and a bit of honor." The staff sergeant actually gave her a nod of acknowledgement. She saw the other eyes of the platoon were on her too. Hernandez even gave her a thumbs-up.

"Alright then. If you want to defeat the enemy, you have to know the enemy. Platoon, on your feet. Do a hydration and then drop your gear. We are going to go over this beast from top to bottom. I want you each to take a turn maneuvering it. I want you all to climb every inch of this. Figure out where the toe and footholds are, where the weak spots are. Know your enemy and you can defeat them."

Falto took a long drink from her water pack tube and rose to her feet. Her ribs still ached, but she shook off the pain along with her gear. She had been beaten, but she had learned from it. And even in her defeat, the nod from Staff Sergeant Rickenburg had gone a long way to soothing the damage to her ego.

She stepped up to the armored hulk of the Grizzly as the staff sergeant began to tell them everything about the monster. *Know your enemy and you can defeat them.* Those words rang in her ears, along with the refrain from the rest of 1st Platoon on her first day: "It's us against the staff sergeant!" Looking at the man as he spoke, she was more determined than ever to be every inch the warrior he was, if not more.

CHAPTER 11

The USS *Virginia*,
south of the Hess Rise, Pacific Ocean

The USS *Virginia* was feeling more like home for Commander Titus Hill. They had been underway for one day after their layover in Pearl to provision and pick up two crew replacements. One of the men had come down with acute appendicitis and, for the sake of the crewman, it was felt best to put into port. During wartime he would have been treated while they were underway, but war seemed a long way off. Patrols were long periods of monotony occasional punctuated by a few moments of nervousness—if they happened to come across any Russian boats.

Commander Hill was gaining a strong appreciation for Captain Stewart. The man knew the importance of training and keeping the crew alert. Some peacetime captains didn't push their crews. Not Stewart. He was not above rolling everyone out for a weapons or fire drill in the middle of Titus's sleep shift. Of course on the *Virginia*, it was always someone's off shift. You easily lost track of the time of day on a submarine.

Captain Stewart wasn't one of those hard-nosed officers often portrayed in movies. He knew the fine line you had to walk between readiness and going too far. Hill personally observed the captain walking that line. The men didn't complain about "the old man." They did their duty and did it well. Hill had witnessed a few times when Stewart's anger erupted. Behind closed doors Stewart did not hesitate to unleash a verbal torrent at his officers. When an enlisted man didn't do his duty, the officer bore the brunt of it.

As XO, his job was to deliver the captain's often brutal feedback to the crew. It was not enviable duty, but it was necessary: the Navy saw it as vital. It was the kind of duty that eventually hardened XOs into good captains. Commander Hill didn't think about advancement much, the very likely scenario of a glut of captains with experience all ahead of him in line for a command. It almost was enough to make a person wish for war.

Almost.

The moment his thoughts drifted to future commands he refocused his mind and concentrated on the duty at hand. Hill stood at the OOD (Officer of the Deck) watch station and surveyed the workstations around him. Behind him, just past the periscopes, the chief navigator was working on the digital plot table. The chief of the boat, Chief Petty Officer Tyrone Simmons, stood just below him, having made his third trip in the last hour to the ship control station to confer with the helm and planesman. The chief was the highest ranking noncommissioned officer on the boat and knew the ship far better than Hill. He respected the shorter, slightly paunchy Simmons; the man had served for years underwater. Every time he had tried to engage him on a personal level, though, the chief only gave him a "yes" or "no" response. *Either he doesn't like me, doesn't like officers, or doesn't like anyone.* He understood the distance common to Simmons's role and permitted it.

Hill watched the digital clock as it went from 0159 to 0200. "Chief, navigation check if you would, please."

"Aye, sir. Navigation—report course and position."

Hill turned to see Lieutenant Jacobson at the navigation table. "XO, we are on course. Running at 300 feet. Changes to thermocline depth. Recommend we descend to 350 feet."

The thermocline, or thermal layers of the ocean, allowed submariners to better conceal their submarines from probing sonar. "Very well," Hill said. "Chief, set depth to three-five-oh feet. Note the change in the log."

"Aye, sir," Simmons replied flatly. "Helm, drop planes three degrees, gradual dive. Take us to three-five-oh feet and level there." Simmons went to the BSY seats, referred to as "Busy One," stations where the vessel's elaborate integrated battle control system was monitored. The BSY system tied in sonar, navigation, and weapons control. It was the heart and soul of the USS *Virginia* and was always manned by officers monitoring the four sonar systems aboard the boat. "Sonar, new depth being set to three-five-oh."

There was a chorus of *Yes, sirs* in response. It was a shallow dive, but Titus could swear that he could feel it. *That's good; it means I'm getting comfortable with this boat.*

"She's handling well, Chief," Hill said casually to Simmons, hoping to spark some sort of small talk.

"Yes, sir," the chief of the boat replied without even looking up.

Several minutes passed when the helmsman confirmed their depth at 350 feet. Hill leaned on the railing at the watch station to give himself a moment of private thought, when a call came up from the BSY. "Conn—Sonar. We have a Sierra contact at one mile out."

Hill moved to the far right rail. "Confirm."

Lieutenant Hawkins at the workstation nodded. "Aye, sir. Confirmed. Designating as Sierra One. Contact is 1790 yards off our port running at three-five-oh feet. Speed is matched with ours, one-eight knots. She's running parallel to us, sir."

Hill glanced over to Simmons and said nothing. The seasoned chief went and checked the reading over Hawkins's shoulder. "Confirmed, sir," he said in a low tone.

"How the hell did it just pop up so close to us?" Titus demanded.

Hawkins didn't lift his eyes from the screen as he replied. "Must have been just below the thermocline or at a deeper depth and rose up quickly. That or she has a profile that makes detection difficult. She just showed up here." While a mile seemed like a great distance to non-Navy men, it was far too close for him or anyone in the control room. It was like having a tick appear on your skin—dangerously close. Such ranges limited combat options if the situation turned into a shooting match.

Damn it . . . we should have spotted this sooner . . .

"Track it," Hill commanded. "I want full TMA on that Sierra." The TMA, or Target Mapping Analysis, would allow him to feed the data into the BSY for possible weapons firing.

"I'm getting some strange readings, sir," Hawkins said.

Hill moved down off the watch station to behind the sonarman. "Strange how?"

"Target's profile is not in the warbook, sir." In other words, she was not demonstrating a sonar reading that conformed to a known submarine. *Perhaps a new Russian or Chinese boat?* "Not only that, she is fading in and out. It reads like a bio target for one sweep, then back to metallic."

"You're not telling me there's a whale out there moving at eighteen knots, are you?" Hill replied.

"No, sir," Hawkins said. Suddenly he leaned forward. "Change in aspect. Sierra One has altered course, sir. Closing. Range now is 1650 yards to port."

From his position over Hawkins's left shoulder he turned to the right where Chief Simmons stood. "That was quick, wasn't it, Chief?"

"That it was, sir." The expression on the rounded face of Chief Simmons seemed to show something Hill hadn't seen there before—concern.

Whoever this ship was, he seemed to be mirroring their movements.

"Comms—Captain to the Control Room." Hill turned to Simmons. "Chief, set us at Condition Two. Check all stations."

The yellow warning light in the control room went on, warning everyone on board of the new status. A storm of commands flew out, including the one to summon Captain Stewart to the control room. After a few moments Simmons responded, "All systems reporting at Condition Two, XO."

Stewart came into the control room looking pristine, as if he had not been asleep and just rousted out, except for a hint of gray stubble. "Captain on the Bridge. XO, sitrep." He cleared his throat slightly as he finished the order.

"Captain, we have a target, designated as Sierra One. She is at 350 which is our current depth. Target is at 1650 yards to our port, matching speed," Hill replied. "We are at Condition Two, sir. The boat is yours."

"What does the warbook say, Hawkins?" Stewart asked.

"Nothing on register, sir." Titus made eye contact with the captain and nodded once to confirm.

"This is pretty far off the normal Russian patrol zones," Stewart said in deep thought, rubbing his beard stubble. He leaned over, his eyes locked on the sonar station where Hill stood. The XO stepped aside to give the captain a better view. "Wilson, get me a cup of coffee, black," he said over his shoulder and the seaman started off for the galley. "She's running parallel to us at our depth?"

"Aye, sir," Hill said. "Sonar reports that the target is drifting in and out of readings. We're reading her one minute as a bio, the next as metallic."

"There's no way that's a whale," Stewart replied. He sighed, took a deep breath, and looked over to Simmons. "Chief, let's see how she responds. Turn us fifteen degrees to port and take us up fifty feet—sharp on the planes. Hawkins, you keep your eyes on that bitch."

A moment later the boat moved, this time noticeably. Commander Hill gripped the back of the sonarman's chair to keep himself steady. "Sir, Sierra One is mimicking our maneuvers. New range, 1578 yards. She's matching our speed and depth just as fast as we're moving."

"That was a pretty damned fast reaction, wouldn't you say?" Captain Stewart asked, mostly to himself, Hill assumed. "XO, have we pinged that target with active sonar yet?"

"No, sir." The ship was currently using its passive sonar system. Active sonar was useful in battle conditions and gave better readings, but it also tended to give away a submarine's position. Stewart's suggestion was low risk. It was clear that whatever was following the *Virginia* had already detected her.

"Hawkins, go to full active. Paint me a picture," Stewart said.

Hill leaned over the BSY station and watched. The active sonar started feeding data to the secondary displays, showing the length of the ship, some basics of her profile. *What the hell? That can't be right.* Sierra One was showing as a massive boat, four times the length of the *Virginia. That's impossible.*

"Sierra One is . . ." Hawkins began. "S1 is now dead stop, falling astern, sir. How the hell did she just stop like that?"

"Bearing to target," the captain demanded.

"Given speed, target is at 142 degrees, sir, falling astern."

"Chief, bring us about to port, 180 degrees, hard-over."

The ship began to turn at the commands barked out by Simmons. The USS *Virginia* tipped into the turn and the crew leaned hard to compensate.

"Sierra One is still at dead stop," Hawkins replied.

"That's impossible," Stewart said. "You can't just go to a dead stop. You getting any cavitation? Her props should be giving us a good reading on her power-plant and class."

"None, sir, that's why it's so . . ." His voice trailed off. On the sonar screen, the dot tagged as S1 suddenly began to move at an incredible speed. It seemed to turn away from the *Virginia*, then moved off. The target profile shifted and sped away like a torpedo. "She's gone off the scopes, sir!"

"Disappeared?" Stewart asked.

"No, sir, she just took off. Let me check the TMA." His fingers worked the old-style keyboard as if he were playing a musical instrument. "Sir, target moved off at over 78 knots, on a course heading of 223.1."

"That has to be an instrument malfunction," he said, taking the cup of coffee from Seaman Wilson and sipping it. "No navy on the planet has a ship that can move at 78 knots underwater."

"Sir, BSY confirms the speed, from both active and passive sonar," Hawkins said.

Stewart said nothing for a few long moments. He cradled the coffee in both hands, seeming to look into it for answers. "This is bullshit on a stick. XO, get the boat to the surface. I have no intention of playing games down here with faulty sonar, that's a recipe for a train wreck. Mister Hawkins, I want a full diagnostic run on our sonar systems—top to bottom. Chief, pull me printouts of the data. Set us to Condition Three, stand us down."

* * *

The data was spread out in the tight space of Captain Stewart's fold-down desk. Hill stood next to him as the captain looked at the information. Titus had seen the data himself twenty minutes earlier. It was disturbing, to say the least.

"So our systems are 100 percent?" Stewart said after several minutes of looking at the data.

"Yes, Captain. Lieutenant Hawkins and his team have checked them all."

"You looked at these?" he gestured to the printouts.

"I did, sir."

"It was a good thing you got TMA tracking it as soon as you did," the captain said, pinching the bridge of his nose and closing his eyes. He drew a breath and looked back at the stack of data.

"This . . . *thing* . . . pops up out of nowhere within rifle distance; that much alone concerns me. And you've seen the data on that target? That signal was a target painting at 480 yards long," he said looking at the numbers. "She had the ability to stop on a dime, a goddamn dead stop, mind you. Her breakaway speed was clocked at 78 knots."

Hill nodded. "Seventy-eight point seven, sir."

Stewart shook his head. "She read one minute with biological readings, then as metallic. To me that sounds like a new hull composite, something we've never seen before."

"Yes, sir."

The captain looked up at him from his chair. "Grab a seat, Commander." He gestured to the bed. Titus sat down.

"There isn't a shipyard in the world that can build a deep sea submersible vessel the length of an aircraft carrier. And no sub or whale could perform those maneuvers that we saw on the screens," Stewart said, keeping his voice deliberately low.

"No, sir."

"Tell me what you think, Commander."

Hill was caught off guard. "The easy solution is to claim it's a software or hardware malfunction—but we were checked out before leaving port. Regulations would say we log it as an anomaly and transmit the data to SUBRON 15 for them to analyze." SUBRON 15 stood for Submarine Squadron 15, the *Virginia*'s current assignment.

"That's what the book says." Stewart leaned back in his chair. "But I asked you, what do you think?"

Hill shook his head. "I'm not sure. If you go by the book, it's a software glitch of some sort. And while everything says that those readings," he glanced at the paperwork, "are likely wrong, we were there—we saw what we saw."

"Which means?"

"There is a ship out there—a big one. With capabilities beyond ours."

Captain Stewart's eyebrows lifted and he nodded once. "If you want to sit in the big chair someday, you sometimes have to forget the books and do what you feel in your gut. I could have chosen any number of candidates who could follow the manual. Out here, where we are, sometimes the rulebook doesn't count. That having been said, what do *you* think the intel boys at SUBRON are going to do when we squirt them this data?"

"Write it off as an error. Mechanical or software problem."

"Damned right. Bureaucracy is the heart of the military, Mister Hill. And anyone who would pass that information to COMSUBPAC at Pearl would have to be crazy." COMSUBPAC was in command of all submarine forces in the Pacific. Hill understood completely.

"So what are you going to do, sir?"

"My job. Get this data and flag it as priority. Transmit to SUBRON 15 and COMSUBPAC under my authority." He rubbed the bridge of his nose again. "ONI might get wind of it, but if they do, it will get bogged down in an entirely different bureaucracy. I know an intel guy, Commander Franks, DIA. I'm going to slide him a summary of this. He's bright. If the story of this gets buried somewhere, he'll make sure it surfaces . . . if there *is* a story here." He lowered his hand and opened his eyes, locking them on Titus. "Sometimes the chain of command is more burden than help. Having connections throughout the Navy is important. If you haven't figured that out yet, write it down."

Titus rose and nodded. He liked Captain Stewart a great deal more. This was a man who knew how to do his job. Bypassing levels of command was something that took guts, or connections. Either way it felt like the right thing to do in this instance. There were important lessons here, ones he was absorbing. "Yes, sir."

"What's the worst they can do, Mister Hill? Take my boat from me?"

CHAPTER 12

Santa Monica Coast Guard Base, Los Angeles

Dana Blaze looked at her pad and watched the digital map. Technology wasn't just part of her craft, it was the medium she worked in—and she saw herself as an artist. Her tech-slash-cameraman, Theodore "Fizz" (don't call him Theo) Hart, had hooked her up with the gear she was using, some of the best that money could buy. Fizz was well compensated for his work and made sure he was one step ahead of the competition. He was sharp, but quirky. Fizz was tall, awkward, and always had a three days' head start on a beard. He wore T-shirts, even when they weren't appropriate to the occasion. Dana was pretty sure he owned only two identical pairs of no-name jeans. He had a bit of a paunch and sometimes smelled like Thai food—but he belonged to her and that she found endearing.

It had taken some effort on his part to plant the tracking chip on Veronica Diamond, but it was well worth it. With that chip, Dana could track her every movement, and pick up on her audio if she desired. Veronica seemed to be scooping Dana with unnerving regularity. As soon as Veronica and her tech had torn out of the newsroom a few minutes earlier, Dana got a tip from one of her stringers. Dana was determined to counter-scoop her. *It's time to show the new girl why I'm top of the heap in this biz.*

"Where next, boss?" Fizz asked.

"Right, two blocks up," she said, never lifting her eyes from the map. "You sure she said 'big scoop'? I don't want to waste my time on something minor league."

He nodded. "Came in on the wire service, flash break. She took the feed and purged it so we couldn't see it. Whatever it is, it's a breaking story and she wanted to make sure nobody tailed her."

101

Veronica had been relegated to second chair at Blown Sun since Dana's coup with the Jay Drake interview. It had been exactly what Ryan Jackson had been looking for, something to generate a massive wave of buzz and bring in viewers. Veronica had congratulated her, but Dana sensed the tension coming from her, an unspoken vibe. Ryan had put the two women on the same program, but Veronica clearly had her eye on Dana's seat.

The two reporters couldn't be more different. Dana was busty, blonde, out there—a few steps past the bleeding edge. Her carefully crafted image was in-your-face, blunt, and daring. She projected energy: that's what the focus groups said, and Dana liked that. Veronica, on the other hand, had long, straight, barely styled jet-black hair, was shorter, a hint of Hispanic heritage in her blood. The same focus groups said she was reliable and, when pressed, "feisty." Dana hated that. She didn't like "feisty" applied to anyone other than herself, nor did she want competition. At the same time, though, she had to admit that competition brought out her best work.

Veronica had broken two big stories since Blown Sun Media had launched. One was a congressional scandal. These were a dime a dozen, but this one involved human trafficking, which was a new and twisted angle even for a congressman. Dana dodged political scandals: their ratio of E-ratings to hours expended was too far out of balance for her liking. The other had been a hostage situation that Veronica managed to get to before anyone else. Her coverage on the two stories had bumped up her ratings and E-factor with the viewers, something Dana watched carefully. *This network only has room for one queen . . . and it's not her.*

Dana and her staff began a surveillance campaign on Ms. Diamond. It had taken a while for her people to figure out how Veronica got her leads. They had tapped her phone, pried her email and social media accounts—nothing. For Dana, it was all about the chain of tips: where did they originate? How did Veronica receive them? Who was the source?

When Dana had finally found out the source of Veronica's tips— she had a mole in the Department of Homeland Security who was getting information from the FBI, the Coast Guard, and other sources for her—she was ready to cripple her competitor. The source hid his tips in carefully coded messages that he relayed to her via an antiquated fax printer that no one else in the office even knew was still working. It was a throwback to the old days when wire services would send in their leads. Dana had spotted her one day picking up a printout. Veronica was good—Dana was just better. She had Fizz rig it with a feed to give her a digital copy of everything that Veronica was reading . . . real time.

The van rounded the corner. "How far up, boss?" Fizz asked.

She checked. "Three blocks. She's stopped at the Coast Guard facility up ahead." Fizz was already closing on the security gate.

He gestured to the security gate at the post. "Hey, boss," Fizz said as he toggled the window down. "Time to strut your stuff."

"Can I help you?" the guard asked.

"Press," Dana said, handing her ID across Fizz. "I know what is going on down at the docks."

"I'll have to call it in," the sentry said. "In the meantime, we will need to check your vehicle."

Three sentries checked under the vehicle and in the back and verified their IDs while the first guard was on the phone.

He handed back her press pass. "Sir, you may proceed to Basin G on the left."

Fizz drove while Dana looked around to see if she could figure out what had drawn Veronica here. Then she saw a ship moored in the basin, snugged into the berth by a Coast Guard cutter. As Fizz slowed to a stop, she surveyed the ship and its shocking damage.

It was an old fishing trawler, painted dingy red. She could see that it had been in some sort of battle. Long jagged cuts swept along the side of the vessel, two inches wide. *Lasers?* The deckhouse was half-missing, not blown off but as if it had been severed, cut by a massive knife diagonally slashing to the deck level. Blood stains were visible on the deck.

The Coast Guard officers spotted her and barked out orders. Bright blue tarps were produced, and the deckhands quickly dropped them over the more damaged portions of the ship.

"Getting this, Fizz?"

"Yup," he replied. "It's almost as if they don't want us to see this."

"Pirates using lasers?" Dana said. Lasers were so expensive and required extensive maintenance . . . private owners were rare.

"Nope," Fizz said. "No burn marks. Whatever cut into that hull was something else."

"You have the device?"

"That's why I make the almost-big bucks."

"Kick it in now. Capture her feed. Cut her off from the network." The marks on the hull were important, but Dana's goal was to slam Veronica with her own broadcast. *Time to seal the deal.*

On Dana's pad, a window popped up. Veronica was standing down by the stern of the ship, just a short distance away, with a Coast Guard press officer standing just off camera, his arms crossed and a scowl on his face. "What you see behind me is all that remains of the commercial fishing trawler *Jonah*, which was apparently attacked today twenty-two miles off the coast. These attackers were unidentified, and by the time the Coast Guard was able to respond, the entire crew of this vessel was found dead or missing . . ."

"Keep buffering her broadcast. Give me time to set up. When you see her go over the edge, send *that* transmission through," she commanded. She checked her hair in the mirror on the passenger side of the vehicle before she bounded out. Fizz followed, his ear wirelessly linked to the black box in his left hand. In his right, he held Dana's camera and sound gear.

"You think you can get her to explode? Wait." Fizz grinned. "Never mind." His twisted smile almost warmed her heart.

The air was rank with the smell of the ocean, fish, and diesel fumes. It was clear that the small clutch of Coast Guard officials on the docks were not happy that the press were there, but there was little they could do. Dana moved along edge of the berth, the battered *Jonah* behind her, stopping ten feet from Veronica. "Alright, we're live in three, two, one . . ." Her face seemed to light up as the camera gave her life.

"This is Dana Blaze with Blown Sun Media. What you see behind me is the fishing trawler *Jonah*, an apparent victim of a high-tech attack that left her crew dead and missing. Pirates right off the Los Angeles coast, or was some other foul play involved?" She gestured for Fizz to pan the length of the ship and the Coast Guard personnel who were on the slashed deck of the vessel taking photographs and measuring. "While reports are still preliminary, it is clear that this is one of the most savage attacks to take place off the US coast in years." Dana excelled in making up facts. She had nothing to base her words on, but she knew how to fill airtime and keep it interesting. "We will be talking to the Coast Guard officials shortly to see if they have any leads as to who may be behind this attack. But as you can clearly see, this was not the result of conventional weapons." She gestured to one of the smooth cuts on the hull that rose behind her where the crew had not yet managed to cover them.

Her hand drifted to the hull of the ship, farther down, and Fizz followed her gesture. There were strange markings on the side of the ship, scrapes in the paint. They weren't rusted, so it was clear they were fresh. The marks were strange, like something had been dragged up or down on the hull of the ship. Two Coast Guard crewman were there, carefully taking pictures of the marks—which told her they were not normal. *What happened to this ship and her crew?*

One of the men called up. "Captain, we need medical investigators. I think we found one of the crew."

"You *think* you found one of the crew?" the officer standing on the wharf replied. "Either you did or you didn't." Fizz tracked the men on the deck with his camera and Dana's ears listened to every syllable.

"Sir, we . . . well, sir, it's hard to explain." Next to the lieutenant who was speaking, a seaman appeared on the deck and leaned over the railing, vomiting down near Veronica. It hit the dock, splattering like oatmeal.

Veronica recoiled from the impact area on the dock and turned to her side, motioning for her feed to stop. "What the hell is going on?" she barked to her own tech/cameraman.

The young man shrugged. "There's some sort of problem with the feed. Nothing is getting through to the home office."

Fizz and Dana could hear the conversation in their earbuds. "What is that bitch doing here?" She pointed at Dana. "This is *my* story!" Her tech/cameraman was still filming, checking his belt-worn transmitter, tapping it in hopes that it would suddenly start functioning. He looked up at her and shook his head.

"That fucking bitch . . . there's no way that she just came across this. She's tailing me to steal the story! God damn her all to hell! I swear I'll slag her the first chance I get!" Her anger swelled as she glared at Dana.

Dana continued to report as if she couldn't hear every word Veronica spewed. "We will try and get you updated information as soon as it comes in. But for now, we have a commercial ship that has been savagely attacked just off our beaches. This is Dana Blaze, on the scene with Blown Sun." She nodded to Fizz—her signal to keep filming, but they were clear.

Fizz grinned broadly. "I got everything."

"You know what to do," she replied.

Using the small black box, he tapped it wirelessly into his own transmitter. Veronica's rage had not gone into the ether, but had been intercepted and buffered into the device. Now Fizz was splicing it into his live feed. What viewers would see was a split screen—on one, the highly professional Dana Blaze breaking a story; on the other, Veronica Diamond exploding in anger, not realizing that her audio and video were being broadcast.

Dana waited until Fizz gave her the thumbs-up. He transmitted the feed into her earbud, so she could hear what viewers were watching and hearing. It took a lot for her to suppress her joy.

Turning, Dana feigned her own anger at Veronica's words—as if they had just been spoken. "Excuse me, Veronica, I'm in the middle of an important story," she replied, as if she were taking the moral high ground. In reality, she had just set up her opposition.

Diamond cupped her ear for her own cameraman's update. No doubt word was coming back from the studio about her outburst being broadcast. Dana watched her for a moment and gave a hand signal to Fizz to stand by, and with a flick of a finger, she hoped he would start filming Veronica. Dana could see color rise on Veronica's face as she lost her temper. She had been burned, hung on her own words, to a world-wide audience. For Dana, this manipulation was a guarantee that she would be picked up by the other media, a bit of digital feed that would be replayed for the next two weeks.

Then it got better.

Veronica tore off her tiny throat mike that was concealed in a piece of jewelry and balled her fists in rage. Dana saw it. Her response was pure Blaze. She flashed a brilliant smile and blew her a kiss.

It was too much for Veronica Diamond. Gritting her teeth, she charged the dozen or so feet between them, her hands reaching for

Dana. Blaze saw her eyes, filled with fury. "You . . ." was all Diamond could howl as she lunged at her.

Dana wasn't sure exactly how she would react, but it turned out to be fairly predictable. She dodged to one side, swinging her own fist hard, hitting Veronica mid-flight in the jaw. Dana had only thrown a dozen or so punches in her entire life, but this was the most solid hit of all. Veronica reeled, coming down hard at Dana's feet. She lifted her head slowly, and Dana could see blood on her lips.

"I hate you!" she spat, rubbing her jaw.

"It's a tough job. It's even tougher when you're stupid," Dana replied. She turned to Fizz. "Please tell me you got that on live feed."

"You bet, chief," he replied.

She turned back to the ship. Tarps now covered most of the ship that could be seen from the dock. The Coast Guard was clearly attempting to hide something, and that caught and held her attention. *Something has them nervous enough to try to conceal it from us.* "Get back to the real story, Fizz. Something weird happened to that ship." She cast Veronica a disgusted look and turned away.

***

Five hours later, Dana found herself in the office of Ryan Jackson. "I don't know how you pulled off what you did," he said angrily as he paced the hardwood flooring. "Veronica's signal got intercepted somehow—her feed wasn't live until *after* you went on the air. Care to tell me how that happened?"

"I assure you, Ryan, I have no idea." It was the truth. She didn't know how the tech had worked, only that it *had* worked. Fizz's fingerprints were all over it, but he would never talk. If Ryan wanted a head to roll, it would be Fizz's, not hers. But she could tell that wasn't where this interview was heading.

"Veronica called me from Santa Monica General," he said, pausing for a moment in his pacing. "Actually, her agent and lawyer placed the call. That little punch of yours broke one of her teeth and fractured her jaw."

Good, my hand still hurts. Unconsciously she massaged her aching fingers at the mention of the punch. "I feel just terrible about that. She was coming right at me, though. I had to defend myself." She didn't even try to sound sincere.

"I saw it live on air, Dana," Ryan said, crossing his arms. "So did a big piece of the country. That little snippet of you belting Veronica is going to be replayed for days. You're going to have our public relations staff busting hump just to keep up with the requests for interviews."

"Forget that—how were our ratings?" Dana said, driving to the point.

Ryan waved his hand over his desk and holographic data appeared in front of him. "Some of our biggest to date. Take a look at these numbers," he said, pointing to the spike on the graph. "And with that unaccountable datafeed of you two—we are trending, strangely enough, with women viewers. Apparently two women punching each other on live feed is a draw for watchers. Only one other news agency was on the scene as fast as Blown Sun. How exactly did both you and Veronica know about this? There wasn't anything on the normal wire services."

"I just have good informants, that's all. As for Veronica, you'll have to ask her." *He's fishing, trying to learn how I did what I did.*

"Well, that won't be happening, at least not anytime soon. I'm putting her on leave until her jaw heals. Assuming there's a lawsuit involved and, given California's wonderful worker laws, I'll probably have to keep her on while she sues my ass. I'm going to move her to another shift, late-late night, as far away from you as possible."

"You need to do what you think is best," she said. *Keep her away from me and away from my viewers.* "Ryan, do you think it would be wise for me to go on the air and issue an apology?"

He rubbed his chin in thought. "Actually, that's not a bad idea. There's no point in trying to hide from this. We may as well get out in front of it. Run it by Bob in PR. If he's good with it, we can run it on the morning feed. Pop it up twice an hour, along with what led up to it—including the clip of you decking her. If nothing else, it will keep the story going and maybe can help reduce what I'll end up paying her in settlement." He crossed his arms again. "I have to assume that you had something to do with this, but I can't prove it. For now, I don't care. What matters is our ratings and the shareholders. If you set

Veronica up . . . well, that's for someone else to figure out. Officially, I'm not going to condone your actions. Unofficially, I can't argue with these numbers."

That night as she settled in at her apartment, she saw the message from Fizz, thanking her for the spot bonus she had deposited in his payroll account. Loyalty came at a price with Fizz, though she was pretty sure that he would have done the same thing even without the money. He would have done it for her for free, but the money assured her that he was in her camp. It was a cutthroat business out there. She had sent a dozen roses to Veronica's house—and had anonymously tipped off several of her rivals that the flowers were being delivered. *That punch was the gift that just keeps on giving . . . the story will live on for weeks.*

Ensconced in her most comfortable chair, she cradled a glass of wine and allowed herself a moment of gloating. She hadn't planned on Veronica getting angry enough to come after her; that was simply a bonus opportunity. Dana had merely planned on hijacking her broadcast and then projecting her reaction. *Sometimes the story just falls into your lap.* That night, Dana Blaze herself was the story, overshadowing what had happened to the crew of the *Jonah*.

The small ship bothered her, though. She and Fizz had hung around as the Coast Guard removed the remains of the crewman from the ship. On the stretcher, the body was just a lump, not even appearing big enough to be an adult human. It was covered with a sheet that was spotted in blood soaking through and something else, something black, almost like oil. She had pressed the officers for comments, but they finally organized enough to usher her off the scene. Whatever had happened had been so disturbing, it had stunned the Coast Guard. Their stunned state allowed her to get footage before being escorted off post.

She pulled up her mobile and called Jay Drake's private line. "Hello, Dana," she heard him say. "I saw your broadcast today. Congratulations."

"I just wanted to call and thank you for that wonderful little magic box you loaned me."

"It worked well from what I saw," Drake replied confidently.

"Indeed it did," she replied, taking a sip of her wine.

"I'm glad I was able to help. I take it we're still on for dinner Friday?"

"Dinner," she replied, putting down the wine. "And for your help with Veronica Diamond, I have a special dessert in mind." She felt the warmth of the wine and much more at the thought of seeing Drake again.

This is a relationship made in heaven.

CHAPTER 13

North LA Veteran's Hospital, Los Angeles, California

The VA hospital on the north side of LA had the appearances of a good facility, but it was staffed by government workers—an observation not lost on Antonio Colton. Every war generated veterans, men and women scarred either physically or emotionally by battle. Congress and the FedGov always made bold statements after the war about how they were going to take care of the veterans who had shed blood for their country. But between the words and actual action was a deep valley where nothing happened. Veterans were always left to fend for themselves in a mind-numbing wash of bureaucracy and frustration. *This isn't just about the FedGov . . . I'll bet the Romans treated their veterans like hell too.*

Antonio was required to come to the VA once every three years for adjustments to his bionic right leg. The leg itself was exceptional—not exactly top-of-the-line, but solid technology. It didn't bother him. They would pry it open, check it out, replace any worn parts—it was routine maintenance. It was what followed that Antonio hated. The psych evaluation.

He was ushered into the sterile examination room and told to strip down and put on a gown. The air stung his lungs with chemical disinfectants and an aroma that he could only call "hospital stink." His bulky physique barely fit in the gown, which hung open in the back; he didn't even bother to try to tie it. He sat on the white paper covering the examination bed and closed his eyes. There was nothing to read or check. His digipad was in his pants pocket, tossed over the chair. Most guys would have killed their time reading messages from friends, responding, making arrangements for the evening. Antonio didn't bother. His circle of friends was small and he had no plans for that night.

111

In fact, going to the VA hospital was the highlight of his week—which both angered and frustrated him.

There were two quick knocks on the door and it opened before he could say anything. The doctor walked in. The portly man was short and out of shape. He looked uncomfortably hot in his white coat. Glancing down at his digipad, he pushed up a smile and extended his hand. "Mister Colton, I'm Doctor Raymond."

Antonio gave him a cursory handshake but said nothing. "So then, how is this Mark III holding up for you?" he said, pulling over a stool with a squeaky wheel and sitting down beside him. The doctor reached out and touched his right leg. Antonio got some feedback of sensation, the closest that he could come to "feeling" the doctor's hand.

"It's just fine," he said flatly. "No real problems. When it gets hot, like in the sunshine, I can feel it. Not that leg, but my own. It's like a throbbing."

"I'm sure you've heard this before, but that's perfectly normal."

Funny that men with both legs get to define what is normal for me.

"Alright, I need you to lay down on the bed so I can open it up and check the servos."

Antonio complied.

Dr. Raymond went over to the small desk and returned with a toolkit. The small screwdriver-like device in the doctor's hands hovered over the knee and chirped. A panel on Antonio's leg popped open and the doctor peered inside with a small maglight he had pulled from his breast pocket. He squinted, looking inside the leg for a long minute. "Well, your knee actuator looks just fine. What kind of work do you do, Mr. Colton?" he said as he took a small probe and inserted it into the leg.

"I sell stuff," Antonio responded with a hint of anger. "Why?"

"Oh, it's nothing. The amount of wear and tear here is minimal. It doesn't look like you were on your feet a lot in your job or I'd see some scoring. These Mark IIIs are like that." He took out a small pencil-like lubricating tube and pressed the stud on it, feeding one end into the interior of the leg. Then he closed the panel on the knee and moved down to the ankle, using the same device to open it up. "You're not a runner," he said, peering at the ankle joint of the artificial leg. "That much is for sure."

"No. I stopped doing calisthenics when I mustered out," Antonio replied. He didn't hate the workout routines, but was not a fan of running. *Why run and go nowhere?* Antonio needed a reason or purpose to undertake that kind of activity.

Dr. Raymond closed up the ankle joint then took his digipad and stabbed at it with his sausage-like fingers. "You having any issues with the neuro-connection? Sluggishness? An occasional limp that comes and goes?" He was clearly running some sort of diagnostic on the leg.

Antonio knew the issues. When he had first gotten the bionic prosthetic, it had taken him weeks to master the neuro-connections. It took a lot of trial and error to adjust the settings. "Nothing since the last time I was in, Doc. She purrs like a kitten." The comment was not an idle one. The leg would occasionally have a low-level hum at night when it was recharging.

"Please lift your leg for a moment and hold it," the doctor said as he squinted at his pad. "Thank you." He fumbled with the pad for a moment then put it down on the small desk. "Well, Mr. Colton, I am pleased to tell you that your leg seems to be holding up just fine. Any issues with the utility compartment?" The compartment was a small storage space on the inner thigh. Whoever had designed the leg had included it, for reasons that only they seemed to know. Antonio could open it with the right thought. A lot of veterans used it to carry their medication, a small pistol, a knife, or nothing at all. Cash was almost dead . . . everything was a transfer of funds. Only those dealing with illegal goods actually used physical money. Antonio didn't use his storage compartment much. It was a small empty space that seemed to have no use for him. "I barely use it, but it seems to work just fine."

"Any questions or concerns?"

"Nope," he replied.

"Alright then," Dr. Raymond said. "I don't see anything to give me concern. You've passed your twenty-five-thousand-mile checkup," he said, grinning at his own joke. Antonio didn't smile, but sat up, swinging his legs toward the floor. "I'll log that in your file. I also see that you are due for your psych check-in. Go up to the fifth floor and the reception kiosk will get you to the right place." He reached out again and shook Antonio's hand. "Good luck, Mr. Colton."

An hour later, Antonio sat in a small sterile white room. It didn't have the anesthetic smell like the hospital room where he had his leg checked. Instead, this room had just a hint of body odor in the air, sweat.

The room was small and had sound-deadening panels on the walls. There was a small, very plain table and two chairs. Antonio sat in one, resting his elbows on the table, patiently waiting. *This room looks more like a police interrogation room than an evaluation room.*

There was a single knock at the door and a slender woman entered. She wore a doctor's white lab coat, unbuttoned. It hung on her depressingly ordinary clothing. Antonio looked up at her and saw her glasses and the way her eyes never seemed to lift up and look at him.

I'm just a number here . . . one of the walking wounded. And this broad is just doing her job . . . nothing more, nothing less.

She sat down opposite him at the tiny table, her eyes flitting over the data on her pad.

"So . . ." she said slowly, finally looking up and into his face. Antonio was a full head taller than she was, and she had to lean back ever so slightly to see his eyes. "I'm Doctor Franco and you are Antonio Colton," she said more as a statement than a question.

"Yes," he replied. He hated these examinations.

Dr. Franco put her pad down and rested her hands together on top of it on the desk. "You know why we're here today, correct?"

"Psych exam," he replied coolly.

"We prefer to think of it as a 'Stabilization Verification Session,'" she replied.

"Like I said, psych exam."

She cocked her head. "I take it you don't think much of these tests, Antonio?"

"I do not."

"Why is that?"

He crossed his arms and leaned back in the chair. "Seriously? This is bullshit and you know it. You want to know if I have PSTD? I don't accept your labels. I don't have a disorder, I just have issues, that's all. I don't sleep most nights. I wake up sometimes in a cold sweat. I have issues holding down a job. Let's see, the last time I was here, the shrink said I had 'issues with authority figures.' Truth be told, I only have issues with assholes who don't know what they're doing." For the first time since he had arrived at the VA hospital, he felt a little better. *Let her soak all of that in.*

Dr. Franco, for her part, did not seem to be shocked or taken aback. "You know we can prescribe medication that can help you with the sleep and mitigate the anxiety symptoms."

"If you've read my file, you know I tried that. I prefer to keep my personality intact." The drugs did allow him to sleep, but they didn't quell the nightmares—those visions of white-clad Russians firing at him as he clawed his way free of the vehicle as it burned. His leg had been crushed when the vehicle had contorted on its side. Then the Russians had appeared, firing into the wreckage. It wasn't enough that they had blown it up; they wanted to kill anyone who might still be alive. He had gotten away, barely, his leg leaving a long bloody smear on the pavement as he moved.

The drugs had worked, but they made him *different.* He was like a zombie during the day. Nothing made him mad, but nothing made him happy either. Antonio hated that feeling. He wasn't himself when on the drugs, he was someone else. The drugs took away the last thing he had, his soul. No, he had given enough to the Army—they weren't going to take his personality, his mind, his soul.

Dr. Franco glanced down at her pad. "So I see. How are you coping?"

"I live in a Torn District in an abandoned church. Everyone in my neighborhood is either a criminal or a victim. I'm a vet and I can't find and hold a job. I do what I must to get by."

"Is that illegal activity?"

There it is, the VA spying on me.

He paused for a moment. Just how much trouble could he get in? "Yes."

"How do you feel about that?" she said with a bit of grit in her tone.

How do I feel about what—being a drug dealer? About not having a life that is worth a damn? He felt his jaw clench at her question, if only for a moment. "You want to know how I feel?"

"Yes." She nodded quickly. "I do."

He shook his head. *No you don't—not really. At night you leave this place, you go home to your apartment in a good neighborhood. You cuddle with your cat and watch the news and order delivery sushi. Your life is nothing like mine.* "Okay—fine, I'll play along. I'm not proud of my life, not anymore. I pick up an odd job here and there. The rest of the time I do things you don't want to know about."

She made no notes on her obsolete digipad but kept her green eyes locked onto his own. "Do you use drugs?"

"Hell no!" he responded quickly.

"Why not?"

"I'm not that kind of person."

"You sell drugs, don't you?"

"I do. But I don't use them."

"Why not?"

He hesitated, wetting his lips as he thought for a moment. "I do what I do to survive. I don't take drugs because I've seen what they can do to a person. I don't take your medications either. I don't want my personality changed. I'm comfortable with who I am, without enhancements."

That seemed to satisfy Dr. Franco.

"Then why don't you sleep at night?"

He said nothing, then, "You're an ass, you know that, don't you?" It wasn't mean. In fact, he respected her for popping the question when she did. *She's more crafty than most of the shrinks I've dealt with. She at least has better timing with her questions.*

"You didn't answer my question."

"The answer is pretty simple, really." Antonio uncrossed his arms and put his hands on the table. "I don't sleep at night because I've been through some serious shit in the war. My friends were all killed and I somehow survived, despite a Russian patrol trying to finish me off. I dragged a bloody mess of what had been my leg behind me for fifty feet before I got to cover and managed to tie it off. I hear the screams of my squad at night. I should have died that day and I didn't. And I don't know why. Not knowing why I survived—that's what keeps me awake." *There, I said it. Maybe now she'll stop with the questions.*

She paused. "How do you cope with it?"

"I go for long walks. In my neighborhood, that's dangerous. I work on the church where I live, patching holes, fixing it up."

"Are you a religious man?"

"No," he replied. "Not since I was a kid. The church is just a building to me, a place to live."

"Is it?"

Why did he keep the pews set up like services were still going to happen? Antonio didn't know. There seemed to be something about respecting what the building had once been—what it represented. He didn't want to disturb that. "I don't know. Maybe it's more than that. Working on the building makes me feel useful. I can see what I accomplish when I'm done."

"So you like a sense of accomplishment?"

"Who doesn't?"

"You might be surprised. A lot of people with PT—er, *issues*, don't even have that. It's like the war took away parts of them, or locked it away deep in their minds. The fact that you can feel accomplishment is good."

She paused and tapped the digipad a few times. "Alright then, I think we're done here."

That was fast. He had undergone many of these sessions in the past. They were never over this quickly. "We are?"

She nodded. "Unless there's something more that you want to talk about."

"No . . ." he paused. "I take it you don't think I'm insane or a threat to society?"

"If I did, I would have signaled security. Too many veterans take matters into their own hands. If I thought you were dangerous, you'd be locked up for a more detailed examination."

"So what do you think about me?" he asked, unsure where the words had even come from.

Now it was her turn to lean back and cross her arms while she thought. "You're a principled man. You have rules you apply to yourself, even though those around you don't obey the same rules. You're proud . . . not arrogant. You are looking for something in life, something to give you purpose. Until you find that, you are building a world around you."

117

Am I looking for something to give me purpose? Her words burrowed deep. She might be right. *At least in the Army, I had a reason to get up every day. Now . . . not so much.*

Antonio rose to his feet. "Sure, Doc, sure. But if you want to know the truth, I'll tell you. I'm just trying to get through my life without screwing it up any more than it already is."

CHAPTER 14

Jay Drake entered the Hard Hat facility and heard the thick sound-proof door slide and hiss shut behind him. The room was dimly lit and was built like a bowl, with his entrance at the top level. The circular room was filled with analysts working with terabytes of Super Data streaming in holographic space around them. Images flew around the room as analysts shared them with each other. From the steps at the top of the room, Drake could see everything. He took the stairs down to the center dais. All around him was knowledge, information, power. He paused to drink it in. *I am master of all I survey.*

Hard Hat had been his idea, and he considered it one of his best. Given his background, that was saying a lot. Built like a bunker in a patch of Arizona desert, the facility existed but was invisible to the state and FedGov authorities. It didn't exist. There was no record of its construction, materials, or the incredible datafeeds that ran to the facility. Anyone driving up to the facility found only an old 1960s style motel called The Star Lite in the middle of nowhere. It was a façade to mask the deep underground bunker that Jay had constructed. It was so convincing, there were times when lost travelers actually stopped and tried to rent a room. Now The Star Lite always had a "No Vacancy" neon light flashing.

Hard Hat was the epitome of power. The FedGov was a monstrously huge and cumbersome organization. While the president of the United States was the nominal executive manager of the FedGov, the reality was that the government was too big to manage. Every branch and every agency operated on its own, within their legal parameters, like administrative silos. All the US president did was create the illusion that it was being managed.

119

Jay Drake understood this better than most people. But where some saw bureaucracy, he saw opportunity. His contractors worked in every agency of the FedGov and most of the state governments as well. Other nations contracted with him, giving his company even more depth. *Spying on the spies . . . a game no private citizen had ever tried before.* His hardware, his operating systems, his tech, was in every home in the United States and in many other countries around the globe. A missile didn't fire, a tank didn't move, money was not transferred that wasn't in some way touched either by his people or his technology. Yet most of this was unknown. Sure, JayTech was well-known, but he owned or controlled countless subsidiaries which controlled other companies and firms everywhere. Anyone attempting to sort through it all would find a spider's web of connections that would take years to fully unravel.

The Hard Hat was designed to tap the data that was out there, classified and otherwise, and allow Jay Drake to analyze it. The facility was illegal, certainly, fed by an army of contractors that were more loyal to him than to their nation. Here his top analysts could crunch the data, look for trends, provide insights into decisions and directions that he could exploit. In the dimly lit cool air of this facility, massive amounts of data could be manipulated and processed in ways that were bleeding edge. He had companies under his wings that did nothing but build the special computers that the Hard Hat used. Hard Hat drove innovation, new technologies, all for the purpose of furthering Drake's own ambitions and power.

This was *real* power. Not the stuff that made its way into the media or movies. Presidents, prime ministers, petty dictators, they all believed *they* possessed power because they had the authority to apply military and economic actions. Hard Hat gave him, Jay Drake, the power to crash economies, to cripple and destroy nations, and devour economies. From this room, and two others identical to it, Jay Drake could control a significant portion of the world. And almost no one knew that it was happening or that the true power of nations sat buried deep in an Arizona desert.

Hard Hat's director of intelligence, Rajin Borra, stood at his side. The short, skinny Indian was a genius in his own right. Drake had purchased not just his company, but the man as well. He owned Borra heart and soul, and both men knew it.

"You had something you thought I should see?" Drake asked. Information came into Hard Hat but it never left. It had been designed that way to eliminate inadvertent probing by the NSA or competitors who were after Drake's secrets. Hard Hat required a live visit—it was all part and parcel with the security protocols. A few hacks had tried to penetrate his security. *They won't be doing* that *ever again.*

"Indeed, Mr. Drake," he said, waving his hand in the air. From the myriad of holographic screens a series of images appeared and moved down in front of the dais where the two men stood. "DIA has been pulling in data from a number of sources on something that is trending . . . something odd."

"Define odd."

"We don't have everything yet, mind you, but it looks as if there have been a number of unexplained naval and coastal events around the world. I should clarify—an abnormal, statistically significant number of unexplained events."

"Show me." Jay leaned forward on the railing around the dais, staring at the data floating before him. Reports appeared, images, graphs. He reached out and touched the holographic data, burrowing into it for a few moments, extracting photographs of a rogue wave hitting an ocean liner—of a French submarine going missing in the South Atlantic. Jay brought both hands into play, manipulating the data. He spun it in the air, using his neurolink to not only see the information, but to process it.

Something is happening . . . something we don't comprehend. "Has the DIA pieced all of this together?"

"No, sir," Borra replied. "Our sources are much, shall I say, broader." Drake didn't look at him, his eyes and mind were still wading through the data.

"Everything here seems to indicate that we didn't have the numbers or types of activity until five years ago."

"Four years, ten months, fifteen days—yes, sir," Borra replied. AFSPC reported the loss of two satellites in a ten-day period; that seemed to be the first statistical glitch.

The Air Force Space Command monitored all satellites and space debris in orbit. For them to lose two satellites in ten days would have caused a little stir.

"Let me guess—they ignored it."

"Indeed, sir. In fact, until two months ago, we didn't start seeing this pattern, either. We saw the data that the DIA was pulling, along with the Office of Naval Intelligence, and we started to piece it together here as well."

It was fascinating . . . the number and type of events. Some had been in the media—like the ferry sinking off the coast of India. Others had been overlooked. "Is there more?"

"Our software developers working for the Navy have been getting a number of issues with submarine sonar arrays. They are picking up biological readings that are showing up as glitches."

"What do I care about whales?" Drake said.

"If these are whales," Borra said, pointing to the data and highlighting it in yellow, "then they are unlike any others we have ever seen. Look at the sizes and speeds of these readings, sir."

Jay leaned forward just a little farther and saw the readings. Borra was right. These were not whales. In fact, from what he saw, his analysts had no idea what they were.

What does all of this mean? His mind raced through the logical explanations . . . but none of them seemed to hold water. This was something else, something *bigger*. He couldn't make it out, not just because of the amount of the data, but because it was a level of complexity that went beyond what he knew. It had been a long time since he looked at something that he didn't fully understand . . . and Jay Drake found it wondrous and scary all at the same time. *When was the last time I was challenged?* He couldn't remember.

"There are no land-based phenomena that parallel this data?" he asked.

"None that we have been able to determine, sir. And we have been looking *very* hard."

You should—for what you are paid. Borra's compensation was not just monetary. What Jay was doing for him, and for several members of his family, was beyond money. Such actions ensured loyalty—and fear.

"I assume that you have had some of our best and brightest attempting to come up with answers as to what or who is behind this?"

"Since we came across this data stream, we have had teams looking at this, twenty-four hours a day."

"What are their findings?" Jay asked, turning to face his director of intelligence.

He gestured to a secure room, almost invisible in the darkness of the bowl-shaped room. The two men stepped down from the dais and moved into the room, not speaking until the door hissed shut behind them. "Sir, our analysts believe that the source of these anomalies is extraterrestrial in origin."

Jay said nothing for a moment. "Are they sure? The Chinese have surprised us in the past with ship-building programs that skirted the intelligence agencies."

"It is not the Chinese, sir, or the Russians. The data on these under-sea readings indicates technologies that do not exist. We have ruled out other sources. Even if the Chinese possessed the technology, there is no way that they could have built a vessel on the scale that those various submarines have detected. A submarine as large as an aircraft carrier? The facilities to build such a vessel would be difficult if not impossible to hide, sir. And the CIA, MI-6, and everyone else is looking for them; we've tracked their orders to the field operatives. If the source of these readings were terrestrial in origin, some intel asset would have found it. We haven't found it because, according to our people, it doesn't exist."

"Extraterrestrial in origin . . ." Jay said slowly. "I have to admit, Borra, you have a flair for the dramatic."

"Sir, this is not grandstanding. This is what our people believe is the source of these occurrences."

Jay looked the shorter man in his dark brown eyes. "I was joking, Rajin."

"My apologies, sir."

"Don't apologize. So tell me, has the DIA or anyone else come to this conclusion yet?"

He shook his head. "Not that we know of, sir. The DIA has compiled the most data on this to date, according to our sources. But we do not have a view into their detailed analysis—only some summary reports that they sent to the DHS that one of our employees scanned."

"That is something we will need to remedy in the future," he replied. "What about the other countries—are any of them close to coming to the conclusion our people have?"

"Not yet. We estimate they are a year from reaching that point. The United States, Russia, and China are the only ones with the intelligence apparatus big enough to amass this kind of information and look at it the way we are. We have very few company assets infiltrated in Russia. In China—well, sir, they have seen the trend but appear to be ignoring it as an error. That or they are hiding their findings in such a manner that our assets are not getting them."

Which is likely the truth. The Chinese had been difficult to penetrate as a government. *So we are ahead of everyone else in coming to this realization. Now what do I do with that?* Should he reveal what Hard Hat had discovered? Was there a way to exploit this situation?

"What do we know about these aliens?" he finally asked.

"Remarkably little. They only have an interest in our oceans. The fact that they have been here on Earth for five years and have not made contact must be attributed to an inability to communicate with us, or a lack of desire to communicate with us."

"Is this an invasion?"

"Unknown. They may be harboring their strength and true intentions until a time of their choosing. We don't know at this point, sir. In fact, there are more unknowns than knowns."

Drake had become one of the most powerful and wealthy men on the planet by overcoming vague unknowns. That was what White Monday had been to him. And in the unknown aspects of life were the greatest opportunities. "We have the advantage right now, among humans at least. We know more than anyone else. We also know that whatever these extraterrestrials are, they are an aquatic race or races. We will need to dramatically increase our spending in deep-sea exploration, communications systems, everything. I own several small deep-sea mining interests . . . and they are about to get a massive influx of capital. I'm going to have our people start hiring experts in linguistics, biosciences, and anything connected with Marine biology. I'm going to purchase some exploration ships—anything to give us an edge. We need to get on top of this, Borra."

"Yes, sir," his director replied.

"I want from you, in the next three days, a comprehensive list of what you need for Hard Hat to learn more about these visitors. If it's people, facilities, hardware—you've got it. If we can, I want to communicate with these *things*. If we can't, I need to know what their intentions are. At some point, the FedGov is going to come to the realization of what they are facing. When they do, I want to be in a position where they have to turn to us. Understood?"

"Yes, sir."

"It's just a matter of time before the government wants some of the same answers—and when they ask, I will have something for them—for an outrageous price."

They'll pay it: they won't have a choice. I can even create the circumstances that force them to react. The whole world will be afraid. Who knows, we might even be at war. They will want weapons for fighting an undersea enemy too.

"I also want our people to analyze how people will react when this is eventually made public. Are we looking at rioting in the streets? I need to make sure assets are protected against every contingency." Most people could be replaced easily enough. The majority of his people were disposable, their skills could by bought elsewhere. Some rose above this level, with a combination of skill and talent that raised them to the level of an asset. *I'll need to make sure I have a plan to protect and evacuate my key people.* The rest . . . they would have to fend for themselves. *I'm not the government; I only need to take care of people who are useful to me.*

The thoughts of what would happen when the reality of this race became known was not lost on Jay. *Fear will consume most people when they learn the truth.* He knew that. Governments could topple. "We are going to need to learn more. *When this does hit the fan, and everyone is shitting their pants, we are going to be a voice of reason and comfort. Just like when White Monday happened, people will turn to us once again to lead them out of the darkness. This time, however, we will be more prepared. We will have a leg up, and by mastering the intel, they will come to us like Duke users, craving another fix.*

". . . and when the dust settles, I intend to be on top of the heap."

CHAPTER 15

Fort Myer, Arlington, Virginia

Fort Myer was an almost invisible base just outside of Washington, DC. Formally designated as Joint Base Myer/Henderson Hall; Army insiders still called it Fort Myer. It had been part of the ring of forts that had surrounded Washington during the Civil War. It was small, discreet, tucked away on prime real estate atop the hill that adjoined Arlington National Cemetery. It had long been the home of the Third United States Infantry Regiment—the oldest regiment of the US Army, known lovingly as "The Old Guard." Assignment to the regiment was considered an honorary posting. The tiny brick chapel at Fort Myer was where many of the nation's honored dead were officiated prior to their burial at Arlington. The Old Guard provided high-profile security for official state functions and the honor guard at the Tomb of the Unknown Soldier and the burial details at Arlington. Her band, "Pershing's Own," was the official band of the US Army.

Master Sergeant Adam Cain had been on a lot of military bases around the world, but Fort Myer was distinctly different. It was incredibly small. He saw stables with actual horses being prepared with a caisson for burial duty. The entire fort appeared pristine; even the parade grounds were brilliant green. The red brick buildings with their big old-fashioned porches harkened to a different era. Getting on-post had required several checks of his vehicle. Terrorists were still out there, despite the response they courted when they attacked. *There's always someone out there wanting to knock the US down a notch, even her own people.*

After he parked his car, he pulled out his dress uniform jacket and put it on. The campaign ribbons and medals made it heavy. He buttoned the jacket and stepped outside. There was a hint of freshly cut grass in the air. Adam followed the signs to the officer of the day's office. He was ushered in by a corporal. Cain stood at attention and saluted the major who rose and gave him a response. "Master Sergeant Adam J. Cain reporting for duty, sir," he said in a low tone.

"Have a seat, Sergeant," the major said. Cain removed his hat and took the old wooden chair across the desk from the major. "I'm Major Malloy. Welcome to the Third Regiment."

"Thank you, sir."

Major Malloy looked down at his Army-issued digipad, heavily padded and reinforced for battle. He looked at the pad, scrolling with his fingers. "Your orders came through two weeks ago. I have been expecting your arrival. The colonel gave me a head's-up. From what I was told, you've had a fairly colorful career."

"Thank you, sir." *This kid has probably never even seen action.* That was the curse of being in the Army so long—younger men with rank.

"You were promoted twice to warrant officer, I see," he said, looking at the information on the pad.

"Yes, sir."

"And busted down twice. In fact, you were supposed to get a battlefield commission to second lieutenant and were broken back to master sergeant. That was a heck of an honor you seemed to toss away."

Honor? What did this young major know about battle and honor? Cain knew the incident and it brought back memories—some good, some not. He had protested the field promotion at the time, but Colonel Carpenter—called "Colonel Clusterfuck" by Cain and the men—had insisted. He had gotten his wish five weeks later for punching some shit-for-brains first lieutenant. A part of him wanted to explain his career to Major Malloy, but he kept his mouth shut. He learned a long time ago that retelling the story didn't help make his case. Officers like Malloy never understood what it was like to be a sergeant on a battlefield. "Yes, sir, that is correct, sir," was all Cain offered.

"Your combat record is . . . impressive," Malloy said as he studied the data. He had to scroll through it—several times, in fact. Cain was difficult in the chain of command, but no one could contest his results in battle.

"I did my duty," he said.

"Three Silver Stars. You were wounded on six different occasions. You have the Army Distinguished Service Cross, a Bronze Star, and I see here you were put in for the Medal of Honor for your action in the Battle of Anchorage. On top of that, you were ASHUR I and II qualified."

"I piloted a Mongoose originally, then a Rhino."

"It's impressive, I'll grant you that. Most of the younger enlisted men would be fortunate to qualify on even one rig, let alone two. I guess that's a benefit of being in the Army so long."

Adam felt his jaw lock momentarily. *He sure has a shitty way of delivering a compliment.* "As I said, sir, I did my duty." The mention of the Medal of Honor nomination felt like a detraction from his ASHUR qualifications. For Cain, it was something he was embarrassed about. His nomination had never been processed, mostly due, he assumed, to his record of insubordination. He knew of other men who deserved it more than him—most of them were buried on the other side of the hill opposite Fort Myer.

The ASHUR qualification was something he *was* proud of. The first generation of power armored suits were slow, bulky, hot, cumbersome, and deadly. Men in them either learned to fight with them or they died, usually in the thick of battle. He had survived. When the second generation of augmented combat armored suits had come out, he was glad to get them. Some armchair generals said they turned the tide of war. But that wasn't the complete truth. The war was turned because the Russians could not match the prowess of US combat infantry, plain and simple. The ASHUR rigs were simply tools; every person who piloted one knew that from their rigorous training. The men wielding those tools, *they* had won the war.

"So, do you know why you are here, Sergeant?" Malloy said, setting down the digipad on the old wooden desk.

"I was transferred here. I'm nearing the end of my career in two years. I assume this posting was a 'reward' for a decent career. I didn't ask for the transfer, but recognized it for what it was." Cain spoke the words with pride.

Major Malloy said nothing for a few long moments, leaning back in his chair which creaked, showing its age. Fort Myer was one of the few places where the Army didn't upgrade to new desks and chairs. There was a sense of history in this place—where even time was held at bay by honor and duty. "A reward? I take it your last CO never fully conveyed what a pain in the ass you were?"

Cain felt his jaw set again. "No, sir, he didn't." That wasn't quite true. Captain Jameson and he had exchanged words, on several occasions. *I don't like where this is going . . .*

"Well, Sergeant, I'm afraid you were sent here to be put out to pasture, and not in a good way. Frankly, you've passed up the early-out offers in the past. With your combat record, your CO couldn't just do a forced retirement. At the same time, you were proving yourself to be insubordinate, disrespectful of senior officers," he glanced back at the pad to refresh his memory, "and 'indifferent to the command structure.' Captain Jameson's words of course, not mine."

"Sir, I knew that this was going to be my last posting—I understand that. Captain Jameson's opinion aside, I intended this to be my best duty station in my career. I'm proud of my service in the Army—I just want to end my career on a high note." *I was right to think of him as Captain Jackoff.*

Major Malloy shook his head in disagreement. "Sergeant, it's a little late for that. Your attitude demonstrates itself all over your Service Record Book. I'm not sure, but you may have set a record for days in the brig during your career."

There were incidents that came to mind. Fort Irwin—well, that lieutenant should have known better. Fort Leavenworth—well, that was just stupid on that major's part. *He should have known not to order a free-fire exercise on a course that was in use. Hell, I saved lives that day. Sure the major lost a few teeth, but he learned an important lesson in the process.*

"Sir, I know I'm a pain in the ass. There are times in my career where I have prided myself on that attribute. I eat, sleep, and shit US Army green. I just want to wrap up my career with a top-notch assignment, something worthy of my experience and expertise."

Malloy didn't appear to be moved. "I respect the fact you fought in the war, sergeant. But this is the new Army. We do things differently. You've become an antique. You're obsolete. You're here because your last CO got fed up with you and couldn't come up with a better solution for dealing with you. Apparently he and Colonel Reed, our commanding officer, were old friends and Reed owed him a favor. You're not here as a reward. Essentially, he's dumped you in my lap. The real question now is what will I do with a washed-up old combat soldier in a peacetime Army post—one of the Army's most prestigious, I might add?"

Cain felt his face go red as he held his anger in check. *There's no point in validating what this weasel-assed little shit thinks of me.* After a few seconds he spoke up. "Sir, I was hoping that I could be posted to an honor guard detail, at the White House or State Department. Given my background and record, I thought it would be a good assignment for someone with my experience."

Major Malloy actually chuckled. "You're kidding me, aren't you? Those are the prime postings, Sergeant. I have a list a mile long of men ahead of you that have absolutely pristine records. Not that I would put you on that list. Given your past 'incidents,' I would never put you in a position where you might embarrass the Regiment. If I did, Colonel Reed would have my ass in a sling. I didn't become a major by making rookie mistakes."

I have been set up—damn it! More embarrassingly, it had been by Captain Jameson, a man Cain considered terminally unintelligent. He had told him that he would have his choice of assignments in the Third Regiment. Adam had been tricked by someone he had underestimated. The transfer had never been about Adam's desire to end his career with one moment in the sun, it was about Jameson pawning him off. He was angry at his predicament, frustrated that someone had fooled him. Especially a dimwit like Jameson. No, he wasn't stupid. He was smart, and that hurt. He had outfoxed Cain, plain and simple. *The Army is breeding officers who are cunning—behind a desk, anyway . . . damn it!*

For the first time in many years, he felt like a raw recruit in boot camp. That was one of the last times in his life when he didn't understand why he had been picked on by the drill sergeant. The feelings he was battling in his head were just like that . . . the fact that someone had the upper hand on him. Even the Russians had never gotten at him like this. This was not professional. This was personal.

"I was led to believe that I would have the option to pick my assignment once I arrived here, sir."

"That simply isn't the case, Sergeant. You've been in the Army a long time. This shouldn't come as a surprise to you."

He felt himself brooding. *I moved away from my family to come here, and for what? Nothing?* "Sir, surely there is a posting where you could take advantage of my experience?" He was keeping his anger in check—but barely.

"The Third Regiment is elite, Sergeant. It is a post to be aspired to. We are the face of the US Army to the public. But this is peacetime, and our president has little use for the trappings of the military. Into that mix, I now have you. If our roles were reversed, what would you do?"

Cain knew what he wanted to say. *I'd probably put a bullet into my head if I was ever as arrogant as you.* He wanted to hold his tongue, to keep his frustration and anger in check. Old habits die hard, though. Adam knew that once he started talking, his mouth would get far ahead of his brain. "I would look at the man sitting across from you and re-member what he has done for his country. I would remember that this man has shed his blood, multiple times, to save his brothers' lives and to protect his nation. I would acknowledge that this soldier has been in battle, something that you have probably never experienced. I would note that this soldier sitting across from you has been entrusted by the Army to pilot its most sophisticated combat armor, something that is a mark of distinction.

"And, if none of that works, I'd remember that this man you have been so casually disregarding is capable of kicking my ass and has a known disregard for officers who have not demonstrated respect." He allowed a stiff, flat grin to rise to his face.

Major Malloy was caught off guard by the thinly veiled threat. He sat upright in his chair and his face now took on a red glow. Clearly he was not used to being talked back to by someone under his rank and command. "I warn you, Sergeant, your borderline insubordination will not be tolerated," he finally managed to say out loud. "If you're not careful and a little more respectful, I can arrange for you to be trans-ferred to Florida."

God's waiting room! Hell no! Sergeant Cain kept his weathered pok-er-face intact. "Sir, you were the one who asked me to switch roles with you. I was only answering honestly."

"I can see why Jameson had you transferred," he curtly replied. "For what it's worth, I *do* respect your experience. At the same time, we both have duties to fulfill."

"Sir, where should I report?" Cain said, thinking that changing the subject might help diffuse the major's temper.

Malloy took on a thin smile. "I'm putting you on honor guard for burial detail at Arlington," he said with a ring of victory in his voice.

"Sir?"

"You heard me, Sergeant. You will command a burial detail. We have veterans that die every day, and you will lead a detachment to properly inter them with the military honors they deserve. I can think of nothing more honorable for an NCO with your experience than overseeing the ceremonies to intern our honored dead."

"Grave detail, sir?"

"It's not 'grave detail.' It is one of the most respected postings in the Regiment. We butt right up to Arlington and one of our primary missions is to help our veterans on their final journey with dignity and ceremony. You'll need to brief yourself on the procedures and processes that we adhere to. I'll give you two days before putting you on rotation. In the meantime, you'll likely need to go over to the stables and review the proper tacking procedures for the horses and the processes for care of the caissons."

"Horses? I've been in the Army most of my life and I have never had any experience with horses before."

"Good." Major Malloy flashed a smile. "A man with your experience is probably used to taking on new challenges. Command Staff Major Jones will walk you through our drill and can get you settled into your quarters." Major Malloy rose to his feet. "Welcome to the Third Regiment, Sergeant Cain," he said with a caustic, snide ring in his voice.

The conversation was over. Cain rose to his feet and went to attention, if only for a moment. "You are dismissed, Sergeant."

"Yes, sir," he said through gritted teeth. In a few moments, he was outside where the warm Virginia sun greeted him. *Damn. I should have known better.* He had been manipulated into taking a transfer. This was never about anything more than the US Army using him as its diaper. *They have shit all over me one last time. Now I'm in command of a burial detachment. Horses? What the hell?* Years of service and he was now in charge of dead men and women.

For the first time since he had driven across the country, he was glad that his wife and daughter were not interested in coming to visit him. He had hoped they would see him in the right light, standing on duty at the White House or Congress. That was never going to happen—he was sure of it.

The Army had little use for him in peacetime. When there was war, he was useful, a tool, an instrument of death and destruction. *Now I'm obsolete. I'm only fit to lead horses through a graveyard and bury other brave men and women.* He understood the heritage, the honor, but it wasn't what he had wanted at this stage of his life.

This was not the Army he had joined. He was a dinosaur, one of the last of his kind. Soon he would be one of those who would be taken over the tombstone-lined hill he saw in the distance across the post, under the shade of the magnificent oak trees.

And the part that hurt the most was, it was his own damned fault . . . and Major Malloy's—*no, Major Catastrophe's. That's how I'll think of him from now on.*

CHAPTER 16

Yorba Diamond,
outside of Los Angeles, California

"Cassidy, honey, your father is going to vid-in for you in just a minute," Cassidy's mother called from the family room.

CC was on with Isis, one of her friends from school. "I have to go, it's my dad."

"Isn't he in India or Thailand or something?" Isis responded. Her video image was dominated by her slender face, wearing makeup that CC's parents would never allow.

"It's Guam."

"Where is that?"

"In the Pacific," she replied. "Really, Isis, I need to go."

"I just Bonked it. Wow, Guam is in the middle of nowhere."

"Goodbye . . ." she said, stressing the farewell before she cut her off. Isis was in her close circle of friends. Not the brightest girl in terms of schoolwork but very in-the-know about the latest social and fashion trends. And trends were everything—they determined who was popular, who wasn't, and they changed almost hourly. Her mother was a doctor and made sure that little Isis had everything she ever wanted. *If only my mother was like hers.*

CC looked down at her digipad's tiny clock and noted that her father's call was only one minute away. It was one of the things she loved about her dad—he was always on time. Her mother was always either too early or too late. Her dad, however, managed his life by the clock, and she was the same way. As it ticked down, his transmission connect came on her screen. She accepted and saw his face appear.

"Hi, honey," he said, flashing a smile. Behind him, she could see a brilliant blue sky and palm trees swaying in a gentle breeze. For a moment, she wondered if he was in La or still on Guam. The wind seemed to toss his jet-black hair and as he lowered the camera view, she saw the stunning beach and the vastness of the Pacific framing his face. "How's my little girl doing today?"

"Fine, Dad," she replied. "Are you outside?"

He adjusted the camera feed on his pad. What she saw was the bright flowing sands of a beach and waves cascading onto the coast. "I'm at Asan Beach—it's our one day off. It feels good to be off the work site, even for a few hours. You said on our last call you wanted to see something other than me in my hotel room, so I thought I'd show you some of the most beautiful places on the island."

The camera readjusted to her father's face. "It looks beautiful," she said. La had beaches too, but they always seemed crowded. To enjoy any degree of privacy on a beach, you had to drive for a few hours. "It must be nice to spend your evenings on a beach like that."

"I don't get much time for that, kiddo. By the time I'm done at night, I usually just go back to the hotel and crash. I know the view looks great, but I don't get to enjoy it very much."

"How's your project, Dad?" It's not that she wanted to know, but she *did* know how to get her father to open up. Mention his work and sometimes you couldn't shut him up.

"It's going fine. We're doing a refurb on the command post here. It's a little tricky, working on an active military base. The Navy is pretty easy to work with. The Marines—well, they're Marines. I'm sure they're great when you need something blown up. When it comes to construction projects . . . not so great. Enough about my job—how has school been?"

"Good," she replied. *Please don't ask about math.*

"Including your algebra?"

Grak!

"Well, we had a test two days ago," CC replied, searching for a good way to tell him the news.

"And . . . ?"

"I got a C." When she spoke, disappointment rang in her words.

"CC—you are smarter than that." His tone wasn't scolding. It was worse. It was the sound of his expectations not being met.

"I'm *trying*, Dad."

"You need to ask your teacher if you can stay late and get some one-on-one time with her. We've had that discussion."

Yes, but you didn't listen. "Dad, they may have done that when you were in school, but not now. Our class is virtual. The teacher is in San Jose or somewhere like that, I don't remember. I can't get time with her after school. This isn't like when you were a kid."

"There are math teachers at your school, hon. You just have to go in and ask."

"I feel so stupid asking for help from the school. And I don't know any of them." It was that, and the fact that getting help would consume what little free time she had in the day. *I have a life too, Dad.*

"It may shock you, but I was young once too. I know that every kid feels the way you do at some point. But your grades are part of what will get you into college."

"I got an A in history," she offered up, hoping to change subjects.

Her father flashed a broad smile. "I bet you did. You and your mother are incredible on subjects like history and English. But math is important, too."

"To you. I asked our teacher if anybody uses algebra for their job. She said engineers did, but even *they* didn't have to manually calculate the solutions. They use modeling and sims to validate their results. Learning algebra is a huge waste of time."

"It's not about using it in your job someday, CC. You struggle with math. What do I always tell you?"

"'It's not about the math—it's about the logic,'" she replied in a bored tone of voice. "You keep saying that, but I don't get how understanding and solving polynomials will help me think differently." It was an old discussion, one that in her mind, she had won long ago.

"CC—I will grant you I don't use algebra on a daily basis, but I use the problem-solving techniques almost every day of my life."

"But I don't know if I'm going to be an engineer like you."

"Hon, I don't care what you become. You will deal with problems throughout your life. Knowing how to break them down and solve them is important."

"I just don't see it, Dad." Problems? Her biggest problem was that JZee was upsliding her social media posts and CC and Isis were flatlining. It was a real-world problem that she knew for sure algebra wouldn't solve. Mathematics had no place in the world of school and soc-media trending, where your popularity rose and fell on an hourly basis.

"You will . . . someday. You've been pretty lucky in life. You didn't have to deal with the rioting and downturns of White Monday and the war. My generation had that to deal with. So far, you kids have had it easy. I hope you never have to deal with anything like we did during that first year of the war."

And there it was, the White Monday reference. CC had heard it before from her parents. It was a big deal to them, when the net came cascading down. She understood—there was that time when the local connections were down for almost an hour during the last quake. *They keep holding White Monday over my head.* Sure, it was a big deal to her parents—but to her it was just a date and event she was forced to study.

"I get it, Dad," she said flatly.

"Talk to the learning coordinator in your center and find a math teacher at the school who will meet with you—okay? I know you don't want to stay after school, but your math grades are dragging you down."

"I'd rather do my math homework with you," she said softly. When her father was not on the road, he always made the time to help her. He had a way of explaining complicated things that made them seem simple. It was a trait none of her teachers seemed to possess. They were teaching so many kids virtually, they didn't have time to respond to every question. School just seemed rushed to her, like the teachers didn't care.

"I know. I miss doing homework with you too, CC. But until I get back, I want you to get help. We both know your mom hates math more than you do. That means finding a tutor to help." She could tell by the tone in his voice that he missed doing her math homework with her too.

"You did hear me say that I aced my history test, didn't you? In fact, I'm As and Bs in every other class." She tried again to change the subject.

Her dad nodded. "I did. Congratulations. You're a smart girl. But even the smartest people have to ask for help from time to time, honey. It's never an easy thing to do. No one wants to admit that there're things they can't do or don't understand. Ignorance is never easy to own up to. But the smartest people I know are those who are smart enough to admit what they know and what they don't—get the help they need, and learn."

"I will," she conceded. It was clear that attempting to wear her father down was not going to change his position. If anything, he was digging in.

"What was the history test on?"

"World War One—early twentieth century stuff."

"I have to admit, I don't know a lot about that period."

"It was actually kind of interesting. The whole world ended up at war because of a weird bunch of alliances and connected royal families. Everyone thought that the war was going to be quick but it lasted years. The technology changed everything. Did you know they used to fly airplanes made of wood and canvas—with open cockpits?"

"Yeah. I actually used to build model kits of some of those planes when I was your age."

"What is a model kit?" she asked, cocking her head humorously.

Her dad smiled. "Something we used to do when I was young. It was all the parts to build a model—a toy, really, of something. I built some German airplane kits. They looked just like the real thing. You painted them and put them on display."

"For what?"

He shrugged. "I don't know. It was something to do."

"Couldn't you just sim up a 3D model and print it on the replicator?" Every home had a sophisticated 3D printer/replicator for making things you might need in the house.

"I *could* have done that CC, we had the tech, but that wasn't the point. I just found it kind of fun, working with my hands, putting all of the little parts together. Technology helps out a lot in life, but many of the most rewarding things are the ones you do with your hands and your brain."

"Seems slow and boring to me."

"It might be. But not everything is tied to the net and your trends or E-rating."

Only the things that are important. "If you say so."

"I do. Do you think you can shoot me a digi of your history test? I'd like to see the results."

"Sure," she said. Her father, no matter where he was in the world, always had time to look at her schoolwork. Sometimes he made comments about it, sometimes he explained it. One thing that she knew for sure, he did read it.

"I'm hoping to be coming home in a few weeks. It'll be just for an extended weekend, but we're coming up on a milestone that is going to allow me to get away from this place."

"When?" True excitement rang in her words.

"Hopefully next month, if all goes as planned. When I get back, we'll get some time together, just you and me. We'll go south down the coast for an afternoon, hit the beach. It'll be just like old times."

CC suppressed the urge to roll her eyes. Her father loved to take her to the beach. When she was seven years old, it was a blast. She wasn't that age anymore. She wanted to tell him, but couldn't bring herself to say the words. *He'll never understand. I have things to do, too.* "Sure—that will be great." Her tone was less than convincing.

"CC—I know you're not jacked about it, but it will be fun. You can bring some of your friends—we'll grab some subs on the way there— make an afternoon of it."

The thought of bringing JZee and Isis made her feel a little better about the prospect. "That would be awesome, Dad."

"So," he said, pausing for a moment. "Whatever happened with this boy you met at the dance? What was his name? Luxor? Trevor?"

"Arnold, Dad. Arnold Fletchman. His tags are Spiked and Arno." The prospect of talking about boys with her father was worse than talking about math.

"Arnold—that's right. So, have you talked to him?" Her father refused to use tag names.

"That depends on what you mean by 'talked to him.' We're in class together, so we talk. It's just not very long conversations." Since the dance, she had connected with Arnold's social media feeds. He occasionally looked at her stuff and even commented from time to time. She had hoped for more after they had danced together, especially that slow dance. Arnold seemed interested in her, but he was not a conversationalist.

"Hon, he's the same age you are. He's just as nervous about talking with you as you are with him."

She shrugged. "I don't know, he just doesn't seem interested in me since the dance."

"Well," David Chen said slowly. "Maybe you can invite him along to the beach when I'm in town."

"A date?" *You are suggesting a date? What happened to my* real *father?*

"It's not a date. For God's sake, don't say that, your mother will come unhinged. This isn't a date. It's just you and a friend for a few hours at the beach—under adult supervision."

"I don't know, Dad."

"Why?"

"Well, I mean, I'd have to ask him."

Her father nodded. "Yes, generally that's part of this, CC. Otherwise, how's he going to know to go?"

"You know what I mean."

"It's scary . . . I get that. I was nervous as heck when your mom asked me out for the first time."

"I didn't know Mom asked *you* out. I assumed you had asked her the first time." It hit her that there were things about her mother and father that she didn't know.

"We were your age once. As much as I hate to admit it, you're growing up. I can't fight time."

"Dad, I—" Her digipad beeped. "Uh oh. I think we're going to lose our signal in a few seconds."

"Yeah, I got that here too. CC—I love you, kiddo. Think it over. When we talk next week, we can firm up plans and you can think about how you want to talk to this Arnold kid."

"I love you too, Dad," she replied, blowing him a kiss with her hand like she used to do when she was a kid.

David Chen waved to her just before the video image went red with the signal loss. CC leaned back and sighed. She missed her father deeply. She knew a lot of her friends spoke about their parents like they were the enemy—but she loved hers. Her mother tended to be a hard woman—crisp, professional, argumentative. But her dad was, well, her dad.

Her mind quickly moved on to bigger, more important issues—like what was she going to say to Arno?

CYCLE III

The sailboat *Living the Dream*, twenty-eight miles southeast of the Florida Keys

Arthur Craig was enjoying his day sailing off the Florida Keys. He was sixty-two, and his sailboat, *Living the Dream*, was the one place where he felt he could get away from it all. Years of hard work for dozens of different employers had left him worn out and exhausted. He was still years from retirement, though—the FedGov made sure of that, constantly raising the retirement age as opposed to fixing the Social Security system. He didn't mind . . . much. The weekends were his to enjoy.

Arthur had planned on sailing out on Friday night and heading back Saturday evening to Key Colony Beach. He had taken down the sails for the night and stood at the wheel, looking up at the brilliant stars. This made all of those years of work worthwhile. For a few long minutes, he drank in the smell of the sea and the breeze. *To hell with work . . . fuck my boss . . . this is where I want to be.*

Something in the sky caught his attention. It was reddish orange and seemed to be just slightly south of him. It wasn't a star; he could see that it was larger and glowing. It seemed to be getting larger each passing moment. *A meteor?*

Arthur's hands tightened on the wheel. Whatever it was, it was getting bigger, closer. He toyed with firing up his engines but wasn't sure where he would go. Unconsciously, his left hand let go of the wheel and touched his life vest to make sure it was on.

At about a mile out, it was huge—a plummeting fireball of immense size. *Is it an asteroid?*

Then it did something he didn't expect at all; it altered its descent. It arced in the sky, angling its flight path slightly with an increased downward bend. Arthur stared at it, his mouth hanging open.

He braced himself, fighting the instinct to jump overboard. Fear made his body go rigid. Arthur felt alone in the night in the Keys, in the middle of some sort of disaster. *It is going to hit!* While it was a good mile or more away, he knew the impact was going to be deadly. As it raced through the sky, Arthur felt a surge of hot air from the fireball, even at this distance. *Living the Dream* rocked hard from the ripple of heat in the air. The wind became hotter every second. There was a boom—perhaps a sonic blast? Fear enveloped him.

Arthur flinched as the object was about to hit the water, but it did not just collide. There was a massive blast in front of the fireball, like rocket thrusters. He had seen satellite launches at the Cape and knew what they looked like. The fireball slowed, then collided with the water.

There was a huge concentric blast at the moment of impact. It raced out across the sea straight at him. His hat flew off and his sails stiffened instantly. Then a wall of heat hit. *Living the Dream* rocked from the wall of superheated air. The air (or perhaps the ocean itself, he couldn't tell) hissed as the air came at him. Arthur lost his iron grip on the wheel and was thrown into the air, spinning and flailing wildly in a disoriented blur. Heat seared him, and then he plunged into the waters of the Caribbean, giving him a moment of relief.

He flailed under the water, struggling to determine which way was up. Finally he broke the surface and gasped hot air. He splashed around, looking for his boat. He saw it on its side, twisted and contorted. It was dwarfed by a massive wall of water surging toward him, obscuring his field of vision. The hot wave roared and smashed into him and the boat. He hit the sailboat, he felt the thud of the collision as the darkness and water churned around him. Arthur held his breath and tried to keep his calm. Bubbles were everywhere and he felt a rush of water as if he were going over a waterfall. Which way was up? He saw a shimmer in one direction and paddled toward it as a roaring filled his water-clogged ears.

Arthur broke the surface, gasping for air, sucking in a half-gulp of seawater in the process. Debris from his deck was everywhere in the water, though most of it was unidentifiable. He spotted his cooler and swam toward it. The plastic container was slightly gnarled and warm to the touch, but still floated. Looking into the starry night, he saw *Living the Dream*, or what was left of her, lying on her side. Her fiberglass hull was discolored and blistered from the heat wave that had preceded the impact. She was sinking. *My boat . . . I worked so hard for her . . .*

As it slid into the black sea below him, Arthur felt his face sting in searing pain, as if he were being poked with a hundred needles. Touching his face, he felt peeling skin on his cheeks and brow. *What happened?* He wasn't sure in the darkness, but he thought there was blood on his fingers. *I've been burned.* With that realization, suddenly the salt water made his arms and face feel as if they were on fire.

Arthur Craig clung to his cooler in the darkness and tried to process what had happened. That was no meteor. It had changed direction and slowed its descent. If it had been a meteor of that size, he'd be dead . . . he knew enough about physics to comprehend that.

If it wasn't a meteor, what was it? Suddenly, he realized it didn't matter. If someone didn't find him soon, they would never know what had happened. His mind turned away from the strange fireball and began wondering how he was going to get to shore.

Baton Rouge, Louisiana

As Deputy David Lowry arrived at the dock at Baton Rouge's south side, he pulled out his digipad to log the complaint. The call had come in about a stolen boat. These were relatively rare occurrences but did happen. Usually it involved alcohol, someone taking a boat out for a joy ride, usually abandoning it somewhere else. Trying to find the culprits was difficult, except for those rare occasions when the perpetrators left evidence or passed out on the boat.

In his sixteen years on the job, he had seen it before. *It's either damned kids or someone drinking.*

He quickly noted that there were no boats moored in the small marina, but there were a lot of people standing on the docks. It struck him as odd. He had been there countless times before and there were always boats tied off. To see it empty was strange. Deputy Lowry stepped out of his car and the people on the docks rushed toward him. All this for a missing boat?

"Officer," the first man to reach him, a sixtyish man in floral shorts, spoke in a tone of voice reminiscent of a schoolboy attempting to get the teacher's attention. "My boat, the *Mabel*, is missing."

"Sir, just a moment." David loaded up the report form on the digipad. Other voices cut in. "My boat is missing," another man added. "Mine too," a third chimed in. Lowry surveyed the crowd as the voices overlapped, each one claiming their boat had been stolen.

"Wait a minute," he said, pushing his hand in a downward gesture to quiet them. "Please—one at a time. How many of you are here to report your boat missing?"

Over a dozen hands shot up.

What the hell is going on?

He tapped his collar comm link. "Dispatch this is zero-three at Bell's South Side Marina."

"Go ahead, David," came back the voice of Gracie at the sheriff's office.

"We're going to need at least two more officers down here."

"I thought it was a stolen boat?"

"It's more like a stolen marina," he responded.

The logistics staggered him. This wasn't a bunch of kids out for a joyride. Someone had taken ten to twenty boats, some of them quite large. And what could they do with them? *You couldn't sell them, no one is in the market for* that *many boats. This has to be a prank . . . it has to be.* This was going to be a long morning.

Three hundred miles off the west coast of Ireland

British-Lufthansa Air Flight 210 was the overnight flight from Washington's Clinton National Airport to London Heathrow. Amy Barrow loved working these flights. For a flight attendant, things were remarkably quiet. Most of the passengers slept, or tried to sleep. This flight had been routine for the most part, almost boring. There was a mother with a sick baby in Travel class that was a bit of a problem. The child had been throwing up, crying, and repeatedly filling his diapers. But now, only an hour or so from the Irish coast, even that tiny passenger had drifted off to an exhausted sleep.

She dropped into her foldaway seat in the prep area between the Elite and Travel class sections, giving her aching feet a few minutes' reprieve. Amy automatically fastened the seat belt. Six years of experience had ingrained in her the need to be secure in the air. There weren't any weather issues reported, but one never knew what a plane might encounter.

Most of the passengers were asleep and there was still an hour before they had to prep breakfast. The Airbus Sleekcraft 5's windows were black with the night. Someone was snoring eight rows up. Other than that, it was serene. One of the other flight attendants, Kathy, was walking the aisle, checking on the slumbering passengers. The only lights came from the few passengers awake with their digipads or the entertainment systems on.

Suddenly the aircraft felt like it was going into a sharp, diving turn. Things shifted in the food prep area and she saw something outside filling the windows with a dull red, then orange, then bright yellow light on the port side of the aircraft. *What is happening?* She leaned forward to get a better look out the window and saw something, just for a millisecond, that stunned her. The windows seemed to bow outward, as if they were melting. *What the—?*

All hell erupted. In her mind, everything seemed to happen at once. The aircraft rocked hard, harder than any turbulence she had ever felt. Those not strapped in were tossed around the cabin like a child's doll thrown into a dryer. Overhead luggage compartments opened in some places and bags launched like deadly missiles, slamming into passengers and seats. All of the windows on the port side of the airplane blew out in a maelstrom of air that turned the cabin into a tornado.

Kathy had been thrown to the ceiling of the airplane then tossed unceremoniously into a row of seats. For a few seconds, the air of the cabin filled with papers, cups, and anything else that was loose. The depressurization alarm went off, wailing loudly. Oxygen masks dropped, and the plane rocked hard, as if it had been punched. The air was supposed to be cold, but Amy could feel warmth all around her. Even with her ears popping, she heard a chaotic mix of banging and thumping mixed with the muffled screams of passengers roused from their sleep by the explosions. There was the sound of debris flying about the cabin. The aircraft wall near her seat felt hot, enough for her to lean away from it. In awe, she watched as the plastic appeared to melt. A rivet from the outer skin of the aircraft popped, punching through the plastic a foot in front of her.

Screams muffled by the rush of hot air seemed to grow louder and fill the dropping airplane with terror. Passengers flailed about, all grasping madly for the oxygen masks, crying out in stark fear. The plane throbbed around her, quaking. She leaned forward and saw the bright light fading, diminishing back to a red glow, then darkness again. Air ripped through the open windows.

The Airbus Sleekcraft 5 angled down steeply, metal groaning audibly. Amy felt the unyielding seatbelt dig into her body. There was something wrong with the plane, that much she knew for sure. She grabbed the telephone handset behind her on the bulkhead and brought it down. "Ladies and gentlemen, please secure your oxygen masks by placing the yellow cup over your face and tightening the elastic straps. Secure your masks first, then those of your fellow passengers!" She saw that two-thirds of the people either had gotten their masks on or were in the process. Some passengers who didn't have their masks on were already passing out as the air stung their faces. She could see their heads go limp on their necks and drop, one by one.

The engines on the starboard side of the aircraft surged—she could hear that through her popped ears. The nose rose, slowly.

She turned behind her and toggled the cockpit. "This is Amy—what happened?"

"Something passed near us—a meteor or asteroid," the copilot, Aubrey Daniels, replied with a voice muffled by his own oxygen mask. "We have emergency warning lights across the board."

"Like hell it was a meteor," the pilot snapped. "That was something else, I'm telling you."

The copilot ignored his partner and kept his focus on the aircraft. "Port engines are out. I have a fire warning in avionics. She's fighting my attempt to turn." The copilot's voice was strained, as if he were pulling with all of his might. He was not talking to her, but to the pilot. "Amy—we are declaring an emergency. We are going down in the water. Have them brace for impact and prepare for a water landing."

Water landing? Planes don't land in the water—they crash. That was an old joke from her flight attendant training—only now it didn't seem so funny. She leaned over far enough to look through one of the missing windows. One of the engines on the port side of the plane was gone. Not ripped away like she would have expected, but simply missing. The remaining engine was there but looked warped, almost melt-ed. The wing itself was missing a panel or two of aircraft skin, some of those that remained were peeled up, vibrating madly with the rush of air. The wing itself was distorted, twisted upward, curling at the far tip.

Amy felt the color drain from her face. *Oh God.* How long would they last in the cold waters of the North Atlantic before help could ar-rive? She paused for a moment, regained her composure, and activated the microphone. *I trained for this . . . Now let's see if that training can save some lives . . . including my own.*

Coast Guard cutter *Unimak*, twenty-two miles off the coast of Baja, California

The new US Coast Guard cutter *Unimak* (WAVP-379) cautiously ap-proached the cruise ship in the heat of the afternoon sun. Four hours earlier, they had received word that the Norwegian Star ship, *The Star of the Sea*, had sent a garbled message to the Coast Guard base in San Diego with the word "attack" in it, then it had gone silent. The cruise ship operated on a regular run between San Diego and Acapulco. The idea that a big cruise ship would suddenly drop communications was only made stranger when she did not to respond to the visual signals and audio hails from the *Unimak*. When she came into view, the ship was dead in the water, listing slightly to port.

The *Unimak* sent out her two launches, led by Commander Hargis, to board the seemingly crippled ship. Captain Rebecca Donavan stood on her bridge, looking at her displays from the cameras that her board-ing parties carried. Her links to the twenty men she sent aboard the cruise ship gave her an up-front and personal view. When she had set out to intercept the ship, it was presumed *The Star* had some sort of communication or power issues. What she saw on her display made her stomach knot up instantly.

"You getting this, Skipper?" Commander Hargis said, angling his view down to the deck. There was a bloody smear there, like a body had been dragged. The trail ended mysteriously, but not with a body.

"Boarding party, weapons free," she replied to the cheek-mike she wore. Her words were immediately picked up by the earbuds worn by the boarding party. The blood looked dry in the hot sun, and there were no signs of other ships alongside the *Star*. That didn't mean that whoever had done this wasn't still aboard.

Hargis acknowledged and ordered the boarding parties to ready their weapons. "Andrews—secure the bridge," Donavan ordered from *Unimak*. "Hargis, you make your way aft and into the engine room."

Lieutenant Andrews's feed from the bridge five minutes later was disturbing. There were no signs of life. Manuals, coffee cups, and papers were tossed on the deck like some sort of struggle had taken place. "Andrews, check internal power."

"Aye, sir," he replied. "Skipper—ma'am, I got zip here." He angled the camera on his headgear over the control station. Black smoke stains streaked up from the access ports. "Some of their equipment looks like it was just hauled away, like someone cut it and took it off. The environmental control systems are missing entirely. What equipment is left is messed up. From the looks of it, something fried the electronics. I just checked the non-digital compass; the needle's spinning."

Captain Donavan tipped her head in thought. *Why would anyone be interested in the equipment on a cruise ship?* Looking over at *The Star of the Sea*, she saw strange marks on her hull paint. Scrapes, like something had been dragged up or down along the hull. Once she noticed them, her eyes drifted down the entire length of the ship. The marks were everywhere. "Fisher," Donavan barked over the mike. "Get your camera gear and get pictures of those marks on her hull." As she studied them, she tried to picture grapples or ladders from boarding parties, but the marks didn't match up. And boarding parties wouldn't have been able to hit the huge cruise ship from so many places; these marks were all along the hull. Donavan trusted her gut. *This isn't at all what it seems on the surface.*

It took Commander Hargis and his team ten minutes to reach the engine room. The only lighting belowdecks came from the boarding party's external helmet lights. When Hargis got there, Donavan saw ankle-deep water on her display. On the stairs leading down, there was more blood, large pools of it now dried and cracking where they were above the waterline. Someone had been injured—no, killed. These were not small puddles. *Who killed them?*

"She's taking on water, sir," Hargis said.

"Get her pumps going," Captain Donavan ordered. "The bridge reports no power there—all the systems are fried."

Hargis checked the gauges. "We've got the same here," he said, flipping several switches in the darkness, to no avail. "Even the emergency lights are not operational."

"No sign of the engineers?" If there had been a terrorist attack, the safest place for the crew to secure themselves was the engine room.

"No, sir, the doors were open. She's listing. Wherever this water is coming from, I estimate we only have about three hours or so before she capsizes."

Donavan considered the words she heard, thinking through her options, which seemed to be dwindling. Her first inclination was to use the intercom to see if they could identify any survivors who might be hiding. There had to be people hiding somewhere. This was a big ship. *There just has to be someone who survived.* Captain Donavan turned her focus to the bridge crew. "Andrews, have two crewmen pull the hard drives of every system on the bridge. Take the rest of your men and search the ship, deck by deck, room by room. Hargis—take half of your men and dedicate them to restoring power; get those pumps working. Send the rest forward to help Andrews."

Captain Donavan stepped off her bridge and walked to the deck door, lifting her bullhorn and turning to face the cruise ship. "This is the US Coast Guard. We have secured this ship. We are here to help you. Please come out and we will assist you. I say again, this is the US Coast Guard . . . if there is anyone aboard this ship, please come out now."

Donavan stared at the screens showing Hargis's team as they tried to deal with the incoming water. "Skipper, it looks like there are leaks all along her keel. I can't imagine what she may have hit out here to cause this kind of damage, though. One thing is certain: we need to get her into port soon."

"How about using our pumps?" she offered, suspecting the worst.

Hargis had a degree in naval engineering. "Not enough, sir. She's going to go down unless you can get another ship out here."

Donavan cringed. *Unimak* was the closest ship; she had checked. There wasn't enough time. They were at least five hours from a ship that had the kind of power needed to keep the cruise ship afloat. Even a visual check of radar didn't show anything close. "I'm going to put in the call—but we're out here alone. You're my best hope for restoring power. In the meantime, we will ring for towing and see if we can get her closer to shore at least."

"I'll do my best, Skipper."

Captain Donavan checked the data on the ship from the Coast Guard's database. There were 613 passengers and 162 crewman on *The Star of the Sea*'s manifest. With the blood on the deck and in the interior of the ship, it looked like a terrorist attack. *Why not just sink the ship? Why take the bodies of the dead? Were the survivors taken hostage?* "Helm, bring us alongside that ship and order the crew to ring for towing. Communications, get me San Diego on the comm. Relay our boarding party's transmissions in a squirt to them. Tell them I will need another vessel out here immediately. Further, have the Air Station launch flights over this area. I want every ship large enough to hold potential hostages tagged."

As her crew sprang into action, Captain Donavan looked up at the massive cruise ship that towered over her cutter. "What happened to you?" she muttered.

CHAPTER 17

The DIA Board Room, the Pentagon

Captain Ashton Slade made sure his uniform was in order as he stood outside the "Board Room." The DIA's largest conference room was where the heads of the agency met weekly for their briefings. Despite being buried deep under the Pentagon, the Board Room was sealed for acoustics and had sensors that detected any unauthorized electronic emissions. Security swept those who entered the room and the room itself before every meeting. It seemed like overkill—until the last few months of his research.

Slade was nervous. He had presented to the Joint Chiefs more than once and had been just as edgy. The word he used to describe the JCS was "demanding," and today's audience, the heads of the DIA, were likely to be the same. Today his nervousness was a little more than the normal terror of speaking with the top brass. This time he was going to deliver a report that was unlike any other he had ever presented. *They'll probably have me in a straitjacket before I even finish. Psych eval at Wally-World.* The thought of going to Walter Reed for mental evaluation made him chuckle.

He had, at the urging of Admiral Frost of Naval Intelligence, sent the report up as red-flagged—the highest potential threat level that could be given to a report. For three days, he had heard nothing. Then a request came that he was needed to respond to questions regarding his report. It was akin to being put on the witness stand. *Given what I put in that report, they are going to be looking at me like I've got a bag of cats for brains.*

The aide at the door, a young lieutenant, tapped his earbud. "They are ready for you, sir," he said, opening the door. The door hissed softly open. Ashe braced himself. He understood the skepticism he was going to face. *In the end, I stand by my research and analysis—do or die.*

The conference table was round, with the center open for holographic displays. Seated around the table were Lieutenant General Martin Quartermain, the somewhat crusty director of the Defense Intelligence Agency; the Director of Naval Intelligence, and their counterparts from the US Air Force and the Army. His boss, Colonel Harper, was there, along with Major General Horace "Cutter" Guttman, who was in charge of Army Intelligence. Colonel Clark Harper gave him a nod of reassurance as he entered the room, as did Colonel Hastings, who sat next to Air Force General Ryan Buchwald. General Bradly Holland, commander of the US Space Force was the youngest face in the room. General Florence "the Axe" Hatcher stood out—she was the only female in the room and the first female commandant of the USMC.

Ashe had prepped with Colonel Harper and the Navy team prior to arriving. That didn't mean it was going to be smooth sailing. His analysis was sound, but he knew the conclusions were destined to raise some ire. Most men in his position would have been worried that they were flushing their career down the latrine—but Ashe knew he was right. *The worst thing they can do is keep me in the Army and take away my Navy desk responsibilities.*

The door hissed shut behind him and green lights appeared in the corners of the room at the ceiling, an indication that the room was indeed secure. "Next on the agenda," Admiral Darien Frost of the Navy said, "Red-Flagged Report 105-A; report from our section leader, Captain Slade." He turned to Slade. "Have a seat, Captain." He gestured to the guest chair at the big circular table. Ashe sat down and wondered if the seat was really that uncomfortable, or was it the situation?

His report appeared on the holodisplay in the center of the room, with various notations on it. The holographic image rotated slowly so that everyone could see it as it passed.

Quartermain glanced at the report then at him. "You're an Army captain reporting on a Navy issue?"

Colonel Hastings spoke up. "If I may, sir, Captain Slade is filling in for Commander Franks at the Navy desk. He is one of our best and brightest."

"That remains to be seen," General Quartermain said in a low tone, pausing the report's slow spin so he could re-read a section. "We received this report a few days ago. It's either brilliant or the product of science fiction."

"It is accurate, General," Ashe replied. "I have gone over the incident reports with not just the Navy desk but the other teams as well."

The gravel-voiced Colonel Hastings spoke up. "I had my reservations at first too, sir. But we cross-compiled and re-cut and sliced the data. Much as I regret it, Captain Slade's work is solid in regards to the Air Force reports on those incidents."

Admiral Frost looked at his hard copy of the report, then took off his glasses. "His analysis is solid, Marty," he said to General Quartermain. "I was skeptical at first, so I had a separate team from ONI crunch his information. If anything, they found additional incidents that could be added to the stream that Captain Slade had compiled."

The tension evaporated. *I missed something?* That bothered him more than the pressure of his current situation. He was going to have to talk to Admiral Frost. *I hate mistakes, no matter how small they are.*

"Captain," General Quartermain said in a clear tone of voice. "I read these reports and I'm frankly disturbed. We're talking about an unknown force having submarine capabilities far above our own. These incidents with the USS *Virginia*, for example. If they are correct, we have potential enemy submarines larger than ours with advanced maneuvering and propulsion capabilities. Darien, are those kind of subs even possible?"

"We don't have that technology," Admiral Frost replied. "Captain Stewart is a seasoned combat commander, though. If he put it in a report, it's authentic. We have other, similar reports from both Seventh and Second Fleets. This isn't an isolated string of incidents we can simply write off as a geological disturbance or something else natural."

General Quartermain was still not convinced—Ashe could see that. "Is somebody going to tell me how the hell we have ships bigger than aircraft carriers landing in our oceans, which we detected, and we never scrambled a single drone to see what it was?"

Air Force General Buchwald responded. "Simply put, sir, we screwed the pooch on this. Those readings were so large, our men followed procedures and wrote them off as glitches. Let's face it, if any of us saw readings like those indicated on page sixteen, we would have done the same thing. They did what they were trained to do."

"We've fixed that—correct?" Quartermain pressed.

"Yes, sir. Now we're looking for these kind of incidents and responding."

General Holland of the Space Force spoke up. "Our surveillance is focused almost entirely on objects we know to be in orbit or about to be—not from a threat that is extraterrestrial. This was simply a contingency we never factored in."

"I'm just shocked that no one has snapped video of these ships," Colonel Hastings chimed in. "I mean, you can't jaywalk at an intersection without getting a ticket because so many cameras are covering your every step."

Ashe leaned forward. "I think I can answer that, sir," he said. "A week ago I started combing the digital gossip magazines. As it turns out, they have run some of the images I think we are looking for. We all just wrote them off as trash journalism or fictional stories with doctored pictures. Since our formal policy is to not acknowledge or investigate UFO sightings, well, they just got dismissed by the general public."

"Can you show us what you've found?" the general asked.

"Yes, sir," Ashe replied. He put his thumb on the table surface then leaned forward for a retinal scan. When he saw the authorization flash, he barked out the commands. "Open file Red 105-D. Authorization Tango-Bravo."

The copy of his annotated report disappeared off of the screens to be replaced with three video files. Each showed blurry, distant images of the ships that civilians had seen and captured with different devices. One was close enough for them to make out some of the faint details. It was big, almost three aircraft carriers in length if not more. Billowing clouds of steam rolled away from it as it touched the ocean—obscuring the image. The other vid-images were more distant and blurry.

"What the hell?"

"Even the mainstream press wrote these off as fakes, which worked to our advantage. But the similarities are there."

"What else can you tell us about their ships?" Admiral Frost asked as he rotated the image so he could see it.

"Remarkably little," Ashe replied. "There are three vessel types we've come across so far. The smaller ships—about the size of a cruiser. These have a distinct angled nose. They are flight and sea capable. The sonar readings we got with them seem to fluctuate between biological readings and metallic, which may be a clue as to their composition. We think these are the ones our submarines are picking up. Their speeds and turning capabilities far exceed what our forces can do. The medium-size ships, like those in that image, appear to be longer and taller. They are remarkably sleek in design but we have not picked these up under the surface. Either we haven't encountered them, or they are positioning themselves in such a way that we cannot locate them.

"The last class of ships are more like small cities. These we have picked up on radar but haven't seen. They are monsters in terms of size, running in excess of 4,000 feet in length. These ships don't seem to maneuver but simply descend into the oceans."

Admiral Frost added an important detail, "That is four to five times as big as the USS *Gerald Ford*, gentlemen." His words rang like a bell in the room.

There was as long moment of silence while General Quartermain considered those words. "Damn," he muttered, either at the size or his frustration. "Let me ask this—is this a trick on the part of the Russians or the Chinese, or anyone else for that matter?"

"I wondered the same thing," Colonel Hastings said. "But how do you fool radar *and* sonar? Add in these images that Captain Slade has found—if it is a new form of ECM, it's like something we've never seen before."

"Sir," Ashe replied. "This has been going on for the past five years. Before that—we have nothing. We're not the only ones picking up the anomalies. The British and French and Russians are reporting them too. Everything from strange sea life to attacks on beaches or ships. That incident three weeks ago with the cruise ship off Baja . . . all passengers and crew missing. The holes in her hull looked like cuts, not random damage."

"You're telling me that incident is tied to this?" General Quartermain asked. "DHS said that a terrorist group claimed credit for that attack."

"Their lie gave us perfect cover, sir. That attack fits the parameters, sir. Strange phenomena, unsolved, tied to the world's oceans . . . right down to the damage to the ship," Ashe replied.

The general tipped his head down and rubbed his brow for a few seconds before speaking again. "Do we have estimates of the numbers of ships we're talking about?"

Ashe had dreaded that question. "I don't have a definitive number, sir. If we go with just what our Air Force has detected, it is over forty of the smaller ships, at least ten of the medium ships, and four of the larger ships. But bear in mind, we have no way of knowing how many other readings have come in that other countries have tracked."

"An . . . invasion," General Buchwald said, almost hesitantly.

"Is it?" Admiral Frost asked. "We don't know what it is. We just know that something is happening here."

"*Is* this an invasion?" General Quartermain asked, looking right at Ashe.

He felt his face turn red. He wanted to say yes, but he remembered his coaching: Don't say anything you are not sure of. "Sir, I don't know. But we have to assume that their intentions are not entirely friendly. Some of these attacks by the UAs have been fatal. We've lost ships, airplanes, and people. So far, we don't have any indication that they have tried to contact us. That doesn't mean that they haven't tried—we just don't know how they communicate."

"UAs?"

"Sorry, sir," he replied. "Slang we've been using downstairs. Unidentified Aliens."

The DIA director winced a little. "So it is definitely extraterrestrial?" The general drove the point home.

Ashe paused. This was the moment he had known was coming. "Yes, sir, I believe so. The data we have gathered does not indicate any kind of technology that mankind currently possesses." General Holland gave him a nod, which was reassuring.

Quartermain scanned the room. "I want all of you to chime in here. What do you think?"

Admiral Frost spoke first. "Marty, I am forced to concur with Captain Slade on this."

The general turned to Buchwald. "Alright, Ryan, what's your take?"

General Buchwald glanced over to Colonel Hastings, who gave him a single nod, making it clear they had discussed the material at some length. "I'm hesitant, sir, but the indications are we are dealing with something not of this Earth. Our data matches that of the Navy, and that is something I can't overlook or deny."

"Brad—what about Space Force?"

"I'm prepared to start redirecting our orbital assets based on this information—that's how solid I think it is," General Holland replied. "We can't afford to not explore it further."

"General Guttman, you've been quiet on this."

"Yes, I have," he said solemnly. "First off, Army intelligence hasn't picked up a thing—but we're on dry land, so that's no surprise. Second, I never have bought into all of this science-fiction bullshit about aliens—and these grainy pictures from the *National Sentinel* don't sway me either. Everything in my gut is telling me this is a hoax. The only thing I *do* know for sure is Captain Slade is one of our best analysts. He's batting a thousand with the DIA and is obviously good enough for our colleagues in the Navy to trust his work too. I had him checked out when I first saw this report—and the captain, aside from apparently not having any sort of personal life outside of this building, is one of our best. Aside from that, I'm on the fence. I need more, plain and simple."

General Guttman hadn't hung him out to dry; Ashe felt good about that. *He had me checked out . . . how creepy is that? Given what I turned in, it makes sense.* At the same time though, he had not won over his own branch head.

General Quartermain rubbed his brow again then raised his head. "I've got a meeting with the Joint Chiefs in an hour. For the first time in a long time I have something to report that isn't boring or typical. They'll probably hand me my ass on a platter when I pass this onto them. We simply don't have a protocol in place for this kind of thing. We're going out into uncharted territory."

Ashe was a little surprised. Science fiction always pointed to the government as being prepared for aliens, or having some sort of inside track on alien menaces. *This is the real world, and in the real world we get caught with our pants down.* A part of him was disappointed. He was hoping to hear about Roswell or some other deep buried military/UFO secret.

General Quartermain continued. "They're going to ask me for next steps. What do we recommend?"

Admiral Frost spoke up. "We need to change our patrol patterns for subs and surface vessels. We need to send out our ships to search for the missing vessels and aircraft—see if we can gather additional information on, well, whatever these things are. We will need procedures for this and a way to report so that DIA has the latest and greatest in terms of intel. As General Holland said, we start looking for them. Any strange incident comes in, we deploy and investigate for now. Nothing threatening, we just need more information."

"Agreed," Quartermain replied. "For now we take this slowly. What about NATO?"

Heads shook around the table. "You share this with NATO and the press will be all over it," Colonel Hastings replied.

Admiral Frost countered. "We need to check the other naval commands—but that requires a hell of a lot more staff. Initial indications are that this is bigger than the Pacific."

"The press is going to pop this at some point, so we need to prepare for that inevitability too," General Buchwald replied. "Those reporters always have some source somewhere that spills the beans. Washington leaks like a sieve. We have to assume we are on borrowed time."

"Good point," General Quartermain said in response. "We'll need to pull in our best public affairs people and have them start preparing a response. I will be forwarding a copy of this report over to the CIA and DHS heads once I get the green light from the Joint Chiefs, so be prepared for them to weigh in and offer their opinions. "

"Gentlemen, I am required to ask this question—and I have never had to do it before—but protocol makes it a necessity. Do we need to recommend to the JCS going to DefCon Four or lower?" His words hung in the room.

General Guttman shook his head. "We don't have enough information yet, sir. If the JCS wants us to, we can do it, but you're inviting the press to ask questions as to why, especially with the Russians and Chinese doing nothing. You can't cover up something like this with some BS response like a training exercise. If Captain Slade is right, these *things* have been here for half a decade already. No point in putting your finger on the trigger right now . . . not until we know more."

"Agreed. Anything else?" General Quartermain asked.

There was quiet in response.

"Very well then. I am going to go upstairs and tell my bosses what is happening. Be prepared for the JCS to want a full court press on this. As such I am sanctioning an additional seventy-five analysts to Red 105A, effectively immediately. Captain Slade, you just became the biggest project in the DIA. We'll need to enable our backup facilities and set up there. This building has a lot of prying eyes and ears and when word of this gets out, everyone will want a piece of the action. Captain, pack your bags and be ready to move when we give the word."

"Yes, sir," Ashe responded. He didn't even know that the DIA *had* a backup facility.

General Quartermain looked over at him. "Most officers wouldn't have had the intestinal fortitude to do what you did, Captain. They would have played it safe. Good job. Dismissed."

Ashe rose and left the room. As soon as he reached the darkened hallway, he drew a long deep breath of the filtered air. *What have I started?* He realized in that moment that his actions had set things in motion, forces that he could not imagine.

His mother had always said that one man could make a difference. *I only hope my difference isn't a step down the road to Armageddon.*

CHAPTER 18

US Marine Corps Training Grounds,
US Naval Magazine Complex, Guam,
the Pacific Ocean

Lance Corporal Natalia Falto sprang forward into the sand, falling flat with her Remington ACR-25 out in front of her, RTF stance (Ready to Fire). She felt her STF (Shear Thickening Fluid) stiffen for a moment on impact, then flex as she dug in. She was wearing STG J (jungle), the standard body armor of the Army and Marine Corps—which was much better than the older BA/2 gear. The STF armor packs it mounted for protection were a thick reactive gel. Before kinetic impact, they were highly flexible and lighter than the few pieces of ceramic plate she wore. The least amount of energy hitting them turned them into bulletproof plates. They allowed lightweight flexibility for a Marine, with top-technology stopping power when it was needed. Topped off with thin armored ceramic plates over vital organs, her gear gave Falto that false sense of safety that every combat soldier was forced to embrace.

The staff sergeant was running a simple drill, but she had learned over the last few months that nothing was simple with "Hannibal" Rickenburg. This was a drill against staff sergeant Parker's 3rd Platoon. They had the high ground, a ridge that ran across the US Naval Magazine (aka the Ordnance Annex)—where the 7th Fleet stored armaments and expendables. Nestled on the southern portion of the island, the reservation was one of the more popular Marine training areas.

"A5 on point. Path is clear. I'm advancing." She rose to prepare for her next move forward as her platoon fanned out in a split V-formation behind her. Falto had taken point, not because she was good at it, but because she wasn't. The staff sergeant had taught her to always train against your weaknesses until they stopped being a hindrance. He preached turning weaknesses into strengths. It was not an easy lesson, but it was one she embraced.

She felt the ground "thump" behind her and saw Rickenburg burst through the foliage in his ASHUR II Lion-class rig. She could see his face behind the thick semireflective armored glass of the curved front breastplate, and she swore she could see him smiling—a rarity. He paused for a moment as the rest of his platoon formed up on him. Standing eight feet tall, the ASHUR II commanded respect by its presence alone.

The ASHUR II was the latest class of combat armor for the US military. The Marine Corps outfitted their rigs differently from the Army—but that was to be expected. ASHUR I gear was cruder, with less armor and less staying power, but potent firepower. The new rigs allowed relatively rapid mobility, and carried the fuel cells and weaponry to hang in a fight longer than their predecessors. The spine of the ASHUR systems served as a support for the entire system. The driver, referred to as the pilot (just to irritate Marine and Air Force aviators) stood in the torso of the man-shaped armor, with his or her feet reaching down to the middle of the suit's thighs. It was armored in layers of STF, carbon-weave, and thick ceramic plates, much more rounded and sloping than the Russian Grizzly counterparts.

Its massive flattened feet gave it good firing stability. With modular weapon mounts, its only standard weapon was a M478 Scythe short-barreled chain gun mounted to the right arm. Every other weapon could be rapidly attached, detached, and field-configured as needed. Staff Sergeant Rickenburg had mounted two shoulder-launched disposable LAW 98A rockets, designed for anti-tank attacks, onto his shoulder racks. The LAWs were short, less than two feet long, and about three and a half inches. The acronym traced its roots back to its Vietnam-era counterparts, the Light Antitank Weapon rockets were vastly different. Triangular in shape, they had collapsible fins that popped out when they fired and a deadly shaped charge. Their range was shorter than the conventional LAW 98—but if you were close enough to be the target, you could consider yourself DOA. On the rig's right arm, he had rigged a canister-fed rapid-fire M275 grenade launcher, and on the left he had attached a L-101 medium laser. The laser was bulky and fired in two-second bursts. It devoured power but was devastating against armored targets.

When Falto had first been schooled on the L-101 laser, she had expected something out of a sci-fi thriller. Real lasers didn't work that way. The L-101 could tie into the suit's armor and be used to paint targets for the new LAW 98A rockets, or it could be used as a direct-fire weapon. There were no bursts of light like in the vids, though—the beams were invisible. The L-series were powered by shotgun-like shell charges that fed from a magazine. When fired, the specially designed explosives gave them a burst of energy. Lasers left only small marks on their targets, but they were weapons of deep penetration. They could fry electronics and flash-boil human flesh, with barely a mark on the armor. In exercises, they would be low-powered bursts. On the battlefield, they were not a dominant weapon, but one to be respected and feared—even by other power-armored troops.

ASHUR operators were allowed to put some sort of custom painting on their chest armor plates, much like World War II bombers had crew insignia on the nose of their aircraft. The staff sergeant's Lion-class rig was adorned with a bulldog, standing on its hind legs, firing a chain gun spewing empty casings—with the words "Devil Dog" in bright red above it. The image was nice, but would be invisible when he turned on his adaptive camouflage system. Once the system was engaged, the entire rig would be a blur to the human eye in the jungle.

The forward armored breastplate popped with a hiss and the platoon could see him, complete with neural feeds on his forehead, drenched in sweat. "Alright, people," he said through clenched teeth, "Sergeant Parker is up there with her people on that ridge." He pointed to the rise in front of them. "They have the high ground and likely have an improved position with the rocks there. We do not have air support on this exercise. Let me walk you through how we crack this nut.

"Carson—you've got the Greyhound drones. I want you and Nunez to swing out along the right flank of that ridge. Run the GRDs around all over that hillside and make a lot of noise. Fire off some grenades and a few magazines of ammo. Get their attention."

"But, Staff Sergeant," the burley Frank Carson said, "the hounds are for tactical battlespace feeds, to give us a full tactical view." The military employed the Ground Robot Drones (GRDs) to fulfill a number of missions. They were created to be semi-autonomous drones; point and click and they fulfilled that mission by handling most of the processing on their own. The Marines referred to the drones loosely as "dogs" or "hounds." Greyhounds (GH-9s) were primarily used for sensor sweeps, to provide a three-dimensional image of the battlespace. Huskies (KH-2s) were used mostly by heavy weapons specialists to carry their gear. Bernards (BN-4s) were used to carry supplies, water, and so on, allowing the Marines to carry their weapons and ammo. They could also be used to pull the wounded from the battlefield. Pit Bulls (PB-05s) were rarer, but were used for tactical operations, and were the only GRDs fitted with weapons and programmed to kill, or to carry explosives and become the implements of death themselves.

Drone operators were an integral part of every platoon they worked in. A single operator could control four to six non-armed GRDs like Bernards, Greyhounds, or Huskies. Pit Bull operators usually commanded only one drone, since they were essentially tiny armed tanks that could run, jump, and fire. They commanded them using a specially designed digipad worn on the operator's chest for easy access. Bernards, Huskies, and Greyhounds looked vaguely like dogs, with streamlined, sleek torsos and head-like sensors with cameras for operator control.

Bernards were typical four-legged drones, just over knee height and a yard long, with carrying straps and compartments for gear and non-battle supplies. Their torsos were slightly elevated to allow them to carry injured troopers in a harness for evac from a combat zone. Greyhounds were smaller in size, sleeker in appearance, with a skinny torso carrying radar-absorbing sloped armor plates to protect their sophisticated sensor head gear. Huskies had thick legs, with bigger actuators for lifting and speed with a slight bump for a head.

Pit Bulls, well, they were different altogether. They had four legs, but they were more spiderlike in their arrangement. Their bodies were not streamlined—they were built for combat, with strangely placed armored plating. They had what looked like a shark fin on their back. It was thick, filled with anti-personnel rockets with a launcher at the top—like a Pez dispenser of death. They mounted a single modified ACR with a belt-fed mechanism, and a three-shot grenade launcher. The Army liked to call them Land Sharks, but the Marines called them Pit Bulls because of their rugged design and deadly bite.

"I know what they are for, Private. Today, you're going to use them as my bait. Sergeant Parker will shift some troops toward you. You are to fade back, draw them with you, string them out. Bobbi Parker knows me pretty well and will sniff a diversion. That's when you," he pointed to Foster, "are going to come up the left side of the hill. Bring your Huskies carrying the LAWs and the chain guns and pick two members of the platoon to come with you. I want you to move about halfway up the ridge, find Sergeant Parker, and fire at her with the heavy stuff."

"How will I spot her, Staff Sergeant?"

Rickenburg grinned. "Oh, don't worry about that. You'll find her. She's going to think for a few minutes that the noise you generate is me in-suit, and will pull everything she has to the left. So you will need to fade and fade fast. I'm coming up the middle with everyone else. Porter, Hernandez, Falto—you are following me up the center. We engage and destroy—close quarters. Everyone got that?" Falto nodded. In a pinch, one or two soldiers could use the hand and shin mounts on the suit for short rides. Carrying riders ate the precious power of the suit, though, and three of the fuel cells that powered the combat suit were on the back where you were clinging. They were hot, even with the insulation and cooling systems, making the hop even more uncomfortable. Following on foot was going to be hard, but in the long haul, it might be better than hitching a ride.

She walked up as the platoon began to move out and shifted to the rear of the staff sergeant's rig. "Porter, you're going to need to hoof it. He's likely to move fast and we can't afford to have you lagging behind." Reid Porter was already wringing wet with sweat and looking even more scrawny in his STG U armor. The kid had been a burden since she had met him. The staff sergeant turned on his adaptive camouflage and moved forward to the ridge; Falto, Reid, and Hernandez did the same. Even invisible, the ASHUR II was a presence to be reckoned with. Each deep thud of the ASHUR II Lion on the ground quaked the sand and rock as if a herd of cattle were charging.

They were rushing the hill in three minutes. The ridge was a steep hill, and the staff sergeant stopped at the bottom, no doubt waiting for the rest of the platoon to get into position. Natalia's legs ached as she scrambled up the hill, trying to keep up with the power-armored suit. She was hot, wet, and could taste the sting of salt on her upper lip—and loved it. She turned and saw the shimmer of Reid's outline just behind her. She grabbed at him, pulling him the final eight feet up the hill. *This is hard enough of a climb without having to pull his ass up here too.*

There was an eruption of fire off to the right—Carson was getting their attention. She could feel her heart pound in her ears as the first simulated shots went off. The diversion dragged on, when she heard the muffled blasts of simulated rocket fire on the left. *That would be Foster . . . right on cue.* The staff sergeant kept his gear low, just below the line of sight to the flat hilltop, waiting for the right moment to pounce.

Rickenburg's "Devil Dog" suddenly lurched forward up the hill—not on any trail, but through the dense jungle growth as if it wasn't there. The suddenness of the lunge caught Falto off guard and she charged into the hole he was making, as did Hernandez. Porter's blurry image was slapped with a branch of a thick bush and he staggered, his balance shattered, as if he was going to spill back down the hillside. "Shit!" she spat, grabbing him with her left hand. He fell but she pulled at just the right moment, her shoulder and neck aching as she managed to keep him upright. *Come on, Sergeant Rickenburg . . . engage these bastards!* Behind her and on her flanks, she could barely make out the camouflaged images of the rest of the platoon moving up alongside.

She was tempted to let Porter fall down the hill, but only for a moment. That wasn't the Marine way. She wouldn't want anyone dropping her. "Porter," she said in a low tone. "You have got to shag it, damn it. Focus, Marine!"

She heard the purr of automatic-weapons fire as they reached the top of the ridge—*we're engaging.* The Devil Dog swung out into a clearing and she heard the muffled purr of the Scythe chain gun mounted in its armored arm come to life. *We're engaging!* She killed her adaptive camouflage gear, as did her comrades. At this range, with thin volcanic dust being kicked up, it wasn't of much use. Some penetrated her visor and she could taste the grit in her mouth.

As the combat armored suit swung around, she saw the target. It was big, larger than any suit she had ever seen in person—and clearly not US in manufacture. Her mind identified it immediately. *A Russian*

Mammoth. The Grizzly seemed daunting enough. The Mammoth—well, her mind raced with the stats and the threat it represented. *Where the hell did they get a Mammoth?*

Mammoths had a driver and a gunner, with the gunner mounted higher and to the rear—almost a cross between a tank and an ASHUR II Rhino-class rig. It moved on four legs, with the back two being huge. The Russians built her to be dominating, but Natalia remembered studying it—they were slow beasts, ponderous. Its armor was typical Russian, sharp edges, nothing but utilitarian use. They didn't use adaptive camouflage, so this Mammoth was painted with jungle patterns, as if you could hide something almost twice the size of an ASHUR II suit.

The Mammoth's trio of chain guns roared and Falto grabbed some brush for cover, pulling Porter with her. She saw Hernandez roll into the brush and fire with her ACR 25, but Falto knew that was folly. Mammoths laughed at American bullets. The staff sergeant fired two simulated LAW rockets at it while it was distracted. Both hit with a burst of white powder marking the hits, but the Mammoth seemed unfazed, indicating that the battle computer did not register them as killing shots.

Staff Sergeant Rickenburg swung to the left with amazing speed, leaving the trio on the ground as it did a dance of death with the Mammoth and shifted to her flank. Falto was stunned at how fast the Devil Dog ran: it was as if the staff sergeant wasn't even wearing armor. The slightly raised shoulder plates looked like a lion's mane—hence the nickname for the armor class. The rest of the platoon was pouring in fire, but she knew that was pointless unless the battle computer registered a lucky shot. She tossed her rifle and pulled out a dummy grenade.

The Mammoth had the same weaknesses as the Grizzly (and the ASHUR II suits for that matter)—her actuator joints. The Russians didn't armor their hydraulic hoses or actuator joints because it was complicated to do so and in some ways limited movement. Falto looked over at Hernandez and tapped Porter so they could see what she was doing. Hernandez mimicked her movements, pulling out a grenade and giving her a nod. Porter—well, he had a look of sheer terror on his face. "Come on, Reid, we have to go for the joints." The kid nodded slowly and fumbled with his grenade.

Falto crouched low and waited for the right moment. The staff sergeant swept to the right and as he did, Sergeant Parker's Mammoth turned to keep him in her sights. Good. In a pair of heartbeats, the Mammoth's left flank was exposed to her. "Now!" she barked. The three of them ran forward, grenades in one hand, the other hand free to climb.

A burst of small-arms fire roared off to her right. Some of members of 3rd Platoon fired at her. Her armor simulated one hit, in her right leg, causing the STF armor to instantly harden and tighten there, pinching her slightly, giving her a not-so-simulated limp.

"I'm hit!" Reid Porter howled and dropped, mowed down in a burst of ACR fire. *No loss there . . . maybe he took a bullet meant for me.*

The Mammoth loomed in front of her. She had never been this close to one before, and now realized just how big it was. She sprang at the massive bent rear leg while Hernandez went for the front leg, right next to the driver's cockpit. Behind the Mammoth's bulk, she heard the hum of the staff sergeant's laser simulating a slice on the Russian battle suit.

Natalia's fingers found the edge of a piece of armor and hung on to it. Sergeant Parker must have seen Hernandez right near her, and perceived the threat. She juked the Mammoth hard in a sidestep. Hernandez flipped the safety on the grenade and hit her stud. She fumbled with it, trying to wedge it in with the hoses. Falto saw her drop as it went off, a puff of white simulated explosion marked the damage.

Hernandez called "I'm hit!" but there was nothing that Falto could do for her. The Mammoth stopped its sideways move, a possible indication that the hit had simulated leg damage to the beast. She reached up and duplicated the moves with her grenade on the massive rear leg, jamming it in between two hydraulic hoses. She dropped and rolled as soon as she hit. Turning, she saw the grenade go off, white powdery smoke rising from the knee joint.

The Mammoth stopped all movement and firing. The same could not be said for the Devil Dog. While his rig was limping horribly from simulated damage, the staff sergeant broke off from the Russian combat armor and fired his grenade launcher with wild abandon, spraying the foliage where the remnants of 3rd Platoon were taking cover. Their suppression fire seemed to falter as the Russian battle suit shut down and they realized that the staff sergeant's Lion-class rig was still able to fire. Falto flattened herself—realizing she had tossed her ACR in the brush when she had made the run for the Mammoth. *Stupid move, Natalia!* She was in the middle of the battlespace with no firearms. For now, her solution was to lay as flat as possible and play dead. As the grenades from the ASHUR II went off, she heard a chorus of "Aw shit," and "Oh fuck," from the 3rd Platoon.

It was over in a matter of minutes. The battle computer that tracked the exercise deactivated the STF in her simulated leg wound and signaled into her earbud the order to cease fire, and secure all weapons. She reached up and undid the chin strap to her Mark III ECH helmet, taking it off and tucking it under her arm. Hernandez walked over and retrieved their ACR-25s and handed Falto hers and Porter his.

She rose from the gritty volcanic soil that stuck to her sweat-soaked gear. The front hatch on the Mammoth popped and hissed open and Natalia saw Sergeant Bobbi Parker rise up from the driver's seat. The staff sergeant looked over along the side of the Mammoth where the attacks had taken her out and made eye contact with Falto. "Damn it! I should have known I had someone on the rear leg too." Parker gave her a thumbs-up. "That was a hell of a move, Marine."

"Thank you, Sergeant." Falto's head throbbed and she kinked her neck until she heard a pop.

Staff Sergeant Rickenburg popped his hatch and stood in his cockpit as well. "Good job, Hernandez and Falto—damn fine work. I want 1st Platoon to assemble here. We need to get to know the Russian Mammoth up close and personal."

Reid Porter lumbered up next to her, his skinny frame soaked in sweat and dirt. "Falto, thanks for grabbing me back there on the hillside. He caught me off guard when he charged off like that." His voice was worn and weary, where she was still feeling the edge of her adrenaline rush from the simulated battle.

She looked over at him. "You have got to start pulling your weight, Private," she spat. "I can't be there every time to save your ass. Everyone in this platoon has a job to do, we can't afford to have someone who's dragging us down."

"I understand," he said, sounding like a young boy being rejected after asking for a date.

"Do you?" she responded.

"Will you help me?" he asked, his tone serious.

Natalia rolled her eyes. "Alright, Porter. I'm going to try to get your skinny ass into shape." There was a part of her that wondered if it was the right move. Not everyone was cut out to be a Marine. *I just hope Porter doesn't get me or someone else killed someday.*

CHAPTER 19

USS *Virginia*, south of Jarvis Island, the Pacific Ocean

Commander Titus Hill watched as Captain Stewart paced the control room of the USS *Virginia*, scowling and grumbling as he moved. He had been "in a mood," as Master Chief Simmons called it, since they had picked up a message on the ELF (Extremely Low Frequency) system. "I'm not a big fan of these snipe hunts," the captain muttered just within earshot of Hill.

"Sir?"

"DIA and ONI diverting us off our patrol route to look for a missing cargo plane. I pulled her stats from the mission file. This was a drone-piloted aircraft, Commander—no loss of life. Her cargo manifest was nothing critical. Why divert a billion-dollar boat to look for a missing cargo aircraft that went down months ago?" The gruff captain kept his voice low, so that only Hill could hear him.

Commander Hill understood. Most cargo aircraft were drones at this point, removing hundreds of pilots from the risk of a crash. FedEx had a massive facility in San Francisco for flight operations over the Pacific, and this was one of their birds. "Maybe we're the closet ship to the crash area?" Hill offered in a hushed tone.

"Doubtful, Mr. Hill. If you've been around as long as me, you start to learn how to read between the lines when it comes to orders. Our mission here is peculiar. Damned peculiar." For Captain Jacob Stewart to be edgy was something worthy of notice.

Titus had his own suspicions. They had passed on those unusual sonar readings only a month and a half ago, and now they were being diverted from a normal patrol. After the war, NOAA had thoroughly mapped nearly all of the Pacific, a result of submarines chasing WWII wrecks as possible Russian combat subs. Running the new "C-View"

170

sonar, they would be able to compare those digital images to current readings. If that airplane was down here, the *Virginia* stood a good chance of finding it. *Maybe, just maybe, these things are connected.*

"Sir," he said carefully. "Perhaps this is somehow related to our report to the DIA."

Stewart turned to face him, his face solid as if his wrinkles were carved in stone. "I've had the exact same thought. And to be honest," he said just above a whisper, "I think that's *exactly* why we are here. I think we're here because we have spotted something they cannot account for. Maybe it was behind this aircraft going down."

"So how are these things connected, sir?"

Stewart shook his head twice. "I have no idea. I sent a follow-up to our sonar-readings report to DIA during our comms burst two weeks ago. You know what I got back?"

"No, sir."

"Nothing."

"Which means?"

"I've been in this business for a long time, Mr. Hill. When the spooks don't talk, it's time to get nervous." Stewart turned to Chief Simmons. "Chief, are we on our target yet?"

Simmons walked over to the navigator's station. "We'll be there in three minutes, sir."

"Very well," Stewart said. "Take us down to six hundred and twenty-five feet. Sonar, activate C-View, run a standard search grid."

"Aye, sir," Simmons said. "Dive control, take us to six, two, five feet, level the bow planes when we hit that depth. Helm, cut speed to one-third. Sonar, relay grid coordinates to Navigation. Go active on C-View." The control room snapped to life as the chief barked out his orders. The *Virginia* dipped, Hill could feel it, but eventually leveled off. Several moment later, Chief Simmons turned to the captain. "We are at depth, sir, and sonar is mapping."

Searching the ocean floor was a long, drawn out process. When a ship went down, even with all of the feeds to satellites, it could take days or weeks to find the target on the seafloor. When an airplane went down, it was worse. Planes connecting with the ocean at hundreds of miles per hour made the wrecks of even the sturdiest aircraft look like aluminum confetti. Some parts might hang together, like an engine or parts of a wing section, but aircraft generally were nothing more than a long debris field. The currents would further scatter the remains of an aircraft. A cargo jet, filled with containers and packages, would appear more as tiny mounds and bits of debris on the ocean floor.

Hill leaned against the rail and settled in for what could be days of work. Stewart paced the control room around him and the periscopes. Part of being in the Silent Service was the patience. Hill eventually moved around, from station to station. *Chances are, it will be a day or two—*

"Conn—sonar contact on C-View," the shift's sonarman, Lieutenant Nagal, said from her workstation.

"That was fast," Captain Stewart said. "Lieutenant, can you confirm the readings?"

Lieutenant Nagal worked the controls of the workstation, starting at the three digital displays. "Yes, sir. Metallic mass, the pings we're getting are consistent with the metal in aircraft skin. She's not an old wreck, not according to the NOAA database."

Commander Hill moved in behind her. "Those are fairly large readings," he said, pointing to the screen. *It's got to be some sort of error. Maybe it's the tail or an engine—but these look larger.*

"Yes, sir. That's the only thing. Most aircraft are just junk spread out. This target is in a relatively small area."

Hill stared at her readings. Nagal was reading the data correctly; it just didn't make sense. Titus turned to Captain Stewart. "Orders, sir?"

"Dive Control, activate our hover control system and bring us to hover once we are over the target coordinates. Rudder amidship. Helm, transfer control to the HCS at the chief's command. Chief, contact the torpedo room and have them prepare Tempest for launch."

"Aye, sir," replied Chief Simmons.

Tempest—the sub's deep sea submersible. While the *Virginia* was limited in how deep she could dive, the US Navy provided all boats with gear for surveying deep depths. Unmanned, the underwater tethered drone could go deep and capture images and even recover parts.

***

It took the better part of three hours for the Tempest probe to reach the depth where the sonar target had been found. Tempest control was a separate workstation in the control room and Petty Officer McCarthy handled it as if it was a video game. Its tether fed through the forward torpedo room and the submersible reached the bottom relatively quickly. McCarthy was young, but his ability to maneuver Tempest was validated when he swooped it down just a dozen yards above the seafloor, operating almost entirely on its tiny sonar readings.

"Approaching the target now," McCarthy said. Stewart and Hill both stood behind him, leaning forward, watching his screens. It was seemingly endless darkness. To Hill, it was hard to tell that the submersible was even moving.

"Let's light her up," Captain Stewart said. McCarthy hit a switch and the powerful lighting system of the Tempest kicked in. Suddenly the darkness came to life. A dim circle of the seafloor lit up. A few deep-sea creatures scurried out of the beams of light, moving back into the darkness only a few yards away. With the lights on, Hill finally could tell that Tempest was moving—and quickly too.

"What the—" McCarthy said as the first image of the crashed cargo aircraft came into view.

Hill saw the elevated vertical stabilizer. As Tempest came over a small rock formation, the rest of the plane came into clear view. The submersible came up on her port side, giving a full-length profile of the airplane. Hill's own mouth dropped open at the sight of the aircraft.

The Boeing 767 Cargolifter was a massive beast of an aircraft—and this one initially looked strangely intact. That changed the longer you stared at the image. The aircraft was sitting on the seafloor on a flat plain, one devoid of any signs of life. The debris was not spread out like in a normal crash. Instead, it was as if someone had reassembled the fuselage , laying them out as they had been on the plane.

The damage was there. It was clear that the plane had come apart, but someone or something had gathered the parts and laid them out on the ocean floor like in an accident reconstruction. "What the hell?" he managed.

"Take her up a little, then angle the cameras and lights downward," Captain Stewart said. Moments later the camera view was almost straight down.

"Those are the cargo containers, right?" Captain Stewart said, pointing to the large containers that were seemingly lined up just ahead of the nose of the airplane.

"Yes, sir, I think they are," Hill replied. "What is all of that stuff on the seabed?"

McCarthy didn't wait for the orders. He lowered the Tempest closer to the images. They were boxes, packages, packing materials. They had not been jettisoned, but seemed to be laid out, as if a meticulous process had been undertaken to arrange it all on the seafloor. A thin film of dirt covered them. They seemed to be placed near specific containers, as if someone were trying to determine which packages went with which container.

"What does that look like to you, Commander?" Captain Stewart asked.

Hill wasn't sure just how to respond. "Captain, it reminds me of what the NTSB does when there's a plane crash. They reassemble the contents of the plane, lay everything out to inspect it."

"I concur. But we're at the bottom of the ocean," the captain replied. "I've seen aircraft wrecks before. Small planes can be intact after a wreck, but a big cargo hauler like this, it should be almost unidentifiable as an aircraft. Someone has arranged it, almost like they were trying to piece it together."

"Look at that engine . . ." McCarthy blurted. Their eyes focused as the petty officer zoomed in on where the plane's engine should be. The main housing assembly of the jet engine was standing upright. Every little piece of the engine was laid out with a thin film of dirt on them, every fin from the turbine, bent and twisted, was meticulously laid out on the seabed. "Please tell me we've been recording all of this," Hill said, surveying the engine.

"Yes, sir," McCarthy said. "I'm glad too, because nobody is going to believe this."

Hill could see Captain Stewart's face harden and get red, even under the dim glow from Tempest's monitors. "I want you to sweep every inch of this wreck, film it all. Her black box is down here somewhere too. Use the grapples and get that thing removed. It should be easy to find; someone unpacked the whole damned aircraft."

Captain Stewart rose and looked at the control room crew. "No one is to say anything to anyone on the boat about this," he stated. "We are on an intelligence mission and anyone blathering about this while waiting for the shower is going to find him or herself scrubbing toilets for the next ten years of their career." It was less a threat than a statement of reality. The nervous nods told him that the crew understood.

Stewart put his hand on Hill's shoulder and pulled him away from the screen. "I've never seen anything like this, Commander," he said at a whisper, just below his ear. "We're going to capture the images, recover the black box, then we are heading to the surface to transmit this."

"We could deploy the ELF antenna and send now, sir," Hill offered.

"Not with Tempest out there. That antenna array might get caught up by the submersible's control lines. Besides, the ELF has a slow transmission rate—no complex images. No—we'll head to the surface and squirt this to the DIA and ONI boys at COMSUBPAC. I want them to get the full image of what we are looking at down here."

Hill nodded. "Sir, what do you make of this?"

Captain Stewart took a long look at the screens where McCarthy was slowly, methodically navigating the Tempest over the precisely laid out wreck reconstruction site. Stewart shook his head. "I don't know. I've spent a lot of my life underwater, and I have never seen aircraft wreckage reassembled like this. Why go through all of that effort? I've seen her manifest; there was nothing out of the ordinary on board. Most of that stuff is just commercial products and clothing. It doesn't add up—not one bit."

CHAPTER 20

**Dana Blaze's apartment,
northern Los Angeles, California**

Dana Blaze sat at her desk in her decorative apartment in the dim light of the night and surveyed her private datafeeds. Most of her colleagues did this at work, but she didn't want her sources' information flowing through Blown Sun Media's network. She had no reason to suspect Ryan Jackson or anyone there of spying on her. At the same time, she had learned to mitigate her risks and optimize her opportunities.

One of her stringers, a programmer at a Silicon Valley firm, had worked for a time at JayTech in their internal accounting systems, a job that sounded beyond boring to her. Life in Cubeville would be akin to a prison sentence for someone like her. Dana knew that if you understood the financial systems of a company, you could master its secrets. Her stringer, codename "Firestorm," had been her source for Drake's purchase of his former high school. Now he was sending her another burst of information. *Not a bad investment of my time—two discreet dates with an uber-geek.*

Firestorm didn't send her a mass of data, but instead dribbled her some information. Two words stood out to her: *Hard Hat.* She accessed the data burst he had encrypted to her and her eyes danced over the words. Firestorm didn't have a good grasp of what Hard Hat was beyond being an advanced R&D facility in the Arizona desert. Whatever its nature, the facility was costing billions of dollars to build with a modest staff. From what she could see in the wad of data floating in front of her, Hard Hat was part bunker and part data analytics facility, something completely unique, in her experience. *He has more computing power there than the FedGov.* Dana checked her own database of what she was tracking of JayTech and could not find any Arizona operations other than a small field sales office in Phoenix for their contracting business.

So Jay, what are you hiding out there?

She understood the need for security, but with Drake it seemed to be part of his DNA to keep and hide secrets. Her instinct for security was almost as strong, as was her lust for uncovering other people's secrets. She and Drake had been on four dates so far, and while they spent most of the time talking, she had to admit that she knew relatively little about him. At the same time, she had to admit that she had not opened up much to him about her past or her aspirations. *We are undertaking a dangerous dance, the two of us. Neither of us wants to share who we really are.* That was why she respected Jay so much. In many respects he was a male version of herself—tough, constructed, forbidding, driven, intelligent, and cunning.

She responded to Firestorm with a thanks and a promise to meet him for lunch soon. Then she looked over the sparse data on Hard Hat. Why would any private person need that much data storage and computing power? She didn't even have the location of the facility. So much had been procured through subsidiaries and shell companies and rerouted to other divisions of JayTech that it was difficult, if not impossible, to get the full picture of what Drake was building.

Was this a story? She paused for a moment at that thought. Was she looking for an exposé on Hard Hat, or was she just intrigued by the mystery? Normally she wouldn't hesitate. It was always about a story with her—or the next story. That was who Dana Blaze was. But this felt somehow different to her. She had already interviewed him; no, this was something more. This was about who he was as a person. And that bothered her. *I've never let my feelings get in the way of my career before—and I shouldn't do that now.*

She filed the information on her personal secured cloud device and powered down her system. Looking around the neatly furbished, empty apartment, it seemed small. Dana didn't throw parties, she simply attended them. There was no need for a lot of space because she never had anyone over. Her furnishings were expensive, but not over the top. Comfort counted more than looks in this one place in her life. Yet the apartment felt smaller, more empty than before. Dana wasn't sure why she felt that way, but she hated it, pushing the emotions deep down.

I'll bring it up tonight on our date . . . I'll see how he reacts.

***

The Pasadena Drive-In north of La looked like a massive warehouse. It was exclusive, Dana had never been there before, but Jay indicated that he had no problem getting them seats. *Knowing him, he owns this place.* Inside the building, another world emerged. It was dark, windowless. There were rows of antique cars parked on simulated shallow ramps, all facing forward to a massive movie screen. Each of the old cars had been converted into a comfortable booth. The diners were served by waitresses on roller skates and could sit back, enjoy their gourmet meal in the privacy of their car-booth, and watch the film. It harkened back to when America had drive-in theaters. Chef Anders, a well-known and popular cooking-show host, managed the exclusive restaurant.

Jay opened the door to the massive old maroon Buick for her and Dana slid in. The plush neo-leather seats were cold at first, but she enjoyed the strange ambience. Jay climbed into the booth after her, closing the door behind him.

"It's hard to believe that people actually used to go to see movies like this," she said, checking out the interior of the vehicle.

"I like it," Jay said. "It reminds me of a simpler time."

"*You* are nostalgic?" she replied with a broad grin. "I never would have guessed that."

"I'm not," he replied. "I just appreciate some aspects of the past. This place recreates the past, a past that technology eclipsed."

"You've been a part of that eclipse your whole life," she replied.

"I have. But that doesn't mean I don't respect the past. I just don't let it dominate my thinking." His words always seemed slightly off to her, as if they were rehearsed. Then again, this was a man who did not socialize much. Her dates with him had been picked up by a few tabloids and were hot e-news trends because he wasn't seen much in public. How they had been leaked to the press, well, Dana refused to ponder that thought.

The waitress came and they ordered drinks. She asked for a cosmopolitan, and he got nothing fancier than a rum and Neo-Coke. They ordered their dinner and he seemed to relax, as much as Jay ever did, leaning back slightly in the seat. *Now's the time to ask.*

"I got an interesting tip today."

"Oh?"

"About you."

Jay cocked his eyebrows for a moment. "I'm intrigued."

She took a long sip of her cosmo and set it down. "It was about something called Hard Hat that you have out in Arizona."

Jay hesitated for a moment. Her belt contained a sensor that would read his physical reactions to her comments—data she could crunch when she got home. "Hard Hat. I'm familiar with that. Why would *that* place be of interest or newsworthy?"

"What is it?" she asked carefully.

"Dana, it's just a corporate backup facility—our DR center. All big companies like ours have them, especially after the war. Losing your data to a natural or manmade disaster is a risk no company can take these days. Disaster recovery is critical in business. That's all it is."

She ran her fingers around the edge of her drink while she thought. "I know a little bit about technology—just enough to be dangerous. You seem to have amassed more computing tech there than almost any other place on the planet. It sounds like a lot more than just a backup facility."

Jay offered her only a flat smile in response. "I feel like I'm being interviewed here," he replied, only half jokingly.

"No, it's not that," she said. "I just was curious. We've gone out a few times now and I feel like you're holding back from me, that's all."

"And you're not? What about your past, Dana? What about what you've done to advance your career?"

Touché.

"It's hard to argue with you there."

Drake paused and took a sip of his drink. "The truth is that Hard Hat is a little more than just corporate backup. It's sort of an advanced R&D facility. We try to keep it off the books and off everyone else's radar for a reason. I don't need the press or my competitors snooping around out there, trying to pry from the staff what they are working on."

That seemed plausible. But this was Jay Drake. Nothing was ever cut-and-dried with him. "Your competitors seem pretty open about their R&D facilities."

"Yes," he replied. "But JayTech is privately owned. My competition has to account to shareholders for every dime and quarter they spend. Shareholders are like ticks. My company is owned by me and me alone. I am not in the same noose they are." Dana could feel the pride rolling off his words.

"It just strikes me as odd that you would bury this facility, hide it from those in your own company."

"The secrets we keep define who we are." He set down his drink and draped his arm around her shoulders. "It's just like how you found this out. It sounds like I might have a mole in my company, someone leaking information to a certain reporter." She appreciated his attempt at coyness.

"How do you know that my source is someone in your organization? I have a lot of powerful friends in the FedGov. Lately a lot of eyes are looking at JayTech and at you."

Drake gently pulled her close. "I don't believe for a second that it was someone from the outside, Dana. The FedGov isn't smart enough to discover Hard Hat, and they are about the only place with the kind of resources that could. No, your intel comes from within my own company. There's no point in denying it."

There was something in the way he spoke that made Dana afraid for Firestorm. *I'd better cancel that lunch with him.* "Well, if it *was* someone from JayTech, I'd have to keep my sources confidential."

"I understand. Next time you get some info on me, just ask. You know I'm more than willing to share." He reached out and gently stroked her hair. "Now we should stop talking shop for a while and sit back. The movie is about to start."

✳✳✳

When Dana got back to her apartment that night, she was exhausted. Four drinks, a meal, and some gentle petting from Jay Drake had taken more of a mental toll on her than a physical one. He wasn't a groper or looking for sex like so many people in La that she interacted with. No, Drake seemed to be more interested in her as a person, less as a sex toy.

She looked at her decorative belt and opened the back of the buckle. The device could read a target's heart rate, sense his galvanic skin response, and even detect his pupil reaction if it had good line of sight. More importantly, it could record everything said. It was, for all intents and purposes, a portable lie detector.

Dana often wore that belt in her assignments, but had worn it tonight to get a reading on Jay Drake in response to her questions about this covert Hard Hat. The device, which had been developed by the Germans for intelligence work, cost a great deal but so far had proven well worth it.

It wasn't that she doubted Drake's responses in particular, she just doubted everyone. It was a safe habit that had served her well. She activated the IS chip from the back of the belt and loaded up the app on her digipad to get his readings. The pad seemed to pause for a long period of time, then flashed the words *Data Corrupt*. Her jaw dropped at the words as she tried it again, with the same result.

Then it hit her. Drake had been wearing some sort of jamming device. *He anticipated that I would be scanning him.*

"Oh my God," she said out loud as she slumped back on to her sofa. "I think I may be in love with this guy!"

CHAPTER 21

The Torn District of Montebello,
Los Angeles, California

Antonio Colton paced around the rectory office he used as a bedroom, his shirt wet with sweat. It wasn't that he couldn't find an air conditioner, there were plenty to be had in the Torn Districts. He simply had bad luck in choosing the ones he stole. Getting new parts or replacements was not in the cards. Stealing one from an abandoned apartment could be dangerous, depending on who might be living in the building, and it proved to be strenuous work because the ones now left working were all on the uppermost floors. His mother had never been able to afford air conditioning, so he was used to sleeping in the summer heat of La. Besides, it wasn't the heat that kept him awake this evening. It was the dreams.

He could barely remember them—only the fear and terror the nightmares evoked. He didn't need a degree or deep analysis to interpret them; he knew they were tied to his service in the war. Even after a decade, the battles were still attempting to strike at him. In the darkness of his makeshift bedroom, he knew he would not be returning to sleep. Antonio knew he needed some fresh air.

He took a pistol with him, sliding it into the back of the waistband of his green fatigue pants. It wasn't out of fear, it was simply a prudent precaution. The Torn Districts were rough places, and while many in the neighborhood knew him, in the middle of the early morning darkness, you didn't take unnecessary risks.

Stepping out of the church, he made sure that the door locked behind him. The air outside was warm, but cooler than in his room. He could feel the sweat on his T-shirt cool against his flesh. Looking up, he saw the stars, oddly clear that night. In a flash of memory, he remembered looking up at night at the stars in Alaska. There had been so many more of them visible from there, and they were so much more vivid. Ambient light—that was what Sally-Jo told him. Los Angeles had a lot of it. Alaska didn't.

He headed west, walking slowly, attempting to clear his mind. He generally failed miserably at this task. When he finally gained some distance from the anxiety, Antonio tried to remember the nightmare that had awakened him, but he could only remember the fear, not the details. *What did the VA doctors call it? A paradox.* The fragments of the dream seemed to erode with each step. As he tried to focus on the bits he could remember, all that was left was a feeling of fighting—of battle.

Walking up two blocks, he rounded a corner and continued on into the night. No one else seemed to be out. What time was it—2:00 a.m.? He spotted two girls standing under the light of one of the three working streetlights within view. *Working girls—gotta be at this hour.* As he continued to walk, he saw them and gave a nod. Antonio knew them only as Debbie and Donna. They claimed to be sisters, but that was bullshit and he knew it . . . hell, anyone looking at them could tell that. They weren't rollers—the prostitutes who lured their marks to hotels only to have them beaten and robbed. Guys from La would troll in looking for working girls and drugs, 24–7. Debbie and Donna were part of Mr. Wiggles's stable. As a pimp, Wiggles wasn't a bad guy: he was more of a protector than a true pimp. He still took 30 percent off the top, though. *Protection always has a price.* The girls both waved to him and Antonio waved back. They had seen him before on these middle-of-the-night strolls.

He kept going . . . walking in the darkness between the working streetlights, soaking up the early morning air—which stunk of garbage in some areas. Garbage pickup in the Districts was sketchy at best, so many old buildings or lots served as garbage dumps. The mayor often spoke of cleaning up the Districts, but somehow it never happened. Antonio had little use for politicians. They had gotten the US into the last war, fighting the Russians alone. None of their children seemed to find their way onto the battlefields. *The fighting was left to people like me. And when we came back, they cut our benefits.* Politicians were of little use, but always present, always promising.

He heard voices up ahead and slowed his pace. There was an argument of some sort just around the corner, harsh words that he could only half make out. Tense words and cursing at this hour rarely led to anything good. Antonio wasn't afraid, but he wasn't stupid either. He moved slowly up to the small cinderblock building that had been a store years before, but was now just a boarded-up bunker covered with spray paint.

Edging around the corner, he saw the source of the voices in the dim glow of a streetlight. Six youths, all probably under eighteen. Three kids were Hispanic, facing off against two blacks and a white youth. All were tense, hunkered down, their muscles flexed. He saw clubs in two hands, a chain and knives in others, all reflecting the orangey glow of the streetlight.

"Yo Fish, you need to ebb," said the largest of the group, a hulking Hispanic boy. "This is our 'crete—not yours."

"I say this is our 'crete. You the one tressing here, slapper," responded the white boy, nervously jerking his makeshift 2 x 4 club back and forth. He was talking street slang, but his tone and inflection were so lame, Antonio was tempted to laugh.

He stopped in full view of them, only twenty-five feet away. He put his fists on his hips and rose up straight, Army straight. When he stood rigid, he realized just how much he had been slumping. *How long have I been doing that?* One of them turned to him, the kid with the knife. "What're you looking at, drooper?"

Old instincts kicked in. He drew a long breath. *I could walk away from this, but I'm not going to.* "Why don't you 'tenders go home. This piece of 'crete ain't worth dying for."

"It ain't any of your business," one responded. "You a po drooper. Wander on, old man, we got this."

Antonio took a long step forward and drew himself up. He could feel the release of adrenaline in his body. It was a warm, welcome feeling—a rush of strength and emotion he had almost forgotten. Little things like his argument weeks ago with Gio had gotten close to this feeling, but now Antonio felt it galvanize his entire body and mind. Raw, almost animalistic energy surged in him, yet it was under his control—at his disposal. He swore he could even feel it in his bionic leg. It was power combined with heightened senses. No, he couldn't walk away at this point—the feeling was so good. "Look, dregs—go now and nobody gets hurt."

Both groups of kids turned their attention to him, moving several steps closer to him. "This is our fight, drooper. Move on before you get hurt."

Six to one. His mind raced as his hand-to-hand training kicked into memory as if it were only yesterday. "I don't want to hurt you. But I'm not going to let you kill each other either. Go home, and call it a night." With each beat of his heart, he was analyzing the biggest threats, his mind dancing with solutions and attacks. *I want this fight more than they can understand . . .* He was silently waiting for them to start it, craving that moment with every fiber of his being.

The teen with the club, the biggest kid, moved first. He swung the club back and then straight down at him, springing forward. Antonio countered by rushing right at him, springing off his legs like a rocket, coming in under the arc of the club. He hit the kid square in the chest as if he were a linebacker, using his left arm to knock him down. The kid never saw it coming. They hit the broken sidewalk and Antonio drove his elbow into the kid's diaphragm, knocking the wind out of his opponent. Rolling, he came up in a crouched combat stance, his back hurting where the weapon had dug into his spine.

A knife flashed in the orange light off to his right. He sprang forward and used his arm to block the attacker. Grabbing his assailant's wrist, he snap-jerked his foe's arm hard, dislocating the kid's shoulder with an audible popping sound. There was a howl from the would-be assailant, and the knife clattered on the chunks of sidewalk at his feet.

The chain hit him in his right leg, wrapping around his knee. For a normal man, this would have hurt, but the kid had no way of knowing that the leg was bionic. He "felt" the impact of the chain on his neuro-sensors, but no pain. Reaching down, he grabbed the chain and jerked it hard. The kid, who had the other end wrapped around his hand, involuntarily lunged forward right at him. Antonio jabbed at the base of the kid's throat. Unable to catch his breath, the kid reeled, panic filling his face as Antonio unwrapped the chain from his leg. The kid dropped to his knees, clutching madly at his throat.

Another boy came at him with a brick. He threw it and it grazed Antonio in the shoulder, tearing at his shirt and flesh as he shook it off. Without missing a beat, Colton grabbed the brick-thrower by the scruff of his shirt neck and fell backward. Putting his foot in the chest of the kid he rolled, the handgun in his pants once more digging into his lower back—but he could barely feel it, thanks to the rush of the fight. He tossed the kid right over his head as he rolled backward, sending him flying.

Twisting, he rose in a low combat stance and faced his attackers. They were not moving. Four were on the ground, mostly incapacitated, and the remaining two were stunned by the fury of his defense. They stared at him with fear, astonishment, and anger in their eyes.

One of the kids pulled a piece—a slider—a pocket pistol. "Mista, you just made a huge mistake." He grinned broadly.

His mind jumped with alternatives. The kid was twenty-five feet away, inexperienced, at night, his hand visibly shaking as he held the weapon sideways in a gangsteresque pose, aiming low, which showed his inexperience. A fool would rush straight at the kid—it would only increase his odds of being shot. *No, move fast, cross his field of fire, make him sweep sideways to try to get a shot; the kid will likely miss.* Antonio surveyed the terrain and chose his path. "Put down the popper," he warned.

"Screw you, droop!" The kid lifted the pistol to fire, still quaking.

Antonio's legs sprang like steel coils, launching him off to the left. He heard the pop of the weapon firing but didn't feel anything. Aided by his bionic leg, his jump was faster and farther than that of most men. He rolled, pulling out his pistol. When he stopped his roll, he came up in a low firing stance, his pistol in front of him.

When the kids saw they were facing an armed opponent, they were stunned. The kid who had just fired at him was still holding the pistol, but was shaking even harder. They were unsure what they were up against—he could see that in their faces. His whole body was a live wire, surging with strength, focus, and energy like he hadn't felt in a long time.

For a long moment or two, nothing happened. Then he heard the hum of a police drone. "Shit!" spat the kid with a weapon, hiding it in his pants. "Patrol." Both groups of kids limped off into the shadows, heading their separate ways. Antonio stuffed his own handgun into his pants pocket as the drone came into view. *Spy in the Sky drone.* The police used them rather than risk officers in the Districts. He stood up from his firing stance, his ears still thundering with the beat of his heart. By the time the drone was in range, it found only him, standing alone, and moved on.

Antonio turned back the way he had come and started to walk. He could feel his body slowly relax, his fingertips tingling from the adrenaline rush as it subsided. Each step seemed to take away more of the feeling of power. Unlike his nightmare earlier, every detail of the fight was etched into his memory. It was exhilarating and intoxicating.

My God—I loved it!

As he walked home, he felt the power that had flowed through him dissipate to nothing. He relived the fight in his mind, every motion, every detail. Pain came to him. His left leg, the real one, ached. *My muscles are not used to this.* Looking down, he noticed the paunch of his stomach. *I'm out of shape . . . but that is something I can fix.* In that moment, he decided to work out, lose some weight, get back into fighting form.

As he passed the spot where he had seen Debbie and Donna, he saw they were gone. Either they had found some marks or had called it a night. He was alone with his thoughts. The fight dominated every aspect of his mind. The skills were still there, compliments of the Army training he had undertaken. He hadn't needed those skills since Alaska, not like this anyway, against a real threat.

That kid could have killed me. Antonio considered that thought for a few moments. Sure, it was possible—but he had done it right, just like they had trained him to do. *No, the kid didn't have a chance in hell of hitting me.*

He reached his home and unlocked the door and entered. Leaning back against the old thick wooden door, he fully relaxed now that he was in the safety of his home. As he looked into the darkness of the church, up the main aisle to the altar, he wondered why he had gotten into the fight in the first place.

Antonio knew he had been outnumbered. The fight wasn't even his, it was between two small groups of kids. Was it to prevent them from hurting or killing each other? *No, that wasn't it. I did as much damage to them as they would have done to each other.* It sounded noble, to think he intervened to help them, but Antonio knew deep down that wasn't the case.

He walked up the aisle to the steps to the altar and sat down on them. The dim lights from outside trickled through the stained glass casting a spray of different colors across the room. Now, even as he relaxed, he felt something he hadn't felt in a long time—happiness. He had actually enjoyed beating up the kids. Something in his mind must have known that. It was why he had made their fight his own. He flexed his hands, balling them into fists. His right wrist was sore, but it was a good feeling, something that made him happy.

The VA shrinks would have a field day with this . . . the PTSD patient who likes to fight. He chuckled to himself—for the first time in months. He rested his elbows on his knees and sank his forehead into the palms of his hands.

What kind of a monster am I? I attacked a bunch of kids . . . just for the thrill of it. It didn't make sense to him. Being in combat had scarred him. He didn't need the psychologists to tell him that. After what he had been through, and what he had lost in the war, Antonio understood a sense of loss. But tonight . . . tonight had been different. He felt something in those moments when his body surged with strength. There was a power there, a power to overcome the nightmares.

He went back to his room, stripped down to his underwear, and crawled into bed. *If I am a monster, I'm the monster they made me.*

Antonio drifted off to deep sleep, deeper than he had experienced in many months. When he awoke midmorning, the sunlight stung his eyes. His body ached, every joint, even those that were manufactured. It was a new day . . . and it was time for a change. The first step was to start exercising. He would try to make sense of what happened some other time. In the meantime, he had to make sure that he did not get himself killed if the situation presented itself again.

It is time to go running . . . I need to get back into shape.

CHAPTER 22

**The yacht *Determination*,
off the coast of Los Angeles, California**

Jay Drake wasn't particularly proud of his yacht, *Determination*, not like some rich men were with their toys. He wasn't a nautical person at all, in fact. Other than a tour of the bridge of the ship, he knew next to nothing about the vessel. He owned the ship for two reasons. One, it was a place he could go for privacy; two, it was an expected accessory of someone in his station in life. *Determination* was a symbol of prestige, one of the few he embraced. She had a VTOL deck for light VTOLs or helicopters and was more sophisticated than most US Navy ships of the same size. Jay made sure she was armed as well, but none of the guests ever had any idea of just what a weapon *Determination* could be.

The tri-fanned VTOL came over the pad on the aft of the ship and landed gently. From his seat in the dining area, he could see his crewman escort Dana Blaze across the deck. She entered and he leaned forward, giving her a gentle kiss on her cheek.

"Well, Jay, you certainly know how to catch a girl off guard," she said, dropping gracefully into the seat next to his.

"We *did* agree to have dinner together."

"I didn't know you'd send a VTOL to pick me up and fly me out to your private yacht." From the tone in her voice, even the usually guarded Dana was impressed.

"You'll find I'm full of surprises," he said, gesturing for one of the waiters to bring them their drinks. After they were served, the wait staff discreetly disappeared.

Dana took a long sip of her drink—a La Iced Tea. "I will say this, you have flair." She brushed her hair back, but from what he could tell, it was perfect.

"No one has ever accused me of that before."

"I'm not sure you let anyone else get close enough to know you the way I do."

There was truth in that. His relationship with Dana Blaze was one of the few Jay indulged outside his role as CEO at JayTech. Dana was highly focused, which was something he recognized and respected. She was extremely competitive and he was the same. There was a sexy sort of ruthlessness about her. Dana didn't let lesser people get in her way. Jay was the same way in his field. The people who had tried to be barriers in his life were swept aside without remorse.

While parts of his relationship with Dana were clear-cut, other parts were confusing even to him. He knew he could have almost any woman on the planet. So why foster a relationship with a reporter? He held the press in such low regard, why date someone in that profession? She was stunningly beautiful, but he could find that almost anywhere. She didn't seem interested in his money; this was not a relationship of a gold digger attempting to gouge a billionaire. Dana had a lot of money of her own, and didn't spend much of it, according to his intelligence sources.

Drake had thought about it a great deal, and had come to the conclusion that he liked Dana because she was not intimidated by him. She poked at him, prodded at his past and the dealings of his company. There was a strange air of risk about her, that she might turn against him at any moment. He hated to admit it, but he found that exciting. There were no illusions about romance or anything else. Jay Drake only trusted her so far . . . but now he felt he needed her.

Hard Hat in Arizona had been crunching data on the anomalous happenings in the world's oceans and the results thus far had just added to the confusion. From what his vast network of contractors could tell him, the Department of Defense was still wrapping its heads around what was occurring, concentrating their efforts on the Pacific Ocean. Jay's people had processed a much larger amount of data, however, by gathering intel from a number of foreign naval sources around the globe.

He still didn't have an accurate picture of what was happening. In the meantime, he was preparing for some sort of deep-sea contact with an extraterrestrial people. JayTech had laid out billions to purchase deep-sea drilling companies in order to lift their technology, and also other scientific research firms. He had purchased enough ships to make JayTech one of the largest unofficial navies on the planet. Jay had purchased two commercial deep-sea exploration companies and had merged them, dumping in millions for research and new ships. Jay wasn't 100 percent sure what he was up against, but he was more prepared than most countries.

Yet even JayTech had limitations. There were parts of the DoD that he didn't have information from. Either they didn't purchase his hardware systems (which he had the capability to compromise) or he lacked human assets in places from which to pilfer information. There were other agencies possibly investigating these phenomena, but he didn't know for sure. Jay knew one thing that could force the release of information . . . the press. If word leaked out that there were extraterrestrial occurrences taking place, the government would have to respond. The FedGov would be pressured into revealing some of what they knew and would formally begin to dump money into the projects. He could then infiltrate those efforts with his array of contracting companies and staff. Having the media get involved would crack open some of the FedGov's closed doors for JayTech, which was something he desperately wanted. It would also push for spending, which would increase his sales and hopefully offset some of the expenses he recently had been running up.

Most people thought that media leaks came from government officials. Back in the old days, that might have been true. In recent years, though, it had been the FedGov's contracting community that had been the source for most major news leaks in Washington. In fact, Jay liked to think he was an expert at it.

Selecting Dana as his vehicle for the leak was deliberate as well. It was risky; his own involvement would be implied if not assumed, given their relationship. It was a calculated risk that Drake was willing to take. Tabloid sources had already gotten videos of them out in public together. If Dana broke the story, it would be inferred that she had gotten the information from him. It would lend credibility to the leak. In fact, the more she protested his involvement, the better as far as the rest of the media would be concerned. Protests would only solidify the link between the two.

"This is an impressive ship," Dana said, settling back into her seat and looking around, drinking in the expense of it all.

"It is expected that I own a big yacht."

"You rarely do what is expected of you—at least that's been my experience," she said, flashing that infamous smile at him. "It's also expected that you would own a massive mansion, but your home is relatively modest, aside from its security and privacy."

"Having a yacht like this is useful. She's fast, has sophisticated sonar gear, and with the VTOL pad, I have a fairly long range."

"Sounds like you are doing more than fishing."

Jay actually chuckled at her comment. "You could say that. In fact, that's why I invited you here tonight."

Dana looked at him quizzically. "I'm not catching your wave on this. I'm not a fisherman."

"No, but you do like a good tale. And I'm going to share one with you tonight. And if even fifty percent of it is true, you will have a massive story on your hands."

Dana leaned forward, her flirtatious smile becoming thin, firmer. "You certainly know how to get a girl's attention."

"What I'm about to tell you . . . well, you *can't* reveal me as the source. That's the price for admission to this party, Dana. Also, you'll find that my room sensors have disabled your usual recording devices. You get this for your ears only, nothing that can tie me to it."

She looked as if she was about to protest, to deny that she had been trying to record him. Her mouth opened but the words seemed stuck. After a few long seconds, the grin faded away to nothing. Dana leaned forward, putting her elbows on the small table between them and resting her chin in her hands. "Alright then . . . we treat this conversation as a business relationship. You have my word on your confidentiality. I know this routine; it's my job."

Jay nearly laughed. Dana Blaze's integrity had always been marginal. Drake assumed from the beginning that she would try to covertly record him every time they got together. The gear she used was impressive, in some cases better than that used by spy agencies around the globe—but she forgot that most of it was built by JayTech or one of its thousands of subsidiaries, or ran his software. He had even helped her knock out one of her would-be competitors, providing Dana the tech that brought about Veronica Diamond's shift to late-night coverage.

"I trust you, Dana, but know this. There will be a high price for violating that trust." He chose his words carefully.

She stared at him and nodded.

Good. It sank in.

Drake continued. "Very well. As you know, I have resources placed throughout the FedGov and around the globe. My resources have started to pass on some interesting information to me, something that is a potentially remarkable story."

"Go on . . ." she prodded, drinking in every word. He wasn't sure, but he thought she might actually be getting turned on as he spoke. It didn't shock him.

"The Department of Defense has been actively investigating a phenomenon taking place in the Pacific Ocean. Apparently, we have lost satellites and there have been commercial ships taken out by a new threat."

"The Russians or Chinese—no, wait, North Korea again?"

Jay cut his hand in a sweeping gesture horizontally in the space between them. "Nothing like that. No, this source is possibly extraterrestrial in origin."

There was an awkward silence for a moment as she stared into his eyes, then blinked her own. "From space? UFOs?"

"Yes." It was not the reaction he had expected from her. She looked at him as if she doubted what he was saying.

She chuckled. "I appreciate you bringing this to me, Jay, I really do. But two things come to mind. First off, I don't generally cover FedGov scandals. It's a bit on the trashy side for my business in the last few decades. Hell, even the tabloids have more credibility than FedGov does most of the time. Second, UFOs? That's a death blow for any legitimate reporter. It's a fast lane to being labeled as a nut job in my business."

Misinterpreting women was not a new experience for Jay. Having been a shy geek his entire life, females had always been hard for him to comprehend. But this was not what he had expected at all. Dana's understanding of her industry and her place in it was something he hadn't factored in with his plans. *There's more to her every time we talk . . . the hard sell isn't going to work here.*

"Dana, hear me out. This is not your typical UFO story. This is something, well, bigger—at least *I* think it is. The DIA has been digging into this, and if the story is true, well, we may be facing a large-scale alien incursion of some sort."

"But the FedGov will simply deny it. They'll do press conferences in which everyone will laugh at my expense for even bringing it up. It's happened before; that's why the top-tier journalists don't touch UFO stories. My E-ratings drop, my value in the market drops, my income drops. I see this as a lose-lose proposition. And frankly, Jay, UFOs? Seriously? You always struck me as being grounded in reality."

"I am." *More than you can possibly understand.* "That's why this should be of more interest to you." Drake looked into her eyes and knew that she did not believe him. He had been prepared for this contingency, though. "Perhaps you're right, Dana, maybe this story isn't for you."

"Thank you," she said, taking a sip of her drink. "I appreciate you bringing it to me."

Jay leaned back. "But someone is going to get this story sooner or later. You were just at the top of my list . . . for obvious reasons. I understand your reluctance. At the same time, with my resources, I stand able to assist whoever gets the story out by providing evidence. One thing I've learned over the years is that politicians hate facts and evidence." He paused. "Don't worry about it, Dana—someone will pick up the story." *Let that sit.*

She flashed him a smile and took a long sip of her drink. "When you say you have evidence, what are you talking about exactly?"

Jay waved his hand as if to disregard her query. "I have reports of the deaths that the government is covering up, sonar readings, all very technical. It's the kind of stuff that would make them squirm in a news conference." He took a sip of his own drink. "Our dinner should be out in a few. I have the chef making swordfish. I remember that you liked it."

There was a prolonged moment of silence.

"And this data you have is solid?"

"You can't argue against the government's own numbers and reports. Do you have someone in mind for this? I'd love any recommendation you might have. What about that Washington Roundtable host—Clark Thompson?"

"Thompson does talk show stuff, typical Sunday morning. He wouldn't touch this until the story broke. He's a clean-up reporter. He lets others do the investigation then confronts people long after the story is out there. You don't want him."

"Do you know someone I should talk to?"

"Talk to me about these so-called aliens. Where are they? In some secret government hanger or bunker?"

"If reports are right, it looks as if they are under the ocean."

"I saw the *Independence Day* reboot. Are they here to take our water or something like that?"

Jay shook his head. "I don't think so—no. In fact, we don't know for sure what is going on. But it's only been for the last five years. There have been some civilian deaths as a result of this . . . um, incursion." He wasn't sure what word to apply to what was happening. "But this story probably isn't for you, like you said."

"There's been some deaths, eh?" Her eyes widened. "And the government has covered it up?"

"I'm not sure if I'd use the phrase 'covered up.' They are just now starting to piece it together. In the meantime they are keeping a lid on it, keeping the information buried. There are some dark corners of the intelligence community that are starting to figure it out. This has been going on for half a decade, so the amount of information available to the right people, is staggering." There were only a handful of people on the planet who could amass and analyze that amount of data, and Jay felt that he was the only one who had even started. "For example, I have some radar readings of massive ships that the Air Force has picked up, all over oceans around the world. They will likely claim these are normal mechanical or software failures. They can't possibly deny the actual data when confronted with it, though."

"Data like that sure would help someone with making the case for this story," she spoke out loud, but Jay was not sure if she was talking to him or if she was thinking out loud. "Let's say you're right. If they have been coming here for the last five years, and we haven't heard a peep from them, why is it a big deal? Why would people care?"

"I don't know, Dana, I'm just a businessman. You know me, I'm not much of a people person. You know people pretty well. You tell me, how would people react to this? What would the churches of the world say? How would the average person on the street react?" He was lying. Jay understood people all too well. He understood their weaknesses and how to manipulate them.

She paused for a moment in concentration. "Honestly, there might be rioting in the streets once it's proved. People generally like things to remain the same. They hate change. Most people are prone to panic when they deal with the unknown. Fear is what feeds most people's reactions."

"I hadn't thought of it that way," Jay lied. *What about organized religion? How many cults would spring up? How would the Catholic Church respond to an alien life-form clearly more advanced than mankind?* He let those thoughts go. Saying it out loud might trigger the wrong reaction in Dana. It was best to play this soft, with a hint of ignorance. "I was just thinking of this as a big story, you know, a good-sized government scandal."

She cocked her eyebrow and tipped her head slightly in exaggerated disbelief. "Sure, Jay. Let's not forget the impact of the technology that these aliens might have," she added with a hint of accusation in her tone.

Let her think she's busted me. "Oh, *that* was something I've given some thought to. I guess you saw right through me. Yes, if these aliens are revealed, there will be a rush to learn their tools and tech. I want to make sure that JayTech is well positioned to take advantage of that."

"I thought you might have an angle."

"Look, I won't lie to you, I want to be on the bleeding edge of whatever comes out of this. That was why I was willing to offer you the story in the first place. If I control the story, I stand better poised to control the results."

"If this is true, and I'm not saying it is, you won't be able to control the story for long, Jay. It will run amok pretty quick, if you have the kind of data you claim. And what about these aliens themselves? We don't know their intentions."

"Well, I have looked over the data, Dana. I can attribute several hundred people's deaths to this. Governments cover up killings all the time, but this feels larger."

"And you have this data?"

"I have a quite a bit."

"Enough to make the FedGov officials squirm?"

"From what I have seen, they would be hard pressed to argue against the facts. Then again, it's hard to imagine what their reaction to this will be when the story does finally break." He was being coy again, baiting her.

"It's not too hard to guess their reaction. They will be facing a crisis on a scale that makes World War II look like a Sunday brunch. They'll have to scramble to try to deal with these extraterrestrials. They'll throw money at it—one of the few things Congress does do. Spending on science, technology, everything tied to the military, will go through the ceiling—if only to keep the citizens calm."

Jay deliberately grinned and locked his gaze with hers.

"You—you're going to cash in on this, aren't you?" Her tone was not accusatory, but one of acknowledgement. "That's the bigger game for you. JayTech will be there to sell them the personnel and hardware to counter this threat!"

Her words would have stung a lesser man's sense of morality. It wasn't something that Jay Drake felt burdened with. "Actually, yes. The truth of the matter is, Dana, JayTech is one of a handful of firms out there equipped to help mankind through this crisis. That is why I cannot be connected to the information I'm offering you."

"So," he said with a sense of finality in his voice. "You're the expert—who should I turn this story and data over to? Who's going to turn this into the story it deserves to be?"

She licked her lips and shook her head slowly. "I can't let you hand this tip over to some hack. Most of the people in my business are just pretty faces, propped up by corporations or teams. If pressure was put on them by the FedGov—and there will be pressure applied—they will fold. You need someone smart enough to take this and make it into something."

"Who, Dana?"

Her eyes narrowed. "Me."

"Are you sure? What about your E-ratings?"

"Answer me honestly—do you have the data to pull this off?"

"I do."

"I will want to review it before I commit. That's part of the bargain."

"Understood."

She finished off her drink in one deep swig. "Just so we're clear," she said in a matter-of-fact tone, "you're leveraging our relationship to help gouge the people of the world to make money." It was a statement of fact. As such, Jay could not feel angered by it.

"You are leveraging our relationship to advance your career."

"You didn't answer my question."

She's good . . . that's why I like her. He flashed a smile. "I don't have to. You know the answer."

She frowned slightly. "I'm not doing this as a public service, that's for sure. That's a concept that plays well in journalism school, but in the real world, it's a lost cause. Reporters and journalists, we are here for one thing—ratings and the rewards that go with them. If your data doesn't hold water, I'm going to take a pass on it."

"Agreed." Jay pulled out a coin-sized data transfer disk and slid it on the table toward her. "There's enough there for several uncomfortable questions that will make the FedGov squirm." Dana reached out and took the disk, clutching it tightly.

"With all your resources, I'm making an educated guess that you are still holding out on me. You have more information than you are letting on."

Jay drew the final gulp of his own drink. "Smart lady. If you weren't, I wouldn't give you the time of day."

"Alright, Jay, I'm in," she said, tucking it into her small purse. She leaned back in her seat. "Partners?"

Drake reached out and took her right hand in his hands. "Partners."

CHAPTER 23

Fort Myer NCO Club, Fort Myer, Virginia

Master Sergeant Adam Cain cradled his glass of whiskey and soda with two hands, letting the ice chill his fingers. The Fort Myer NCO Club was like everything else on the tiny base—steeped in history. The red brick building dated back well over a century and the outside structure was overly pristine, almost antique. That was the charm of Fort Myer as a whole, a charm lost on the master sergeant. The inside was still a bar, but it wasn't a fun bar, not like those he usually frequented. The NCO Club was too clean, too free of cigarette smoke, too "friendly" to be any bar that Adam usually drank in. After a day of orchestrating three burials and arranging for the Fourth of July activities, it would have to do.

For a few moments, Cain tuned out the sound of pool from the back room and the babble on the television. He tugged at his dress shirt where it dug into the thick muscles of his neck. It felt like it was choking him, just like the Army was. Wearing a dress uniform every day was bad enough. *I am a seasoned combat veteran. Now I order men to clean up horse shit. What has the Army turned me into?*

The hand that slapped his back brought him out of his thoughts and into reality. He turned his head and saw Master Sergeant Clyde Breckenridge standing at his side. "Well, it's a sorry state of affairs to find a nut-buster like Adam Cain sitting in his parade best in such a fine establishment," Breckenridge said in his gravelly voice.

Cain let go of his drink and shook his old friend's hand hard and firm. "Breckenridge . . . if I had known you were coming, I would've baked a shit-cake."

The shorter, stockier man grabbed the stool next to him. "Damn good to see you."

199

"You too," Adam responded. Clyde Breckenridge had a career that had paralleled his own, a rocky one at best. "Last time I saw you we were both standing on top of that Russian Mammoth I toasted."

"You mean the one *I* destroyed," Breckenridge countered.

Adam shook his head. "I'm not going over that argument again. Look, we both went toe-to-toe with that bitch. Let's just say we both took it out."

Breckenridge frowned and signaled the bartender, pointing to Cain's drink and giving him a nod for the same. "If that will make you feel better, but I think we both know who took it down."

"Taking it down isn't the same as taking it out," Adam countered. "Any chimp in a Class II rig could take one down. It's a fine art to destroy it and kill the driver and gunner."

Clyde smiled. "All that matters is the kill." He held up his fist between them. Adam could see the Roman numeral II tattooed on the back of his right hand. He had the same. The Army mark for ASHUR II qualified drivers. He balled his own fist and the two men tapped their fists twice. It was an unspoken handshake between two seasoned combat veterans, both qualified to pilot power armor in battle.

"Hoo-ah," Cain said.

The bartender brought Breckenridge his drink and the shorter man clinked Adam's glass and took a long sip. "Jesus, you're still drinking the cheap shit."

"All I can afford on a master sergeant's pay," Cain said, taking a sip of his own drink. He made sure he had his old friend's eye contact. "It is damn good to see you, Clyde."

"You too, Adam," he replied in a low tone. "How's your family?"

He took another sip of the whiskey at the mention of his family. "You remember me telling you that Julie filed for divorce a few years ago? It turns out we actually got a divorce." Sarcasm dripped in his words. He would have loved to have blamed it on the whiskey, but the reality was it was just raw pain.

Clyde chuckled. "No shit. I know that, everybody knew that but you, Adam. Forget it, it's the past. How are they doing?"

"My wife is moving on with her life. As it turns out, she is comfortable with us being divorced. Who would have thought? My daughter

Amy is fine. She wants nothing to do with me. She thinks I'm a shitty father . . . and she just might be right."

The wrinkles on Breckenridge's face tightened. "Well, you still have 'em . . . and that counts for something." He took a long drag on his whiskey and soda. Adam knew enough not to ask about his old friend's family. Clyde had been a devoted husband and father. A drunk driver, running his car on manual, hit their car before the anti-collision systems could override, killing his wife and son. Adam had been there for him during that horrible three-year period of his career. Their deaths had nearly broken Clyde, and only a tight-knit circle of Army buddies had managed to rebuild him. Even so, there was a part of him that was never quite the same.

"I don't have them, Clyde, that's the thing. I'm nothing more than a cash distribution for child support, and that ends this month. I'm doing what I can to keep contact with them, but it's a one-way street. They are purging me from their lives. Hell, they've probably been doing it for years and I've been too pigheaded to notice it."

"Here's to lost causes and old master sergeants," Breckenridge said, holding up his glass. Cain gladly toasted it, emptying his glass. He motioned for the bartender with two fingers. "Reload."

"Where have they got you posted?"

Breckenridge rolled his eyes back into the thick wrinkles of his brow. "Fort Eustis—Quartermaster Corps. Can you believe that shit?"

"Fort Useless," he said giving the Army's nickname for the Virginia base. "How did you end up in supply?"

"The same way you ended up on terminal burial detail. We are what the Army calls a conundrum. Too damn good to discharge, too stubborn for promotion, too decorated to force out, and too stupid to leave on our own. I got word you were with the Third Regiment, and I figured I'd arrange an inspection over at Fort Belvoir so I could pop in and see your sorry ass."

"I hope it was worth the trip," Adam replied.

"That it was," his old friend replied. "Though I have to admit that when I got word through the old farts' network that you had gotten assigned to the Third Regiment, I assumed it was a mistake."

"It was." Adam almost choked on the words. He hated admitting he screwed up, but there was no way around it. And if anyone would understand, it would be Breckenridge. "I thought I was getting some plum assignment here in DC, you know, covering the president or something like that. Instead they have me burying men we served with. Every day I get to embrace the honor of the Army I used to know, and am reminded of my own mortality. That mix . . . well, it tears you up a little every day. "

"Just getting in the Third is a mark of respect."

"In my case, it was a form of final punishment."

"Their mistake," the stout sergeant replied.

"It's mine. I should've known better. Ten years ago, I would've spotted what they were up to and would have been prepared, I would've outfoxed them. Now I'm on the exact wrong side of the country from my family. There are times, old friend, that I'm too stubborn for my own good."

"That has always been one of your many problems."

The bartender arrived with two more drinks and Adam ignored him, turning back to his old buddy. "I suppose you're keeping a list of my deficiencies?"

"I am at that," Breckenridge said, taking a sip of his fresh drink. "You are stubborn, but you are damn loyal too. When I lost Jenny and Tom, the Army wanted to ship me off for the shrinks to soothe my anger. You understood me and stood by me.

"You're a damned good fighter too. I hate to admit it, but there are times you are a hell of a lot better than me in a powered combat suit. I've seen you do shit in battle armor that should be impossible. And with the exception of one questionable Mammoth kill," he allowed himself a quick wink, "you are one of the best combat warriors in the Army.

"And to round out my list, Adam, you're honorable. The Army is a lot of things in the last few years. They've lost some of that honor and respect. The last war taught them that you can't fight a war economically, trying to expense every damned bullet and grenade. That was a costly lesson for sure. You never lost your honor, even when those above you lost theirs. You stand by your troops and you even stand by officers that, frankly, we'd have been better off fragging ourselves.

"The Army can screw with your mind. It can mess with your life. But they can't take your honor and values away from you, Adam. Fuck the powers that be! Here's to honor." He held up his glass and Adam toasted him.

"Goddamn, it is good to see you," Cain said, putting his drink back on the bar. "We've been through hell and back again."

"We certainly have bled on the same damn battlefields, at least in Afghanistan and Alaska. You know, I heard some shit about veterans offering tours up there, taking people on walking tours of the battle-fields in that tundra. That's when it hit me: I'm old. The places where I have seen good men and women die are being made into tourist attractions."

"You ever think of going back up there yourself?"

Breckenridge shook his head. "Fuck that. That one little town we fought over in Afghanistan, what was that place—Bum-Fuck-Ville? It's a resort now with a golf course and casino. And as far as Alaska is concerned, I've slept on that damn frozen permafrost enough for a lifetime. Don't even get me started on the mosquitos. I don't want to relive my past. I went there once—and fought and killed Russians there. That's enough for me."

Adam wondered. He had toyed with going on a trip up to Alaska. Even an Army shrink recommended it at one point. She said it would help him cope with his "painful memories" of the events there. He didn't believe that. *It's bullshit on a stick.* If anything, he was worried about stirring up any bad ghosts of memories he had of the fighting there. No, there was no going back, not in his mind.

"You hear about Rory Peterson?" he said, changing subject.

"Rip-Roaring Rory? No. The last time I spoke with him was three years ago at Fort Hood. What's the sitrep on him?"

"He drew advanced combat training at Campbell. He got hit during a live-fire exercise. Some recruit with her head up her ass misdi-rected a mortar barrage."

"He okay?"

"Lost a leg and most of an arm."

"Son of a bitch," spat Breckenridge. "Knowing the Army, they'll probably fast-track that stupid-ass recruit. Fucking officer material."

"Here's to the future chairman of the Joint Chiefs of Staff," Adam said, holding his drink up for another toast.

There was a long moment between the two combat veterans where nothing was said. Each held his respective drink. Adam thought back to the battles he and Breckenridge had fought in together. The memories of the bitter cold felt oddly different from the air conditioner that was blowing cool air on the back of his dress uniform. *I've been cold in my life, but never as cold as Anchorage and Fairbanks.* For a moment, his body quaked with a chill at the memory.

"You know what we need, Adam?" Clyde asked. Adam's eyes fell on his friend's service ribbons on his dress uniform. The colors of the campaign and medals awarded were stark against the olive drab of the coat. The colors were almost a mirror of his own. Maybe it was the alcohol tugging at his brain, but he wondered how many men he and Clyde had killed in battle. *How many have we lost?*

"No, what do we need?"

"A war." Breckenridge's words were deep and solemn.

"I thought you were going to say some pussy," Adam said.

"I'm serious, Adam. Men like us, we *need* a war. Peace is no place for combat soldiers like us. The only place we still exist—still have meaning, a purpose in this world—is leading men and women in war. These kids the Army is taking these days, they are Foxtrot Alpha Whiskey Tango Hotels and you know it. They need guys like us, BTDT, or they're just cannon fodder."

It was the slang that made Cain chuckle. FAWTH—fucking accident waiting to happen. *Ah, that takes me back to the old days. We used to call them FREDs—Fucking Retard, Extra Dumb, back before the Army banned the word "retard." God, I hate political correctness.* BTDT—Been There, Done That—was the name of several military NCO clubs across the country. Hearing those buzzwords strung together reminded Adam of the old Army, the one he joined fresh out of high school. It warmed him more than the whiskey. It was a bond, like their fist bump, that separated them from the rest.

"I hear you. I remember when I upped, my first sergeant said the same thing about me. Called me a walking clusterfuck. I carried that name up through my first firefight. Every generation of the Army thinks the new kids are soft. They are. We make them hard."

"We're due for a war," Clyde said, tipping his glass to swirl the remaining contents.

"I hope not. I've had my fill of fighting . . . so have you."

"You know what I mean, Adam. A decade without conflict. The US is overdue for some sort of rumble with another country. Don't you worry, Adam, periods of peace are always punctuated with war. War defines us as a people, as much as the liberals hate to admit it. The Russians are strutting along like they won . . . and don't even get me started on those uppity-ass Chinese. You and me, we've got *one* more good fight left in us. That's the only reason they haven't pushed our withered asses out the door. And as much as I hate war, I'm looking forward to this one."

Adam cocked his head to the side. "Why?"

"I don't want to die in peace. Old fighters like you and I, we need . . . no, *deserve* to die in war. Not inspecting pallets of toilet paper or burying the dead. One more war and that's the end for me. I want one more chance to die like a man, not sitting on some porch somewhere with my memory and bladder failing me, having someone wipe my ass. I don't have a family other than the Army. I want one more chance to prove to the world who I am, what I am capable of." There was a finality in Breckenridge's voice, like an eerie prediction of some sort. Cain understood it. As he spoke, he felt the tug of time and peace pulling at his soul too. His friend's words conjured for Adam a mental image of Clyde in his ASHUR II Mamba rig, on a hilltop, surrounded by faceless dead enemies.

But he didn't see the glory of dying in war. *I've dragged far too many young kids into battle only to never see them return. Clyde may want some glorious final stand, but I don't need it. I have a family still.* War, to Adam Cain, was something to be avoided. Always.

"You and I look at it differently. I don't want another war. I don't enjoy the peace much, but I'll take it any day over battle. I'm tired of sending messages to the parents of servicemen telling them that their kid has died in some Godforsaken place. I don't need a glorious death."

"War is coming," Breckenridge pressed. "It's inevitable. History cannot stand long periods of peace. It's a matter of time."

That was logic difficult to argue with. "You may be right. If it comes, by God, I'll be there—right in the middle of it, regardless of what I want," Cain responded. "You know me, I'm dumb enough to volunteer to go. I won't like it, but I will do my duty and the mission I've trained for my whole fucking life."

"Here's to the last war." Clyde lifted the remains of his drink. Adam clinked his glass and downed the last of his drink. A warmth rose in the pit of his stomach. He wasn't convinced it was entirely the whiskey— he liked to think it was the camaraderie.

CHAPTER 24

Yorba Diamond,
outside of Los Angeles, California

Cassidy got off the school shuttle and shuffled up the walkway to the front door, using her thumb on the security pad to open it. She didn't even remember shutting it behind her, but somehow knew she did. She dropped her bag by the door and heard her digipad clatter on the hardwood of the foyer from inside her backpack. Kicking off her shoes, she walked more like a zombie than a fifteen-year-old. Her mind was elsewhere, a jumble of thoughts from school, things she had to do, the day's conversations. She felt a weariness, a mental blankness from the attempt to mentally process the day into some organized filing system in her head.

"Hi Cassidy, how was school?" her mother asked as she came into the kitchen. CC was almost surprised to see her mom there with her brother, Donny. Even when he was sitting on his booster, Donny's head barely poked up over the edge of the table. Her mother had been working late this week. For a moment she wondered if something was wrong.

"Fine," she responded flatly. School had been long, boring, and amazingly dull for Cassidy. If it had been more about class work, it still would have been boring, but less so. Life at Barbara Walters Academy was mostly about social interaction—much more than when she was in middle school. There were sects or cliques of kids that seemed to attract each other. The jocks, the geeks, the wannabes, the cheer-losers, the S-punkers, the hashers, and a dozen more groups made up the social fabric of the school. Cassidy wasn't sure just where she and her small circle of friends fit in. It was becoming clear to her that they were a clique all on their own, nameless, themeless.

Just sitting down for lunch was a strange social experiment—at least, that was how she would have described it. Which table you sat at was determined by the kids you hung with. Breaking out of that mold caused problems. It drew unwanted and unwelcome attention and scorn. With JZee out sick, CC had sat at a table without giving it much thought. Two of the cheer-losers slid down and asked her what was she doing there. When she told them she was eating lunch, they informed her she couldn't sit there. The table was half empty, but all of the kids sitting there were facing her, glaring at her, as if she had committed some sort of crime.

She had wanted to ignore them . . . no, that wasn't true. She wanted to punch the one girl, Sally Sleight, right in the face. She was so condescending in the way she had spoken to her. But Cassidy held back her anger, picked up her lunch, and moved to another table. She felt the eyes of everyone in the room on her. Silent intimidation over a seat. *There will come a time I don't take that from people like her.* For now, she did what was expected.

"You're home early," CC said, pulling up a chair across from where Donny sat.

"I filed my motion at the District Court this morning and took the afternoon off," her mother replied. "Your father said he'd try to connect with us after you got home. I thought he might like to see all of us."

Donny made eye contact with her and flashed her a smile. She jokingly stuck her tongue out at a moment when she was sure her mother was distracted. Donny responded in kind. Playing with Donny was hard. They were so far apart in age and the ways they played, that CC struggled with it. The things he liked to do were boring to her. The things she thought he'd like were too complicated.

"It's going to be early for him, isn't it?"

"Not too early," her mom assured her.

"What's for dinner?"

Her mother grinned. "I thought after we took his call we would go out and get dinner. How does that sound to you?"

Her father was more the cook in the house than her mother, so CC didn't mind. In fact, she was hard-pressed to remember the last occasion on which her mother had actually prepared a meal from scratch. She didn't think less of her for it. Her mother worked hard in her career and with the commute downtown, there usually wasn't time to prepare a meal. David Chen filled that gap. While he wasn't a great cook by any stretch, CC missed her dad's cooking. "Fine."

Her mother's digipad chirped. "I'll bet that's your father now," she said excitedly, picking up the pad and flipping down the stand. She stabbed her perfectly manicured nails at it and in a second the image of David Chen filled the screen. She moved the pad so that everyone in the room could be seen.

CC looked at her father and saw the bags under his eyes. *I wonder if he's sick?* "Hi Daddy!" she said.

"Wow, everyone is here! Turn Donny around, I want to see his face."

CC's mother shifted Donny and her father began to talk in a ba-by-ish voice. "Hey Donny, how are you doing?"

"When are you coming home?" Donny asked. CC did like that about her brother . . . he was blunt.

"Well, I'm pretty busy here, Donny. I should be home next weekend for a visit."

Donny didn't like the answer. He crossed his arms and pouted slightly, tipping his head down. "I want Daddy home now," he said under his breath.

"I will be soon. How's my little girl?"

CC felt more energy than she had all day. "I'm fine. I got a B on my math quiz today."

"Awesome, kiddo!" As he spoke there was a low rumble behind him. It sounded like a thunderstorm. It was enough for David Chen to turn his head to the window behind him. Outside the window, Guam looked like it had brilliant skies. "Must be a storm coming in." There was no hint of concern on his face.

"How has the weather been there?" CC's mother asked.

"It's been pretty good. We had three days of rain earlier in the week, real drenchers. That set us back a few days." There was another sound that came through the digipad, a popping noise, rapid, joined by another. Once more, David Chen turned to the window over his shoulder. Something was going on, but he was trying to not look concerned—CC could see that.

"What is it, David?" her mother asked.

"I'm sure it's nothing," he replied. "How's your case going, honey?"

Her mother shrugged. "I had to file a motion to dismiss some of the evidence this morning. It will be a few days before the judge rules on it. I think it's pretty strong, but with these kinds of thing—"

A loud crashing sound came from David Chen's digipad, like a car hitting a building, that cut off her mother's sentence. David got up. "Hang on, hon," he said and moved to the window. "God only knows what those Marines are up to . . ." He pulled back the curtain and looked outside. "What the hell?"

"What is it, David?"

"I'm not sure," he said, still looking outside. "I'm seeing smoke coming from the anchorage. There's a lot of people running around." His words were cut off by a purr of popping noises. "What are they shooting at?"

"They're shooting?" her mother asked.

"Something is going on here," David said, moving away from the window and turning back to his family. "Maybe there's been an accident down at Big Navy."

"Shouldn't you get to someplace secure?"

"I'm in the middle of a huge military post, honey. What could happen to me here?"

"What if it's a shooter?"

"I've got a few thousand Marines here, all armed." Then his lights flickered on and off. David looked again toward the window. They could hear more popping sounds.

There was a monstrous roar from outside, deep, long, and loud. It was so deep, so bass, that David Chen seemed to recoil from the digipad. Suddenly his window cracked. The glass didn't shatter, it simply cracked in a bizarre spiderweb pattern.

Her mother took no chances. "CC, take your brother into the living room."

CC protested, "Mom . . ."

David Chen looked at the window. A wailing noise filled the air and came through the digipad. A siren of some sort. "That can't be . . ." he said.

"What is it, David?"

"We're under attack. They told us about the siren during orientation. That is the attack alert."

"David, you have to get out of there," she stammered, as if trying to control her words.

He nodded. "I love you guys. I'm going to head over to the security bunker." Suddenly there was a whooshing sound, a low roar, and his window shattered inward. The room behind him was sprayed with thousands of tiny shards of glass, some clinging in his hair and on his shirt. David Chen curled up and ducked off view of the camera for a moment, then rose, seemingly fine. Noises from the outside were coming in on the digipad's feed—a popping noise, gunfire. How distant it was, CC couldn't say. She knew that sound, though—she had heard it on the evening news programs. To her, it was the sound of war.

David Chen's expression had changed. Gone was the casual father. This was a man who was afraid. CC had never seen her father afraid before, ever. The image burned in her mind. "Honey, I have to go—" Before he could finish, the image cut off and a "carrier lost" error message appeared on the digipad.

Cassidy Chen stared at it. Something was happening, something horrible. She could feel it. And her daddy was in the middle of it. What was it? There were news reports all of the time about terrorists or crazy lone gunmen attacking somewhere. Now one of these things she had managed to ignore was happening to her and her family. Suddenly, to her, Guam felt as if it were on another planet.

Donny Chen felt the tension too. He began to cry. Cassidy looked up and saw the expression of terror on her mother's face. Her hand was over her mouth and tears were pooling under her eyes, looking for a path down her cheeks.

Cassidy didn't pray when she was a child. Her parents were not particularly religious, but some of her friends were and she went to church with them. When everyone bowed their heads in prayer, it seemed a strange concept. She mimicked them, never understanding what they were doing. CC hadn't felt the need to pray before. There were few things in life she wanted and didn't have.

Now things were different. She closed her eyes for a moment and prayed for the first time ever. *Please bring my daddy home okay . . .*

CHAPTER 25

The DIA Boiler Room, the Pentagon

Captain Ashton Slade stood next to his CO, Colonel Harper, and General "Cutter" Guttman. Across the table was the Director of the Defense Intelligence Agency, General Quartermain. The director's office was typical of the inner sanctum of the Pentagon leadership. It was not ultra-modern but old, with deep-grained wooden desks. The room reeked of history, with a well-stocked library filling one wall plus a small credenza with several decanters of alcohol. The director's face had been an angry red since the discussion had started, and his color just kept getting darker.

"Does anyone here want to tell me where our leak is?" General Quartermain demanded. "Because that's what my boss, the chairman, wants. That, and a position on where we stand on this damned story."

Ashe shook his head. "Sir, we were stunned that this Blaze woman released the story. The details she released are nowhere near complete, which tells me that her source might not be with us. If you look at the incidents she cites, it's a fraction of those we have tracked and documented."

"How does that help us, Captain?"

Colonel Harper cut in. "We've talked it over. It means that the leak is probably not DoD. The cited incidents do appear, in condensed form, in the material we released to the DHS and CIA. Sir, we're not the source here. Our halls are clean." There was a hint of pride in his voice. Leaks were not new in Washington DC, but they always were ugly, ungainly beasts, impossible to prevent or stop once they got moving.

General Quartermain's frown lessened. "Good. The chairman likes it when the fuck-up is with another agency. Unfortunately, the DIA was named in that reporter's piece, which means we have to respond."

"Dana Blaze is a mover and shaker, but this is out of her league from what I have scanned on her," Ashton said. "She never rolls in the Washington sty. This doesn't fit her standard MO."

"How does that help us?" Quartermain asked.

Colonel Harper jumped in. "It gives us some wiggle room. If we come out and say 'no comment,' the regular DC press will smell a story and be all over us. We admit that the incidents happened . . . hell, that's hard to deny anyway since most of them were already covered in the press. Then we go after Blaze. Question her lines of logic. Just because these things happened, that doesn't mean they are connected. Slam her credibility. It puts her on the defense and gives us the room we need to deal with this better. The regular Washington press pool will turn on her for pissing in their pool."

General Quartermain pounded his fist on the table. "I like it. Get a summary of this drafted so that I can wave it in front of the chairman and he can get the National Security Council to buy in."

"It's gone that far?" Harper asked.

"And beyond. The president has asked for a briefing on what we *do* actually know. Once he's in the loop, there's no more deniability. I've told the chairman we don't have a lot on these incidents, but now that the cat is out of the bag, we have little choice but to start telling the higher-ups. Captain Slade, you're going to help me prep my deck for the meeting."

"Yes, sir." Ashe realized that for the first time in his life, something he was doing was going all the way to the top—to the president. A part of him was excited at the prospect. Another was nervous. He knew he was not making a mistake in his interpretation of the data, but there were so few answers—and he knew leaders well enough that he knew they hated ambiguity.

Dana Blaze's exposé on the alarming trend of naval incidents and their potential ties to something extraterrestrial had been ignored by most of the powers that be for a week or two, but as others in the media began to crunch the data, it was clear that there was substance behind her story. She had, as Colonel Hastings put it, "stirred up a shit-storm."

"Fill me in on the report from that sub," General Quartermain demanded.

Captain Slade nodded. "The USS *Virginia*, sir. This report is unnerving, sir. We've been going over the data and it certainly is tied to the events we're trending." He pulled out his secure digipad and fired the images over to the general's display.

"What you are looking at is the *Virginia*'s images of the crash of a Federal Express cargo plane, designated as Flight 203C. She went down eight months ago. As part of our increased tracking of the anomalies, we tasked the *Virginia* to investigate the wreckage."

"How deep is this?"

"It's at 1,500 feet, sir."

"So, who the hell laid that plane out like that?" General Guttman chimed in.

"That's the question we all have. A big cargo hauler, fully loaded, should have been a big debris field. Instead, someone or something has taken the time to lay out the plane like an accident investigation."

General Guttman leaned forward to look at the image in front of General Quartermain, squinting slightly. "I have to tell you, that is damned disturbing to see at that depth."

"We concur, sir. What they did took a lot of time and a lot of resources on their part."

"What does it mean?" Quartermain asked.

"Our best guess is that they are attempting to learn more about our technology. We don't know if anything is missing in the cargo, but this doesn't look like a planned robbery. They took the time to reconstruct that airplane deliberately, methodically. We believe it is the action of someone trying to learn about us."

"It seems a bit extreme. If you want to know about mankind, listen to our media," Quartermain snapped.

Ashe shook his head slightly. "You're thinking like a human, sir. We don't know if they even understand how we communicate, let alone *what* we communicate. The more we went over these images and the report filed by the *Virginia*, the more we realized that what they had found was a scientific experiment. They were doing the same thing we would do if we captured one of their ships—taking it apart to learn how it works."

"And they did it at that depth," General Guttman said. "That's deeper than our manned subs can operate, isn't it?"

"Yes, sir," Ashe replied. "They seem to be able to operate at depths that would be a dangerous proposition for our people."

"Captain, tell the general about the trending of attacks," Colonel Harper said.

"Well, sir, we've been analyzing the nature of the encounters. There's a trend in the last six months for more violent attacks."

"Like the cruise ship? What was it? The *Star of the Sea*?"

"Yes, sir."

"We were lucky some harebrained terrorist group took the credit for that," General Guttman added.

"What does this mean?" Quartermain pressed.

"We don't know for sure, sir."

"Captain—you must have some ideas in that head of yours. I've read enough of your reports by now to know you are pretty damned smart. What do you *think*?"

The compliment came with a commitment to say the words. Ashe *had* been thinking about the increase of violence. "Sir, I think they are testing themselves and testing us. It's a prelude to something larger."

"Testing?"

"They are operating in deep water. Their entire environment is extreme pressure, darkness, and cold. They have to adapt to engage with us. They are unsure of what their own weapons can do and what we are capable of doing in response. I think these are probes. They are shaking down their equipment, honing tactics, testing our defenses and how we respond."

"A prelude? As a prelude to what?" Quartermain pressed.

Ashe drew in a long breath before responding. "A larger, more comprehensive test. Bear in mind, sir, this is only an educated guess at this time."

General Quartermain's digipad buzzed. He picked it up and looked at the message. "Goddamn it . . ."

General Guttman's pad buzzed from its pouch on his belt. He pulled it out. A few moments later Colonel Harper's buzzed. Ashton said nothing as the men checked their pads. He knew enough not to ask. If all of them were being buzzed, it had to be an emergency, and apparently one above his pay grade.

"Assemble the seniors in the Board Room in five. I think Hastings is on leave. Get him on a plane and back here, now! I want live feeds in from the affected areas we know of. Get them streamed in there real-time," General Quartermain commanded. "You too, Captain Slade."

"Sir?"

"We're under attack. Apparently your aliens have decided to pay us a visit. Your prelude is on."

***

Seven minutes later, Ashe found himself in the Board Room surrounded by the senior members of the DIA. A banner in red flashed at the top of the screen, scrolling with white letters indicating the commands that were online. There were images flickering on the screen. He wasn't sure where the signals were coming from, but he saw smoke and the scenes of battle . . . something he had experience with. *Where are they hitting us . . . and with what?*

Lieutenant General Quartermain sat in his usual seat. "What do we know? Darien?"

Admiral Darien Frost of the US Navy didn't look nervous at all given the gravity of the situation. He had that kind of calm demeanor that Ashe admired and wished he could emulate. "Approximately forty-five minutes ago, we got word that an attacker of unknown origin initiated an attack on our base at Guam. Apra Harbor is under attack, as is Andersen Air Force base on the north end of the island. An attack of some sort is also taking place in Hawaii, and we have temporarily lost our landline comms with them. We're getting a lot of information on commercial traffic and laser squirts from satellites. The picture of events there is less than complete at this time."

"The enemy being . . . ?" Quartermain asked, the dread in his voice implying he already knew the answer.

"I believe we are facing a new enemy, sir, pursuant to Red 105A." The admiral shot a glance over to Slade.

"We are not alone," General Buchwald added. "The British are reporting attacks as well. Iceland has reported some sort of assault taking place, too."

216

Admiral Frost spoke up. "I just got a squirt from the commandant of the Coast Guard. There are reports in Los Angeles, Boston, Miami, San Francisco, and Savannah of strange creatures coming ashore. They are massive snail-clam things in shape, but these are the size of city busses, definitely alive, coming up on the beaches and making their way ashore. There are over a dozen of these coming ashore in LA alone. This can't be a coincidence."

"What intel are we getting from Guam?"

General Florence "The Axe" Hatcher's face seemed to clench as she spoke. "The USS *Antietam* has been lost at Big Navy; she went down at the start of hostilities. Her emergency beacon was activated—which we got off a satellite feed. That was our first clue, along with some sort of insect attack on Andersen AFB. Word is my Marines are engaging the enemy at the base. Comms is spotty, but we are attempting to patch in some live feeds. I've tried to raise the base commander, Colonel Spearman, but so far, it's a no-go."

Admiral Frost chimed in. "I recommend we get the fleet out of Pearl now."

"I agree," General Quartermain said. "But where can you send them where they will be safe? If the enemy is coming out of the oceans, I can't very well pull the ships ashore."

An aide entered, a lowly second lieutenant. "Sir, we are getting a signal from the Marines at Guam."

"Put it up." The lieutenant stabbed at the table controls and a holographic image appeared in four floating panels over the massive meeting table so that everyone in the room could see the images. It was combat footage, shaky and jarring, but the images were clear.

Ashe saw a squad of Marines huddled low, firing their weapons in short bursts down a street which could have been on any US military base around the world. Smoke rose in the background. When Slade and the other men in the room saw the targets, their jaws dropped for a moment.

At first glance, they were like massive crabs or lobsters—at least, that was how he would have described their bodies. They had greenish-blue plates of shell—and from the flicker of ricochets, it was at least somewhat effective armor against the bullets the Marines were pouring on them. They had long necks and elongated skull-like heads, with strange curves. The way the "tail" plates interlocked reminded him of a lobster or armadillo. Every aspect of the creatures seemed large and menacing. They had six legs, crab-like, each with pincer-like claws at the end. They didn't move smoothly, but seemed to be uncertain in their motions. *They are operating out of their natural environment . . .*

Their "eyes" looked more like strangely shaped reflective plates of polished black rather than eyeballs in the traditional sense. He couldn't tell if this was some sort of visor, or the eyes themselves. They were not round like human eyes; these were long and triangular, with strangely shaped ends that melded into their armored exoskeletons . . . if it was indeed exoskeleton.

What he assumed were antenna jutted backward in a curving arc. It reminded him of the reverse of a lobster. They didn't appear to be sensor gear, though he saw what looked like a vein running from them into the head. *No, these are more organic, oddly natural . . . like they are part of them.*

They moved fast, much faster than Ashe would have expected. One lifted a big front claw and there was a white stream that came from a bulge attached to it. The pencil-thin stream hit a Marine nearby and appeared to cut him in half, along with a big piece of a building next to where he stood. *What was that—a high-pressure water jet weapon?* It was like a laser in its lethal effectiveness. *I knew we used tools like this to cut metal, but never thought of them as weapons.*

Two Marines tried to fall back, no doubt to keep their distance. The alien sprang at them with a speed that was faster than the Marines. It moved to physically assault them with its legs and claws. One leg knocked a Marine into the side of a building, one story up. Another forward leg clamped onto the other Marine and cut them in half, sending a spray of blood into the air.

Suddenly two minigun-armed aerial drones appeared in the distance and fired down at the creatures. Then—in the far background, moving through the smoke, Slade saw something else. It was big, larger than a human and looked as if it was some sort of organic form of ASHUR II armor, but larger and sleeker. It was smooth, wet looking, with gray-and-black splotched patterns on the exterior that seemed to change as it moved onto the street. Where ASHUR II suits had some distinct edges to them, the bipedal alien suit had an oddly organic feel. It was not like a suit of armor, but something that was part of the creature. No open joints, no hoses or hydraulics. *How did they do that?*

The Marines were yelling, firing, and someone was screaming. The bipedal creature raised its arm toward the drones and something launched from it. He couldn't see what it was, but one drone wobbled, then fell.

"First platoon, move to Phase Line Charlie," a Marine officer's voice came over the battlespace feed. "We have ASHUR incoming," another Marine called out. A grenade went off near the crab-like creatures, which seemed to push them back a few steps, more than Ashe would have expected, as if the explosion hurt them more than it did humans. Their retreat was short-lived however, as they surged forward a few heartbeats later. One had two legs missing on the left side, but seemed to move with little impairment on the remaining four legs. *They are tough, that much is sure. With multiple legs, they are effective in battle even when they lose one.*

Suddenly the signal ended and a hiss of static filled the air. The static continued for a few seconds before the lieutenant shut it off. "Sorry, sir, we lost the signal on their end."

Ashton was frozen in place, as if he hoped the image would return. In all his months of doing research on the anomalies, he had wondered what the aliens looked like. Now that he had seen them, he was stunned. He had expected one race, but there was at least two—more if you counted the large snail-like creatures. *Were there more?* Probably . . . it was only a few seconds of combat footage. As a combat veteran, the images of Marines dying stirred old and painful memories from the war. *I have never felt so horrible at being right about something.*

"Captain Slade," General Guttman said. Hearing his name woke him from his thoughts. He looked over at the general, unsure of what he had missed. "You can sit down."

It was then Slade realized he had risen to his feet while looking at the footage from Guam. He nervously nodded and lowered himself back into his seat. His mind was alive with questions—questions that now demanded answers.

"Was that their soldiers?" General Quartermain asked.

There were murmurs around the table as the generals and admirals turned to each other. Ashe couldn't contain himself. "Sir, we saw two different species in that footage. They may have more—many more."

"Those *things* tore my Marines apart," General Hatcher said. "I think we need answers and need them right now."

Ashe shook his head. "You all have the same intelligence we have. I haven't held anything back."

"Why Guam?" Quartermain asked.

"Possibly because it's isolated," Ashe offered. "They don't fully understand us. Remember the ships that have been attacked? Maybe Guam is a testing ground for them, to test our capabilities and their own."

"Are you saying that this was a dry run?" General Hatcher responded with a hint of disbelief.

"Unknown, sir," Slade replied. "I'm speculating, just like you. But if I were here for five years, preparing, I would not just commit everything at once. I'd test us. See how we fare in battle. Then I could make adjustments and corrections based on the data."

"Sir," the lieutenant said. "We are getting a relay broadcast on a secured laser-line from the USS *Abraham Lincoln* outside of Pearl Harbor. It's a direct punch signal off one of our satellites." The image of an iron-jawed naval officer with black hair streaked gray over his ears appeared. The man was like something you saw in a movie when you described a tough naval commander . . . at least that was what Slade thought as he saw him.

"This is DIA, Lieutenant General Martin Quartermain, and the DIA command staff."

"Admiral Jason Dawbs, sir. We have a limited message time on this satellite."

"Understood. We have lost contact with Hawaii and USPACFLT. What is your situation?"

"We are twenty miles out from Pearl. We received messages that some strange things came up on our beaches. They were like giant clams, long bodies. They disgorged some sort of insects or bugs or something. It was slaughter, sir. These things are like carnivorous locusts. Then I got word over short-range comms that Pearl was under attack. The *Lassen* and several other ships put out to sea, but once they hit open water, the *Lassen* went down. No torpedoes, her keel just was rammed or hit with something and they were taking on water. Apparently it was some sort of submarine attack. It just wasn't like anything we've experienced before. The USS *McCampbell* went down in the harbor itself. Her captain sent me a lot of data, which I will have my comms officer transmit to you. The ships that made it out of Pearl are on their way to rendezvous with us now.

"Then they came out of the water. They weren't Russians—they were some sort of creatures. They hit Pearl and Honolulu roughly an hour ago and caught us off guard. Harbor sonar didn't even report detection until they broke the surface. Those insects they unleashed forced ground units into a rout. USMC and the Army were fighting a holding action at Hickam AFB but these bug-like things have forced them to button up in some of the more secure facilities. Pearl's power grid failed shortly after the creatures hit the shore, and Honolulu's went down just a few minutes ago. Initial reports are massive civilian casualties with survivors fleeing the city. We've been getting indiscriminate reports on all military channels; none of it is very good, sir. All landlines into and out of the islands are down. Thank God we have our satellite and microwave relays.

"I've got CAP in the air and we are at Ready One on the flight line, but I don't have a target at this point. PACFLT is silent—I think they've been taken out, or at least their communications capability. I'm operating under that assumption. I'm a little concerned about sending in a strike on Pearl without a good view as to who the enemy is."

Quartermain leaned forward over the table, looking into the face, resting his elbows and talking with his hands as much as his mouth. "Admiral, we received word that Guam is under attack as well. I technically don't have the authority, but I'm asking you to get some of your drones in the air and over Pearl. We need intel, images, everything. This enemy is alien in origin . . . I say again, alien in origin."

Admiral Dawbs nodded in response. "The CNO sent an encrypted burst on the B-channel five minutes ago for us to maintain distance from Pearl but that doesn't prevent us from getting our drones out there. The ships that made it out of the harbor are on their way right now to rendezvous with us. That gives us a pretty good task force.

"Admiral, I don't know where your carrier is safe. Needless to say, whatever intel you can provide us is critical at this stage."

Admiral Dawbs nodded. "I understand, sir. The Navy won't let you down, sir. We'll launch in five." The image disappeared in a flicker as the satellite signal changed.

Ashe took in what Admiral Dawbs had said. "General—sir, he mentioned these clam-like things crawling ashore."

"Yes, Captain."

"We've had the same in Los Angeles and several other cities. We need to get the word out—those things are dangerous."

Quartermain spoke in a low tone. "Crap! We don't even have a procedure to do that . . ."

CHAPTER 26

US Naval Base, Apra Harbor, Guam, Pacific Ocean

"Move it! Head for the armory. Grab your shit! This is *not* a drill," Staff Sergeant Rickenburg barked into the barracks. STG's nickname with the Marines was "shit" and everyone knew it instinctively. "We are under attack. Move it, people! All I want to see is assholes and elbows!" Lance Corporal Falto didn't even think, she just reacted, getting her boots on and sloppily tossing on a fatigue shirt over her OD T-shirt. Somewhere in the distance, she heard the wail of an alert siren. They had just gotten back to the barracks from a run and suddenly there was a rush of confusion. Then came a rumble somewhere within a mile, a mortar round going off. That added a sense of urgency.

"What the fuck is going on?" Hernandez said, grabbing her ACR-25 from the locker as Falto did the same.

"We're under attack," Falto said.

"By who?"

"How would I know?"

Rickenburg hollered again. "Move it—move it—move it!" The cadence in his voice was like a machine gun in her ears. Falto rushed past him and realized that he was only wearing a T-shirt and fatigue pants himself. Whatever was happening, it had caught the staff sergeant off guard as well. *Is it the Russians? Maybe the Chinese?*

As they ran out onto the street in Big Navy, she heard a long metallic groan and the agonized sound of straining metal off to her left. She looked between buildings, and what she saw stunned her. One of the cruisers in the port was sinking. Her stern was down and the bow was lifting up at about a thirty-degree angle as the ship slid into the water. Even from blocks away, above the rooftops of the buildings between the waterfront and the barracks, she could see sailors clambering on the tipping deck, jumping into the water far below. Smoke rose from the dock areas and she heard the distinct popping of ACR-25s firing at some yet unseen foe.

"Falto, move your sorry ass," the staff sergeant barked, snapping her back to the task at hand. She turned her gaze away from the dying ship and ran, faster than she ever had before. *Who is attacking us? It has to be the Russians. Why here, why now?* Memories of the Grizzly and Mammoth tactical suits came to the forefront of her mind. She sprinted around a corner with her rifle in her arms. The armory was three blocks down, and base personnel were already gathering there. *I promised my mother I wouldn't be in a war . . .* She pushed that thought down deep. Now wasn't the time to think of that.

The armory was a scene of chaotic noise and panic, the smell of sweat and fear stinging in the air, circulated by the low-hanging fans that spun so slowly it made everything else appear fast. Marines from various companies were rushing in, grabbing live ammunition, suiting up in their armor. "Bravo Company First Platoon, assemble here!" Rickenburg commanded. She moved without thinking and again felt the rumble of an explosion.

There were Marines everywhere, sergeants barking orders, attempting to sort out where people belonged. The chaos didn't last long as the NCOs did their work. *This has to be what it was like when the Russians came ashore at Fairbanks or when the Japs hit Pearl Harbor.*

For a full two minutes and a half, the staff sergeant held his hand to his earbud as the Marines assembled. *He's getting orders from battlespace command—getting the lay of the land.* Falto kept on working, glancing at Rickenburg as she and the others stood by, awaiting orders. There were several moments where he had a look of awe on his face, a mix of confusion and attempts to clarify the situation. She had never seen that expression on him before.

Slowly he turned to his platoon. "Big Navy is under attack from the sea by an unknown enemy force. Andersen was hit as well, but by some other sort of attack. The Air Force is out of the fight for now because they can't even get to their aircraft. Our Marine joyboys are still good, though, and promise us some air support.

"This is no exercise, people. As of now, we are at war, and I intend for us to take the fight right down their throats. You will get on your full STG urban gear. Everyone, take a full load-out of ammunition and grenades. Foster, treat this as a tactical threat level one, meaning get our heavy support weapons ready and on the Huskies. People, get your shit on. We push out in four."

Falto scrambled to her locker and pulled out her STG U (urban) gear, tightening the straps more than usual. Her heart was pounding in her ears as she snugged on her helmet and toggled it online. At the armaments cage, a corporal scanned her embedded ID chip and doled out her appropriate kit of ammunition. In Falto's case, as a fire team leader, she was handed seven magazines, stuffing six into her utility belt while she took the last magazine and slid it into her ACR-25. The clicking sound it made as it mated with the rifle seemed louder than normal to her. She checked her safety, just like she had been trained to do. She got a standard grenade pack too, hooking it to her utility belt.

One of the Marines behind the table handed her a pistol, the Sig Sauer M18. She was qualified for it, but it was assigned only for certain tactical operations. Natalia tucked it into her pistol pocket under her armor, pocketing three magazines. She moved like a machine, not slowing, not hesitating, returning to her place in line, her rifle in hand. Looking across the armory, she saw Staff Sergeant Rickenburg approach a large podlike cocoon the size of a car standing on its end. He leaned in for a retina scan and there was a pop-hiss as the split door to the sleek gray pod opened. Inside was his ASHUR II Lion rig. Its front armor plate was hinged and open and he slithered into the massive armored suit as if it were a second layer of skin. Two techs moved into the pod while the staff sergeant strapped himself into the suit and put on his comms earbuds and biofeedback strips.

The techs brought over ammunition containers and opened the access ports on the armor, sliding in the canisters of deadly firepower. The dummy exercise LAW 98As were replaced with live rockets, their tips painted red. The two-foot-long rockets had a sophisticated laser-targeting system made them deadly at short and medium ranges. They were a mix of high speed drone and rocket. As they worked to outfit her staff sergeant's rig, Falto saw Sergeant Parker climbing into her ASHUR II suit too, though hers was a lighter Hyena. The other two pods in the bay were already empty, indicating that those pilots were already engaged somewhere on the base.

A voice came over her helmet earbud. "This is battlespace command, Lieutenant Fricks. We have unknown enemy forces coming in from the western side of the base. This is no drill. I have established phase lines for deployment. All forces will be tagged for their deployment zones. These unknowns are unidentified at this time. Priority for now is protection of the civilians and noncoms on the base. The use of live ordnance is authorized." Lieutenant Fricks was assigned to Alpha Company and while his voice was firm, she had an immediate thought flash in her mind. *Why the hell is a lieutenant commanding the battlespace? Where the hell are the other senior officers?* In that moment, she felt like they had been caught with their pants down and it wasn't a reassuring feeling.

The "Devil Dog" throbbed to life as its fuel cell kicked in with a low hum. The staff sergeant tested his arms to make sure they worked, somehow missing the technicians who were still working on rigging and arming the massive battle suit. They checked hose connections at a furious pace and uncoupled the suit from the pod. The staff sergeant stepped forward and moved in front of his assembled platoon and stood for a moment. Falto looked at the cartoonish logo that the staff sergeant had painted on his rig, a bulldog standing on its rear legs, holding a chain gun, chomping down on the smoldering stump of a cigar. His name, "Hannibal Rickenburg," was stenciled in yellow over the "heart" of the suit. It seemed so out of place on the olive drab coating his armored plates, but Natalia found it oddly warming and she felt encouraged. He moved his Lion rig in front of Parker's Hyena and the two seemed to be communicating. *With the staff sergeant here in that armor, what could possibly happen to us that we can't handle?*

He turned to the gathered Marines.

"Listen up, Marines! Alright, First Platoon, pay attention. We have an incomplete battlespace picture at this time, but it appears that the attackers have come ashore at the north end of the base. My command feed shows the enemy has hit Andersen and has effectively taken them out of the fight. The force here appears to be tasked with holding us tight to the base. Another force is reported to have landed at Haputo Beach and is driving right at North Finegayan. We believe that is their ultimate target, to knock out fleet comms. What we have here is a force designed to tie us down, plain and simple. Well, I say we fuck up their plans."

The mention of the North Finegayan Telecommunications Site caught Falto's attention. The site was a key communications facility for the Seventh Fleet and most of the Pacific commands.

"Our senior officers are all at the west end of the base and are currently cut off from us. I got a short message relayed from Lieutenant Fricks, and we have a plan based on an enemy amphibious assault on the base. Right now, Charlie Company under Lieutenant Debbs is engaging with them on the western flank here at the base. We are going to take the center and form up on Phase Line Charlie. Sergeant Parker is going to shift along the right flank. Our goal is simple—form a large kill box, get them in it, and take them out. We will contain their inland push, drive them back to wherever the hell they came from. Then we will move up the shoreline to North Finegayan and hit them there."

Falto nodded—the plan made sense to her. As a Marine she understood the concept of beachheads but in exercises she usually on the other side as the invading force. She felt comfortable with what the staff sergeant laid out for them.

"We are going to head out toward the docks up Sumay Drive and cut over on MacArthur; that's where we will establish our lines. Sergeant Parker and her platoon are going up our right flank and we need to make sure we are linked with her too, so we don't create an opening for the enemy to exploit. Carson, you'll run the Greyhounds out ahead of us, paint us a picture of what is out there. Per tactical plan one, keep the Huskies with our heavy gear to the rear until we need them.

"There's a complication. There are civvies in the battlespace. When we come across them, we move them back to the armory. Get this through your thick heads: the armory is our last line of defense. If things go south, we will fall back to that point. It will be our Alamo.

"All of you: if you see someone who is not US personnel, you *will* engage. We are going to pass a lot of buildings here; you will need to sweep them as we go. We are doing this by the numbers. I want tight fields of fire and make use of good cover. I don't want anyone rushing in until we know what we are up against. Follow my lead." He seemed to look her right in the eyes, as if he was only talking to Falto, then his eyes swept the rest of the Marines.

"I need you people crispy. This is what we trained for." The siren blared outside of the armory, almost drowning out his voice over the small speaker on the suit. "We do this as a unit, and we do it as professionals. You are *Marines*. Never forget that." There was something almost fatherly in his words . . . reassuring. Falto looked at her hand and saw she had a bit of a tremble. *It's not fear, it's the adrenaline.* Glancing to her side, she saw Reid Porter. His face was almost colorless and his eyes looked twice their normal size. *Now that's fear . . .* She had been spending her off-time working with Porter, despite the ribbing she had been getting from the others. He was getting better at being a combat Marine, toughening up. Going into battle would determine if she had been wasting her time. She hoped her hard work with him paid off.

They exited the Armory and immediately her senses came to life in the burst of brilliant sunlight and the smell of something burning. In the distance there was a cacophony of battle, the staccato of gunfire and muffled explosions that were unfamiliar to her. She knew the noises of most of the US weapons, which meant that these were something else. Staff Sergeant Rickenburg took the Devil Dog at a jog at the point position for the platoon. Each footfall on the concrete shook the Marines behind them as the Lion rig moved toward the sounds of battle. After a block, the staff sergeant's voice filled her earbud. "Alright, people, weapons free. Safeties off. Kick on your ACs. Carson, fire up your GRDs, send out the Greyhounds ahead of us, paint us a picture. The rest of you, bounding overwatch until we get into position, either side of the street. Falto, Porter, Appleton, Finch—you four follow me down the middle. Able fire team, you take the left flank."

Falto reached to her hip and turned on her active camouflage system. As the suit activated, she could see herself fade under a dull shimmer as the stealth system adapted to her surroundings, making her only semi-visible. In urban combat environments and in broad daylight, the systems were only partially effective, but if it saved her life, she was in favor of it. Slowly, she reached up with her thumb and disabled the safety.

Staff Sergeant Rickenburg slowed his gait to a walk and swept the streets side to side with the menacing M478 Scythe chain gun. Having the ASHUR II rig ahead of them made Natalia feel safer, but also strangely exposed in the middle of the street as the rest of the platoon split into two lines hugging the buildings. She glanced over at Porter and was surprised he had the presence of mind to turn on his camouflage system as ordered. *That kid is going to get someone killed if he's not careful. I just hope it's not me.*

A civilian rounded a corner, his arm locked around a wounded Marine. He was half-assisting, half-dragging the injured soldier in the opposite direction from where Falto was heading. The Marine's helmet was gone, his armor looked torn, or perhaps parts of it had been cut off in the fight. Wet crimson seeped through his remaining armor and showed in the seams between the STF armor packs on his thighs. His face was pale, almost gray, and she could see the fear and confusion in his eyes. She paused for just a moment as they made eye contact.

"Where do I take him?" the civilian asked. She glanced at his ID badge and only caught his last name, Chen.

"The infirmary is behind the Armory. Take him there and get yourself to the Armory."

"I have to go back," the civilian insisted. "There are other wounded."

Falto shrugged and took off. "Get someplace safe!" she called back to the man. She ran full out to catch back up with her platoon.

A few moments later, the staff sergeant stopped at MacArthur Drive and leaned forward, holding up one arm as a signal for the platoon to halt. "What the fuck . . . ?" he muttered over the open comm link. He slowly stepped back into cover. "Battlespace command—you seeing what I'm seeing?"

Natalia didn't hear the response from Lieutenant Fricks, but she could tell right away that she wasn't going to like it.

It took a moment before Rickenburg spoke again. "People, we are going to deploy out onto MacArthur. Enemy bogies are up ahead. Pull down your tactical displays and get the BS view active." Natalia activated the visor in her helmet. In the upper corner of her left eye, she could see a digital display of the battlespace. There were multiple red targets, at least fifteen, fanned out over a two-block area. There were some friendlies there too, other Marines and sailors who had been tagged. The Greyhounds were doing their job, giving a ground-view perspective of the battlefield.

Zooming out using only eye movements, she could see the larger battle. The enemy had come ashore and had a beachhead from the water's edge in an arc inland about an eighth of a mile. Charlie Company under Sergeant Lee was hitting the left flank of this and was taking losses, which showed digitally on her battlespace display. Sergeant Parker's force was to the far right, just beyond the enemy position. *And we are the center—the bait to lure them in.* Falto zoomed farther out for a more tactical view of her platoon.

Fricks's voice came in her earbuds. "Be advised, Bravo Company, First Platoon, enemy forces are advancing rapidly on your position. They are moving around the BOQ and will be on your flank shortly."

"Alright, we do this by the numbers. Hannibal has the center. Baker Fire Team will cross with me providing suppression fire and hug the building. Then two seconds later, right flank round the corner. I have no fucking idea what these things are. We are moving up past the inlet, one block, then engaging. You see anything that is not US personnel, you shoot it. You see something moving, you keep shooting it until it stops moving. Got that?"

A chorus of "yes, staff sergeant!" came back.

"Time we earn our pay," Rickenburg said. With surprising ease, he slid out into the middle of MacArthur Drive and Falto heard the short bursts from the Devil Dog chain gun purring, sharp streams of fire with the whir of its rotating barrels, engaging targets she couldn't see yet. "Advance!" he barked.

She rounded the corner and started up the street. Then she saw—*something.* They weren't human. They were like a two- or three-yards-tall crab hybrid, with six legs. The forward portion of the body turned upward, like a centaur, taller than two human beings. The front two legs had hideously dangerous pincers, massive, large enough to hold a human by the torso. The carapace was that of a giant scorpion or a lobster, greenish-blue in color. There were little bulges and bumps on their shells in weird places. They had flattened heads with grotesque mawlike jaws. Upright, it was taller than a human being, but it was clearly not of Earth. Some were half-climbing an office building, with three legs up, three on the ground, sticking their armored heads into broken windows. Many were going after troops down the road who had already engaged. Falto saw black smoke rising from one battle off to the west—and she wondered if that was one of their weapons or if it was the result of a Marine counterattack.

They had tails, long thick ones covered with exoskeleton plates that shimmered in the brilliant sunlight. The ends of the tails were scorpion-like, with a hooked spike. Her brain struggled to process what she saw, to make sense of the images. *Aliens. We are being attacked by freaking aliens.*

Even with his camouflage system, the Devil Dog was not easy to hide. The staff sergeant assumed a position behind a concrete barricade set along the street, his chain gun pumping short clusters of shots downrange into the crablike creatures. "Alright, Marines, pick your targets and fire. I want tight fire control." The sergeant's shots riddled one of the creatures, and while it recoiled slightly, it didn't seem phased. Another one he caught with a burst near the raised head torso and it jumped sideways. She saw a greasy green-black ooze coming from the bullet holes. *They bleed . . . good!* The creatures reeled under the gunfire, some falling, others recoiling. The staff sergeant seemed to be unerringly guiding his weapons fire on the aliens; Natalia could track his bursts perfectly as he moved and fired.

Falto hoisted her ACR-25, brought one of the insect/crab things in her sights and squeezed her trigger in controlled bursts, just as she had been trained to do. The bullets hit, but she didn't see ricochets or any sign of damage. The impacts made the target shake—Natalia could only hope they were inflicting pain. The erratic cracks of gunfire filled her ears all around her.

"What are these things?" Carson's voice wailed in terror.

"Shitcan the chatter," the staff sergeant barked. A stream of his chain gun rounds hit one of the legs of the creatures and severed it at the joint. The creature recoiled several steps on its remaining limbs—but then righted itself, ready to continue the fight. One of its limbs was a bulge that was being aimed like a weapon at the staff sergeant's Lion. If it was hurting him, Falto couldn't be sure. It was still moving as if the weapon had no effect. *What the hell are these things?*

The Devil Dog didn't hesitate under the alien's fire; it upped the ante. It unleashed one of its rockets downrange. The rocket snaked out and the creature seemed to try to dodge. The rocket must have lost its laser painting as it twisted down under the creature, because it exploded into the concrete. The impact was still impressive as the crablike monster rose in the air in the explosion and came down hard on its back, two of its legs twitching in the white smoke from the blast. As the smoke cleared, she could see the creature's lower exoskeleton had been ripped open; charred gore was strewn about the explosion site.

Falto took aim at another target, one of three of the creatures that were attacking a power transformer. They were firing a weapon that emitted a narrow white beam of some sort at the dull gray transformer. She targeted the alien's head and fired two shots. She must have hit something vital because the creature stopped firing at the transformer and turned as if to look at her. Its eyes were unlike anything she had ever seen, dark green, almost black, set back in its skin-armor. For a moment, she knew it was looking right through her visor, into her soul. Natalia didn't let her fear capture her, she kept firing single shots, well aimed. Her marksmanship was not off; Marines were the best marksmen on the planet. The problem was the target was shaking off the hits.

The creature lifted one of its front legs that had a bulbous black bulge on it, and pointed it up the street at Falto and the platoon. *A weapon!* She didn't know what it was, but it was being aimed and that made it deadly. "Hit the dirt!" she yelled, reaching forward and grabbing Porter's shoulder as she dove for better cover behind the corner of a building.

She hit the ground hard and her STF armor stiffened instantly on impact. There was a strange, high-pitched whooshing over her head. Twisting her neck she looked up and saw Henderson, only ten yards behind her, taking cover from another structure, get hit with a splatter of what looked like globs of wet green snot. Each hit of slimy goo was the size of a grape. From her position, she saw Henderson's camouflage system fail and watched him contract in pain.

Then she heard him scream.

It filled her ears and everyone else's over the platoon's tactical channel. It was agony, pure and simple. Natalia rushed back to where Henderson fell, with Porter right behind her. Natalia was on her hands and knees, carefully avoiding the globs of goo on the concrete.

Smoke rose from Private Henderson's STG U armor as he flailed at it. "It burns!" he cried as he fumbled with the straps, sliding out of line of fire with the enemy. Falto drew her knife and cut the gray straps, ripping his chest plate free.

Whatever that thing had fired, it was a corrosive. It had eaten holes right through his STF plates, the K-weave webbing and into his flesh. He wailed in pain, grabbing her arm. Looking at his face she saw where splattered droplets had eaten his visor, into and through his cheek. Through the inch-and-a-half-wide hole she could see his teeth and mangled gums and the horrible blisters on his tongue. Another blob of corrosive had hit his stomach, and she could smell the stink of feces, proof that it had torn deep into his guts.

She fumbled at his utility belt and pulled out a Numb-Shot, jabbing the penlike device in his arm. In a matter of moments, the sedative kicked in. His howls became whimpers. "Porter, signal the corpsmen." Gunfire snapped and popped all around her. She slowly let Henderson lay flat. "They'll get you out of here—you're going to be alright." Falto wondered for a millisecond if she had lied to him.

Turning back to the battle, Falto lifted her rifle and took a bead on the creature that had hit Henderson, but it looked as if Sergeant Parker had emerged from the right flank in her Hyena rig to deal with the creature. The Hyena was a lighter battle suit than the Devil Dog, fewer weapons, less armor, much faster. Natalia saw on her tactical display that Parker's platoon was spread out, almost to the water's edge, far more forward than she had expected. Her arrival was a welcome sight. *With two ASHURs here, how can we lose?*

Her Hyena's rail gun operated much like an L-Series laser, with shotgunlike slugs used to generate the energy it demanded. The big gun accelerated metallic slugs to hypersonic speeds with controlled magnetic pulses. It ate power madly, was slow to recharge and load, but when the slugs hit, they tore into anything. Almost at a full run, the sergeant fired one round into the head of the creature that had hit Henderson. The creature's skull exploded in a crimson spray. Just as that happened, though, the transformer that was being attacked exploded in a brilliant burst of sparks and an airborne fireball.

Sergeant Parker reeled around, her suit's rail gun firing every few seconds, tearing into the creatures. One of the aliens made a noise, a screeching howl unlike anything that Falto had ever heard. The aliens seemed to sense a new threat, and instead of falling back, they surged forward right at the Hyena. Sergeant Parker moved like a gymnast, running, shooting, almost dancing through the enemy forces, trying to keep some distance between her and their onslaught. People saw the ASHUR II suits and assumed they were slow and bulky, but Parker did a dance of death with the enemy, like an art form. One of her rail gun shots struck another crab-creature at the base of its neck. Its head exploded out the back with blackish-green mist.

Rickenburg fired short bursts, taking out another one of the creatures in a spray of deadly fire. Falto saw that the enemy was not being lured into their kill box, but was instead hitting Parker's flank and tearing it to shreds. She could make out one fire team falling back as it was slashed by some sort of grayish beam.

Staff Sergeant Rickenburg noticed it too. "Battlespace command, Sergeant Parker seems to be drawing them off to our right."

Lieutenant Fricks's voice came back. "We need them in the box. See if you can get their attention, Hannibal."

"Platoon, hold fast. I'm going to bring them in," he barked into the comm system. Natalia rose slightly, still in cover, and eyed the concrete barrier that had been used by the staff sergeant. It was good cover and gave a better angle on the street. She squatted low and ran for it with Porter right behind her.

Natalia saw another creature emerge from the chaos and smoke of the fighting. The creature was short, only three-and-a-half feet tall, and a greenish color. It had exoskeletal plates on its shoulders, but it looked more like pure muscle than armor. What served as "arms" were long, nearly to the ground, and were the thickness of a human's thighs. Its "hands" were flattened claws, webbed, with sharp white curved nails. The rear legs were short stumps, sharply bent.

The face was something out of a horror vid, making her cringe. Its bony lower jaw was jutting out in front of its head, creating a massive and deadly underbite, like a bulldog. It had thick white fangs curved upward not just in the front, and rows of spikelike teeth along the jawline. The back of the short creature was almost like a turtle shell, but much narrower. *How many of these aliens are there?*

The new creature moved right past Sergeants Parker, turning to the advancing Rickenburg in controlled hops, almost like a running gorilla. The powerful arms flung out in front of it while the back legs thrust hard, like a coiled spring. The creature would fly several yards, land, then spring again, moving at sharp angles. It was amazingly fast. It moved toward the troopers on her left, then suddenly turned to head back to the waterfront.

Natalia fired three bursts, hitting the midsection of the alien in mid-jump. The creature tumbled and for a moment she thought she had killed it. To her dismay, the creature rolled its head toward her and opened its mouth, as if threatening her. It was a hideous sight. The jaw was massive; its fanged mouth reminded her of an alligator. It hissed, grotesque and threatening. Then it rolled to its feet and lunged toward the water, past the fighting and into the smoke.

My bullets didn't even penetrate it.

The staff sergeant had advanced some twenty yards ahead. There were explosions of rockets going off as he targeted another giant crab-creature. As she reloaded, Falto glanced over at the first of the fallen aliens that the staff sergeant had killed. They were much larger than she had thought now that she was closer to it. There was a smell about them too. It reminded her of her childhood and the smell of something rotting on a beach.

No time for this shit. She raised her ACR and squeezed off two rounds into a front leg of one of the creatures. Another explosion cut off her line of sight as smoke rolled in, so she wasn't sure if she hit it. She wanted to follow the staff sergeant, but she knew that their best chance was to bring the enemy to them, engage at long range.

Suddenly Sergeant Parker went down with a ground-shaking thud, tangling with one of the crab-things at point-blank range as she moved forward into the enemy formation. One of its monstrous legs swung around and struck her hard, sending her Hyena rig skidding on the pavement and into a concrete planter, the planter shattering under the impact. The other nearby aliens sensed her weakness, Natalia could see that. They swarmed toward her as she struggled to get up. Another stabbed a leg at her left side armor with its massive tail stinger, scattering pieces of it on the roadway and leaving the majority as a gnarled, twisted reminder of the attack. Another lifted a leg with a bulblike protrusion on it and fired a weapon. A thin white stream stabbed out and cut across Parker's ASHUR suit. Bits of armor and technology peeled off under the hit. *God, that's a high-pressure water stream of some sort!*

Another creature raised its leg and seemed to fire something from a bump on that leg, causing the Hyena to stagger back. "Parker, fall back! My platoon can cover you. Get out of there!" Staff Sergeant Rickenburg called out over the open tactical channel. As Parker turned, Falto could see the extent of the damage. The water, under tight compression, had worked like a laser at close range. It had gouged a gash across the front plates of the Hyena rig, cutting it like a hot knife in butter. A glint of red was visible from Parker's wounds. She staggered three or four steps toward Falto's platoon, fighting gravity, balance and the injuries.

Then one of the creatures came up behind her and pounced.

The assault was savage. It drove its huge, narrow, clawlike front legs into the mangled battle suit from behind, just above the fuel cells, wrecking the armature that held her depleted LAW rack, tearing it into worthless, twisted scrap. It punched Parker's suit onto the concrete, grinding it face-first from the impact, tearing at one of her joints and spraying florescent green hydraulic fluid in the air like blood. The creature struck again and again, madly flailing at the downed trooper, sending pieces of armor and flesh flying into the air with each up-strike. Falto hoisted her rifle and fired, as did most of the squad, in a vain attempt to provide cover fire to Sergeant Parker, as did the remnant of the rest of her own platoon. Rickenburg unleashed another rocket at the same moment. There was a blast above the fallen sergeant, and when the dust and smoke cleared, there were only parts of the creature splattered about the roadway.

Two more of the creatures retreated at least thirty feet, apparently unsure of how to deal with the explosions. *Or maybe what hurts them is more than the shrapnel, it's the sound.*

It was too late. Her battlespace readout showed there was no longer a life signal coming from Sergeant Parker. She was dead. She had died a Marine's death. Civilians liked to think that ASHUR pilots were invulnerable. Watching Parker fall in a pitched battle underscored the mortality of the wearers of the armored tactical suits.

It was as if Staff Sergeant Rickenburg could sense the effect the loss of Parker had on his platoon, and he gave them focus. "Hold tight, people, I'm going to see if I can bring them to you." Huddled down behind the concrete barrier, she shifted her position slightly and rose to fire another shot. She fired at one of the creatures in the distance, fairly certain that she had hit. Her audible alert told her the magazine was empty. Without even looking at her weapon, she hit the release tab and dropped the empty mag, slapping another into her ACR and continued to squeeze off short bursts of three rounds downrange. True to her Marine Corps training, she knew these shots hit their mark—but was unsure if they had done any real damage. Porter lay on the other side of the barrier, firing away as well.

Sixty yards to the west, two of the crablike creatures latched their massive front claws onto a utility pole and clamped it hard. The pole crunched under the strength of their grip and toppled down with a shower of sparks and electrical cables dancing on the ground. Natalia fired several rounds at one creature, but they both moved behind a nearby building off to her left, apparently for cover. As the chain gun roared from the Lion, the aliens seemed to see him has their immediate threat. As they had done with Porter, they surged at him, moving with stunning speed.

Rickenburg tore into the crab-creature leading the charge. He tried to fall back several steps, but it wasn't fast enough. The alien's deadly front pincers tried to grapple with the Lion as he raised his left arm with the L-101 medium laser. She heard the hum and pop of a power shell discharging from the laser. She didn't see the impact—you never did with a laser—but the alien's leg made a hissing, popping noise then went limp, almost toppling the creature in the process. The alien recoiled, only to be caught in the fire from Marines firing their ACRs from Fire Team Baker on her left. It quaked under the impacts then dropped to the pavement.

Natalia saw another of the shorter aliens bounding forward, into one of the buildings on her left. It moved so fast, bounding from side to side, the Marines were having a hard time getting a bead on it. She tried for a shot but held back when she realized the folly. With a crazy twist, it jumped through the glass of a first-floor window and disappeared inside. She saw it emerge from another window, bullets flying all around it. It headed back to towards the Lion, running within twenty feet of Staff Sergeant Rickenburg as he continued to fall back, and aliens rushed towards him.

They're gathering intel—like Marine recon. But where are they taking it? Through the haze of dust and smoke, she saw the creature bound into the water in the distance. Another emerged almost instantly, breaking off to the far left toward Charlie Company. *How many of these things are scouting the battlespace?*

Without warning, a crab-creature emerged from between buildings off to her right, grabbing Private Dane in one of its forward claws and clamping hard. Dane screamed and in an instant was cut in half. The Marines near it fired, ripping it apart, sending bits of its flesh flying—but too late for Dane. Falto felt painfully exposed behind the barrier now that they were being hit on the right. "We need to fall back," she told Porter who only nodded in response.

"Here they come!" Rickenburg called out. "Watch your flanks, make sure we stay connected to Parker's platoon. Ling, take Baker fire team and secure our flank with Sergeant Lee's force on the left flank—there's a gap there now. Watch your fire patterns." His voice steeled their resolve as he riddled another giant crab creature.

She saw five more of the crab creatures burst out of the churning water and rush at the staff sergeant as he continued to step back. Two fired at Rickenburg's Devil Dog with their high-pressure water cutters. One missed, another seemed to hit. The staff sergeant staggered to the right slightly, responding with a burst from his chain gun that tore into two of the creature's legs, pulverizing the exoskeleton and making it look like a crab leg broken open for butter and consumption. "We almost have them," he bellowed over the comm channel.

Fearing another move on their right, Falto tossed a smoke grenade to give them cover. The acrid smoke added to the smells of the base-turned-battlefield, and after a few long seconds, she darted backwards some 20 feet and moved around a building, Porter right behind her. She felt something hit her back but whatever it was, it hadn't penetrated her STG, at least she didn't think so. When she got to the back, she checked with her hand but couldn't feel anything.

Suddenly her battlespace display flashed—incoming air support. *Drones!* They came from the north. The twin, light gray hover drones each carried a pair of tank-busting missiles, marked yellow on their nose tips. Moving off some fifty yards, they floated, acquiring targets, then unleashed their weapons. The missiles engulfed two of the crab-beasts in a blast of explosives, bits of roadway, and death. As they moved off, exhaust and smoke swirling under their rotors, she saw a torn up crater in the road and torn bits of the enemy on the street.

God bless Marine aviators. Those were some joyboys who earned their pay today . . .

"I wish these bastards would get tired of this shit and fall back like they're supposed to," Hernandez complained on the tactical channel.

"Can the chatter," Falto replied as she fired. That crater was excellent cover and close enough to the far side of the street if she had to move again. Falto broke into a sprint and dove for the still-smoldering holes in the roadway. They were not deep, only a foot or two, but it was enough. Next to her landed Reid Porter, his helmet damaged from something, probably his own clumsiness, his reflective blue visor cracked down the middle but in place. Looking at Porter, she felt more alone than ever in the makeshift foxhole.

A pair of crabs rushed past the staff sergeant's ASHUR and headed straight at her position. One of the Marines on the left side of the street, she thought it might be Private Martinson, fired his grenade launcher at the crab that was closing fastest. The results were spectacular as the explosion devoured the left legs of the lead alien. Another explosion sealed the deal, forcing the crab to sidestep between buildings. The other alien creature seemed to recoil, only to be fired on in the kill box the Marines formed. It was being hit on three sides with precise bursts. Within moments both aliens were dead, their bodies wreathed in smoke and whatever the ooze was that came out of them.

Far up the road, near the waterway on the left flank was an olive drab Marine Amphibious Combat Vehicle (ACV). She checked it through her scope and saw that the tank was battered, apparently having tangled with some of the alien's acid spray, but still operational. The front left side of the vehicle looked as if it had been melted, the armor rent. The Marine gunner on the top unleashed the machine gun on the creatures that were still rushing the staff sergeant. Rickenburg fired his laser as well; Falto could hear the pop of the shell and the low-pitched electrical hum of the discharge. Both creatures charging the staff sergeant went down, one twitching its legs furiously. *He's awfully close to the edge of the water . . . does he know that that's where they are coming from?* While the ACV was maintaining distance from aliens already ashore, there was no way to know how many more might emerge.

Natalia's battlespace display in her visor showed a grim picture. The aliens' beachhead was far from contained. They were seemingly unafraid, punching holes in the Marines' lines everywhere. On the left flank, the remnants of Parker's platoon were holding their own but were starting to lose ground. The right flank was fragmented—more enemy signals than Marines. The center, where she was, was still holding. These were clearly not mindless creatures. Their losses were being replenished from the water's edge at a steady pace. The creatures were moving up on both flanks. Once they pressed that advantage, things were going to get dicey. *If we can't consolidate our lines, we're going to be whittled away.*

One crablike creature in the distance raised its front leg and pointed it down the street. The bulbous growth on its leg was large, with veinlike feeds going back along the leg into the body of the creature. The staff sergeant turned to face the new threat—but not fast enough. There was a deep, bone-shaking roar that filled her ears. The ground shook and Falto tried to flatten in the crater, but the ground was vibrating under the attack. Even with the earbuds, her ears popped painfully and the sounds of the battle became muffled. Her vision tunneled for a moment and she was worried she was about to pass out. Dust rained in around her.

As she regained her focus, she saw Rickenburg stagger back from the sonic attack. Her eyes hurt as much as her ears. She shook her head and saw a splatter of blood on her weapon. Her nose was bleeding and she tasted copper on the back of her tongue. There was a small red blur in her right eye that she opted to ignore. A drizzle of blood dripped down the bottom of her visor onto her armor, exposing plates of her adaptive camouflage as a result. *Great—a sound weapon.*

The gunner on the ACV must've been a hardass because the tracked ACV's heavy machine gun focused on the alien, tearing it apart under a stream heavy-caliber fire—though the sound was muffled as her ears ached from the sonic burst. The staff sergeant got his bearing and opened up with his grenade launcher at the new enemy formation, running across the street and firing at the creatures emerging from the waterfront. On impact, the grenades tore into the creatures. One twisted and dodged the incoming grenades, jumping at the staff sergeant and swinging its massive forward claw at the Devil Dog. It hit the staff sergeant's rig hard and sent him skidding and rolling across the concrete only twenty yards up from Falto's impromptu foxhole.

Hannibal needs help! Falto rose from her cover and fired at the attacker. The adaptive camouflage system on the ASHUR II flickered on and off for a moment, then failed completely. Using his toppled rig as cover, Falto fired at the crab, as did the rest of her fire team, tearing at its armored head and torso. It jabbed its claw again at the ASHUR, hitting it hard in the leg, caving in the armor there. Then it flopped over, its big tail twitching. She reached him and saw the damage to the front of his rig. Nasty gashes had ripped through his armored plates. His transparent blast-proof faceplate was spiderwebbed with damage. Like her, he had a bloody nose.

"You okay, Staff Sergeant Rickenburg?" she asked, her voice sounding muffled.

"We need to get them in the kill zone, Falto," he said, struggling, rising up to his knees, then eventually onto his feet. Rickenburg was right. His attempt to get their attention was working. A half dozen of the aliens were forming up, surging at him. "Get to cover—I'm bringing them in," he said as he twisted the ASHUR and rose to his feet. Falto felt a surge of energy as she rushed back to the crater and cover. *This is what victory feels like!* Her ears strained to re-pop.

The staff sergeant stood his ground, firing bursts at the crabs, centering their attention on him. The ACV moved back slightly along the shore, attempting to provide flanking fire for Rickenburg. Smoke curled in the air from the far end of the base where their barracks was located and explosions quaked the ground under her. The battle was consuming Big Navy.

Lieutenant Fricks's voice came to her muffled eardrums. "Watch your right flank. Sergeant Parker's platoon, I need you to retrograde fifty yards and secure a fire position at the athletic center. Sergeant Lee, press forward, tighten your flank. Sergeant Lee—respond—" She could tell from the sound of his voice that things were getting out of hand.

Then, at the edge of the water, Falto saw motion. One of the small hopping recon creatures emerged, just for a moment, then dove back into the deep water. Then she saw what looked like a pair of massive claw-like hands emerge on the concrete edge of the berth not far from the staff sergeant. In that moment of terror, she was reminded of the old movie, *Creature of the Black Lagoon*—that's what the hands of the creature looked like, only much larger and more menacing.

The claws lifted an ebony blur from the water, rising nearly fifteen feet in the air and landing on the concrete of the dock area with such force that she felt the quaking where she stood. The massive creature charged, rushing forward on massive tree-thick legs. It ignored the ACV and darted right at the ASHUR. The impact was enough to nearly topple the Devil Dog's balance; she saw the staff sergeant teeter slightly. The creature's feet crushed into the concrete and they sank nearly six inches on impact. Despite its quick movements, the creature was still taller than the staff sergeant's Lion rig. *It's huge—it must weigh tons . . .*

This is something new, something menacing. It was the first of the creatures that appeared even remotely human, though clearly it wasn't. Its skin . . . *or is it armor?* was jet black. There were streaks on the skin of light maroon and green, no discernible pattern that she recognized. Its hide or skin reminded her of a stingray she had seen once as a child at the aquarium, leathery yet oddly resilient. It was bipedal and taller than an ASHUR rig by at least two feet if not more. From the sound of its landing, it had to weigh much more. Like the ASHURs, it seemed to be outfitted with weapons. These were not attached like the Devil Dog's but seemed to be part of the body, as if they were bundles of additional muscles, elongated bunches that looked like menacing weapons.

It's a tactical suit of some sort . . . it has to be. The head was a flattened oblong shape that in profile looked like a football but was flatter and rounder, vaguely reminiscent of a hammerhead shark with some human features. A glossy black visor-like plate covered its face. The hands were crablike claws with an extra appendage that seemed to work as a thumb. Unlike ASHUR systems, there were no hydraulic hoses, nothing exposed. It was smooth, with muscular ripples. She saw what she thought were hoses, but they looked like thick veins under its fleshy armor. It stepped out of the holes made from its landing and she could see that its legs ended not in humanoid feet, but three claws, spread out, with deep bluish webbing between them and tipped in nasty hooked nails that looked as if they could dig into the concrete if the operator wanted them to.

Staff Sergeant Rickenburg turned on it at point-blank range, firing his chain gun in a tight burst. Unlike the crablike creatures, this massive alien didn't cringe. Instead it swept its huge arm to the side, striking the Lion rig hard, lifting it off the ground and sending it crashing to the concrete yards away. The ACV opened up with its heavy machine gun, its bullets thwacking into the side of the creature, which gave Staff Sergeant Rickenburg time to recover. The large-caliber bullets hit it, marring the skin, but from where she stood, they didn't seem to penetrate it. *Those .50 caliber rounds go through brick walls . . .*

The creature spun slightly and took off, its footfalls sounding like a pile driver on the concrete. It moved amazingly fast for its size, its strides almost double that of an ASHUR rig. It broke into another sprint toward the ACV. The driver started to back it up, trying desperately to get some distance in, but the creature was faster. It was on the ACV in less than three heartbeats. A quick sweep of its arm collided with the gunner in the top mount. The machine gun and the gunner's head went flying. The gunner's head rolled a good thirty feet onto the spent brass and bits of debris in the road.

Rickenburg staggered the Devil Dog to its feet. "New target. Concentrate your firepower, people," he barked, emptying his last canister of grenades into the new enemy. The explosions caused the hulking figure to take a step back, but that was all. Out of the water, two more crablike creatures appeared and charged at the Devil Dog, running the 80 yards or so with a scurry of their hard pointed feet. Their appearance forced the staff sergeant to break off firing at the black humanoid creature and engage the new targets. Rickenburg emptied the ammo drum, leaving nothing more than alien body parts from the crabs. For a second, she heard the empty purring of the chain gun. *He's got a reserve, not much, but some.*

The Devil Dog's L101 laser banged then hummed as Natalia's right ear re-popped. The laser beam was invisible, but she could see from the smoky streak that the staff sergeant had hit the ebony enemy in its left arm. It twisted under the attack, enough to signify some sort of pain. It then turned and raised the injured arm, pointing it at the Lion rig.

Falto emptied her magazine into the torso of the creature, but saw no sign that her shots were affecting it. In the muffled haze of noise, she heard other members of the unit fire around her. It was in their kill box, but was not going down.

The creature kept its focus on the Devil Dog. One of the bulges under its skin puffed out and collapsed, obviously firing something, targeting the Lion rig. The staff sergeant had been hit, but there had been almost no noise from the attack. She didn't see a projectile, there was no retort, but something had been fired. She heard him moan audibly and saw the armored warrior stagger back from the mysterious weapon. "Keep your fire up on this bastard but start to fall back. If pressed, fight a holding action to the armory. You can make a stand there," he spat onto the comm channel, obviously in agony. Natalia checked her battlespace display. Sergeant Parker's former platoon was already starting to fall back to their new position, exposing their flank more than she liked. Rickenburg had spotted it before she had, testimony to his battlefield prowess. *With them falling back, our right flank is wide open and more enemies are coming out of the water.* Staff Sergeant Rickenburg knew what he was doing.

"We won't leave you," Hernandez screamed back.

"Do it. I've got this bastard," he replied. The ASHUR tactical suit lunged forward, slower than before, but charging at the new enemy.

The survivors of the platoon didn't argue but instead started falling back to the rear in good order. Hernandez was just ahead of Falto and Porter was behind her. They were almost to the other side of the street when Hernandez's body suddenly jerked, like a puppet being violently shaken on the end of its strings. There was a hint of crimson mist as she skidded across the pavement, leaving a streak of blood.

Natalia slid next to her, raising her weapon. She saw the attacker, a new crab creature rising on top of the wreckage of the ACV near the massive black armored alien—now 100 yards away. She aimed at its flat head, hitting it with bullets in three controlled bursts that would have made her range coach proud. When her magazine emptied, she dumped it and reloaded, firing half of the new mag as other members of the fire team opened up at it. The creature collapsed on its side, its legs spreading like a massive spider. Falto concentrated the rest of her magazine on the ebony warrior that now turned its attention back to the Lion. It bolted at it again, moving in for the kill.

The staff sergeant punched his arms like a boxer at the black-skinned creature. He concentrated on the head of the alien, using the straight edges where the blast plates were jointed on his armored arms almost like dull knives, concentrating the force of his punches. The blows hit with enough force to rip through the door of a car, but there was no sign of damage on the alien other than it rocking under each strike. Falto reloaded and fired another burst at it, hitting it in the thigh, but it shook it off as if the bullets hadn't hit.

She turned for a moment to Hernandez and saw her arm had been chewed almost into hamburger. There were dozens of three-inch needlelike projectiles sticking out of her. She was ashen in color and her breathing was labored. Porter slapped a freeze pack onto her hemorrhaging arm and pulled the tab. She felt dangerously exposed, something that was instinctively bad. The freeze pack activated, temporarily freezing the wound and stopping the bleeding. Freeze packs damaged tissue, but they were faster and more effective than a tourniquet and often made the difference between life and death. Falto was surprised; Porter had done good—he had probably saved Hernandez's life.

She activated her comm link to battlespace command. "Corpsman on my position," she called.

"None available," came back an audible response from the battlespace command.

"Damn it," she swore.

Porter shook his head. "I already signaled. We're on our own," he said, firing to assist the staff sergeant.

Hernandez spoke in a strained voice. "I can make it." She patted Porter on the arm as a thanks for his aid.

Falto craned her head back around to seek out a target as Staff Sergeant Rickenburg staggered back from a blow from the creature, struggling to keep his balance. He opened up with his remaining chain gun ammunition reserve at his foe, and tried to move back, attempting in vain to keep some distance between them. The chain gun roared then hummed as the reserve ammunition depleted.

The staff sergeant popped the armored forearm cover over the canister of pressurized coolant for the chain gun. Falto was surprised by the move. *What is he doing?* He aimed the arm at the face of the creature and, using his other arm, hit the manual release. The pressurized cylinder fired like a rocket squarely into the face of the creature. The cylinder hit hard, then spun off wildly. *I had no idea a rig could do that.* Rickenburg's prestige went up another notch in her mind.

The chain gun barrage had obviously hit the enemy armored suit in the left forearm. It staggered for a moment. There was a hissing sound and she saw what looked like a blackened water and thick goo squirting out from a hole. *Are their suits filled with water?* The creature reached over to its arm and seemed to twist it . . . *off.* It disconnected at the elbow joint. *It just disconnected its own arm!* Her mind reeled at the concept, trying to process what she was seeing.

The staff sergeant's Lion was drenched with the liquids that had come out of the severed arm. The heat from his rig's fuel cells was so hot that the liquid sizzled and crackled. The creature stepped forward with its good arm, holding its severed limb like a club, and began to pummel the staff sergeant.

The blows to the Devil Dog were savage, mauling his chest armor and armored cockpit glass. Rickenburg lurched back a step under each brutal impact, but the alien closed the distance. The hits made a dull thudding sound, and a few made the metal internal frame of the rig moan under the stress.

Rickenburg stunned Falto again by ducking under one savage blow, using his now-useless chain gun like a battering ram on the creature's neck. The enemy staggered back a step, but only for a second. Falto fired two bursts at the monstrosity, hoping to get its attention, but it was focused on the staff sergeant. She couldn't see Rickenburg's face but she imagined him grinning at his foe.

The creature swung the club again, and on its second blow, the staff sergeant twisted the Lion around, closing the distance between them and coming under the swing of the club. He moved the suit as if it were part of his skin, not hundreds of pounds of armor and firepower. Rickenburg head-butted the Lion into the face of the enemy, cracking his armored glass in the process.

There was a scream from off to her right, and Falto saw Foster hit with a barrage of the needlelike projectiles from one of the crab creatures that had emerged from around the corner of a building. Foster's right leg's armor was ripped to shreds by the impacts and he collapsed, his adaptive camouflage flickering off as he went down. The attack wasn't as severe as the attack on Hernandez, but he was badly injured. Private Rogers jumped up and pulled him back behind a concrete potted planter and laid down fire that drove the alien back around the corner.

Falto surveyed the scene in front of her. The two combatants had somehow gotten some distance between them, only a few yards, but more than she expected. Rickenburg was moving slowly, almost limping. One of the hydraulic hoses behind his leg leaked a sickly green fluid onto the street. Smoke rose from where he must have been sprayed with one of the creature's acid weapons; it was burning through his armor in a hundred places. The staff sergeant was injured, battered but still there. He backed off to her left, trying once more to get some distance between him and the creature. The bipedal alien raised its remaining arm and fired another burst into the Lion, still holding its severed limb in its claw.

Then it swung its arm back and tossed its severed limb at Rickenburg's rig. The severed forearm slammed into him, crunching the armor where it hit. The staff sergeant seemed to shake it off, but his movements slowed even more. She could see on his rig's torso where it had caved in the armor.

Two more crab-creatures emerged, not on the street but on the roof over the office building off to the left. They dropped down about ninety feet from the members of her platoon who were falling back on that side of the street. The Marines there laid down a pattern of intense fire, dropping back to give themselves more distance from their attackers. One of the creatures had a two-foot-long gray pod-looking device in its claws. It held it over its head and fired at the Marines.

There was a hissing noise and a blue-black liquid sprayed onto the members of her platoon on the other side of the street. As the black liquid reached them, it seemed to evaporate into an iridescent, oily blue mist. The Marines caught in it screamed. Foster rolled out of the cloud, his fingers clawing at his throat. He looked as if he were covered in black charcoal. His tongue was huge, swelling in his mouth, and his eyes looked red—then she realized they were bleeding.

Gas! The Marines trained in gas, but no one had used it against the US military since World War I. The battlespace display showed their green lights flicker to black as the three of them died. From the thick black cloud, two troopers, Franks and Kozin, staggered out of the mist, hacking horribly. Their STG urban armor plates fell off with each step, their K-weave webbing seeming to melt in ugly globs down their uniforms that were also dissolving. Their flesh was already looking burned, bright crimson with blisters. *That stuff is caustic.* She tried not to imagine what they were feeling.

Turning to the enemy that had killed her comrades, she fired four precise controlled bursts, aiming at the gas weapon the alien held. She hit it, and could see that it was leaking fluid that almost instantly became the blue-black mist and engulfed the crab creature. The crab flailed about, finally releasing the pod. It craned its ugly head around at her as she replaced her magazine and fired at its eyes. The creature staggered back, blinking a thin gray membrane over its visor-like eyes, then falling backward, hopefully in agony.

Lieutenant Fricks's voice came in her one working ear. "Our lines are folding. All units are ordered to fall back to the armory. Repeat, retrograde to the armory. Evacuate any and all civilians you can along the way." This was a message broadcast to all companies.

Things are falling apart not just here but everywhere. They surprised us, caught us with our officers out of place, and hit us with technology that is different from ours. Damn them!

"You heard the man, Falto," came a ragged voice in her earpiece. It was Rickenburg, fighting for each breath from the sound of it. "The mission is yours now. Take care of the platoon. Get them back to the Armory." She could hear agonizing pain in his voice. He fired the last of his rockets at the armored creature, but the shot went wide and missed, sending parts of an office building spinning into the air. An explosion two blocks away, a mortar barrage, gave her some hope. Fire support meant that not everyone was dead.

"Negative, Staff Sergeant, we won't leave you," she replied through her throat mike.

"Don't make me crawl over and kick your ass," he sputtered. "Get our people out of here, fall back. Save this platoon to fight another day. Adapt. Improvise . . ."

Overcome . . . "Yes, Staff Sergeant." As she spoke, the black bipedal alien moved toward the Devil Dog. Rickenburg rushed the alien with his last burst of strength. The massive creature punched the ASHUR II tactical suit with its remaining arm, knocking it to the ground. It planted a foot on the suit. She heard the staff sergeant's agonized cry as the alien drove its foot down hard, through the suit, into the concrete. Falto could feel the ground shake under the foot's impact. The crunch of the armor made her stomach pitch. She looked at her battlespace display and the staff sergeant's green signal was overlaid by a black X.

The greatest warrior she had ever known was dead.

She centered herself on his last words. "Adapt . . . improvise . . ." and the word he didn't say, "*overcome.*" *It's my first combat mission and I have to cover a retreat.* People liked to believe that Marines didn't re- treat, but in reality they did what they had to in order to achieve the mission objectives—including tactical withdrawals. "Carson, send me the Husky," she said through gritted teeth. Falto grabbed Porter by his helmet strap. "You see that building—" she pointed three long blocks back to the base's records center, "—that's where we're going. We'll use that as a waypoint for covering the street. Move!" Even with the flick- ering adaptive camouflage of Porter's STG gear, she could see that the man nodded his head.

Falto switched to the broader tactical channel, giving her access to the battered remnants of both her platoon and Sergeant Parker's. "I need fire teams to execute a retrograde movement to the east. Our first phase line is the records building. We will hold there. Carson, Porter, Thompson, Mackelroy, I want suppression fire on that *thing* that killed the staff sergeant." ACR fire popped all around her.

Porter grabbed Hernandez. "Marines, we are executing our reposi- tioning. Follow me." He dragged the unconscious form of Hernandez behind him.

In that moment, she felt a sense of pride. *All of those hours of work- ing with the kid, and he looked downright heroic.* The other Marines sprang into action, following him and firing. A recon drone hovered over the Marines—proof that some of the joyboys were still in the fight. *It would be better if it were armed . . .*

The Husky GRD trotted up beside Falto like a faithful dog, obliv- ious to the carnage around it. One of its side protective plates was corroded, no doubt by an alien gas attack—but it seemed operational. The four-legged ground drone carried on its back the massive rail gun. *Why the hell had Carson packed the rail gun? I was hoping for a Carl Gustaf.* That was something that could be sorted out later. *Work with what you've got . . .* that was how she'd been trained. She undid the strap and pulled the heavy free. She had fired one of these in training only a few weeks before. Falto toggled on the power; the gun throbbed to life in her hands. She loaded a large five-round magazine of shells that generated power into the gun. It was so heavy, she could barely move with it. She rose in a hunched stance, resting her elbow on her knee to prop it up. Falto tied the target scope of the heavy weapon into her visor display using the link on the gun's side.

Natalia activated the targeting link to her helmet and focused the red reticle on one of the approaching crab creatures, firing as she drifted the crosshairs across her enemy. The shell exploded in a burst of energy that made the weapon hum. The recoil was light but was still there. The hypersonic slug hit the creature in one of his upper legs, ripping its menacing claw off. "That left a mark," she sarcastically spat. The creature tipped down and stopped its advance. She felt something sting her left shoulder and heard the Husky topple over onto the road in front of her, metal grinding into concrete. Instinctively she moved behind it for cover, propping up the big rail gun and crouching.

Natalia looked at her shoulder and saw her adaptive camouflage had failed on her left arm. Two large needles had penetrated her STF plates and lodged in her shoulder. She pulled them out, but they hurt. "Little fuckers are barbed . . . great." Her arm went numb fast. *Poisoned too.*

She picked up the heavy rail gun and felt the numbness creep into her fingertips and her shoulder. As she moved the weapon, the targeting reticle in her visor moved across the creature that was now walking toward her from remains of the Devil Dog. She slowly squeezed the firing stud and the massive weapon fired a power shot then hummed and kicked as a round went downrange. Even with the light recoil, her balance was thrown off.

It hit the creature mid-torso, sending it toppling backward, its impact shaking the ground around her. *Got you, you bastard!* She twisted, bringing the rail gun to bear on the closest of the crab creatures, now only twenty-five feet away. The moment the targeting reticle crossed the creature's neck, she fired.

The shell discharged and the big gun hummed in a recharge cycle then pulsed, and the creature's head began to flail about wildly, spraying a thick fluid into the air. The creature rushed toward her only to collapse a few yards in front of her, dead.

The numbness from the needle attack started to spread to her upper chest. *It's cold . . . why is it so cold?*

She focused. In the distance she saw the bipedal creature rise. Her shot had hit it, but it was still alive, still in the fight. As if to accentuate its anger, she saw that some of the light-colored stripes on its hide shimmer and glow slightly, some a dull red, others a brilliant green. *What does it take to kill these things? We're going to need more than ASHUR suits, that's for sure.*

"Porter . . . are you and the others in the records building? Tell me you are clear," she muttered into her throat mike as she momentarily collapsed onto the hot pavement.

"Roger that, Falto, we're here and we are positioned to cover you," she heard him scream into her earpiece. She felt a moment of pride. She had done what the staff sergeant had told her to do. She had fulfilled his final order, just not the way he would have envisioned it. Her chest, no, her heart ached. It was like heartburn only a thousand times worse.

The bipedal alien stopped at one of the fallen crab creatures and picked up a leg. It seemed to be adjusting its grip on it. *Oh shit, that's one of their weapons!* She moved with a burst of energy, dropping behind the already damaged Husky as the black creature sprayed globules of deadly acid in her direction. Some hit her shoulder pads, but the Husky she was using for cover bore the brunt of the hit. It smelled like an electrical fire mixed with raspberries as it corroded the ground drone. She used her fighting utility knife to cut off the damaged shoulder pad just before the acid ate through it. The aroma from it stung her blood-clogged nostrils and made her eyes sting.

She battled the numbness creeping through her body. *I've got to fulfill the staff sergeant's last orders.* In a burst of energy, she rose and sprinted for the records center to rejoin the rest of her platoon. The reassuring rattling of gunfire off to her right gave her hope. *We are still in this fight!*

CHAPTER 27

USS *Virginia*, patrol station over the Chinook Trough,
Pacific Ocean

Commander Titus Hill reached the command center as soon as he
could. He had been asleep, but when the call came, he sprang to action.
He was still tucking in his shirt as he strode into the room. Captain
Stewart was on the raised watch station deck with the periscopes, looking over a message. "Reporting as ordered, sir."

"We had Flash traffic via the ELF," Stewart said in a low tone. "I've
authenticated it. I want you to see it before I pass it on to the crew." He
handed the printout to Hill.

> >>>>>TRANSMIT 007.1551 FLASH Level 5 ENCRYPT
> COMSUBPAC TO ALL COMMANDS ... DEFCON 1, WAR
> ALERT CODE 001<<<<<
>
> As of 1045 HRS Hawaii-Aleutian TZ, JB Pearl Harbor
> Hickam and Guam are under attack by forces of
> unknown origin. All Navy vessels are authorized to
> respond to any aggressive operations with war-level
> responses per Revised ROE Document 002.050. This
> is not an exercise. Release of conventional weapons
> is authorized for the duration of the crisis, nuclear
> weapons are LD mode pursuant to ROE. EOM

Titus didn't say anything for a moment. He knew the Rules of
Engagement document; it was new from DoD a month ago. It provided individual boat commanders a great deal of latitude in dealing with
encounters like those the *Virginia* had experienced. Even Stewart said
it must have been a reaction to the reports he had sent up about their
unknown sonar contacts.

"Mr. Hill," Captain Stewart said. "We are about to go into harm's way." Titus gave him a single nod of acknowledgment. Stewart reached out to the comms stack and activated the ship-wide switch, pulled the microphone up to his mouth and drew a deep breath before speaking.

"Crew of the USS *Virginia*, this is your captain. We have just received word that US forces at Pearl Harbor and Guam are under attack by an enemy of unknown origin. The Joint Chiefs have placed us at DEFCON One. We are at war." His words were solid, direct, and oddly reassuring.

"We are going to War Alert Level One, and we have been authorized to respond to any suspicious contacts as if they are a threat.

"The last time we were on this footing was when the Russians invaded Alaska. I know a lot of you are going to be experiencing a mix of emotions right now. Clear your heads and focus on your duty. Rely on your training and our procedures. You are the best attack-boat crew in the Pacific fleet, and this is the finest ship in the Navy. Respond as you've trained and drilled to respond, and we will prevail. I will keep you posted once we receive details." He shut off the mike and put it down.

"Mr. Hill. Set Condition One throughout the ship. Comms, send our confirmation code to the FLASH message, authorization Tango, Alpha, Zero, Bravo."

"Aye, sir," Hill replied, turning to Chief of the Boat Simmons. "Mr. Simmons, you heard the captain. Set Condition One ship-wide. Load torpedo tubes. Extend the ELF antenna for transmission." The ELF system was a slow communications system but allowed the US boats to receive orders while submerged. It was tied to a deep underground antenna array somewhere in the upper peninsula of Michigan.

Simmons barked out a string of orders. The crew snapped into action. In the command center, there were no murmurs of concern or speculation, only action. A yellow warning light went on, a less-than-subtle reminder that the ship was possibly going into battle.

Captain Stewart leaned down from the elevated watch station toward Titus. "I'm going to be counting on you, Commander. Things are likely to get dicey soon. If that happens, the crew needs to know that you and I are thinking and acting as one. Understood?"

"Yes, sir." His mind went to his mother and sisters, and he knew they would be worried about him. For one brief moment, he contemplated his life what could have been. *I never got married and had kids of my own . . . it wouldn't have been fair with me gone so much. Will I ever get a chance at a normal life now?* He could only hope that the members of his family were okay.

No time for this . . . now is the time for duty first . . .

***

Hill was finally on his assigned watch. After the DEFCON One announcement he had gone back to his berth, but sleep was evasive. He guessed that few of the boat's personnel were going to be getting sleep. No other information had been forthcoming over the ELF. *Hell, the war could be over for all we know.* The crew were gossiping, muttering just under their breath about the Chinese or the Russians. Titus wasn't so sure. The vessels that the *Virginia* had tracked over their tour were bigger and faster than any boat ever put in the seas. While he felt assured that it was not the work of the Russians or Chinese, he still didn't know who it was.

The captain didn't seem to sleep at all. Captain Stewart paced the boat. He had been in the command center several times when he normally would have slept. The captain didn't say anything, he just paced, occasionally patting sailors on the back. *Everyone is edgy, I guess.* Captain Stewart leaned against the raised platform and crossed his arms, seemingly lost in thought.

The quiet was shattered when Lieutenant Hawkins spoke up from his BSY workstation. "Conn—Sonar. I have a Sierra contact one-point-nine miles out. Designating as Sierra One."

Titus didn't wait for confirmation. "Sound General Quarters," he replied. "Battle stations." The yellow warning light went red and the comms officer transmitted the alert throughout the ship. Captain Stewart sprang like a cobra, bounding up onto the watch station. "I've got the bridge, Mister Hill."

"Aye, sir."

"Sonar, any ID on Sierra One?"

Hawkins was adjusting controls. "Got her on passive sonar, sir. Vessel is moving parallel to us, three-three-four-one yards off our port stern. Her speed is at twelve knots. Depth is 312 feet, sir."

"Torpedo room, stand by," Stewart said. Simmons arrived at the control center from his berth and relieved Chief Petty Officer Hammond. The grizzled old sailor wasn't about to let his boat go into battle with someone else at con.

"Sonar, I want a firing solution now on that Sierra. Paint me a TMA and do it now," Stewart barked.

"Aye, sir. We're having a hard time getting confirmed readings on the target. It's like that one a couple of months ago, drifting between metallic and bio."

"So our mystery boat is back . . ." Stewart said.

"Shall I go to active sonar, sir?"

"Not yet, Mr. Hawkins."

Five seconds later, the sonarman tensed in his seat. "New signal!" Hawkins said. "Small target, fast moving. She's launched something at us, sir."

"All ahead full," Stewart ordered. Simmons chimed in. "Helm, maximum rotations." The *Virginia* slowly lunged forward.

"Is that a torpedo, Sonar?"

Hawkins shook his head. "Too quiet, sir. It's not any kind of torpedo in the warbook. She's closing with us fast. Busy calculates impact in 30 seconds on my mark—mark!"

"Chief," Stewart barked. "Stand by on countermeasures. Helm, we will be going hard to port, sixty degrees. Standby on the dive planes. I want us taken down to 350 at my command."

The command center was alive, as if it were a living entity. Titus moved in behind Hawkins and watched as the mystery object approached. "She's closing, sir," he said. "Too slow to be a Russian fish. Her readings are only trace metal. She's twenty seconds to impact."

Stewart's voice roared. "Launch countermeasures, hard to port. Take us down, Chief."

The *Virginia* leaned into the tight turn and the crew grabbed onto anything close; Titus put his hand on the rail of the watch station as she made the arc of her turn, leaning into the curve. There was a popping noise and whirring which became distant as the countermeasure deployed. Chief Simmons called out, "Countermeasures launched, sir."

"The fish isn't going after them, sir—but it did seem to slow down when the measures were launched. Impact in 7 . . . 6 . . . 5 . . ."

Stewart grabbed the mike. "All hands brace for impact!" Titus repeated the order, though he doubted anyone in the crew could have missed it.

"2 . . . 1 . . ."

Titus braced hard for the explosion that he was sure would end his life and that of the crew. What happened instead was a dull thud against the hull. It was a hard hit, but not explosive. For a second, he waited, then he relaxed his grip. "What the hell was that?"

"Damage report," Stewart called out. Chief Simmons signaled each of the key stations on the boat to ascertain their status. "No damage, sir."

"A dud?" Titus asked.

"Get me at TMA on that ship, Hawkins."

"Sir, I can't on our passive sonar. I've run through all of the bands, sir. Recommend going active."

"Do it!"

"Active sonar on."

The ping of the outbound sonar signals rang from the speaker. "Whoa! Sir. Target is slowing—but only when they get our pings. It's like it's confusing them."

"Tighten the cycle of the signals then. Get me a lock on that boat."

"I'm working it, sir!"

Suddenly, there was an explosion that rocked the *Virginia* hard, shaking it violently side to side. Titus fell to the deck and he saw Stewart come down head first on the railing of the watch deck just above him. Whatever had hit the ship had gone off, delayed. Warning alerts sounded and the red light flickered on and off. The captain was sprawled on the raised watch deck, his hand hanging just over the edge.

Commander Hill rose as a yeoman bent over the limp form of Captain Stewart. The older man's head was limp, wobbly. His neck seemed bent at an odd angle. "I think he's dead, sir."

Titus ignored that for the moment. "Damage report, Chief!"

Simmons worked furiously at the controls, and Titus caught bits of his conversations.

"How bad, Chief? Can you seal it?"

Chief Simmons turned to him. "We have a leak in the torpedo room, sir. It's like something burned a series of tiny holes in the hull. We're taking on water but the pumps are running. We cannot stay down too long before we have to seal it." The concern was made more serious by the fact that the torpedo room was directly under the command center, one deck down.

"Is the reactor still online?"

"Still active, sir," called the lieutenant manning the power systems. Nuclear reactors, no matter how they were reinforced, were dangerous beasts—that's what he had been taught since he joined the Navy. The fact she hadn't automatically shut down was a good sign.

Titus looked down at his dead captain and shook his head once. *This is not how I intended to get my first command, damn it.* "Get a medic up here for the captain. Hawkins, get me a firing solution on that boat."

"Sir, she's drifting in and out of registry. I can only give you a probable target."

"That will have to do. Set our fish to go full active. If that sonofabitch doesn't like active sonar, he'll probably hate our torpedoes coming at him generating all that noise."

"Solution loaded and dumped to the fish, sir," Hawkins responded.

"Chief, fire tubes one and two."

"Aye, sir," Simmons responded, wiping the sweat from his brow with his forearm. "Fire one and two."

Nothing happened. "Where're my torpedoes, Chief?" Hill demanded.

"On it, sir," he said, holding the headset to his ear. He heard the chief of the boat bellow at an unseen crewman, "I don't give a goddamn! You fire those fish now!"

There was whooshing sound, then another as the torpedoes launched. Hawkins called from the BSY workstation. "Both fish are active and pinging, sir."

"Chief, what's going on there?" Hill demanded.

"Flooding, sir. The crew was working on the holes."

"Get them out of there and get that room sealed." It wasn't an easy decision. Sealing the room would take away the *Virginia's* torpedo firing capability. *If we don't seal it, we sink.* Simmons nodded and took off for the forward access hatch to the lower deck, his jaw clenched like a prizefighter going into a bout. Hill moved over to the helmsman. "Take us up fifteen degrees on the planes and level us off at 100 feet. Bring us to starboard and run a Sigma pattern." Hill turned back. "Hawkins, paint me a picture."

"Enemy vessel is moving erratically, sir. She seems uncertain, like our active sonar is confusing them. The torpedoes are on general track, but they keep losing their lock between the pings."

"Aspect to target?"

"She's in our aft starboard aspect, 1042 yards, rising to 300 feet."

"Time to impact?"

"Thirty seconds—wait, sir. Target has fired. Incoming torpedo. This one is moving slower than the first one. She'll be on us in 42 seconds."

Just great. "Stand by on countermeasures. Helm, swing us to port 15 degrees. Angle up on the bow planes five degrees more. Ballast tanks, get ready for a full blow on my command."

Chief Simmons came back into the command center soaked from the knees down from the leaked water he had been wading in. His shirt was wringing wet from his own sweat on the chest and armpits. "Torpedo room sealed, sir. Two men unaccounted for. We have twelve men in the forward missile room who are cut off by the flooding. They are alive and not taking on water yet."

In command for three minutes and I've lost the captain and two crew . . . this is just great. "Thank you, Chief."

"Sir, our torpedoes are losing target lock intermittently."

"How close are they to the enemy boat?"

"Closing to eighty yards, but they are drifting every ten yards and the enemy is starting to accelerate."

His mind raced back to his Prospective Executive Officers training, the explosive effects of torpedoes underwater. Underwater blasts were devastating, more so than on the surface because of the dense ocean water and the incredible concussive force. Eighty yards seemed far, but the size of the warheads on the torpedoes might just do some damage. But time was running out. *Better to use them than lose them.*

"Blow them!"

"Sir?"

"Manual override. Blow those fish, Lieutenant!"

Hawkins's fingers danced over the controls and he hit the red detonation studs for the two torpedoes. There was a muffled pair of "whomps" as both went off a mile distant. "Both torpedoes blown, sir."

"Any damage to the enemy boat?"

"Sierra One has stopped accelerating, sir. Wait—no, she went dead stop." Subs, when damaged, can make all sorts of sounds as compartments flood or implode under damage. "I am getting some strange popping sounds—but I cannot tell if it is damage, sir."

Let's hope we injured her.

A medic, Lieutenant Donavan, appeared and cut his way across the command center to the downed captain, whose skin had already taken on the pallor of death. Titus ignored him. *In a few minutes we might all be dead.*

"Twenty-five seconds on that inbound fish, sir," Hawkins called out.

"Launch countermeasures. Chief, get us to the surface. Full blow." Once more he grabbed the handrail over the fallen form of Captain Stewart.

Simmons barked out the command loud and clear. A chorus of "Aye, Conn" told him the crew were reacting as they had been trained. Bringing a boat like the *Virginia* to the surface on an emergency blow was tricky work. The ship was not what one would call agile, and Titus knew she had taken on a few tons of water just beneath him. "Countermeasures launched, sir. Full blow on the main ballast tanks." The massive bulk of the submarine angled slowly upward and seemed to surge faster. Hill could feel it under his feet. But something didn't feel right. It was the angle. The *Virginia* should be coming up much steeper—and faster. She wasn't rising the way he expected—and that was bad news.

Hawkins called out. "Sir, countermeasures ineffective."

"Mr. Simmons," a seaman called from ballast control. "Problem with the forward ballast tanks. We can't get pressure. We are not going to make the surface."

The damage was worse than we thought. Titus bit his lip. "Quick-deploy the ELF antenna. Comms, emergency message. Give our position and inform COMSUBPAC that we are engaging an enemy vessel and are damaged. Stand by to deploy the emergency locator buoy." His last words rang like a knell for the crew. The emergency locator was only to be used when a boat went down. In these depths, it was akin to Hill announcing a death sentence for the crew. He could see the fear in their faces.

"Aye, sir," the comms officer, Lieutenant Wynne, said. "ELF antenna clear, transmitting now."

"Sir," Hawkins cried out. "Incoming fish has gone to dead stop."

"What?" Hill jumped over to Hawkins's BSY workstation.

"Incoming torpedo is dropping astern, sir."

Why had they stopped? Something changed—"It's the ELF. Comms, keep transmitting."

"Yes, sir."

Goddamn it—*the ELF signal, it has to be disturbing them in some way. How can I make this work for me?* "How many channels are there on the ELF bands?"

"Four we can transmit on. We are on the Alpha channel now, sir."

I wonder if they will react to these. "Wynne, can you transmit on all the ELF channels simultaneously?"

"Sir?"

"Can you?"

"We can, but we were taught in training to not do it. It causes some garbling with COMSUBPAC's receivers at the relay stations."

COMSUBPAC isn't here. If they react at all to ELF signals, I have to try to take advantage of it. "Forget what you were trained to do. Transmit on all channels. Send anything, send garbage. They reacted to the ELF signal; let's see how they like this."

The lieutenant at the comms station started to sweat but did what he was told, his fingers racing over the systems. "Transmitting, sir."

"Hawkins, what about Sierra One? Are they reacting at all?"

"Aye, sir. She is breaking off, moving at 43 knots, on a bearing due northeast."

"Not nearly as fast as the last time we tangled with her, maybe those torpedoes did some damage," Hill said, more to himself than the crew. "What about that enemy fish?"

"Sonar shows that it is dropping, sir, down to 400 feet and continuing to descend. It's like it shut off or something," Hawkins said. Hill didn't care how deep it went, just as long as it wasn't tracking his boat any longer.

Hill realized for the first time how tense he was, how his hands ached from holding the guard rail. His eyes made contact with the kneeling Lieutenant Donavan. "Sir, Captain Stewart is dead. It looks like his neck is broken," he said in a low, respectful tone. Titus already knew that, but the confirmation by the ship's chief medical officer seemed to hit hard. *I had just started to know the man, now he's gone.* "I understand, Lieutenant. Get a couple of crewmen and take him out of the command center."

"Chief Simmons, organize a repair crew to get down to the ballast tanks and get them working. We need to get on the surface so we can get the trapped crewman in the forward missile room out." The soaking wet chief of the boat nodded and took off toward engineering. Hill turned to the communications officer. "Keep transmitting on the ELF, Lieutenant. Tell command that outbound ELF signals seem to disrupt their weapons systems."

As he stood in the command center, Hill felt his hands tremble slightly. The rush of adrenaline from battle started to ebb from his body. He felt the beads of sweat on his brow and wiped them with his hand. Lieutenant Donavan returned with two men and they lifted up Captain Stewart, his head seeming to dangle off to the side. Titus moved to join them and cradled the dead man's head until one of the seaman moved forward and took his place.

We have been damaged and need a sub repair station. Guam and Pearl were out of the mix because they were under attack. Sasebo, Japan, was an option—but it was in the same general direction as the enemy boat headed. *We're in no condition for another fight, not with the torpedo room flooded.* That left Kitsap-Bremerton in Washington state. It was a haul halfway across the Pacific, a sea filled with unknown enemies.

"Navigation—plot us a course for Kitsap. Helm, lay in that course, three quarters speed."

Perhaps the best course of action was to get back home . . . and hopefully find out what the hell was going on.

CHAPTER 28

Blown Sun Media headquarters,
Los Angeles, California

Dana Blaze was furious. "Goddamn it, Fizz, you have to find me a way to Guam or Hawaii!" She threw her stapler across the room in Hart's general direction, but nowhere near him. It landed near her "away bag," the one she always had packed and ready to go, for a trip that broke on a moment's notice, like this story.

"Boss-lady, I'm trying," he responded, lifting his eyes from his top-of-the-line digipad. "Things are bungle-fucked since the news of the attack broke two hours ago. All commercial flights over the Pacific have been grounded."

"Find me a private plane," she spat.

"Trying. Oddly enough, people are apprehensive about flying to an island that is under attack."

Usually she found his wry sense of humor reassuring, but today it just made her angrier. "I will pay a hundred and fifty thousand dollars. Get me in the air."

The sound of the dollar amount made Fizz nod. "That helps. Money is the best lubricant in the world. Let me see what I can do." He left the room, his fingers still tapping at his digipad. She could hear him starting a call in her outer office, which meant he was on it. Fizz was more than a technician. While he lacked social graces, he had a way of bonding with some people quickly, the kind of people Dana usually wouldn't give the time of day. Fizz had connections who had connections, some of which were actually legal. He had negotiated her into dangerous places before, and she hoped that he could pull it off again.

The skinny form of Ryan Jackson appeared in the open doorway. *Oh great, this day keeps getting better.*

"Dana," he said in a heavy breath, as if he had been running to get to her office. "What are you doing here?"

"Trying to get a ride out to Hawaii or Guam," she fumed, crossing her arms. "Tell me you know somebody who can get me out there."

Ryan seemed flustered at the instant demand. "Uh, no. That's not why I came here."

"Argh!" she growled. Ryan was lucky she had already thrown the stapler.

"Dana, you need to get down to the shore." Ryan stepped to her desk and waved his hand. A holographic image came up of Long Beach, patched in from a camera drone. Thousands of people were gathered around the . . . *things* that had crawled from the water and onto the shore in the last few hours. Dana saw the images, but in the back of her mind she wondered how Ryan had such control over her desk. That was something that Fizz was going to have to resolve.

The creatures had come ashore all along the LA coastline, emerging from the surf simultaneously like a pod of whales beaching themselves, intent on mass suicide. Only they didn't stop at the beach. They were slightly larger than a city bus. They looked like a massive cross between a clam and a snail, with a snail body on the bottom and a massive vertical clam shell on their back that rose like a fin. The snail-like body slithered on shore, leaving a wet sticky trail behind it. From the air vid shots, they looked and seemed to move like giant snails, like some sort of promotional gimmick for an upcoming movie. The shells themselves were oddly beautiful. They had a luminescent quality when the sun went behind clouds, showing strange striped patterns and a reddish-pink glow, and the press had made some comparisons to angel-wing clams that reportedly glowed in the dark. At the same time, their appearance was grotesque. The snail-slug bodies had eyes on three-foot stalks, and there were additional antenna growths. Marine biologists and every tree-hugger in La went down there, forming bucket brigades to keep the creatures wet with seawater. As they slinked ashore, it was apparent they were intent on moving off the beaches and into the city.

Ryan pointed to the images. "Every reporter in the city is down there. FedGov says that the president is going to be making a comment on the situation sometime soon. Since that initial broadcast about the attacks on Guam and Hawaii, the net has crashed three times and it's become impossible to hold a cell conversation for more than a few minutes. This is chaos, a chaos you happen to be closest to. You're my best. I need you down there covering this story."

She shook her head. "Like you said, every reporter in the city is there. Anything that happens there will be covered instantly by everyone else."

"Look," Ryan protested. "You broke the story globally on aliens. We caught a lot of flak on that, but you look like a freaking genius now. Now we have aliens coming ashore and you're not down there covering it. I *need* you there."

She didn't relent. "Hawaii or Guam. That's the real story. They reported being under attack and we're having a hard time getting and maintaining communications with Hawaii. The local island power grid was either damaged or shut down. Guam still has power but there's no one there to cover the story. FedGov has ordered all commercial ships to port and have grounded flights out there. Every local hack and idiot with a digipad will capture what happens downtown. What is happening out in the Pacific, *that* is something no one else can cover. That's where the *real* story is. Not covering a bunch of giant clams."

"They're technically snails," he began, and she only glared more at his correction. "Look, over a dozen of these things have come ashore." He pointed to the camera drone's coverage. As the camera swept back, she could see the gathering thousands of spectators and the police lines attempting to hold them back only fifty feet from the creatures. "The one that came in at White Point has already crossed West 25th Street and is moving north on the 213. The two at Redondo Beach are over a quarter mile inland already. The mayor has asked people to evacuate the areas around the aliens, but the streets are crowded with spectators. It's a *huge* story."

"I agree," she conceded. "But the bigger story is Hawaii and Guam. Just the fact that the FedGov isn't answering questions about what is happening there makes them the bigger story. That's where I should be."

"I want you down there." He stabbed his finger at the holographic image.

"I need to be somewhere else."

"You'll never get out there. The government is going to keep a lid on what is happening there; we've already started to get that vibe from them. Dana—you're my queen when it comes to these aliens. I need your face on the net with the aliens looming behind you." Jackson was practically pleading with her. *How quaint.*

Things had changed quickly with the fragmented reports of the attacks in the Pacific and the arrival of . . . whatever those things were . . . in Los Angeles. Up to this point, Dana had suffered criticism from FedGov communications specialists. She had been labeled as "alien-crazy" by one trade rag. The Washington, DC, press corps was far less kind, openly mocking her. Most reporters would have backed off. She went on the offensive, referring to the DC press corps as "a good-old-boys club of old farts with sagging gray ball-sacks." Censors edited it, but the quote went far and wide and her E-ratings shot up as a result of her short counterattack.

The criticism didn't bother her. People paid attention to the story because of her reputation. The first few weeks had been rough, but more and more reporters hopped on the bandwagon and did research of their own. Slowly, methodically, the evidence began to mount, much of it courtesy of the information that Jay Drake had provided. After a month, the FedGov was reeling from questions posed by reporters and the public about what was happening in the world's oceans. Other governments began to acknowledge what had been denied by the United States. Slowly the crack had formed. Dana went from being the lone voice, to being nominated for a D-Emmy for her coverage of what might be the story of the century.

"Just getting down there is nearly impossible," she said. "Look at those crowds." In typical La style, the arrival of the aliens, no matter what potential danger they represented, was an excuse for a party. Most of the people there couldn't even see the creatures, they were there because everyone else was there. *Lemmings. They have no idea what those things are, but they're down there drinking and dancing. No . . . not lemmings . . . idiots.*

"We have rented a VTOL," Ryan said. "I can get you in the vicinity within fifteen minutes." Hope rang in his voice.

Dana pondered that. If Fizz couldn't get her out to the islands, it didn't make sense for her to be entirely on the sidelines of this story.

Every fiber of her being said that the story was out where no one could reach. But the proverbial bird in the hand was tempting too. As much as she hated to admit it, Ryan had made some good points.

"Look, I have my guy trying to get me out to where the *real* story is. If he can't get something in the next hour, I'll go down and do a live broadcast. But the minute I get a ride out of La, I am out of here. Do we have an understanding?"

Ryan nodded. "Fantastic. I'll have the VTOL on standby. I'll be back in an hour."

He pivoted and turned as Fizz entered. The two men gave each other a passing glance. Ryan looked up at the bulky tech and flashed a geeky smile. Fizz looked down on him like an annoying mosquito. He stepped in and shook his head, with a hint of shame. "Boss-lady, you know I have contacts up the ass out there. I've had no luck. I found one guy with a VTOL, but it doesn't have the range to reach Hawaii. With the communications blackout and the warnings from FedGov, no one is willing to risk their lives to get out there."

Dana uncrossed her arms. "Keep looking," she said. "Otherwise we have to go down for a close encounter of the idiot kind." She pointed to the holographic image, turning it so he could see it.

"What is that, spring break?" Fizz asked. "Looks like fun."

"Knock it off. Go and keep knocking on doors." Fizz left the room and closed the door.

Suddenly her own digipad buzzed and she heard a familiar voice. "Having problems getting out to the islands, eh?" She looked down and saw Jay Drake's face with a wicked grin on it.

"How did you do that?" He hadn't called her, he had just tapped right into her pad.

"My company wrote your operating system and one of my factories provides the communications processor nodes in the pad. I can do this with almost any digipad I want. I just usually don't want to do it. But this is a bit of an emergency."

He has more power than any one man should. Oddly, it made him more appealing to her. "So how did you know I couldn't get a ride out?"

"I activated your microphone a while ago."

"You know, Jay, this is borderline creepy. It's like you're living in Stalkerville—population you."

"Call it what you will, Dana. I know you pretty well. I knew you'd be trying to find a way out to where the real action is. What would you say if I can get you to Guam?"

"Seriously?"

"I have a number of ships moving into position now. All have heli-pads and most have VTOLs with pretty good ranges. They are already at sea and I have a VTOL at LAX with extended-range fuel tanks. My logistics people are crunching the numbers right now. I can get you out to Guam in roughly thirty-six hours."

"Why not Hawaii? It's closer."

"Guam," Drake responded. "That's where you need to be. Trust me."

Do I trust him? What does he know about Hawaii that I don't? She paused for a long moment and realized that she had little choice. "Okay, Guam."

"There's a price for this shuttle service, Dana," Drake said as he templed his fingers and leaned back in his chair.

"Whatever it is, I'll pay it."

"First, you have to thank me for giving you the story of the century." Jay flashed a narrow smile.

"I thought I already had," she replied with a hint of sultry in her voice.

"I want to hear it from your lips," he replied coolly.

"Thank you, Jay, for turning me on to a story that may redefine my career." She said it with conviction, as if she actually believed her gratitude herself.

"Good," he replied. "The second thing is that when you get to Guam, I want you to secure samples of the aliens and their technology."

"What do you mean?"

"I'll be blunt, since you appreciate that. I want you to steal any-thing you can lay your hands on that is tied to the aliens. Weapons would be of key interest, but I will take anything you can get. I have arranged for biological sample cases to go with you in case you can get alien body parts. I want to learn everything I can about these things. You'll be there, on the battlefield. Pick up anything you see that my people can analyze."

His request was strange. "Won't the DoD folks be securing every molecule?"

"They will try, but battlefields are big messy places, and if I am right, you will be the first press person there. It puts you in the perfect position to secure me samples of the alien technology."

"What are you going to use it for?"

Jay responded by widening his smile slightly. "Dana. I don't think you really want to know that. Let's just say I'm not entirely comfortable with the FedGov being the only source of information on these aliens. It's better that the people have more than one source of data about these creatures . . . don't you think?"

She studied his face for a moment. Jay Drake had always been an enigma, but more of his true nature was emerging every time she dealt with him. There was a ruthlessness hidden behind his geeky persona. Drake was using these attacks for profit and power. And he was willing to do it behind the backs of the FedGov. Jay was a dangerous man. When the rest of the world was panicking, he was seeing opportunities.

"I agree," she said.

"I will get you the details in the next few minutes."

"Aren't you going to tell me to be careful out there?" she asked coyly.

Jay chuckled. "Careful isn't a description I'd use for you." Her digi-pad went black as he terminated his signal.

"Fizz!" she called.

Her tech and cameraman came back in. "Still working my magic, boss-lady."

"We have a ride. Jay Drake is setting us up."

"Seriously?" he said. "Awesome."

"You'll need your body armor on this one. I don't know what we'll find on Guam when we get there."

Fizz smiled. "Boss, you know I'd kill for you, but I have no intention of dying for you. Damn right I'll be armored up." He turned and jogged out of the room to get ready.

Dana watched him leave, and wondered for the first time what she would find when she got to Guam. *With any luck, a story that will paste my face on every screen on the planet . . .*

CHAPTER 29

Huntington Beach, Los Angeles, California

Antonio Colton could not understand why everyone wanted to see the big creatures that crawled out of the sea and into Los Angeles. Gio had insisted on going down and joining the crowd. Gio didn't care about the aliens, he was moving in the crowd selling Duke and Wire. When you had a lot of people gathered together, drugs were always in demand. Even with all of the police down there, they would be concentrating on crowd control, not on what the crowd itself was doing.

He had come with Gio, not out of wanting to clear his meager inventory, but to watch out for his friend. Crowds could get out of hand quickly and no one had any idea what these creatures were that had come ashore. When they finally got off the bus in Huntington Beach, the crowds were already packed in the streets. It was like a wild block party. *Anything is an excuse for a party for those living in La.*

They mingled quickly; there was no other way to do it. The creatures had come ashore and the news media was all over them. Initial rumors were that it was some sort of publicity stunt. No one knew what they were, but when he saw them on the newsfeed they reminded Antonio of an upright sea clam shell. The more he looked at them, though, he realized they were more like massive snails, with slug bodies dragging the massive, elongated shells into La. Their shells were beautiful. When a cloud rolled by you saw a glimmer, as if they were painted with glow-in-the-dark paint. The shells themselves shimmered a pinkish-to-deep red in color. Streaks of other colors, greens, browns and yellows, appeared like random artwork. Everyone was waiting to see them at nighttime, anticipating a lightshow.

Despite all the noisy people gathered around them, the giant snails continued crawling inland from the beaches, which Antonio found disturbing. No one knew what they wanted or what they were doing, but they seemed intent on moving down the streets, following the paths of least resistance. People were making sure the massive slugs were kept wet. Every Marine biologist in California was down there capturing vid and talking with the news media. Theories were all over the place, from mutations to some long-lost prehistoric creatures on some sort of migration. The prevalent thinking was that they were somehow tied to the strange incident in Hawaii and Guam, but media coverage of that was sparse. The net had some videos of Honolulu in flames and panicked people running about—but they lacked any real detail.

Antonio was tall and finally, after an hour, he got his only live glimpse of the creature. It was moving up the six lanes of Warner Avenue, forcing traffic to be diverted to the packed side streets, creating gridlock for blocks in every direction. The police were attempting to form a cordon around the creature as it moved, but trying to move the masses of people was a nearly hopeless task. The Meadowlark Golf Club had turned into a party ground, with hundreds of people camping out for a view from the fourth green, much to the chagrin of the club owners. The beachside homes and yards were overflowing with spectators too; Antonio's only advantage was his height. Five blocks away he saw it, just the top part of it, and only for a moment before someone blocked his view.

He had to admit, what he could see of the massive seashells did look pretty. The press had said each one was the size of a bus, but this one looked bigger. The closed shell rose like a fin above the crowd. The gathered mass of people blocked his view of the snail itself, but the shell alone was impressive. The newsvids had reported a noise the shells made, a constant, moderately high-pitched scraping or clicking, almost like a droning. Now and then it was loud enough for him to hear over the din of the people.

"Did you see it?" Gio asked. Somehow, Gio had secured a cold Miller Sledgehammer beer.

"Yeah—can we go now?" Antonio surveyed the crowd. All these people together were tweaking his senses.

Since the street battle over a month ago, he had been working out. Exercising was the only thing that came close to the rush he'd felt in the fight. He had taken long runs in the Torn District. It wasn't the kind of place where people exercised, and his running had gotten him strange looks, but he didn't care. When he pushed himself hard, he felt a tinge of the emotional release that he had felt in battle. That feeling was more seductive than any drug or drink he had ever tried. He began to drop his spare tire. His biological leg ached, but in a good way. It felt like when he was in Basic Training again, and that memory seemed to add to the feeling. *It's probably wrong for me to feel good about that fight, but I don't care.* For the first time in a long time he was feeling good about himself.

Being in a crowd of people elevated his nerves and made him edgy—flirting with the same feelings he'd had in the fight. He hadn't expected that. Large groups never gathered in his neighborhood. That hint of tension in the air, even with everyone partying around him, gave him comfort. *Maybe I shouldn't have been so fast to criticize Gio for wanting to come down here.*

But seeing the creature tempered that thinking. The press had said there were attacks by non-Earth forces in Hawaii and Guam, the lack of images seemed to make those attacks seem irrelevant. Those animals across the big blue waters of the Pacific were not friendly. *Why does everyone assume that these big creatures are any different? Just because they look nice? If they attacked us there, why do people assume they can't do the same here?*

Gio seemed stunned. "Why should we leave, man? Everyone in La is down here. This is the place to be. Look at all of these people. It's a party, man."

Antonio shook his head. "Look, I don't know what these things are, but they can't be good news."

"If they are so bad, where's the National Guard? The police are here already—it's as safe as it's going to get. You're just paranoid."

No, he just knew differently. Even if the National Guard were called in, it would take hours to get them mobilized, and even longer to move into the city. With the attacks elsewhere in the Pacific, he knew the Guard were likely getting prepared to move out—but no one knew it yet.

"I am telling you, staying down here is a mistake. We need to leave."

"You are the biggest buzzkill to walk the planet, man," Gio said with a raised voice as the crowd tightened around them. "Why not just enjoy the party?"

Because this isn't a party. His mind went back to his time in the war. Crowded places were killing zones: mobility was limited, and movement was often the key to survival. *If these things are hostile, they have drawn us out for the slaughter.* "Gio. I'm not asking. We are leaving."

"We've only been down here for a few minutes. I haven't even seen the big snail yet." Someone cranked up a portable media boomer box and started cranking music, the theme to Disney's *The Little Mermaid,* forcing him to raise his voice.

"I did. You aren't missing a thing. We need to leave." As he spoke, he surveyed the crowd. It was an impromptu street party to everyone else. For Antonio, it was a recipe for disaster. *If something goes down, these people are all going to be sheep for the slaughter.* His mind calculated potential threats and dangers. He began to evaluate where he would go if something went wrong. Rather than debate with Gio, he grabbed his friend by the arm and dragged him away from the massing group of people who were arriving from all over the city.

"Dude, what are you doing?" Gio asked when they got clear of the crowd. He twisted hard, breaking Antonio's grip.

"We're going to get on the bus and get back to the hood."

"I'm staying."

"Something bad is going to go down here. I can feel it."

"You have been more whacked than usual since that street fight. Did one of those bangers hit you in the head?"

"Everything tells me this is wrong," Antonio said flatly. He could feel the excitement in his body, the tension—and he embraced it. It reminded him of the war, of the street fight—of a bit of happiness. *Maybe I came down here knowing I would feel this way . . .* As soon as he had that thought, he suppressed it.

"This is awesome," Gio countered. "You are going to miss the party of the century. I'm going to make a killing here."

Antonio looked at his friend almost longingly. In the Army, you never left a man behind. He had to remind himself that this wasn't the Army. *I hope I'm wrong—but my gut tells me I'm right.* "I can't help you once I leave."

"You ain't my big brother. I can take care of myself." Gio turned and took a step away, then looked back. "I'll catch you tomorrow."

"I hope so."

Suddenly the crowd made a noise, an "ahh" in unison. Something was happening. Antonio stretched up to get a better view. He couldn't see much other than the massive snail seemed to stop moving. He could still see the sweeping, almost decorative shell poking over the heads of the crowd. It had changed. The green and yellow striping on the shell seem to shimmer, even in the direct sunlight. Gio stopped a few yards in front of him, getting his first good glimpse of the creature.

The massive shell fell open, surprisingly fast. There was a white and black mass inside, filling every crevice of space. The mass was alive. For a millisecond he thought it was the internal organs of the creature, but then everything changed. The mass erupted out and upward into the crowd, like a silent explosion. Then came the noise, louder, the clicking noise . . . followed instantly by screaming.

Antonio glanced around. Behind him, nearly a hundred feet away, was a city bus, trying to move but unable to maneuver because of the throngs of people. Turning back, he saw the sea of people running away from the opened shell, screaming, arms flailing. Some dropped out of his field of vision. The screams were not just panic—they were pain, he knew from his time at war. His heart pounded in his chest.

"What the fuck . . ." Gio said, backing up toward him, his eyes fixed on the now-fleeing mob of people. There were bits of white, almost like popcorn, flying through the air from the mass that had been in the shell. The bits were fanning outward in every direction from the creature.

Antonio's instincts told him to run for the bus. But his training kicked in. *We have to save these people—as many as we can.* He grabbed Gio by the shoulders and snapped him around. "Get to that bus. Get people inside, as many as you can. Wait at the door."

"Right . . ." Gio said, still stunned as the mass of people started to press around them.

"Now, Gio—move!"

Gio didn't have to be prompted again. He sprinted for the bus. Antonio wanted to follow him, but he knew what he had to do—he had to try to help these people. His body surged with adrenaline. He embraced the mad hot rush of energy. Reaching out, he grabbed a man. "Head for that bus!" he jabbed his finger to where Gio was already sprinting. In the panic, most people were so afraid they were running right past it.

The man he grabbed nodded and obeyed. Antonio snagged a middle-aged couple and gave them the same order. Glancing over his shoulder, he saw Gio at the bus doors, helping people onto the bus.

Looking at the crowd, he could see now that what was coming out of the shell were white balls, the size of golf balls, and they were only fifty feet away. The screams nearly drowned out the clicking noise. He saw one man run by, his hair soaked in blood, making his ponytail paint crimson on the back of his shirt. Antonio grabbed a woman and her two young children. "Get over to that bus—it's safe." The mother scooped up both children and ran for the bus. *I hope I'm right . . . I hope that bus is safe.* He faded back a few steps to get closer to the bus.

A couple of women ran near him and he told them to head to the bus but they ignored him, seeming to swat at their hair. *What are they running from?* He moved closer to the bus, grabbing a teenager and ordering him to the vehicle. The kid's eyes were as big as quarters and he numbly agreed, running for the bus. Antonio glanced back and saw that Gio was working hard getting other stragglers on the bus—it was already pretty full.

A woman staggered and half-collapsed onto Antonio. Her sundress was soaked in blood from a golf-ball size hole in her back. Her breath was ragged. Antonio scooped her into his arms and yelled out, "Everybody, into the bus!" He took off for the bus, carrying the injured woman. He could feel her hot sticky blood on his flesh thigh. He reached the bus in thirty strides and handed her to Gio and another man who were already on the bus. By the time he got there, she had passed out and was turning pale from blood loss. *What kind of weapon made that hole in her back?*

Turning back, he saw the white balls seeming to hop from person to person. Some landed on the ground, others flew through the air. Antonio ushered several more people onto the bus and as he watched, he saw other wounded emerge in the crowd. Some looked as if they had been bitten, blood was flowing. Others staggered, then fell, only to be trampled by the crowd. The white ball-creatures seemed to spread as fast as people ran, hopping from person to person. *What the hell are those things?*

People, in their panic, collided with the side of the bus, then ran around it. *I can only save a few more.* He grabbed a teenage boy holding a skateboard who seemed to be lost in the turmoil and practically tossed him onto the bus steps. A woman tried to make her way to the door of the bus but was staggering, almost like she was drunk. He wrapped his arm around her and noticed one of the white ball-creatures at the base of her neck. He moved her onto the landing of the bus and barked out to the driver in his best military-command voice. "Close the door!" The driver didn't argue. The door hissed and slowly closed.

He looked down at the last woman he had pulled aboard. The back of her white top was soaked in blood from the neck downward. The thing on her back was wiggling, digging and biting into her flesh. She let out a horrible, deep moan of agony. *It's not a weapon, it's alive.*

Antonio didn't think, he acted, grabbing and pulling at the alien. Whatever it was, it was dug into her flesh hard. His fingers were instantly slick with her blood. He managed to tear it free of her skin. It looked like a cross between a demonic human skull and a giant sand flea. Its nasty bloodstained maw snapped at his fingers but couldn't reach them, making a clicking noise like the gnashing of teeth. Its hiss seemed angry as it tried to get a bite of his flesh. It twisted, its little legs stabbing at his hand.

He sidestepped the injured woman on the landing and the passengers screamed at the sight of the thing he held in his hand. Someone yelled, "Kill it!" *Yes!*

He slammed it onto the floor of the bus. It hit but didn't die. It turned on its spindly crab-like legs. He knew in his mind what it was going to do; it was going to spring at him or one of the other passengers. That was what he had seen, the creatures were attacking and moving from one victim to another.

In a flash he stomped hard on the creature with his artificial leg. He hit it before it could jump, driving it into the floor of the bus and shoving his foot almost through the floor in the process. His mind and body were alive. It was like the street fight—like being in battle. He felt the surge of energy light up his senses and he embraced it for a moment. Then he bent down and helped the woman up.

"Did you kill it?" Gio asked from behind him.

"Oh—it's dead. What happened back there?"

The woman was shaking from fear and pain. "That big clam-thing just stopped and opened up. Millions of these things came out. They were all over us in a few seconds. They were everywhere!"

Antonio took off his shirt, folded it into a pad and pressed it to her torn skin. "You've got to get to a hospital." The injured woman went limp in his arms, blacking out. He felt her blood soak his left leg.

"All of those people . . ." someone asked. "What will happen to them?"

As if on cue, the aliens hit the bus. They sprang at the windows and the closed door. It sounded almost like automatic gunfire as dozens of them flung their little white shell-like bodies at the windows. The passengers screamed and recoiled, moving to the other side of the bus—only to draw the attention of the aliens there, who bombarded the windows to no avail. *If they get in, they will kill us.* He wondered for a full beat of his pounding heart if getting on the bus was the right decision. *I hope I haven't gotten everyone here killed.*

Then the little creatures seemed to move on . . . though a few still tried to get at the passengers. In a few seconds their attack was over, they were bounding and hopping after running people. While some inside the bus still were screaming or crying, Antonio looked outside. The aftermath of the attack was staggering. Bodies were everywhere. Three lay near where he had been standing when the shell had opened up. *If I can see hundreds, there must be thousands.* Some of the little creatures were straggling, hopping to anyone who still had a spark of life in them and tried to move. Blood pooled everywhere—on the street, the sidewalks, and in the yards. In a few moments the only noise on the bus was heavy breathing and crying.

Antonio remembered the woman who had collapsed in his arms earlier, the one with the hole in her back. "What happened to that injured woman?" he said, grabbing Gio's shirt to get his attention.

Gio pointed. The woman lay on her stomach, her sundress and the black floor stained with her blood. Someone had put a T-shirt over her wound, but the wifebeater already showed a bloodstain the size of a football. Antonio pulled back the T-shirt to look at her wound. The bloody hole was nearly circular. Inside he saw, covered with a film of gore, a white ball, twitching. As he exposed it, the wiggling stopped. *Aw, shit . . . it's one of them! It's burrowing into her body.*

It must have sensed him. The creature sprang from the deep hole right at him. It hit his right thigh and its nasty little maw tried to sink into his bionic leg. Someone else saw it jump and screamed. Antonio fell back and the creature attacked the source of the noise, landing on a man's arm and tearing right through his shirt and into his flesh with a single bite. Panic returned to the inside of the bus as the occupants screamed and tried to scramble away.

Not Antonio. He went after the creature. But it had hopped again, landing on a teenage boy who managed to knock it aside with his hand. The creature landed on the floor as Antonio jumped at it. He landed on the injured woman and he grabbed at the creature. It bit into his hand and he instantly felt an ache up to his elbow. He didn't let go, though every impulse he had was to do so. In agony, he reached out and grabbed the teenager's skateboard. He smashed the insect-like creature onto the floor, then hammered it with the skateboard. He used so much force that he broke the board, sending part of it flying. Moving the skateboard off the creature, he made sure it was dead. A sickly green ooze, what he assumed was its blood, spread out from the crushed, skull-like body-head.

Antonio's fingers tingled and pain racked his hand. The bite had been deep and blood was flowing, but not gushing. Gio took his shirt off and handed it to Antonio. He wrapped it tightly around his hand. "I think there was poison in that sucker," he muttered to his friend. Gio patted him on the shoulder. "Man, you saved my life back there."

The bus rumbled and lurched as it tried to move, as if it were going over a curb. Antonio sat on the floor and didn't try to stand as the bus rocked again. He didn't want to look outside; he knew the driver was forced to drive over the bodies of the victims . . . it was the only way to get away from the scene of carnage. *I don't need to see that—no one does.* He reached down to the injured woman on the floor of the vehicle and felt her neck. She had a pulse—not much of one, but it was there. His own hand ached and felt as if it were on fire. Looking at his bionic leg, he saw where his synthskin had been torn by the maw of the little creature that had attacked him.

These were not creatures . . . they were a weapon. His initial fears had been confirmed.

"Get us to a hospital!" he bellowed to the driver, tucking his injured hand into his armpit and squeezing it to hold the T-shirt bandage in place. One person was still crying as the bus rocked and lurched every so often. He realized it was the driver.

CHAPTER 30

Fort Myer, Arlington, Virginia

Master Sergeant Adam J. Cain had been in his office preparing for a burial detail when the word came in that the United States was under attack. The DefenseNet was getting live streams from Guam and Hawaii about the attacks there, but nothing about the scale and scope of the attacks. Hawaii's commercial communications, other than satellites, had gone down when their power grid failed, which limited the feeds of the regular news channels. Even the DoD information from Hawaii was mostly a jumble of conflicting data and reports. Pearl Harbor was under attack, but from the images, other than a few twisting black plumes of smoke and a sinking ship, there were none of the traditional signs of a big battle. There was a marked lack of people, except for dead bodies. It was eerie to see from the drone images. To Cain it looked as if the battle was over—and we had lost.

Guam was still sporadically online, but the details were sketchy at best. Word was that the attack had come from the sea. Not an amphibious assault. No, these invaders had come right up out of the depths of the ocean. The Marines on Guam were putting up more of a fight. That battle looked right—with images of Marines and ASHUR rigs rushing in—mortar rounds going off—and other than the strange spider/crab-like aliens, it was how a battle should look.

The images of the aliens reminded Cain of a mix of insect and lobster—or a crab. He studied them, trying to learn their formations, their weapons. He saw some unleash what looked like a gas weapon, others fired weapons that were nearly silent but seemed to take down the battling Marines. *They are in the fight of their lives, but this isn't the enemy we've trained for.* His experience told him that meant the military was going to have to adapt, and fast.

279

Then from around the globe came images of big bus-sized clam-snail-like creatures crawling ashore in major cities around the planet. The Italians had not messed around; they had fired on one of them. That proved to be a big mistake. It opened its huge shell, disgorging millions of carnivorous large sand-flea-like creatures. The images of the police and camera crew being attacked were horrific. When they burst out, it was like a bomb going off and they moved fast, striking at random. Entire neighborhoods had been devastated in hours, and there didn't seem to be an end to the devastation.

Of course the Italians had held those images, preventing their release from fear of panic. It would have helped if the rest of the world had known. At the same time all around the planet, the snail-like creatures had opened, releasing their deadly cargo. Cities found themselves fighting an enemy that was a mass of tiny eating machines that swarmed and attacked without fear. Chaos was erupting around the globe. *It should be reassuring that we are not in this alone, but it's not.*

Cain had ordered his men to focus on the jobs at hand, but he too was struggling with what was happening. His wife and daughter were in Los Angeles, where a dozen or so of these things had unleashed their biological terror. There had been so many people crowding near the waterfront to see the aliens, it had become a scene of carnage and death. Now came word that everyone was trying to flee the affected cities all at once. Roads had become parking lots in a matter of minutes. Gas stations were already running out of fuel. Riots were breaking out as people looted stores for food and water. The scenes coming in from Boston, where several of the strange clamshell-shaped snail-creatures had arrived, were of a city in flames, as panic turned to rioting and basic systems started to fail. In between his burial assignments, Adam tried to reach his family, but the net was overloaded across the world. Getting a net signal for a call was impossible.

They will be okay. Julie never would let Amy anywhere near those things . . . she is smarter than that. He didn't worry about them as much as he worried about other people. *If they hunker down and don't panic, they should be okay.* He kept telling himself that, but with each passing hour, he doubted it more and more. Amy was a headstrong kid. He had struggled to keep her in line, and that was his function in his career. Evacuating LA was going to be nearly impossible—and those bug-things were everywhere.

What the fuck is happening? Every movie he had ever seen about aliens said that they came from space, not from the oceans. When he had seen news reports weeks earlier about the potential of aliens in the sea, he had written it off as a hoax. Now people would be looking at those news reports in a new light. Now everyone was claiming they knew the government was covering up the aliens. *Only that one woman, Blaze, had the balls to come out and make the accusations. Hindsight makes the other reporters look like hypocrites. Hindsight will do that to you.*

As he sat in his small quarters on the base, he continued to try to redial his wife, to no avail. "If these assholes want a fight, they came to the right place," he muttered to himself. As the newsfeeds painted a story of gloom from around the globe, his mind was back in Los Angeles. All the aliens had done so far was cause a lot of chaos. And out of that chaos, there will be war. Cain knew that. War was the response to this kind of attack. *Oh, there would be calls by politicians to try to reason with these bastards. Hell, we don't even have a name for them yet. They would want to try to negotiate. That was a pussy response. They came to the surface looking for a fight.* "I say we give them what they want—give them a taste of war," he murmured.

He settled back in the lone chair in his room and tried again to call but got an "all circuits are busy" message. Then came a long wailing sound from every direction on the base. *The alert siren.* Fort Myer was going on alert!

Adam took off his dress uniform shirt and tie that he wore for burial detail and replaced them with his fatigue pants and shirt. They felt good, comfortable, reassuring—and they fit as if they were tailored for him. An alert was a prelude to war. War was the one thing he knew, the one thing he was the master of. Adam actually felt good as he buttoned his olive drab fatigue shirt. Dress shirts were starched, stiff, stifling. Today reminded him of wearing a similar shirt when the Russians began swarming ashore in Alaska. It was a shirt of duty. The shirt of a soldier. He looked down at the tattoo of II on his hand. *I need my rig . . . an ASHUR to pilot. That is where I am most effective.*

Fifteen minutes later, Cain assembled his squad on the grassy green lawn where the Army band spent its afternoons practicing. Seeing everyone in their combat boots and fatigues reminded him that the Third Infantry Regiment was more a ceremonial posting. Some of these men and women were highly decorated in their careers, but they were often by-the-book warriors. Most of them had been posted to the regiment as a reward, unlike him. He could see the ones who were not kiss-asses, the ones who had seen battle. There weren't a lot of them, but he could see each one. It showed in their faces and the way they stood rigid at attention, the determination they showed. Unfortunately, most of the men and women in the regiment were nervous, sweaty, pale, unseasoned in the art of warfare. The members of the Army's band, Pershing's Own, were the easiest to spot. *Hell, that one kid looks like he's about to shit his pants. Probably a drummer.*

For months he had viewed his posting to the regiment as punishment, being sent to an American equivalent of Siberia. Now there was an enemy—a fight was coming. Suddenly he was no longer a ceremonial decoration, he was going to be in battle again. *All wars begin with alerts, with grandiose words—but they all end in battles and death.*

Major Catastrophe Mallory stepped forward in front of the assembled troops, holding a printout in his hands. He was one of the ass-kissers, Adam was sure of it. What gave it away was the slight quiver of fear in his fingertips as he held the orders. "Attention. As most of you are aware, the United States was attacked earlier today on the islands of Hawaii and Guam. What we know is limited at this time, only that fighting continues on both islands. What few messages have gotten off the big island indicate that the fleet at Pearl Harbor has been hit and the Navy has lost a few ships. Honolulu and the military bases on the island have also been attacked, both by the biological weapons the attackers have used, as well as some of their troops.

"Likewise many of our coastal cities have come under attack by strange big flea-like creatures released from other alien carriers. These unprecedented attacks have cost thousands of lives and have caused panic in the civilian population. Even cities not impacted, such as Chicago, have reported looting and rioting as people begin to secure supplies in case of an attack. July 28, 2039, is likely to be remembered in decades to come, along with December 7, 9/11, and April 2, 2029."

The major paused and drew an unsteady breath. "The president will be going on the air shortly and will announce that our coastal cities are under martial law. The Third Regiment has been assigned to security and civilian control in Arlington, including the security of all approaches to the Pentagon from the Potomac. You will be issued armor and weapons. Under the conditions of these orders, you are authorized in the use of deadly force if matters violate the rules of engagement which your NCOs will be provided.

"Make no mistake, people, we are at war. The president, as part of his announcement, will be informing the American people that our foe is not from Earth but extraterrestrial in origin. We have been aware of their presence for some time. They have advanced technologies and we do not know their intentions, only the results of their actions." His voice wavered for a moment as he read the orders.

Wimp-assed wuss—kill the drama and get on with it.

"This is our planet, and the US government is pledging the entire might of the nation in this fight.

"We are counting on all of you to do your duty and protect our part of the nation's capital." He stopped and folded the paper, seemingly thankful to have finished. "NCOs will muster for their orders. All units are to assemble at the armory and draw their shit." There was a pause as he surveyed the troops. "Dismissed!"

Adam joined the other NCOs to receive specific orders and the rules of engagement. As the other sergeants dispersed, Adam stayed behind and moved in close to Major Mallory. "Sir, may I make a request?"

"Today isn't the day for your usual demands, Sergeant," the flustered major responded.

"I'd like to transfer to a combat unit, sir."

"I don't have time for this bullshit, Cain," he snapped.

"Sir, I'm ASHUR qualified." He twisted his hand to show his tattoo, the mark of an ASHUR II pilot. "I've seen more combat than my entire squad added together. You hate my ass. This is your chance to get rid of me."

"No transfer, Sergeant Cain," he said, glaring.

"Sir—my wife and daughter are in Los Angeles. Fighting is the one thing I do and do well. It's in my best interest and that of the US Army that you assign me to a combat division."

Mallory stared into his face. *Come on, asshole, say it!* The major shook his head. "I need you here. I hate saying it out loud. But I need you here, *now*."

"Looter patrol? Sir, that's a pile of horseshit for a soldier like me. I'm not a policeman . . . I'm a trained killing machine." *It's what the Army has made me.*

"Watch it, Sergeant, you are bordering on insubordination. You've taken that hill more than once."

You have no idea what insubordination looks like, you steaming turd. "Sir, I ask that you reconsider," he responded through gritted teeth.

"Denied. Get to the armory and get your people their gear. We have a mission to perform."

"This isn't a 'mission,' sir. I've been on those. This is just a show of force. This is to make the locals feel safe and comfortable and make them think that our no-balls commander in chief is tough and strong. For *you* this may be a big deal. For me this is a fucking parade without the band—oh, wait, the band will be out there with us!" Even the men and women of Pershing's Own were being outfitted in combat gear. *I never have been in a combat situation with someone whose MOS was playing the fucking tuba.*

"Goddamn it, Sergeant!" Mallory snapped. "You can't talk to me that way, I'm your superior officer."

"Transfer me or lock me up, Major Catastrophe," he said angrily, loud enough for only the major to hear.

"No, you miserable old withered piece of shit." The major had finally hit his breaking point. "I won't do that because it's what you want. For now, I need your damned combat experience here. I hate it. I hate admitting that I need you under my command. It would be easy to ship you out, make you someone else's problem. That's the story of your whole career. But we are going to war, and you are needed here. Some of your troops need your experience if these aliens decide to move on the District. I know you think I'm a moron, but I'm smart enough to know that having you here will save lives if these bastards attack. I might chafe at every conversation we have, but I have been trained to analyze a situation and put the right resources in place. In this case, despite my personal feelings—that's you. Now get your ass in gear and get ready to get on the trucks. We move out in an hour."

"Sir," he said, as he reined in what he wanted to say. "If you won't transfer me, can you at least get some ASHUR II rigs assigned to the regiment? I'm qualified and I'm pretty sure Sergeant Mackie is too. If something goes south and these things decide to go after the Pentagon, I don't want to take my men in without the proper fire support."

"ASHUR gear is not part of our TO&E."

No shit, Sherlock. I know it's not on our Table of Organization and Equipment . . . but this is war and wars are not fought by the book. He tempered his response after a moment of consideration. "I know that. That doesn't change my request, sir. A four-star shitstorm is coming. You are going to need that gear here. We are defending the capital of the United States; you'll have no problem in getting the hardware authorized. One thing politicians do well is protect themselves, and that gear is the best defense we have if those fish come ashore in the Chesapeake Bay. You said you recognized what I bring to the table: then you have to trust me on this, as a combat veteran. Get me a rig to pilot."

Major Mallory paused for a moment. He studied the older man's face but didn't speak. "Alright, Sergeant. You are right. We get hit without that kind of firepower, a lot of men and women will die. No promises, but I'll see what I can do."

He bit his tongue and flashed a salute. Adam Cain felt a surge of pride, a feeling he hadn't enjoyed in a long time. Maybe Major Catastrophe wasn't the moron he had thought. Cain had to admit, the major's thinking was sound . . . it was Army thinking. *I can make a difference today—and if he gets me a rig to pilot, I can make a bigger difference tomorrow.*

CYCLE IV

The Oval Office, the White House, Washington, DC

"Ladies and gentlemen, the president of the United States," said the White House press secretary from off-camera. The president appeared in his blue suit with his red and blue tie and his perfectly starched white shirt. He sat behind the Resolute desk, a little unsure, but doing his best to portray the image of a man in control of a situation that defied all control. The Oval Office gave that false image of control. Gone were the smiles from the campaign. He was dripping with the presidential aura.

"My fellow Americans, the question we have long pondered, are we alone in this universe, has been answered. We are not. But they do not come in peace: we, and other nations of the world, have been the victims of savage attacks—attacks that have killed thousands of innocent men, women, and children.

"Like you, when I learned of these attacks, I was stunned by their brutality. But your nation was not entirely ignorant. Within the last few months, the Defense Intelligence Agency determined that there was an alien presence in our oceans. We were unsure of their intentions and chose to use what time we had to learn all that we could about these visitors from another world. We had hoped to be able to communicate with them at some point. We had chosen a peaceful approach to their intrusion on our planet. We had few indications of a hostile intent.

"For reasons unknown to us, these aliens have attacked our nation, and many nations around the world. The initial attacks came on the island of Hawaii and our military bases on Guam. The fighting on Guam is still raging, the US Marines with assistance from the Navy and Air Force are engaged in a deadly struggle for control of that island.

286

"On the island of Hawaii, we have only sketchy information as the island has lost all power and their underwater communications lines have been severed. What we do know from satellite feeds and microwave relays is that our fleet has been badly damaged and Honolulu and the immediate surroundings are under attack. We do not yet have an adequate picture of the events unfolding there but our prayers are with the brave men and women on these besieged islands who are fighting for not only their survival, but for survival of the human race. To them I say, 'Hold on—help is coming.'

"Additionally, the invaders unleashed other weapons, biological in nature, on our coastal cities, an invasive species of insect-like crustaceans that has already killed thousands of our people and has forced the evacuation of several cities. Los Angeles, San Francisco, New York, Boston, Savannah, and Miami have all experienced these attacks. We believe similar attacks were unleashed on Guam and Hawaii.

"We know little about these aggressive invaders or their ultimate intentions. What we do know is that we will resist them, as have other nations around the world. I have spoken with leaders of many countries and the measures we will be taking are in line with those that most of our allies are undertaking."

President Bobrow paused for a moment, then intensified his stare into the cameras. He spoke without the aid of the teleprompter, that much was clear to everyone in the room and watching via the net around the planet. "Our destiny as a nation—a people—and a race is at stake in this conflict. I call on the American people and urge members of both parties to unite in this single cause. We will send a message to these invaders with our actions; we will not cower, shirk, or submit. We will fight! Our petty differences be damned. We need to set aside those past differences and work as one people—one race, against this threat. We have tools and technologies superior to those of any other time in the history of mankind that will enable us to triumph. Our response to these attacks will send them a clear message: 'You have attacked the wrong people—no, the wrong *race*.'

"To our enemy, I say this directly: Any fleeting moments of terror you inflicted on us will pass. Your attacks on our people will be remembered and repaid a thousand times over. You do not know the hardships our forefathers have endured to survive and thrive as a nation.

You have underestimated our will, strength, determination, and drive to survive. If you believe victory is possible, you are *sorely* mistaken. While we cherish peace, when war is brought to our doorstep, we respond with righteous fury and fortitude that you cannot comprehend. Your day of reckoning is coming. We will not be satisfied with anything short of complete victory.

"You have begun this fight . . . but I assure you, *we* will end it." He seemed to pause for a moment, reining in his emotions, never quite crossing the line from being presidential.

"As such, I call upon Congress to declare war on this new enemy.

"As of an hour ago, I have placed all US military personnel on a wartime footing. I am declaring martial law in all communities within twenty miles of our shoreline. I have called for the immediate federalization of all National Guard forces and have asked the governors to call up all troops for immediate mobilization. I have also activated all Reserve forces, ordering those personnel to report for immediate duty. This will take time but will ensure our domestic security.

"As a result of reports of rioting in major cities, I will use my powers as president of this nation to put down such looting and authorize the use of deadly force. This is not a time for us to fight each other, this is a time for us to come together as a people. If you are contemplating illegal activities to exploit the chaos caused by these attacks, you will be treated with the same force as these aliens that have chosen to assault our great nation.

"I have ordered FEMA to engage in relief efforts for those cities that have been attacked. But, to be blunt, the scale of these assaults stretches FEMA beyond its capabilities. I have ordered the Army Corps of Engineers to assist in their efforts. Orders have gone out to recondition and reopen many of our decommissioned military bases. These will serve as refugee centers for those citizens who are moving away from our coastal areas. It will take time before these are ready—and I ask the American people for their patience and assistance in these efforts. I further ask that we all open our doors and offer aid to those who are displaced by these attacks. It is time for America's legendary generosity and values to shine through and to help our neighbors who have suffered in this conflict.

"Governors have contacted my office and I have received reports of some people already trying to profit from this horrible series of events. No American should take advantage of this situation. As part of my executive order tied to this attack, I have frozen all prices and all wages. In order to ensure no financial panic, I am shutting down all stock trading for two weeks—and other security exchanges around the world will be doing the same. Those who attempt to exploit the deaths of our people by profiteering will be dealt with severely.

"The full force and weight of the federal government will be applied to dealing with this issue. For the first time since World War Two, we will mobilize the entire weight of this country to deal with a threat. The lives of the thousands of people who have been killed and injured as a result of these dastardly and cowardly attacks will be avenged.

"Make no mistake, we are in this battle for our very way of life. We are fighting an enemy with technological capabilities we do not have, but we are resilient. Humanity is bred for surviving, and we will prevail over these aliens.

"In the coming hours and days we will all need to confront our fears and rise above them. And we will. While war has come to us from the depths of the ocean, we shall take the fight to these invaders. They will come to rue the day they thought to battle our species.

"We shall overcome the darkest of our thoughts and emerge into the light of victory."

CHAPTER 31

US Naval Base, Apra Harbor, Guam, Pacific Ocean

Lance Corporal Natalia Falto had one thing in mind: fulfilling the last orders of Staff Sergeant Rickenburg and getting the platoon back to the armory. "Save this platoon to fight another day." The order to retreat stung her ears and gnawed at her mind. The staff sergeant's plan of luring the alien force in and slaughtering them had died when he did. A large bipedal alien had emerged from the ocean, and it was like a walking tank. It had crushed the staff sergeant's Lion-class rig after a hard-fought battle. The odds tipped at that moment and the initiative was lost.

She half-walked, half-dragged herself along the exterior of the records building on MacArthur Drive. The roar and pop of assault weapons fire from the remnants of Sergeant Parker's unit surprisingly appeared on their right flank. It seemed to have caught the alien's attention. Falto started to enter the building and hands grabbed her, pulling her inside to supposed safety.

Looking around, she saw what was left of the platoon. Of the thirty-nine personnel of the platoon, only a dozen or so remained. She popped her visor for a moment and let the cooler air hit her face. "Sitrep," she said as she looked around the foyer of the office where the remains of the platoon—*her* command—were spread out.

"Not good," Porter said. "Low on ammo. We've got five wounded," he glanced at her own injury, "six, counting you." The fact that Porter was the one speaking for the survivors impressed her. Porter was no longer the weakling—he was in full battle mode.

Private Carson chimed in. "Both Huskies are out of commission. The crabbies went right after the Greyhounds too—the dogs' signals

290

must have been an issue for them. I saw both of them get torn in half in the claws of those things."

"The staff sergeant's last orders were for us to fall back to the armory. We also have to evac any civvies along the way. That's what he wanted and that's what we are going to do. That's where we'll make our stand."

"They have hit the command center—or at least the comms hub. We have lost our overall battlespace feed, we're down to tactical feeds only," Private Robertson said. *Our officers never made it on the field. Someone is going to pay for that foul-up.* A lot of responsibility had fallen to Lieutenant Frisks and now he might be one of the dead.

"They seem to have a hard-on for our power poles too," Private Cox added. "I saw them tear down two of them." Natalia remembered the creatures hitting the transformer as well.

"Alright, we'll figure out what they were targeting and why later," she said. "For now, we need to get out of here. We're going to have to assist the wounded." *That thing that killed the staff sergeant is still out there.* "Robertson, you and I will provide cover fire for the others. We'll fade back along MacArthur and round the corner two blocks back onto Sumay Drive. That intersection is your waypoint. Hold up there— we'll join you, then we can move right down the street to the armory."

Suddenly two of the troopers grabbed their ACRs and raised them. Natalia swung around and saw one of the shorter, combo gorilla-bulldog aliens behind her, looking in at the window. It had a menacing under-bite jaw with white fangs pointing upward and was only a few feet from her. Its body, greenish in color, seemed like the underbelly of an alligator at this range. The arms on creatures were massive bundles of muscles, with a hide that looked tough enough to shake off bullets. While the creatures were short and seemed to be unarmed, it appeared like a predator at this range. Gunfire barked from the confines of the foyer and the window exploded outward as the creature dove to one side. The creature disappeared out of her field of vision. *Shit—it's seen us!* Moving to the window, she looked down and didn't see blood.

"We need to move," she said. "Toss me a magazine." Someone threw one to her, and she snatched it with her good arm. Her left arm, which had been hit with the needles, was numb but usable. She slid the magazine into her utility belt and hoisted her ACR to check the ammo count. Eight more rounds remained in the magazine in the rifle.

The wound was not painful as much as it was inconvenient. The needles that had been fired into her shoulder had been tipped with something that paralyzed her muscles. The left half of her upper body was limp, even her face. It felt like when she had her wisdom teeth pulled, her face felt like it sagged. Her breathing was labored—she was sure whatever had hit her had paralyzed her lung on that side of her body too.

Natalia fumbled with her utility belt as the platoon made its way through the sea of cubicles. She opened the pouch that held her Marine Corps-issued meds. She pulled out the energy boost pack. Peeling off the safety cover with her teeth, she jabbed the tiny needle into her numb wrist and squeezed. Closing her eyes, she waited to feel the rush of energy, that burst that might drive away the numbness and give her enough strength to reach the armory. The numbness didn't abate, but it didn't get worse.

Looking around the foyer she focused on the door leading to the inner offices. "Alright, Marines, let's move." She tried the door but it was locked. Private Robertson was more direct. He hit the doorjamb with his big beefy shoulder, shattering it and swinging the door open. Falto suddenly saw the advantage of his taking the issued drugs and being a pumper.

"We need an egress to the south," she said as the sounds of gunfire outside increased. *The fight is coming our way and we are hemmed in.* A check of her battlespace display showed that the Marines' lines were eroding by the moment as everyone fell back to the armory.

"There's a set of doors on the east side," someone called out. Outside there was a muffled explosion that sounded like a mortar round coming down. One of the windows on the north side of the office shattered.

"We only have windows to the south," Private Walters said. "Got no egress here."

She headed in that direction to see if she could improvise a solution when suddenly she saw movement. She raised her ACR and swung it over, her finger on the trigger. She saw two women on the floor of a cubicle next to her. They were curled up in tight balls, hiding on the floor.

"Shit!" she spat, lowering her gun. "You idiots almost got slagged! Jesus!" They were shaking, slowly starting to stand. "Porter, get over here. We've got two civvies."

"We didn't know what to do," one of the clerks stammered in a fearful, shaking voice.

"You can't stay here," Falto replied. Porter took charge of them, and Falto headed to the south side of the building to check for herself. She didn't want the doors to the east, leaving that way might expose them to the advancing enemy.

South was a wall of windows that led to a narrow street between Records and the next building. This was going to have to do. The staff sergeant had said "improvise," so that was what she would do. "Break out the glass, Walters—we'll make a door. Porter, you take the civvies with you, they are *your* responsibility. We're going out this way and then head south to the armory. Everybody got that?" She looked around; even the walking wounded gave an assuring nod. "Robertson, you and I have the rear guard." The hulking wall of muscle nodded once, checking his weapon's ammo count.

"Alright, break it out!"

Two of the Marines broke out the glass with the collapsible stocks of their ACRs. The moment the glass shattered, it let in the sounds of battle, making it seem even closer. Using their weapon butts, they took out the few remaining shards of glass still in place.

Her training took over her actions. Inexperienced Marines might just rush out pell-mell, but she knew there was a slight tactical advantage in coordinating their movement, and it reduced the risk of leaving someone behind. "We go on three. Keep your heads down. Check your six every now and then. Robertson and I are right behind you. Porter, you keep those civilians close and make sure nothing happens to them. They are *your* responsibility," she repeated. The scrawny Marine nodded, his face pale. *You can do this, Porter. I trained your ass for weeks for this moment. You won't let me down.*

"One—two—" Falto never reached three. The north side of the building erupted, as if a truck had rammed the office building at full speed. Standing there in the hole it had made in the brick wall was the black-skinned alien that had killed Staff Sergeant Rickenburg. It was so tall that it hunched over in the office, ripping down the hanging ceiling as it entered. It took a step forward, ignoring the wall, the debris of the office and everything else, moving as if the structure was little more than Styrofoam. Falto knew it was the same alien because it was missing one forearm, the result of the damage that the staff sergeant had inflicted. The strange streaks of color that seemed to be part of its armor or body seemed to pulse crimson and yellow as it made eye contact with her.

"Go! Go now!" she said, raising her ACR. She fired off her rounds as did Robertson, catching the creature in a crossfire. Their shots were on target, but didn't seem to have an effect. A light dropped on its electrical cable from the ceiling, swinging into the line of fire with at least one shot hitting it and sending the light spinning. She activated her visor and it dropped in front of her face, as if that was any sort of protection against the creature she faced. *It killed the staff sergeant, and he was in an ASHUR rig . . .* Falto knew she couldn't take on the creature alone but that wasn't her mission. Her last set of orders was to get the platoon to the armory and save any civvies they found, and that was what she was going to do, one way or another.

The hulking creature glared at her and she felt it in her brain, as if it were looking right into her soul. She dropped the empty magazine and reloaded. "Move it, Marines!" she barked to the shattered platoon behind her.

The alien lurched forward as if the cubicle walls and filing cabinets were not even there. It hit them and just kept moving, barely slowing at all, as if it were wading in shallow water. Private Robertson fired controlled shots, emptying his magazine in a matter of seconds into the creature. Her own shots were aimed at its head and neck. The bullets seemed to hit; they left small divots and grayish groves in the creature's flesh. None seemed to penetrate its armored skin.

Falto stepped backward one step, toward the shattered window where the platoon had evacuated. Robertson didn't. He emptied his magazine and reloaded, firing precise shots. Where she stepped backward, he strode forward. Pumpers . . . their military-grade steroids made them dangerously aggressive at times.

Robertson rushed toward the creature, firing as he went. "Robertson, fall back!" she called, firing and yelling at the same time.

The biped moved two steps forward, ripping the office apart as it went. It got to close-quarters range with Robertson, seeming to ignore the bullets he was firing. It stabbed its webbed hand-claw straight at the muscled Marine, one of its three claws stabbing into Robertson's torso. Its black claw-nail punched through his STG armor and out the back, slicked black with blood. *There's no help for Robertson now.* Falto stepped one more step back, standing on the crunching broken glass at the window.

Robertson moaned and seemed to shift on the impaling claw. The creature shook its massive arm twice, sending the body of the big Marine flying into a cubicle like a rag doll.

Falto's last bullet fired and she heard the ping in her earbud telling her she was empty. She dropped the ACR and pulled her M18 Sig Sauer and held it in front of her, aiming carefully at the visor-like element on the head of the alien. Her bullets found their mark, but didn't seem to have any effect, other than to draw the alien's attention. It ignored the fallen body of Robertson and turned to her, wading into the office, crushing the last walls, chairs, and filing cabinets between them.

She emptied the magazine. When she dropped the empty to reload the M18, the alien moved to point-blank range. "No!" she screamed as it swung its massive arm at her like a scythe. She flew through the office and onto a desk. Natalia felt her chest ache and her breath seemed ragged. *Broken rib—shit!* She rolled around to see the creature—or find her pistol, or both.

The M18 was gone but the alien was there, right in front of her. It found her gun in the debris. With remarkably maneuverability, it picked it up with its one massive clawed hand, its black nails as nimble as fingers, though many times the size. It held the gun between two of them, seeming to look at it and her at the same time. A wave of agony stung Falto in that moment.

It dropped the gun to the floor and stepped on it with its massive foot, grinding it down. When the creature moved its foot, she saw the gun flattened by the incredible weight.

The creature flicked it aside. Natalia fumbled for her fighting utility knife, which she was laying on. It was a pointless gesture, but she had to try something.

She didn't find it in time.

The alien raised its remaining forearm and she saw the needle-firing weapon embedded into its skin. He slowly, methodically swept it across her. She felt a stab in her torso, right above her crotch and near her broken rib. Momentary pain—then numbness followed, within the same heartbeat. Her ears roared. Falto's vision tunneled. She struggled to breathe again, and popped open the visor on her helmet in hopes that would get her more air. Her body felt hot, tingly, wet with sweat. She wanted to close her eyes but didn't. In her mind she heard the staff sergeant say, *Good girl . . . don't let him see your fear. Be a Marine.*

The face of the enemy moved to within a foot of her own. It was tilted slightly, as if it were studying her. Her lips burned and tingled and her vision narrowed even more. She could smell it—not a fishy smell at all, it was sweet, almost alluring.

A voice reached her—Porter Reid, still in her left earbud. "Falto, we are clear of the building but are under fire and falling back. Where are you?"

Looking at the alien face in front of her, Falto summoned the courage to defiantly smile. *I win! They will make it to the armory. I didn't let you down, Staff Sergeant Rickenburg.*

"Porter, you have the mission now. Get those people to safety—go . . ." Then the darkness of tunnel vision took her away, though she struggled to the last.

* * *

The darkness ebbed, though she didn't know how long it had been. She felt motion, as if she were being dragged. The heels of her boots were scraping on concrete. The motion stirred her back to semi-consciousness. A wave of nausea hit her, and a violent spinning sensation. The paralyzing agent must have faded. Natalia tried to move but her joints ached and her arms and legs felt as if they were encased in concrete. As she cracked her eyes open, she saw the clouds moving above her. *I'm alive! How am I alive?*

Falto forced her eyes to open. She saw towering over her the massive black-skinned alien that had knocked her out. Its remaining hand was clamped onto her right shoulder and it was dragging her as it walked.

She could barely feel the points of its black claws gouging what was left of her armor. A mortar round went off nearby, she could hear the blast and felt, despite the numbing agent, the concussion rack her body with deep vibrations. It didn't seem to faze the creature dragging her. It towered over her, unswerving and unshaken by the battle around it.

It stopped for a moment, then lifted her into the air. She couldn't see what was happening. Suddenly she felt the release of the claw on her shoulder and her body dropped a good foot into some sort of coffin-like case. The black-skinned alien was gone from her field of vision. Falto tried to move her head to the side but could only manage an inch or two. It was as if her muscles wouldn't respond. Natalia tried to lift her arms, but they too seemed to weigh a hundred pounds each, barely responding to her efforts to move them. She twitched, but it took all her strength. *What have they done to me?*

She felt a cool, wet ooze rise up around her body, starting in the middle of her back. It hit her fingers and lifted her hand slightly. The goo seeped into her armor, hitting her flesh with an icy chill. It came up around her body and her tingling fingertips flexed a little, and she thought it felt like snot. Feeling was coming back to her body, but too late. The substance was squeezing her fingers together and was all over her back, and was getting thicker. *What have they put me in? What is this stuff?*

Something loomed over her, a massive shell-like covering, like the lid of a coffin. It cut out the brilliant daylight and returned her to darkness. Her reaction was to try to reach up, to push the lid off, but every motion made her throb with pain. There was a hissing noise . . . *is the lid sealing shut?*

Then came a gurgling sound from under her near-limp body. The cool ooze rose up around her body, higher and higher. The air pressure increased for a moment, making her ears ache, then it subsided instantly. She jerked her body with all of her might, hitting the lid-like covering, but could not move it. She was surprised she had been able to move that much. The shell covering her was soft on the underside. The goo rose and rose to the point where she was straining her nose and mouth into the last little pocket of air. Then that disappeared.

Panic took over. Falto's battle-racked body thrashed as she held her last breath. The cool slime covered everything. There was nothing she could do. A little gasp of air escaped her lungs and she could taste the ooze seeping into her mouth as a result: it tasted like spinach, almost minty. *Oh God . . . I'm drowning . . .*

The goo penetrated her ears and every orifice of her body as she rocked side to side. Then she could no longer hold her breath. She sucked the sickly liquid into her mouth. Some went to her stomach, but the rest slithered into her lungs, filling them. She tried to scream but opening her mouth only forced more fluid into her lungs. *No!*

CHAPTER 32

Virginia, patrol station over the Chinook Trough, Pacific Ocean

Commander Titus Hill of the USS *Virginia* was having the worst three days of his career as a Navy officer. First had been the message from COMSUBPAC putting the ship on a war footing. Then had come an attack from a boat that performed handstands underwater compared to his boat. The ensuing battle had cost Captain Stewart and two other crewmen their lives. The torpedo room on the deck below the command center had been flooded but sealed. The forward ballast tank pumps had been damaged and the boat couldn't surface.

During the peak of the battle, it seemed that the ELF transmissions were disruptive to the enemy, so Hill had kept the communications station transmitting, relaying information that he never would have sent using the ELF array under normal circumstances. It had been a hasty decision, the kind he had been trained to make throughout his entire career. Messages came in as well, a lot of war alerts and Flash traffic. COMSUBPAC was not responding to any messages at all, a sign that the submarine command for the Pacific might have been an early casualty. There were other messages about strange attacks on coastal cities by the same enemy they had tangled with, and the enemy was now being referred to as "alien." *Well, at least we no longer seem crazy for those sonar readings Captain Stewart sent.* The picture that Hill was beginning to develop was not entirely clear, other than the United States and most of the world was at war with aliens in the oceans . . . where he and his crew did their job. *Wrong place at the wrong time . . .* How many Navy careers had been built on that foundation?

The reality of the situation was grim. Without being able to pump the ballast tanks, the *Virginia* couldn't surface. As long as she kept on moving, she wouldn't sink, and with a nuclear reactor, that meant a long time underwater. So, it meant either repair the damaged pumps, which was difficult to do without a dry dock, or attempt to scuttle the boat in shallow water so that the crew could try to evacuate.

The engineers had tried to repair the ballast pump, but couldn't. According to them, the damage was of an unknown nature. The ship had been hit by something that had burned holes into the ship and subsequently the pump. The holes were not big, but they were not something that could be simply welded. The system was trashed. How the enemy had burned holes in his boat was something for the experts to contemplate. Hill's immediate task was to come up with a work-around or risk losing the vessel and most likely some of the crew.

He had been on the verge of giving up when Lieutenant Dahlgren proposed a radical solution. The nuclear reactor's water circulation system had an auxiliary pump. It could potentially be jury-rigged to serve as a pump for the forward ballast tank. *We have challenges to overcome; no, that isn't the right wording—what we have is "potential hopes."* The reactor was designed to shut off if the aux pump went off line, so a jury-rigged bypass had to be put in place so that the reactor didn't scramble. Doing so violated the Navy regs for safety, but this was war as far as he was concerned. *Manuals and regs can go to hell.* The pump was weaker than the one it would be replacing. The adaptors for the pump didn't match those of the ballast tanks. The auxiliary pump couldn't be removed, so hoses would have to be run through the ship to the ballast tanks, making the control point the reactor room. There was also a risk that the tanks themselves had been damaged in the attacks, rendering the entire effort a colossal waste of time. *There are a dozen reasons it should fail. We've thrown out the book when it comes to repairing battle damage at this point. That's why we've taken the better part of two days to get it rigged and have tested it as best we can.*

It only had to work for ten minutes, enough to fill the ballast tanks. Once filled, the valves could seal it off. It was a tricky decision to make, with a lot of variables. He wasn't sure if this was something that Captain Stewart would have approved—but Stewart was dead. The boat was his now. There was no safety net, no chain of command to help him make the tough call. It fell to him to decide to move ahead with the attempted fix. *I won't scuttle this ship off of home port without at least trying to save her.* Despite the complexities of the decision, it was an oddly easy one for him to make. That didn't mean he didn't have doubts.

Titus remained in the command center with an open comm channel to the reactor room where the engineers and one of the ballast controlmen were posted. "Are we good to go, Chief?"

Chief Simmons, like Hill, hadn't slept since the attack . . . not more than a few minutes at a time. No one on the crew was sleeping. The attack had shaken them good, and they still were not out of danger if this duct-taped wonder failed. "We are as good as we are going to get, Skipper," the veteran replied. Titus was not yet comfortable with his new title.

"Comms, put me on ship-wide," Titus said.

"This is Commander Hill to the crew of the *Virginia.* You are aware of our issues with the ballast pump. We're about to try our work-around. There is no guarantee that this solution will work, but we must try. Even if it does work, we are hundreds of miles from safe harbor in a sea that is at war.

"But we will try. And if it doesn't work, we'll try again. We will continue to try because we are the best boat in the US Navy, and you are the best crew. Thanks to Captain Stewart, we've tangled with the enemy and have given as good as we got. We will honor him with this attempt, and we will continue to try until we succeed. I will keep you posted—Hill out." *Captain, if you're out there, please let this work.*

He nodded to the comms officer. "I'm turning communications over to ballast control."

"Aye, sir," spoke up Lieutenant McBride at the ballast control station. "Awaiting your word, sir."

"Fill forward ballast tanks. Helm, up five degrees up on the bow plane, maintain course and speed."

McBride leaned forward into her microphone. "Reactor room, activate the pump at 25 percent power."

A muffled voice responded, "Affirmative."

Commander Hill moved in behind McBride and looked at the ballast control. There was no reaction on the readout on the ballast tank. "Crank her up slow and steady, Lieutenant," Hill said.

"Reactor room, any leaks or issues?" McBride asked.

"Nothing so far," came the voice of Lieutenant Dahlgren.

"Take her to 50 percent," McBride said. The forward ballast tanks registered something for a moment, then went back to zero. *Is that proof of a leak in the tanks?*

McBride didn't look at the Hill, but she must have felt his eyes tracking behind her. "It does that, sir, when we start pumping. Sometimes there's a lag in the readings here." She activated her mike. "How are we doing, reactor room?"

"Holding—no leaks, pressure is steady."

"Take her to 75 percent."

A moment later the ballast tank reading went up, but only 1 percent. "How do we look, reactor room?"

"We are running a little warm. You can take her up more."

"Take her to 90 percent." Hill felt sweat form on his upper lip.

The ballast tank reading didn't change. He dipped his head. *It must be the tank was damaged in the attack. There was no way to repair them at sea. What is our next step? There has to be something we haven't thought of.*

He raised his head and was surprised to see that the ballast tank reading was at 10 percent and rising. *It's working!* He held back his enthusiasm. At any moment something could go wrong.

McBride called the reactor room. "She is running hot down here. We can only do this for another twenty minutes or so," Dahlgren said.

"Sir, we are at 100 feet and rising, sir!" the helmsman called out.

McBride spoke up. "We are at 26 percent, sir. If we can get them to 80 percent, our calculations put us on the surface."

"Come on, Lady V," Hill said, patting the back of McBride's chair. "Get us to daylight."

It was a long fifteen minutes before ship broke the surface. The crew could feel the change as the conning tower reached the surface. There was a subtle lunge as the ship settled back into the sea slightly, a momentary feeling of almost weightlessness as the ship dropped back down and rocked slightly. It did not leap out of the water, but slowly, almost methodically, broke the surface. Titus looked out the periscope. The *Virginia* was on the surface, but in the middle of a rolling Pacific storm. The crew could feel the sway with the waves. It wasn't violent, but they felt it and everyone settled in, making sure they had a good handhold.

"Sir, recommend we shut down," McBride said.

"Do it." Word came from the reactor room that the pump had shut down and was still operational. If needed, it could be pressed into service again.

"Put me on ship-wide," he said to the comms officer. "This is the XO. We are on the surface. My congratulations to everyone on the boat who took part in this repair. But I remind you, we are not out of this yet. We are a long way from drydock and our home has been badly damaged. We're no longer under the waves but we have surfaced in a war zone. I need all of you to be alert, well-rested, and ready to respond if called upon. Hill out."

He turned to Chief Simmons. "Chief, go get some sleep. And tell Lieutenant Dahlgren and the others they can expect commendations once we reach Kitsap."

"Aye, sir, Skipper. Might I recommend you get some sleep too?"

Hill waved his hand in the air between them. "I'm going up on the mast and get some fresh air."

"Sir, we are back online with comms. Defense traffic is high. New orders for us are coming through—in the open, sir."

"In the open?" Usually such orders would be heavily encrypted. *Things must be getting pretty bad for them to broadcast in the open.*

"To all vessels, Seventh Fleet. We are to make for the nearest continental port or Japan."

"No word on Pearl or Big Navy?"

The comms officer nodded his head. "Yes, sir—marked "Eyes Only" for the captain—er, you, sir. There's a big bundle of traffic and orders for me to wade through, sir, but we are ordered back to the US."

"Get processing. I'll be back in a few minutes."

"Sir," the navigation officer spoke up. "Meteorological shows that we are in the middle of a squall. Satellites are still on-line and feeding us telemetry of the storm." As if on cue, the *Virginia* rocked slowly with a wave. Hill made sure his grip on the railing of the command center was good. He noticed that he was holding the same spot where Captain Stewart's head had hit. He moved his hand quickly to another location.

"I know. I just need a minute in air we didn't manufacture," Hill said. He moved up into the mast and grabbed his rain slicker. *The last time I was here it was with Captain Stewart. Now he's dead and his boat is beat up.*

"I hope I don't let you down, sir," he muttered to himself as he began to work the hatch.

CHAPTER 33

DIA, the Board Room, the Pentagon, Virginia

Captain Ashton Slade stood alone in the Board Room. The evening shift of analysts had come in early as a result of the war alert. The DIA command structure was off compiling information on the alien attack from sources around the world. They had left him alone a while ago, he no longer knew how long. Alone with what live feed information he could pull from drones or soldiers in the field. The holographic image, sans the audio, hovered in front of him. Every now and then he would pause the images to zoom in on the aliens. *My enemy now has a face.* Despite his weariness, he did not stop looking at the images. His mind was doing what he had trained it to do, looking for patterns, seeking order in the chaos. *Everything I can learn may be critical.* For the last few hours, he felt as if the entire weight of the world was on him.

He had done all of the second-guessing already. "What if I had discovered them earlier?" "What did I miss that might have saved lives?" Slade had mentally kicked his own ass several times, but each and every time he ended up at the same place . . . the Board Room of the DIA. There wasn't anything that he could have done differently. *The enemy had the upper hand and had pressed their advantage, plain and simple.* The initiative in this war was on their side . . . for now.

The "official" word on the events in Hawaii was that the DIA and other intelligence agencies did not have a complete picture of events. That wasn't entirely true. In fact, it was the NSA that had cut off the communications lines from the island to prevent mass panic, back when they held the delusion that they could control the flow of events. It was part of some plan they had created decades ago for events that had nothing to do with aliens. The pretense that the NSA could control communications in an emergency of this scale was now gone, but the NSA hadn't turned the lines back on yet. The word Ashe had heard from the DIA director was that they couldn't. *Someone's going to get their ass handed to them in front of Congress . . . if we survive this.*

Hawaii was an unfolding debacle. Initially the aliens had disgorged their horrible sand-flea-like creatures. Like swarming piranhas, they came ashore striking at any organic material that moved or made noise. They were followed by the alien crab-like creatures and a small number of black bipedal creatures. There were others, small aliens, which fanned out in advance of the troops, seeming to act as scouts.

Many ships made it out of Pearl Harbor, but a few went down right in the harbor, never even getting a chance to fire their guns. Those that made for open waters found themselves attacked by what he reluctantly called "submarine forces." Ashe's hesitation came from the fact that they were not normal submarines.

The Naval Base at Pearl Harbor was under siege in a matter of minutes, and the might of the naval force was impotent to stop it. Those Marines that did resist did some damage, but had been forced to fall back to the interior of the island.

The weapons the enemy used would keep the military scientists and contractors working for months to fully decipher. Some cutting weapons were actually high-pressure water weapons. At close ranges they were as effective as a laser in battle. The aliens used a form of chemical-biological warfare. In some of the fighting at Pearl, they had fired weapons that dispersed an ugly black cloud of mist that poisoned anything biological that came into contact with it.

In close quarters, the aliens were even more vicious. He had seen whip-like weapons used by some of the aliens that seemed to be electrically charged, capable of nearly cutting apart humans in STG or ASHUR gear, and apparently able to damage armored vehicles. The crab-aliens had frontal claws that could sever human limbs and torsos when they clamped on. *They are intimidating warriors.* It was a sentiment that he would never say out loud, not with the emotional wounds from the fighting still fresh in so many officers' minds.

Their ranged weapons were formidable as well. There were acid-spray devices, and others they would not fully comprehend until they laid hands on them. *Our tactics are going to have to evolve fast to counter these weapons systems.*

The battle for Oahu's Hickam Air Force Base had been equally one-sided. The aliens had come ashore. Drones had gotten into the air but were outnumbered. Perhaps not so oddly, the attackers did not seem to know how to deal with air assets. Despite that advantage, the base's personnel had been devastated. A few drone bunkers held out, somehow ignored by the aliens, but the drone assets were dwindling in numbers and support staff. The arrival of a SEAL team in ASHUR II gear had temporarily returned control of the AFB to the US, but only long enough to evacuate personnel. The ASHUR rigs were proving to be the best defense against the aggressors. *They are only good on the surface. At some point we are going to have to take the fight below the waves. We'll need a new generation of gear to deal with deep-sea conditions.* Ashe's mind was already six steps ahead on this; he had already begun to mentally sketch out the kind of gear that the Navy and Marine Corps were going to need.

The attackers did not seem to distinguish between civilian and military targets. Honolulu had been swarmed by large crab-scorpion creatures, which appeared to be the bulk of the attacking forces. Slade and his people, just by reviewing drone footage, had identified almost a half-dozen different kinds of aliens. This was not a single race attacking mankind, it was an attack by numerous species of aquatics. *Or, we are facing one enemy race that has other creatures doing some of its grunt work for them.*

Hawaii had not fallen entirely. Oahu's civilians and military alike had fallen back to the island's interior. Battles were raging everywhere, but the suddenness of the alien attack had shattered and scattered the defenders. *No surfing contests this year . . .* The Navy was already talking about a relief mission, and Slade found himself the lone voice recommending against it. "How can you send a naval force to the island when the enemy controls the seas?" The Navy top brass, at least so far, was headstrong in their convictions. *They are fighting as if the enemy is the Russians. The brass are fighting the wrong war. This is a new enemy, which will require new tactics and defenses.*

Guam had been a different story, but almost as grim. The aliens had hit Big Navy hard, as they had in Pearl Harbor, but in Guam the Marine Corps had been able to respond faster. The battle had been more even. Andersen Air Force Base had been overrun by their killer sand-fleas or "goblins" as some analysts had already dubbed them. They were weapons of terror, effective at driving even the most hardened soldiers into a full rout. But the Marine drone aviators had sealed themselves in and had given the ground forces good air support. Air superiority had helped, but the ASHUR rigs again had proven instrumental in the fighting. *We won't be able to keep air superiority for long. The enemy will adapt. They came from another star, so flight is something they already know. This slight edge will be fleeting.*

The battle for Guam was not over. The aliens appeared to be in retreat, but only after inflicting staggering losses. Most of the Marine units suffered 40–50 percent casualties. In the last war, units were considered combat ineffective with 15 percent losses. *But this is nothing like the last war.* The US had not suffered these kinds of losses since the Korean Conflict in the last century. The fighting was still going on in some parts of Guam, including Andersen Air Force Base and near the North Finegayan Telecommunications Site, which had apparently been one of their objectives.

As the holographic image changed to a new drone feed in another part of the Guam battlefield, Slade once more hit Pause to zoom in on a group of the aliens coming ashore. They moved in a circular pattern, apparently centering on a bipedal alien. *Were these the leaders? Is this one of their standard combat formations?* He made notes on his digipad. *We will need people to study their organizations and formations. Maybe there's something significant in how they came ashore.* He set down his digipad and rubbed his eyes. They were dry and burning. He couldn't remember the last time he ate or drank. The battles had consumed him, lighting up his mind with thoughts of how to deal with this enemy.

The attacks on the US mainland mirrored those from the Pacific. The creatures had sent their Trojan horses ashore slowly, so that they appeared to be massive benign snails, their decorative shells the size of an RV. There was nothing benevolent about the massive snails. A dozen had appeared in Los Angeles alone. They had slowly crawled inland and the local officials, in most jurisdictions, did nothing to stop them. Then the giant crawlers burst open, spilling out millions of carnivorous killer sand-fleas. Their legs resembled sand fleas and their bodies were actually tough exoskeletons shaped like human skulls. They were the size of ping-pong balls, and from a distance when they moved, they looked like a hopping sea of popcorn. Of course, if you were close enough to see that, you were doomed already.

The goblins functioned like a cross between frenzied piranhas and locusts. Their tough shells made them difficult to crush and they burrowed deep into your flesh once they attached themselves to your skin. The more you moved or screamed or ran, the more you seemed to attract their attention.

Crafty little bastards. Unleashing the swarms of these creatures killed thousands and cleared huge parts of the attacked cities. They spread out rapidly, ravenously. The rest of the human population tried to flee the affected cities. While the generals characterized the hideous attacks as WMDs, Ashe saw them for what they were: effective. They were the biological equivalent of bombing a jungle with napalm. They had managed to clear the cities for easy attack from the seas.

The whole world had been victim to the alien assaults. Japan had suffered several devastating attacks in Tokyo both by the sand fleas and a small number of aliens that made incursions into the city, then mysteriously fell back. China said little, but it was known that Hong Kong had gone dark both physically and electronically, indicating that the aliens were doing something there. The northern French coast in Normandy had been probed as well, with alien incursions then retreats.

Lieutenant General Quartermain had asked him flat out what he made of the pattern of attacks. Ashe had pondered the question for a long minute before responding. "These are probes. They are testing themselves against us, probing at our points of resistance. They are analyzing what weapons and tactics they possess that are most effective. They clearly have the resources to inflict more damage but have not concentrated them. They are testing us, General, testing our resolve and how effective our weapons are against their own."

When asked why, he had responded with what he felt in his gut. "They will adapt." He must have said the right thing. Within two hours, he had been flown to the White House to brief President Bobrow on what he knew. General Quartermain had applauded his work to the commander in chief. "If it wasn't for this officer, we would have been caught with our pants completely down." President Bobrow didn't have any compliments. He demanded answers, answers that Slade and the rest of the intelligence community simply didn't have. It had been a day that most officers of his rank would have been thrilled to be a part of. Ashe wasn't. For him, it had been like a prolonged root canal with no anesthetic. Slade wasn't looking to score brownie points with the president. This was no steppingstone in his career. Every hour of this attack tore at him, making him wish there was more he could have done to prevent it. His weary mind tried to remember the details of the meeting in the White House, but they were a blur. There was a barrage of questions and damned few answers.

He agreed with the need to federalize the National Guard and activate the Reserves, but he knew the public didn't fully comprehend what that meant. The National Guard was on the scene for disasters and limited wars. They responded quickly to crises. The scale of this emergency was massive. Many cities were dealing with fleeing refugees. Getting the Guardsmen to their armories, getting them outfitted, and arranging for transportation was a staggering logistical effort. Even with dedicated fuel supplies, they couldn't move more than a few units quickly . . . and standard deployment plans didn't take into account alien attacks from the sea. There were no plans that dealt with a contingency on this scale. *The public thinks the National Guard will be on every street corner in a day or two. In reality, it will take months to get them properly deployed. In the meantime, we are here, as General Quartermain said, with our dicks in our hands.*

The Defense Logistics Agency was already throwing up a red flag. The stockpiles of ammunition and expendables the DLA had were meant to last for three to six months in a limited war situation, enough time for industry to begin to replenish stocks. An all-out war would quickly drain the tools needed to wage the war, and some of the required factories were in cities that had been targeted by the aliens. *We're fighting a war no one had contemplated—even after the Russian incursion in Alaska.* There were going to be some dark days ahead, Ashe could see them coming.

The door to the Board Room hissed open but Slade didn't look up. "Slade, what are you still doing here?" Army Major General "Cutter" Guttman asked.

"Sorry, sir," he stirred from his deep thoughts. "I was just watching some of the vid that we captured today."

"We have the next shift going over all of that," Guttman said. "You need to get some sleep."

"I was thinking of grabbing a cot and crashing in one of the conference rooms."

Guttman frowned. "I think you should go home and sleep there. The DIA will function just fine if you are not here. Besides, you have another big day tomorrow. I need you somewhat rested."

"It will take days to crunch all of this into something meaningful," Ashe said, pointing to the paused holoimage.

"True. But you have a briefing with the president at 0900 tomorrow. You need to hit that with a fresh brain."

"I'm going back to the White House?"

The usually gruff General Guttman laughed . . . the first time Ashe had ever seen that. "Of course you are. Like it or not, for the time being, you're the intelligence expert on these creepy-ass aliens. I'm sure as hell not going in there to brief the president. I'm taking in my best person. For the next few weeks, if not more, you're going to be the man on the spot."

"Me?" He allowed himself a small chuckle as well. "Sir, my entire military career has been in intel. I went to the White House and the only detail I remember, other than the president, was the blue carpet with the gold stars and the presidential seal. You would think I'd remember more than that. Now you're telling me I'm the best intel asset on an alien assault . . . it's just a bit hard to believe."

Guttman moved in and took a seat at the conference table. "The first time I went to the White House, I tripped on a chair leg. Almost fell flat on my face. I felt like an idiot. You'll do fine. The president was impressed. He hates bullshitters and you separated fact from your best guesses. He's asked for you to be there. So don't worry about the décor. Go in and do what you do best."

Ashe nodded. "Yes, sir. I just assumed Colonel Harper would be the one doing the briefings going forward."

"It's now General Harper. The Chiefs authorized his promotion this afternoon. Congress still has to approve it, but they wouldn't think of not approving it on the heels of this attack. The man knows how to pick people to do a job, and we're facing a big task. We're going to mobilize on a scale that would make the Manhattan Project look like a trip to Disney World. Harper's going to have a key role in that."

"Wow."

"He's not alone," Guttman said. He dug his right hand into his pocket and tossed out a pair of major's clusters. "If you're going to be seeing the president, we need to make sure you have a rank befitting the burden. Congratulations, *Major* Slade." He held out his big beefy hand and Ashe shook it, stunned by the turn of events. "You should know, Admiral Frost is going to make you an honorary commander in the US Navy. The JCS usually doesn't approve of these things, but it's important that you know he's doing it."

"Thank you, sir."

"Don't thank me. Your job is about to become a hell of a lot bigger and more complicated. USARC is calling up reserves in the middle of cities being clogged with refugees. There are three commands vying to be in charge of what is unfolding in the Pacific. The Navy is champing at the bit to get into the fight, even though they're feeling a little vulnerable at the moment because the oceans are hostile territory. All the branches need intel, and they are all going to look to you. We're bringing in over three hundred more analysts to get started, and we're moving them to our Aux location for now, until we can get them to more permanent facilities. With that rank comes a lot of responsibility."

Three hundred analysts! Just organizing them into something productive would take weeks . . . weeks he didn't have. Slade's mind raced. "I'm going to have to start pulling together my materials, sir."

Guttman shook his head. "Go on down to the analyst pit and tell them what you want for your briefings tomorrow. The DIA command knows you're on the spot for the president. Pin on those damned clusters and start using them. Tell them what you want and get out of here . . . get something to eat and go to sleep. The war will be here for you tomorrow. It's going to be here for a long while." The general pulled himself up. "Don't make me make that an order."

"No, sir. You're right," Ashe said as he picked up his new rank insignia. They felt oddly heavy in his hand. "And thank you again, sir." *It wasn't that long ago that I was thinking about leaving the military. Now I have to brief the president daily with an entire world at war.*

Things had changed . . . and they would never be the same.

ACKNOWLEDGMENTS

This book is the first of a trilogy establishing an exciting and dynamic fictional, comic, and gaming universe.

To say that this was Brent's idea would be an understatement. That was where it all started, Brent Evans saying, "Let me bounce an idea off you for a kick-ass IP." But to say it was just Brent would be downplaying the roles of the entire Creative Juggernaut team. Everyone's fingerprints are on this book, on the characters, and in this series. This was a true team effort. The debates were awesome, the decisions were great, and the results . . . well, we'll let you decide.

Thanks go out as well to our new friends at WarGate Publishing for making it possible to bring this series to life.

Welcome aboard. Your rig is prepped and loaded. Time to suit up!

ABOUT THE AUTHOR

Blaine Pardoe is a *New York Times* bestselling and award-winning author. He has been an author and designer in the gaming industry since 1985. He has written countless sourcebooks for games including the Star Trek RPG, Space 1889, the Robotech RPG, BattleTech/MechWarrior, Twilight 2000, Renegade Legion, and Leviathans. He has authored numerous science fiction novels in the BattleTech/MechWarrior universe. His political thriller, *Blue Dawn*, was an Amazon bestseller in its category. Outside of the gaming industry, he is an accomplished historian and bestselling author in the military history, business management, and true crime genres. He has twice won awards from the Military Writers Society of America and was awarded the Harriet Quimby Award from the Michigan Aviation Hall of Fame for his contributions to aviation history. He has been a guest speaker at the US National Archives, the Smithsonian, and at the US Naval Academy.

ABOUT THE CREATOR

Brent Evans is a long-time Illustrator and award-winning Art Director. As an artist, he began Freelancing in 1987 and worked in many genres including political cartoons, comics, and children's books. In 2005 he was hired by gaming visionary Jordan Weisman to work on several games, and immediately distinguished himself as one of the core illustrators for the *BattleTech* franchise. His creative design and project management style inspired his elevation to Senior Art Director in 2009 for many legendary gaming franchises including *BattleTech*, *Shadowrun*, D&D's *Dragonfire*, *Valiant RPG*, and many more. From 2017-2019, he took on the additional role as Line Developer leading the overhaul of the *BattleTech* product line, catapulting the brand into the industry-leading global success that it enjoys today. Of Brent, it is said that his "superpower" is the ability to recruit and develop creative talent.

Additionally, Brent is a graduate of and serves as a Board member for the Game Design & Development program for the University of Washington.

SNEAK PEEK OF

BOOK 02

RIPTIDES

CYCLE I

Brockatonorton Bay, Maryland, East Coast, United States

Estes Thorn settled into the big chair in the cabin and shut off the satellite-fed e-unit. For weeks, all that had been on the net were news reports of the massive alien attacks around the globe. The press hopped from one harebrained theory to another to fill the gaps in the actual news. Media speculation only seemed to make matters worse. All that the actual news vids showed was images of death and destruction as the enemy from the depths of the ocean lashed out at mankind. She watched the news every night at the cabin, but she didn't see any real value in it. *We're just guessing at this point. All I know is that the trip to Hawaii I'd been planning is on indefinite hold.*

She adjusted the chair so she could see the gently pounding surf of the Atlantic Ocean through the screened front door. Her family had owned the cabin for the last seventy years, and it was still considered "young" by the standards of some on the Delmarva Peninsula. Estes found it hard to think of the ocean as dangerous or threatening. She had been coming here her whole life. The family cabin was where she went to get away from the stress of working in Washington, DC. Sure, it was a pain to get there every weekend, but within the four walls of the tiny cabin, she could power down, and work seemed like it was on another planet. Though with autumn looming, soon she'd have to close it up for the winter. What was relaxing and therapeutic in the warm months became bitter cold in the winter. *For now, I still have plenty of weeks to enjoy it.*

For the better part of an hour, she just sat and watched night deepen. The breeze picked up; she could see the weeds whip in the wind in the dim light coming from the cabin. Eventually she rose from the big chair and closed the heavy wooden door. She locked it, not out of fear but from habit. Living in Washington, DC, locking was a necessity. Here in the isolated cabin, there was no need. *No one was ever wandering the beach at this hour.*

She grabbed her digipad and prepared to settle in with some reading when she heard a scraping sound outside, like something rubbing on the screen door. She unlocked the wood door and cracked it open, curious about what was making the noise.

What she saw were three large crab-like creatures, at least two times larger than a Maryland blue crab. Their bodies were almost pearlescent, an opaque white. Their legs seemed odd, then it hit her: they had more than a normal crab should. There were eight—no, ten legs on them. She expected them to scurry from her presence at the screen door, which they apparently were clawing at with their oddly enlarged front claws. But they didn't react at all to the light from inside the cabin or her presence. *It's as if they are ignoring me.* Looking out into the darkness, she could see others moving in the sand—closing on the cabin.

One of them swung its claw above its body, bringing it down on the screen. It tore into the plastic mesh, not like a knife, but like a blunt object ripping the screen. Estes slammed the wooden door shut out of fear. She reached up and locked it. *Whatever those things are, they are not crabs . . . not normal crabs.* Her mind quickly made the connection. *These are aliens!*

The old, thick wooden door, a survivor of six hurricanes, seemed secure to her. She moved back several steps as she heard claws dragging on the wood. *It will hold—it has held for years.* Despite that thought, she continued to back up.

Then a stream of translucent material penetrated the base of the door. She jumped to the side, avoiding it easily as it cut the door with laser precision. Was it a laser? . . . no! The penetrating stream hit one of the dining chairs at the far end of the tiny cabin and sent it flying. Estes realized it was not energy, but water. *They are using water to cut through.* Estes whipped her head around and saw another two holes appearing in the door, the wood sliced as if they were using a precision saw. The hole was irregular in shape, but covered most of the base of the door. The piece of wood flew into the cabin, as did a blast of cool ocean air.

Then they came in.

A half dozen of the crab-like creatures crawled through her door and fanned out with surprising speed across the cabin. They moved with purpose, as if they were looking for something. Two moved past Estes and she curled up near her heavy chair in a ball of pure fear. The crabs paused next to her, but moved on, intent on something else.

They moved into the kitchen area of the cabin, which was really more like a kitchenette. Mounted over the small stove surface was a microwave. The crabs focused on it, swarming the microwave as if it were some sort of food source.

The crabs seemed to trace the outline of the microwave with their claws, and she could hear a cutting noise, not like a saw, but a popping and hissing. The lights in the cabin flickered for a moment, adding to her terror as she watched from her position on the floor. She saw sparks and smelled a hint of ozone in the air as they cut electrical wiring. Suddenly the microwave fell on to the stovetop with a crashing thud. They moved with purpose, with intelligence, pushing it to the floor. The microwave door was shattered, its wiring severed by their cutting. It was a worthless hunk of plastic, electronics, and wiring. *Why are they interested in that?* It made no sense.

The crabs scampered around and on top of the battered microwave oven. Then they moved, almost in orchestrated unison, lifting it up, some sliding beneath it. It shifted, and she saw that they were carrying it on their flat backs.

The aliens moved to the door. Two ran ahead and cut the hole wider, then they swiftly scampered through the hole and off to the beach, into the darkness. The wind caught her battered screen door and she could hear the parts of the torn screen flapping against the doorframe. A strange silence fell over the cabin.

Estes Thorn relaxed slightly, slowly climbing to her feet. She looked at the gaping hole where the microwave had been and could even see to the outside, where the water-lasers had penetrated the exterior of the cabin. Then, slowly, she turned to the ruined front door.

Grabbing her iPhone X2, she tried to dial 9-1-1, but her fingers were shaking too much.

Del Norte County Sheriff's Department, Crescent City, California

Deputy Sharon Braxton felt as if she was hip-deep in paperwork, all because of a dead body. Del Norte County was not a crime-free county; it had a small number of murders every year and a nagging drug problem, especially Duke. This crime was different, though, making her life more complicated than she felt necessary.

A local retiree, Fred Dobbs, had found the remains floating in the water near the docks, where the locals continued to spend their time despite the warnings of aliens in the ocean. People in Crescent City were nervous about the alien attacks; they asked for patrols along the shoreline, which the sheriff tried to accommodate to calm their nerves. There were far too few deputies for the amount of shoreline in the county. *And if the aliens come, we don't have enough firepower to do much more than piss them off.* It was a public relations move, nothing more.

The coroner had determined that the victim Dobbs found was one Sublieutenant Anthony James Talbot, a sailor in the Royal Navy, who had been dead for almost a day. The sublieutenant was in a duty uniform complete with his wallet and a soggy set of written orders that were unreadable. The cause of death was not drowning, which is what she had expected. In the face of the news coming in from Hawaii and Guam, she presumed a British ship had gone down at the hands (or fins) of the aliens, and Talbot merely a victim. The coroner had shattered that thinking.

Sublieutenant Talbot had died of a form of toxic shock. There was a bizarre cocktail of chemicals in his bloodstream, which had overloaded his immune and lymphatic systems. Death had been painful. The capillaries in his face and extremities had burst at some point, making his face horribly distorted. *It didn't look like an alien attack; it looked like a lab experiment gone bad.*

Sharon had reached out to the British Embassy with word that one of their sailors had been found dead. At the same time, her boss, Sheriff Daytona, had reached out to the US Navy to let them know. The US Navy had requested a full dump of the autopsy. Then they wanted an official report. Then the British Embassy wanted all the same material plus photographs of the poor sublieutenant and his fingerprints. This was followed by the US State Department chiming in, saying that the

Brits wanted dental x-rays of the victim. Suddenly, a dead body had become a federal case that seemed to be taking up all her time. *I'm waiting for the FBI to call next.* At this point, nothing would surprise her.

As she worked on the appendix of her report, detailing who she had spoken with and what they had requested and when she had sent the material, her phone rang. "Two-to-one, it's the FBI," she muttered out loud to herself. "Deputy Braxton speaking," she said in a weary tone.

"Good day," a crisp British accent replied. *Okay, it's not the FBI—it's worse.* "This is Captain Keith Richardson, Royal Navy, Naval Intelligence Division. I trust you are the officer currently handling the case of Sublieutenant Talbot?"

"Yes, Captain, I am." *What do they want now, tissue samples?*

"I trust we are on a secure line, Deputy?" Richardson asked.

"Sir, we are a small office. I'm afraid we don't have secured lines."

"I see." She could hear the disappointment in his voice. "Well then, we shall simply have to press on. We were able to confirm that you indeed have Sublieutenant Talbot, based on the copies of the fingerprints you were able to send us."

"Good. From the ID on the body, we assumed we had the right person."

"Yes, well, I need to ask you, Deputy, has any debris from a boat or ship shown up on your shoreline where the body was found?"

Braxton shook her head. She hadn't considered this question. "I've had no reports from the locals of anything washing up."

There was a pause. "Well then, we are faced with a bit of a dilemma." Sharon knew one thing: when someone says "we," it usually meant "she."

"You're going to have to be a little more clear, Captain."

He cleared his throat as she watched the blades of the ceiling fan over her desk slowly spin, filthy with caked-on dust. It had been years since the sheriff's office had been properly cleaned. "Deputy, this is sensitive information. I cannot impress upon you strongly enough that this cannot be leaked to the press. I don't want the Royal Navy to get gobsmacked by the media, if you catch my meaning."

"The local net-news already covered the fact that we recovered a sailor from your navy. It's not exactly a secret."

"Yes, well, the part I'm going to convey to you next has *not* been released. Do I have your assurance that it will stay that way?"

This is starting to sound interesting. Her mind swirled with various scenarios of the sublieutenant skipping out on his wife, or having some sort of second life. "You have my word, Captain."

"Well then. Sublieutenant Talbot was stationed aboard the HMS *Triumph.* We lost contact with her five days ago, presumed lost to these bloody creatures that have been attacking both of our countries."

"Okay . . ." She still didn't see where he was going. *I was right about one thing: it's tied to the aliens.*

"Well, this is the sensitive portion. We have not released the fact that we lost contact with the *Triumph.*"

"Oh, I get it, you don't want the press to notify the families before you get a chance. I understand completely."

"Not . . . quite, Deputy Braxton. You see, the *Triumph* had just set sail out of Scapa Flow when we lost contact with her."

"I'm not following you."

"In the North Sea, Deputy. You are on the US West Coast. Even at top speed, there's no way that the *Triumph* could have reached the Pacific Ocean."

"But his body . . ."

"That's right. Somehow he has shown up on the other side of the world from where he should be. We are uncertain if the aliens took his body, or the whole boat. But somehow he has ended up in the most peculiar of places given the distances and the speeds you'd have to travel to get there."

It hit Sharon at that moment. Suddenly the world seemed bigger to her. *It would be impossible for him to show up here. How did they do it—and why?*

"That's incredible."

"That, Deputy, is an understatement."

She paused. "What do I need to do?"

"Her Majesty's government would appreciate the return of the sublieutenant's remains. In the meantime, if it is not asking too much, can you conduct a search of your shoreline for any other remains or debris that may be from the *Triumph*?"

"Of course."

"And I cannot stress enough, discretion is critical."

The world gets weirder for me every day.

Made in the USA
Middletown, DE
12 September 2024

60349930R00198